WHIT

WHIT

OR
ISIS AMONGST THE UNSAVED

Iain Banks

LITTLE, BROWN AND COMPANY

A *Little, Brown* Book

First published in Great Britain in 1995
by Little, Brown and Company
10 9 8 7 6 5 4

Copyright © 1995 by Iain Banks

The moral right of the author has been asserted.

A CIP catalogue record for this book
is available from the British Library.

ISBN 0 316 91436 3

Typeset by Palimpsest Book Production Limited,
Polmont, Stirlingshire
Printed in Great Britain by
Clays Ltd, St Ives plc

Little, Brown and Company (UK)
Brettenham House
Lancaster Place
London WC2E 7EN

For Pen and Rog.

CHAPTER
ONE

I was in my room, reading a book.

I turned a page. The curved shadow of one candle-lit white surface fell over another and the action made a small sharp rustling noise in the silence. Suddenly, a dizziness struck me, and I was acutely aware of the paper's thin dryness, rough against the skin of my fingers and seemingly conducting some powerful, disorienting energy from it to me. I sat as if stunned for a moment, while the unbidden memory of my first Healing coursed through me, suffused with the light of a distant season.

It was a hot summer's day; one of those close, still afternoons when distant haze over the hills or across the plain might become thunder before the evening, and stone walls and outcrops of naked rock will give off small bursts of sweet, heated air when you walk close by. My brother Allan and I had been playing daringly far away from our home at the farm, and daringly close to a main road. We had been stalking rabbits in the fields and looking for birds' nests in the hedgerows, all without success. I was five, he a couple of years older.

We found the fox lying in a just-cut field on the far side of the hedge from the road, where cars and trucks roared past in the sunlight.

The animal was small and still and there was dried blood round its nose and mouth. Allan poked the fox's body with a stick and pronounced it long dead, but I looked and looked and looked at it and knew that it could still live, and so went forward and stooped and raised it up, gathering its stiffened form into my arms and burying my nose in its fur.

Allan made noises of disgust; everybody knew foxes were covered in fleas.

But I felt the flow of life, in me and in the animal. A strange tension built in up me, like a blessed opposite of bottled-up anger,

3

germinating, budding and blossoming then flowing out of me like a glowing beam of vitality and being.

I felt the animal quicken and stir in my hands.

In a moment it jerked, and I set it down on the ground again; it wobbled to its feet and shivered once, looking shakily around. It growled at Allan and then leaped away, vanishing into the ditch before the hedge.

Allan stared at me wide-eyed with what appeared to be horror and – for all that he was the boy and two years my senior – looked very much as though he was about to cry. The muscles at the hinge of his jaws, beneath his ears, quivered, spasming. My brother dropped his stick, shouted incoherently and then also ran off through the brindle stalks towards the farm.

I was left alone with a feeling of unutterable contentment.

Later – years later, with the benefit of a more mature perspective on that vivid childhood instant – I was to recall precisely (or at least seem to) what I had felt when I'd lifted the fox off the ground, and, troubled, ask myself whether whatever Gift I had could act at a distance.

. . . The dizzying moment passed, the turned page settled against those read before it. Memory – the gift we all share, and which certainly does act at a distance – released me back to the present, and (though I didn't know it at the time) what was the start of my own tale.

*

I shall introduce myself: my name is Isis. I am usually called Is. I am a Luskentyrian.

*

I shall begin my story properly the day Salvador – my Grandfather and our Founder and OverSeer – received the letter which set in motion the various events described herein; it was the first day of May 1995, and all of us in the Order were already caught up in the preparations for the Festival of Love due to take place at the end of the month. The quadriennial Festival, and especially the implications it would involve for me personally, were much on my mind then, and it was with a sense of impending relief and only a hint of guilt that I was looking forward to departing the Community for my weekly walk to Dunblane, its cathedral, and the Flentrop organ.

Our home lies in a loop of the river Forth a number of miles upstream from the town of Stirling. The river – rising from a confluence just above Aberfoyle – meanders like a brown rope the Creator has dropped haphazardly across the ancient green flood-plain which forms the eastern flank of Scotland's pinched waist. The river curves, swerves, doubles back and bows round again in a series of convoluted wriggles between the Gargunnock escarpment to the south and the long, shallow slope of collectively untitled hills to the north (my favourite of which, for its name alone, is Slymaback); it passes through Stirling itself, swelling gradually, and continues to snake its way to Alloa, where it broadens out further and begins to seem more like part of the sea rather than a feature of the land.

Where it passes us, the river is deep, not yet tidal, smoothly flowing unless in spate, often soupy with silt and still narrow enough for a child to throw a stone all the way across, from one muddy, reeded bank to the other.

The pouch of raised land where we live is called High Easter Offerance. The Victorian mansion, the older farmhouse, its out-buildings and associated barns, sheds and glasshouses as well as the various abandoned vehicles that have been pressed into service as additional accommodation, storage or greenhouses, together take up perhaps half of the fifty or so acres the river's loop encompasses, with the rest given over to a small walled apple orchard, two goat-cropped lawns, a stand of Scots pine and another of birch, larch and maple, and – where the old estate slopes down to the river – a near-encircling wilderness of weeds, bushes, muddy hollows, giant hog weeds and rushes.

The Community is approached from the south across a bow-arched iron bridge whose two main girders each bears an uniden-tifiable coat of arms and the date 1890. The bridge was once quite capable of supporting a traction engine (I have seen photographs) but its wooden deck is now so thoroughly rotten there are numerous places where you can see through its eaten timbers to the swirling brown waters below. A narrow pathway of roughly nailed-down planks makes a pedestrian route across the bridge. On the far side of the bridge, set amongst the crowding sycamores on the raised bank opposite the Community proper, is the small turreted house where Mr Woodbean and his daughter Sophi live. Mr Woodbean is our gardener, though the house he lives in belongs to him; the estate of High Easter Offerance was gifted to my Grandfather and the Community by Mr Woodbean's mother on condition she and her descendants possessed title to the turret house. I am fond of telling people Sophi is a lion-tamer, though her official title is Assistant Animal Handler. She works at the local safari park, a few miles across the fields, near Doune.

Beyond the Woodbeans' house, the overgrown driveway winds through the trees and bushes to the main road; there tall, rusted-shut iron gates look out over a semicircle of gravel where Sophi's Morris Minor sits when not elsewhere, and the postman's van parks when he comes to deliver mail. A single small gate to one side gives access to the dank, tree-dark driveway within.

North, behind the Community, where the coiling river almost meets itself at the draw-string of our enpursement, the land dips towards the line of the old Drymen to Bridge of Allan railway line, which describes a long grassy ridge between us and the major part of our policies beyond, a rich quilt of flat, fertile arable land comprising some two thousand acres. There is a gap in the old railway line where a small bridge, long since removed, had given access to the fields back when the line had been operational; my route to the cathedral that mist-bright Monday morning would begin there, but first I would break my fast.

*

Our secular lives tend to centre around the long wooden table in the extended kitchen of the old farmhouse, where the fire burns in the open range like an eternal flame to domesticity and the ancient stove sits darkly in one corner, radiating heat and a comfortingly musty odour, like an old and sleepy family dog. At this point in the morning at this time of the year, the kitchen is bright with hazy sunlight falling in through the broad extension windows, and crowded with people; I had to step over Tam and Venus, playing with a wooden train set on the floor near the hall door. They looked up when I entered the kitchen.

'Beloved Isis!' Tam piped.

'Buvid Ice-sis,' the younger child said.

'Brother Tam, Sister Venus,' I said, nodding slowly with mock gravity. They giggled embarrassed, then returned to their play.

Venus's brother, Peter, was arguing with his mother, Sister Fiona, about whether today was a Bath Day or not. They too stopped long enough to greet me. Brother Robert nodded from the open courtyard door, lighting his pipe as he stepped outside to get the horses ready; his nailed boots clicked across the flagstones. Clio and Flora ran yelping and screaming around the table, Clio chasing her elder sister with a wooden spoon and followed by Handyman, the collie, his eyes wide, his long pink tongue flapping ('Girls . . .' the girls' mother, Gay, said with weary exasperation, looking up from the Festive banners she was sewing, then seeing me and wishing me good morning. Her youngest child, Thalia, stood on the bench beside her, gurgling and clapping her hands at the show her sisters were putting on). The two children hurtled past me, shrieking, with the dog skittering across the tiles behind them, and I had to lean back against the warm black metal of the stove.

The stove was built for solid fuel but now runs on methane piped in from the waste tanks buried in the courtyard. If the fire, with its giant black kettle swung over the flames, is our never-extinguished shrine, then the stove is an altar. It is habitually tended by my step-aunt Calliope (usually known as Calli), a dark, stocky, dense-looking woman with beetling black brows and a tied-back sheaf of thick hair, still raven-black without a trace of silver after her forty-four years. Calli is particularly Asian in appearance, as though almost none of my Grandfather's Caucasian genes found their way to her.

'Gaia-Marie,' she said when she saw me, looking up from her seat at the table (Calli always refers to me by the first part of my name). In front of her, a knife glittered back and forward over the chopping block, incising vegetables. She rose; I put out my hand and she kissed it, then frowned when she saw my travelling jacket and my hat. 'Monday already?' She nodded, sitting again.

'It is,' I confirmed, placing my hat on the table and helping myself to porridge from the pot on the stove.

'Sister Erin was in earlier, Gaia-Marie,' Calli said, returning to the slivering of the vegetables. 'She said the Founder would like to see you.'

'Right,' I said. 'Thank you.'

Sister Anne, on breakfast duty, left the toasting rack at the fire and fussed over me, dropping a dollop of honey into my porridge and ensuring I got the next two bits of toast, plastered with butter and slabbed with cheese; a cup of strong tea followed almost immediately. I thanked her and pulled up a seat beside Cassie. Her twin, Paul, was on the other side of the table. They were deciphering a telephone scroll.

The twins are Calli's two eldest, an attractive mixture of Calli's sub-continental darkness and the Saxon fairness of their father, my uncle, Brother James (who has been performing missionary work in America for the last two years). They are my age; nineteen years. They both rose from their seats as I sat down. They quickly swallowed mouthfuls of buttered bread and said Good morning, then returned to their task, counting the peaks on the long roll of paper, converting them into dots and dashes and then gathering those into groups that represented letters.

A younger child is usually given the task of collecting the long scroll of paper from the Woodbeans' house each evening and bringing it back to the farm for deciphering. This had been my duty for a number of years – I am a few months younger than the twins, and even though I am the Elect of God I have, quite properly, been brought up to be humble in the sight of the Creator and to learn some of that humility through the accomplishment of common, simple tasks.

I recall my scroll-collection duties with great affection. While the trip to the house on the far side of the bridge could be unpleasant in foul weather – especially in the winter darkness, carrying a wind-swung lantern across the decaying iron bridge with the swollen black river loud below – I was usually rewarded with a cup of tea and a sweet or a biscuit in the Woodbean household, and there was anyway the fascination of just being in the house, with its bright electric lights shining into the corners of the rooms and the old radiogram filling the sitting room with music from the airwaves or from records (Mr Woodbean, who is a sort of fellow traveller where our faith is concerned, draws the line at television; his concession to my Grandfather's strictures on the modern world).

I was under instructions not to linger in the house longer than necessary, but like most of us charged with the scroll run I found it hard to resist staying a while to soak in that shining, beguiling light and listen to the strange, distant-sounding music, experiencing that mixture of discomfort and allure younger Luskentyrians commonly endure when confronted with modern technology. This was also how I came to get to know Sophi Woodbean, who is probably my best friend (before even my cousin Morag), even though she lives mostly amongst the Blands and – like her father – is what my Grandfather would call Only Half-Saved.

Cassie ticked off another group of signals and glanced at the grandfather clock in the corner.

It was almost six o'clock. Unless the scroll looked like containing an especially urgent signal, Brother Malcolm would be calling the twins away to their work in the fields soon, where up to a dozen others of our Order were probably already working. At the far end of the table, the primary-age youngsters were trying to eat at the same time as feverishly copying each other's homework before Uncle Calum rang the bell for class to begin in the mansion house across the yard. The secondary-school children were almost certainly still asleep; the bus which would stop at the end of the driveway to take them to the Gerhardt Academy at Killearn wouldn't arrive for another hour and a half. Astar – Calli's sister – was likely busy supervising bed-making and laundry collection while Indra, her son, was probably to be found tinkering with some piece of pipework or joinery, if not attending to the Festive Ale being prepared in the hop-fragranced brew-house in the barn beyond the courtyard's western corner. Allan, my elder brother, was almost certainly already in the Community office, also across in the mansion house, keeping the farm records up to date and giving Sister Bernadette or Sister Amanda letters to type.

I finished my breakfast, gave the plates to Brother Giles, who was on washing-up duty that day, said a general Goodbye to all in the kitchen – Sister Anne fussed over me and thrust an apple and a couple of pieces of haggis pakora wrapped in greaseproof paper into my pocket – and crossed the yard to the mansion house. The mist above was only faint, the sky beyond clear blue. Steam rose from the wash house, and Sister Veronique called out and waved to me, a laundry basket piled and heavy on her hip. I waved to her, and to Brother Arthur, holding one of the Clydesdales while Brother Robert and Brother Robert B. adjusted its harness.

The men called me over to look at the horse. Dubhe is the largest of our Clydesdales but also the laziest. The two Roberts reckoned he was limping a little but weren't sure.

I have a way with animals as well as people, and if I have anything that can be said to resemble a duty in the Community it lies in helping to soothe some of the pains, injuries and conditions people and beasts are prone to.

We walked the horse round a little out of his harness and I clapped his flanks and held his head and talked to him for a while, rubbing my face against his while his breath thundered out of his black-pink nostrils in hay-sweet clouds. Eventually he nodded once, taking his huge head out of my grasp and then holding it high, looking around.

I laughed. 'He's fine,' I told the men.

I crossed to the mansion house; this is the rather grand title given to the dwelling Mr Woodbean's father had built to supersede the original farmhouse at the turn of the century. It is built of chiselled grey-pink sandstone rather than the rough, undressed stone of the earlier building, and its three storeys stand taller, better lit and devoid of whitewash. It was reduced to a burned-out shell some

10

sixteen years ago, in the fire that killed my parents, but we have rebuilt it since.

Inside, Brothers Elias and Herb, two muscular American blonds, were on their hands and knees, buffing the hall floor. The air was filled with the sharp, clean smell of the polish. Elias and Herb are converts who came to us after hearing about our Community from Brother James, our missionary in America. They both looked up and smiled the broad, perfect smiles which they have assured us (almost proudly, it seemed to me) cost their respective parents many thousands of dollars.

'Isis—' Elias began.

'*Beloved*,' Herb snorted, glancing at me and rolling his eyes.

I smiled and gestured to Elias to continue.

'Beloved Isis,' Elias grinned, 'would you kindly cast some light into the poor occluded mind of our brother here on the matter of the co-essential nature of the body and the soul?'

'I'll try,' I said, suppressing a sigh.

Elias and Herb seem to thrive on interminable debates concerning the finest points of Luskentyrian theology; points so fine, indeed, that they were almost pointless (at the same time, I have to admit to a certain feeling of gratification at having two such glowing examples of Californian manhood – both a couple of years older than I – on their knees before me and hanging on my every word). 'What,' I asked, 'is the exact nature of your dispute?'

Elias shook his yellow duster at the other. 'Brother Herb here contends that if the Heresy of Size is to be fully rejected, then the soul, or at least that part which receives the Voice of the Creator, must effectively be the *skeleton* of the believer. Now, it seems obvious to me that . . .'

And on they went. The Heresy of Size came about when a few of Grandfather's original followers, misunderstanding his teachings on the physicality of the soul, decided that the bigger and fatter one was, the larger a receiver one presented for God's signals and so the better one would hear God's Voice. Perhaps the fact that Salvador had filled out somewhat over the previous few years to become an impressive and substantial figure had something to do with the Sizist Heresy; the disciples concerned had only known our Founder as a big, bulky man, and did not know that his rotundity was entirely a result of both blissful inner peace and his wives' extravagantly generous cooking; had they been able to see photographs of Salvador when he first appeared on the sisters' doorstep, when he was, apparently, quite skinny, they might not have deceived themselves so.

While Elias and Herb argued on, I nodded with all the appearance of patience and looked fleetingly round the wood-panelled hall.

Hanging in the hall and on up the gleaming walls of the broad stairwell there are various paintings and one framed poster. There is a portrait of the elder Mrs Woodbean, our benefactress, several landscapes of the Outer Hebrides, and – almost shockingly, given the way Grandfather feels about the contemporary media – a bright purple and red poster advertising an event in something called The Royal Festival Hall in London two years ago. The poster publicises a concert on the instrument called the baryton to be given by the internationally renowned soloist Morag Whit, and it is a measure of Grandfather Salvador's love of and pride in my cousin Morag that he suffers such a garishly modern thing to be displayed so prominently in his sanctum. Cousin Morag – the jewel in the crown of our artistic missionary work – was to be our Guest of Honour at the Festival of Love at the end of the month.

We are not a wealthy Order (indeed part of our attraction for outsiders has always been that we ask nothing from our followers save belief, observance and – if they come to stay with us – honest toil; all donations are politely returned) but we are more than self sufficient and the farm produces a decent surplus each year, part of which it pleases our Founder to spend supporting missionary work. Brother James in America and Sister Neith in Africa have saved many a soul over the last few years and we hope that Brother Topec – currently at Glasgow University – will become our envoy to Europe after he graduates and receives suitable instruction from Salvador. Cousin Morag is not a missionary as such, but it is our hope that her fame as an internationally famous baryton soloist, when combined with her espousal of our faith, will help turn people to the Truth.

Additionally, it has been Morag's expressed desire since the last Festival of Love to take a fuller part in this one, and we were happy to hear a couple of years ago that she had met a nice young man in London and wanted to marry him at this year's Festival.

When Elias and Herb had both explained their positions I looked thoughtful and answered them as best I could; as usual it was a dispute about nothing very much resulting from them making two subtly different but equally profoundly mistaken interpretations of Grandfather's teachings. I assured them that the answer would be found in their copies of the *Orthography*, if they only studied them properly. I left them still looking puzzled and ascended quickly to the first floor before they could think of any supplemental questions (that they would in any event I had no doubt, and could only hope that they would have moved on to another part of the floor or a different – and preferably quite distant – task entirely when I descended again).

The rattle of the Community's ancient Remington typewriter sounded from one of the old bedrooms, now the office, to the left at the top of the stairs. I could hear my brother Allan's voice as I reached the landing, where the floorboards creak. Allan's voice cut off, then I heard him say something else, and while I was walking towards the double doors which led to my Grandfather's quarters, the office door opened and the broad, flushed-looking face of Sister Bernadette poked out, framed in crinkly red hair.

'Sis – ah, Beloved Isis, Brother Allan would like a word.'

'Well, I'm a little late already,' I said, clutching the handle of Grandfather's anteroom and knocking on the door with the hand in which I was holding my travelling hat.

'It won't take—'

The door swung open before me and Sister Erin – tall, greying, primly elegant and looking somehow as though she'd been up for hours – stood back to let me in, sparing a small smile for Sister Bernadette's crestfallen face on the other side of the landing as she closed the door behind me.

'Good morning, Beloved Isis,' she said gesturing me towards the door to Grandfather's bedroom. 'You're well, I hope?'

'Good morning, Sister Erin. Yes, I am well,' I said, walking

13

across the polished floor between the couches, chairs and tables while Sister Erin followed. Outside, beyond the partition at the courtyard windows which screens off Grandfather's private kitchen, I heard the school bell sound as Brother Calum called the children to their studies. 'And you?'

'Oh, well enough,' Erin said with a sigh it was hard not to suspect was fully supposed to sound long-suffering. 'Your Grandfather had a good night and a light breakfast.' (Sister Erin will insist on talking about Grandfather as though he is a cross between royalty and a condemned prisoner; admittedly he does encourage us all to treat him somewhat regally, and at the age of seventy-five may not have *all* that long left with us; but still.)

'Oh, good,' I said, as ever at a loss to respond suitably to such portentousness.

'I think he's had his bath,' Erin said, reaching round me to open the door to Grandfather's suite. She smiled thinly. 'Marjorie and Erica,' she said crisply as I took off my shoes and handed them to her. She hauled the door back.

The door opened to steps which led up onto the surface of Grandfather's bed, which is composed of six king-size beds and two single beds squeezed hard up against each other and which entirely fills the bedroom itself save for a single raised table near the far wall. The bed surface is covered with multitudinous quilts and duvets and several dozen pillows and cushions of varying shapes and sizes. The curtains had not been drawn, and in the gloom the bed looked like a relief map of a particularly mountainous area. The air was thick with the smell of incense candles, scattered everywhere along the single shelf which ran round the walls; a few were still lit. Gurgling noises and voices came from a half-open door ahead of me.

My Grandfather's large round wooden bath lies in the spacious bathroom beyond his dressing room, which is in turn beyond the bedroom. The bath-tub and its surrounding platform, constructed for him by Brother Indra, fills half the room; the rest contains an ordinary bath, a shower cabinet, washhand basin, toilet and bidet, all supplied from a tank in the mansion house loft which is itself fed from our river water-wheel (based on an ancient Syrian design,

Indra says) via various filters – including a raised slope of reed-bed – a tangle of pipes, a methane-powered pump, roof-mounted solar panels, and, finally, a methane-boosted hot-water tank immediately above the bathroom.

'Beloved Isis!' chorused Sister Marjorie and Sister Erica. Marjorie, who is three years my elder, and Erica, who is a year younger than me, wore peach-coloured shifts and were drying the bath with towels. 'Good morning, Sisters,' I said, nodding.

I pushed through the double doors into the lush and fragrant space which Grandfather calls the Cogitarium, a greenhouse which extends from the end of the mansion house's first floor and rests on the roof of the ballroom below, where we hold our meetings and services. The Cogitarium was even warmer and more humid than the bathroom.

My Grandfather, His Holiness The Blessed Salvador-Uranos Odin Dyaus Brahma Moses-Mohammed Mirza Whit of Luskentyre, Beloved Founder of the Luskentyrian Sect of the Select of God, I, and the Creator's OverSeer on Earth (and patently unembarrassed when it came to bestowing extra and religiously significant names upon himself), sat in a modest cane chair situated within a splash of sunlight at the far end of the greenhouse, up a chessboard-tiled path between the in-crowding fronds of multitudinous ferns, philodendrons and bromeliads. Grandfather was dressed, as usual in a plain white robe. The long, whitely curled mane of his hair had been dried, and with his dense white beard formed a nimbus round his head which seemed to glow in the misty morning sunlight. His eyes were closed. The leaves of the plants brushed at my arms as I walked up the path, making a gentle rustling noise. Grandfather's eyes opened. He blinked, then smiled at me.

'And how is my favourite grand-daughter?' he asked.

'I am well, Grandfather,' I said. 'And you?'

'Old, Isis,' he said, smiling. 'But well enough.' His voice was deep and sonorous. He is a handsome man, still, for all his years, with a powerful, Leonine face and skin that might grace a man half his age. The only blemish on his face is the deep, V-shaped scar high on his forehead which is the original emblematic mark of our Order. That deep, rich voice, which rings out above us all when we sing during a service, is identifiably Scots, though tinged with a hint of public-school English and the occasional American vowel sound.

'Blessings to you, Grandfather,' I said, and made our Sign, bringing my right hand up to my forehead and administering what might best be described as a slow tap. Salvador nodded slowly and indicated a small wooden seat by the side of his cane chair.

'And blessings to you, Isis. Thank you for coming to see your old Grandfather.' He put his right hand slowly up to the back of his head, and winced. 'It's this neck again.'

'Ah ha,' I said. I put my hat down on the seat he'd waved at and went to stand behind him, putting my hands on his shoulders and starting to massage him. He let his head drop a little as I kneaded his muscles, my hands working across his smooth, lightly tanned skin.

I stood there in the hazy sunlight, its glowing warmth twice-filtered by mist and glass, and ran my hands over my Grandfather's shoulders and neck, no longer massaging but simply touching. I felt the strange, welling itch inside myself that is the symptom of my power, felt its tickle come rising through my bones and go tingling into and through my hands, and knew that I still had my Gift, that I was Healing.

I confess that a few times in such situations I have attempted to discover if touch is really necessary for my Gift to work; I have let my hands hover just over some afflicted animal or bodily part, to see if mere proximity is sufficient to create the effect. The results have been – as my old physics teacher would have said – indubitably ambiguous. With animals, I simply am not sure, and with people, well, they can tell you aren't touching them, and touching is what they seem to expect for the Gift to work. I have always been coy about taking anybody into my confidence concerning the exact reason for my interest in this matter.

'Ah, that's better,' Grandfather said, after a while.

I took a deep breath, letting my hands rest on his shoulders. 'All right?'

'Very much so,' he said, patting my right hand. 'Thank you, child. Come now; sit down.'

16

I lifted my hat and sat on the wooden seat at his side.

'Off to play the organ, are we?' he asked.

'Yes, Grandfather,' I said.

He looked thoughtful. 'Good,' he said, nodding slowly. 'You should do things you enjoy, Isis,' he told me, and reached out to pat my hand. 'You are being given the luxury of time to prepare for you role in the Order, once I'm gone—'

'Oh, Grandfather—' I protested, no more comfortable than usual with this line.

'Now, now,' he said reasonably, patting my hand again. 'It has to happen eventually, Isis, and I'm ready and I shall go happily when the time comes . . . but my point is that you should use that time, and use it not just to study and sit in the library and read . . .'

I sighed, smiling tolerantly. I had heard this line of argument before.

'. . . but to live your life as young people need to, to seize the opportunity to *live*, Isis. There will be time enough to take on cares and responsibilities in the future, believe me, and I just don't want you to wake up one morning after I'm gone with all the weight of the Community and the Order on your shoulders and realise that you never had any time for enjoyment and freedom from cares while you were young and now it's too late, do you see?'

'I see, Grandfather.'

'Ah,' he said, 'but do you understand?' His eyes narrowed. 'We all have selfish, even animal urges, Isis. They have to be controlled, but they have to be given their due, as well. We ignore them at our peril. You may make a better and more selfless leader of the Order in the future if you behave a little more selfishly now.'

'I know, Grandfather,' I told him, and put on my most winning smile. 'But selfishness takes different forms, too. I indulge myself most shamelessly when I'm sitting reading in the library, and going to play the Flentrop.'

He took a deep breath, smiling and shaking his head. 'Well, just never forget that you're allowed to enjoy yourself.' He patted my hand. 'Never forget that. We believe in happiness, here; we believe in joy and love. You are entitled to your share of those.' He let go of my hand and made a show of looking me up and down. 'You're looking well, young lady,' he told me. 'You're looking healthy.' His grey, abundant eyebrows flexed. 'Looking forward to the Festival, are we?' he asked, his eyes twinkling.

I brought up my chin, self-conscious beneath the Blessed Salvador's gaze.

I suppose I must describe myself at some point and now seems as good a time as any to get it over with. I am a little above average height and neither skinny nor fat. I keep my hair very short; it grows in straight if allowed to. It is surprisingly blonde for my complexion, which has a hue roughly in keeping with my 3:1 racial mix (though in my vainer moments I confess I like to think I inherited a little more than my fair share of my grandmother Aasni's high-boned Himalayan handsomeness); my eyes are large and blue, my nose is too small and my lips are too full. They are also inclined to leave a slight gap through which my unremarkable teeth may be seen unless I deliberately keep my mouth firmly closed. I believe I developed late, physically, a process that has at last ceased. To my great relief my chest has remained relatively non-pneumatic, though my waist has stayed narrow while my hips have broadened; at any rate, I have at last gone one full year without once being referred to – at least in my earshot – as 'boyish' in aspect, which is a blessing in itself.

I was dressed in a white shirt – reverse-buttoned, of course – narrow black trousers and a long black travelling jacket which matches my broad-brimmed hat. My brother Allan calls this my preacher look.

'I'm sure we're all looking forward to the Festival, Grandfather,' I told him.

'Good, glad to hear it,' he said. 'So, you're off to Dunblane, are you?'

'Yes, Grandfather.'

'You'll come round this afternoon?' he asked. 'I've been having more thoughts about the re-draft.'

'Of course,' I said. I had been helping Grandfather with what we all suspected would be the final version of our Good Book, *The Luskentyrian Orthography*, which has been undergoing a kind of divinely sanctioned rolling revision ever since Grandfather began the work, in 1948.

'Fine,' he said. 'Well, have a good . . . whatever it is you have playing an organ,' he said, and smiled. 'Go with God, Isis. Don't talk to too many strangers.'

'Thank you, Grandfather. I'll do my best.'

'I'm serious,' he said, frowning suddenly. 'I've had this . . . *feeling* about reporters recently.' He smiled uncertainly.

'Was it a vision, Grandfather?' I asked, trying to keep the eagerness out of my voice.

Visions have been important to our Faith from the beginning. It all started with one which my Grandfather had all those forty-seven years ago, and it was the series of visions he had thereafter that guided our Church through its early vicissitudes. We believed in, trusted and celebrated our Founder's visions, though they had – perhaps just with age, as he had been the first to suggest – become much less frequent and dramatic over the years.

He looked annoyed for a moment, then wistful. 'I wouldn't put it as strongly as a revelation or a vision or anything,' he said. 'Just a feeling, you know?'

'I understand,' I said, trying to sound soothing. 'I'll be careful, I promise.'

He smiled. 'Good girl.'

I took my hat and left the Cogitarium. The Sisters had left the bathroom looking dry and smelling clean. I ascended into the up-thrust landscape of the bedroom and crossed to the far side through the gloom. I picked my boots up from the floor of the sitting room.

'How is he this morning?' Erin asked from her desk near the double doors as I did up my laces. Sister Erin looked at my boots with an expression consistent with having seen something unpleasant on the soles.

'In a jolly good mood, I'd say,' I told her, to be favoured with a wintry smile.

*

'Hey, Is,' Allan said as we exited doors on either side of the landing at the same time.

My elder brother is tall and fit, and fair both in hair and skin; we share eye-colour, though his are apparently more piercing. He has a broad face and an easy, confident grin. His gaze is prone to darting about, shifting all the time as he talks to you with that winning smile, coming back to your eyes every now and again to make sure you're still listening and only zeroing in on you when he wants to convince you of his sincerity. Allan claims he clothes himself by way of the Stirling charity shops like the rest of us, though some of us have wondered quite how he seems to find perfectly fitting three-piece suits and smart blazers with such remarkable regularity. If we occasionally ungraciously suspect him of Vanity, however, we are content that when he travels out-with the Community he favours frayed, tatty country clothes. That morning he wore a pair of faded jeans with a crease and a tweed jacket over a checked shirt.

'Good morning,' I said. 'Bernie said you wanted a word?'

Allan shrugged, smiling. 'Oh, it was nothing,' he said, walking downstairs with me. 'It was just we heard Aunt Brigit wouldn't be coming back for the Festival, that's all; thought you could have mentioned it.'

'Oh. Well, that's a pity. But you'll see Grandad today; you tell him.'

'Well, yes, but it's just that he takes these things better from you, doesn't he? I mean, you're the apple of his eye, aren't you? Eh, sis?' He nudged me and favoured me with a sly grin as we reached the bottom of the steps. The smell of polish lingered and the floor looked like an ice rink, but Elias and Herb had departed.

'If you say so,' I told him. He held open the front door for me and I preceded him into the courtyard. He pulled on his tweed jacket. 'You off to Dunblane?'

'I am.'

'Right.' He nodded, gazing up at the gauzy mist as we walked across the damp cobbles. 'Just thought I'd take a saunter out to the road-end,' he told me. 'Give whoever's on the post-run a hand.' He adjusted one shirt cuff. 'Expecting some fairly heavy parcels,' he explained. 'Hamper, perhaps.' (We do all our food shopping by post, for somewhat ridiculous reasons I shall probably have to explain later. There are hidden intricacies and interpretative choices associated with the post-run itself, too.) We stopped, facing each other in the centre of the courtyard.

'How's, ah . . . how's the revision going?' he asked.

'Fine,' I told him.

'He changing much?' Allan asked, dropping his voice so slightly he probably didn't realise he was doing it, and unable to resist a furtive-looking glance at the mansion house.

'Not really,' I said.

Allan looked at me for a moment. I suspected he was debating with himself whether to be sarcastic. Apparently the decision went my way. 'It's just, you know,' he said, looking pained, 'some of . . . some of the others are a bit worried about what the old guy might be changing.'

'You make it sound like a will,' I smiled.

'Well,' Allan nodded. 'It is his legacy, isn't it? To us, I mean.'

'Yes,' I said. 'But as I said, he isn't changing much; just tidyings up, mostly. So far we've spent most time explaining false signals; the early self-heresies; he's been trying to explain the circumstances behind them.'

Allan crossed his arms then put one hand to his mouth. 'I see, I see,' he said, looking thoughtful. 'Still think all this will be ready come the Festival?'

'He thinks so. I'd imagine so.'

My brother flashed a sudden smile. 'Well, that sounds all right, doesn't it?'

'I'd say so.'

'Good. Well . . .'

'See you later,' I said. 'Go with God.'

'Yes, you too.' He smiled uncertainly and walked away.

I turned and headed out of the Community.

CHAPTER
TWO

The main buildings of High Easter Offerance form the shape of an H with one end walled off; I went from the enclosed courtyard through the gateway into the open yard beyond, where chickens clucked and jabbed at the ground and the wheeze of the bellows serving Brother Indra's forge sounded from the blacksmith's shop (I looked for Indra but could not see him). Past the animal sheds and barns lay some of our collection of long-immobile vehicles; half a dozen old coaches, one double-decker omnibus, four pantechnicons, a couple of flat-bed lorries, ten vans of varying capacities and one small rusting fire-engine, complete with brass bell. Not one is younger than twenty years old and all are so surrounded, and in some cases invaded, by weeds and plants it would probably take a tractor or a tank to rip them free, even if their tyres and wheels were present and intact and their axles not rusted solid. The vehicles shelter some of the less hardy crops for which there is not sufficient room in the glass houses to the south of the main buildings and provide extra dormitory and living accommodation, or just additional dry storage space. They also make a wonderful place to play when you are a child.

From there the road leads to the fields through the gap in the railway embankment where a single-span bridge used to carry the railway above; I struck off from the track there and ascended the grassy bank.

*

The raised bed of the old railway line was crossed by swollen bridges of golden mist, slowly moving and changing in the cool morning sunlight and offering glimpses of our cattle, sheep and wheat fields; a group of Saved digging out a ditch in the hazy distance helloed and waved, and I flourished my hat at them.

As I walked, I felt the usual feeling of calmness and dissociation

25

creep over me, perhaps enhanced on this occasion by the shining, intermittently enveloping veils of mist, cutting me off both from the Community and the outer world.

I thought of Grandfather Salvador, and his warning regarding reporters. I wondered how serious he was being. I have never doubted that our Founder is a wise and remarkable man, and possessed of insights that justifiably put him on the same level as the great prophets of old, but as he himself has said, God has a sense of humour (who can look at the work that is Man and deny this?), and my Grandfather is not above reminding us of this by way of taunting our credulity. Still, some of us trust a prophet the more when he admits to teasing us on occasion.

It has to be admitted that my Grandfather suffers from a spasmodic obsession with the media, and has done ever since the founding of our faith. The trouble with the media – and certain government agencies – is that they are liable, on occasion, to refuse to be ignored. Getting away from most aspects of the modern world is simply a matter of avoiding them (for example, if one refuses to enter shops, shopkeepers can generally be relied upon not to come and drag you in off the street) but the media, like the police or social workers, are capable of coming to seek you out if they think they have just cause.

Probably the worst time was during the early eighties, when there were a number of so-called exposés in the press and a couple of television reports on what they were pleased to call our 'Bizarre Love-Cult'. These were usually highly distorted pieces of nonsense about strange sex rituals disseminated by lapsed converts – sad cases to a man – who had found that the farm work in the Order was too hard and gaining access to the female body rather less easy than they had heard, or imagined. The most worrying of these lies hinted at the involvement of Community children in such practices, and threatened the involvement of the authorities.

I was only a child at the time but I am proud that we responded as sensibly as we did. Educational inspectors and health workers confirmed that we primary-age, home-taught children were better educated and healthier than most of our peers, and secondary schoolteachers practically fell over themselves to praise the exemplary work and discipline of the Community children who came to them. We were also able to point out that no under-age girl had ever fallen pregnant while in the care of our Order. Reporters, meanwhile, were offered the chance to stay and work within our Community for as long as they liked, providing they brought a willingness to work for their keep, notebooks rather than tape-recorders, and a sketch pad in place of a camera. Grandfather Salvador himself was the epitome of openness, and – while politely deflecting questions about his upbringing and early history – so concerned with the souls of the few reporters who did turn up that he took it upon himself to devote several extra hours each night to explaining his ideas and philosophy to them. Interest waned almost disappointingly quickly, though one journalist did stay on for half a year; I don't think we ever did trust her, however, and indeed it turned out she was only researching for a book on us. Apparently it was no more accurate than it was successful.

(Luckily, none of this prurient interest coincided with our four-yearly Festival of Love, when things are more focusedly carnal and we do tend to behave a little more like the popular image we acquired then . . . though I can honestly report that despite the fact I was fifteen years old at the time of the last one – and physically sexually mature – far from being involved in any way I was quite firmly excluded from the proceedings precisely because I had not reached the age of consent the outside world deemed appropriate. At the time I felt a degree of annoyance and frustration, although now that the next Festival is almost upon us and I am liable to be as much one of the centres of attention as I desire, I admit my feelings have changed somewhat.)

At any rate, we are always on guard whenever some new seeker after truth appears on our doorstep, and whenever we venture outside the Community.

My thoughts turned to my maternal grandmother, Yolanda. We had been warned to expect one of her annual visits sometime over

27

the next few weeks, before the next Festival of Love. Yolanda is a sun-weathered but leanly fit Texan in her early sixties with no shortage of funds and a sharply colourful turn of phrase ('Nervouser than a rattler in a room full of rockin' chairs' is one expression that has always stuck in my mind). She joined our Order at the same time as her daughter, Alice (my mother), though she has never stayed at the Community for longer than a couple of weeks at a time, save for two three-month periods after first Allan and then I were born.

Perhaps because they are both such strong characters, she has never entirely got on with Salvador, and over the last few years she has taken to staying at Gleneagles Hotel – only twenty minutes from here, the way Yolanda drives – and coming in each day to visit us, when she organises self-help classes, usually for women only; it is to her that I owe whatever skills I possess when it comes to accurate long-range spitting, Texan leg-wrestling and prompt bodily self-defence with special reference to the more vulnerable and sensitive parts of a man. Thanks to her, I am also probably the only person in my neighbourhood to own a combined knuckle duster and bottle opener, even if it does languish forever unused at the bottom of the underwear drawer in my bedroom.

I suspect Yolanda has at least partially lost her faith (she is untypically coy on the subject), but I could not deny that I was looking forward to seeing her, and experienced a pleasant glow of excitement at the prospect.

I thought, too, about Allan, and how he had changed over the past year since Sister Amanda had borne him Mabon, a son. It was as though he had refined himself in his dealings with the rest of us and with me in particular, treating us all somehow more formally, less warmly, as if his reserve of care and love was too drained by the demands made on it by Amanda and the baby to spare us what we had come to think of as our due portion. He seemed also to have developed a habit of asking me to deliver any bad news to our Grandfather, claiming – as he had that morning – that my elect status, and perhaps my gender, made Salvador look more kindly upon me than him, so increasing the chances he might accept ill-tidings with less equanimity- (and health-) threatening distress.

Somewhat past the boundary of our land, I tutted to myself and stopped a moment, reaching into my pocket and taking out a small vial; I opened it, dipped my finger inside and smeared a little of the grey substance inside onto my forehead, in a tiny V-shape just under my hairline, then replaced the vial and continued on my way.

The mark dried slowly in the humid air. It was written with nothing more exotic than ordinary Forth mud, taken from the banks of the river where it rolls past the Community; just silt (and quite likely largely cow silt and bull silt, given the many herds farmed in fields upstream from us). It marks us all with our Founder's stigmata and reminds us that our bodies come from, and are destined for, the common clay.

We imprint ourselves so for our own and not for others' benefit – certainly not to advertise ourselves – but the mud anyway tends to dry a shade barely lighter than my skin and is often hidden by the half-inch of hair that hangs over it.

I strode along the old track, alone in the drifting golden mist.

*

I negotiated the A84 by means of a muddy foot tunnel, and the river Teith via the broad curved top of an otherwise buried oil pipeline.

It was here by the side of the A84 I'd first Healed, that day Allan and I found the fox lying in the field. Whenever I passed this spot I always looked for a fox and thought back to that high summer day, to the feel of the animal in my hands and the smell of the field and the wide, prized-open eyes of my brother.

When I'd returned to the farm later, sauntering back chewing on a length of straw, I'd been taken straight to my Grandfather. He'd shouted at me and made me cry for playing so close to the road, then cuddled me and told me I'd obviously inherited a way with animals from my late father, and if I ever brought

29

anything else back to life I ought to let him know; it might be that I had a Gift.

Ever since then I've been smoothing away aches and pains and limps and assisting at births in the byres and barns. Out of the numerous hamsters, kittens, puppies, lambs, kids and chicks I've been brought over the years by tearful children, I think I've coaxed one or two back to life, but I would be loath to swear to it and anyway, it is really God who does the Healing, not I (regardless, still, I wonder: *does it work at a distance?*).

My ability with people I am even more sceptical about, even though I know that I certainly feel *something* when I lay my hands on them. Personally, I am more inclined to believe it is their own Faith in the Creator that heals them, rather than any real power of mine, but I suppose it would be wrong to deny there is something mysterious going on, and I hope that what I call humility in myself is not faintheartedness.

*

I attained the Carse of Lecropt road between the farms of Greenocks and Westleys and crossed over the M9 motorway and under the Stirling-Inverness railway line on my way to Bridge of Allan, already bustling with school, commuter and delivery traffic. Bridge of Allan is a pleasant, ex-spa town at the foot of a wooded ridge. When I was younger I believed my brother when he told me that it had been named after him.

The path up the east bank of Allan Water continued through the woods of the Kippenross estate in a cool, sunken track before skirting the bottom edge of Dunblane golf course – where a few early golfers were already swinging clubs and lofting balls – before depositing me near the centre of Dunblane, with only the dual carriageway and a few small streets between me and the cathedral. The mists had lifted, the morning was warm and by this time I had my jacket over my shoulder and my hat in the other hand; I held the hat in my teeth while

I used my fingers to comb my damp hair forward over my forehead.

I dallied just a little in the town, looking in shop windows and glancing at the headlines of newspapers displayed outside the newsagent, fascinated and repelled as ever by the gaudy goods and the loud black letters. I am well aware at such moments that I resemble the proverbial small child with its nose pressed against a sweet-shop window, and hope that I draw some humility from this realisation. At the same time, I have to admit to a sort of thirst; a hankering after some of these vapidities which makes it a relief to recall that as I have not a single penny in my pockets, such goods (so ill-named, as my Grandfather has pointed out) remain entirely out-with my reach. Then I shook myself and strode towards the long, weathered-sandstone bulk of the cathedral.

Mr Warriston was waiting in the choir.

*

I learned to play the organ in the mansion house's meeting room when I was still too short to be able to reach the highest stops or depress the pedals without falling off the seat. I could not read music, though my cousin Morag could, and she taught me the rudiments of that skill. Later, she would play the cello while I played the organ, her reading from her score while I extemporised. I think we sounded good together, even though the ancient organ was wheezy and in need of the sort of professional and expensive repairs and refurbishment even brother Indra could not supply (I learned to avoid certain notes and stops).

I believe it was God who brought me here five years ago on one of my regular long walks, shortly after the Flentrop had been installed, and had me stare so admiringly at its pipe-gleaming, fabulously carved wooden heights and so greedily at its keyboards and stops in the presence of one who could appreciate my admiration that that person, Mr Warriston – one of the cathedral's custodians and an organ enthusiast himself – felt moved to ask me if I played.

31

I assured him that I did, and we talked a little while about the abilities and limitations of the organ I had learned on (I did not mention the mansion house or our Order by name, though apparently Mr W guessed my origins from the first; to my relief he has never seemed either unduly interested in or appalled by us or the lies and rumours associated with us). Mr Warriston is a tall, gaunt man with a pinched, grey but genial face and a soft voice; he is fifty years of age but looks more elderly. He was invalided out of his job with the Hydro Board some years before I met him. He had been about to test the organ for a recital to be given that evening; he let me sit on the narrow bench in front of the three stepped keyboards, pointed out the pedals and the stops with their odd, Dutch names – Bazuin and Subbas, Quintadeen and Octaaf, Scherp and Prestant, Salicionaal and Sexquilter – and then – by God, the glory of it – he let me play the gorgeous, sonorously alive thing, so that, hesitantly at first, only gradually finding my way about the first small part of the great instrument's abilities, I filled the mighty space around us with rolling swells of sound, shrilling and booming and swooping and soaring amongst the timbers, stones and glorious glass of that towering house of God.

*

'And what was that you were playing today, Is?' Mr Warriston asked, setting down a cup of tea on the small table by my chair.

'I'm not sure,' I admitted, taking up my cup. 'Something my cousin Morag used to play.' I sipped my tea.

We were in the Warristons' sitting room, in their bungalow across the river from the cathedral. The window looked out over the back garden where Mrs Warriston was hanging up the washing; the cathedral tower was visible over the spring-fresh greenery of the trees around the hidden railway line and river. I sat on a hard wooden chair Mr W had brought in from the kitchen for me while he lounged in a recliner (soft furnishings are forbidden us). This was only the third time in as many months I had visited the Warriston household, though I had been invited to do so that first day I played for Mr W, and often enough thereafter.

Mr Warriston looked thoughtful. 'It sounded rather . . . Vivaldi-ish at the start, I thought.'

'He was a priest, wasn't he?'

'He took orders originally, I think, yes.'

'Good.'

'Have you heard his Four Seasons?' Mr W asked. 'I could put on the CD.'

I hesitated. Really, I ought not listen to something as sophisti-cated as a CD player; my Grandfather's teachings were clear on the matter of the unacceptability of such media. A clockwork gramophone was just about acceptable if one plays serious or religious music on it, but even a radio is considered unholy (for general or entertainment use, at least; we did keep an ancient valve set for the purposes of Radiomancy, and for years after the move from Luskentyre the two branches of the Order kept in touch by shortwave radio).

While I was dithering, Mr Warriston got up, saying, 'Let me play it for you . . .' and moved to the stacked black mass of the hi-fi equipment, squatting looking compact and complicated on a set of drawers in one corner of the room. He opened a drawer underneath the dark machine and took out a plastic case. I watched, engrossed, even though at the same time I realised I was clenching my teeth, uncomfortable in the presence of such technology.

A sudden noise in the hall made me jump. My cup rattled in its saucer.

Mr Warriston turned and smiled. 'It's only the phone, Is,' he said kindly.

'I know!' I said quickly, frowning.

'Excuse me a moment,' Mr W went out to the hall, putting the plastic CD case down on top of the player unit.

I was annoyed with myself because I had blushed. I know with every fibre of my being I am the Elect of God but I feel and act like a confused child sometimes when confronted by even the simplest tricks of the modern world. Still; such instances inspire humility, I told myself again. I nibbled on the digestive biscuit that had accompanied my tea cup on its saucer and looked around the room.

33

There is an inevitable fascination for the Saved in the trappings those we call the Blands (amongst other things, though in any event, hardly ever to their faces) surround themselves with. Here was a room with immaculately bright wallpaper, voluminous, billowy furniture that appeared capable of swallowing you up, a carpet that looked as though it was poured throughout the house – it extended with apparent seamlessness into the hall and bathroom and stopped only at the doorway to the tiled, spotlessly clean kitchen – and a single huge long window made from two vast sheets of glass, which reduced the sound of a passing train to a distant whisper when outside it sounded like shrieking thunder. The whole house smelled clean and medicinal and synthetic. I could detect what might have been deodorant, aftershave, perfume or just washing-powder fumes.

(Most Blands smell antiseptic or flowery to us; we are happy to indulge Salvador and his tub on account of his age and holy seniority, but there is simply not enough water – hot or cold – for each of the rest of us to bathe more often than once a week or so. Often when we do get our turn it is only a stand-up bath, and we are anyway discouraged from using perfumes and scented soaps. As a result of such strictures and limitations and the fact that many of us do heavy manual work in clothes we cannot change or wash every day, we tend to smell more of ourselves than of anything else, a fact which the occasional Bland has been known to comment on. Obviously, I myself am not expected to undertake much menial labour, but even so I try to make sure I have my big wash on a Sunday evening, before I walk in to Dunblane and meet Mr Warriston.)

Plus, there is electricity.

I glanced towards the hall, then leaned across to the small table beside Mrs Warriston's armchair, where there was a pile of hardback books and a reading lamp. I found the lamp's switch; the light clicked on; just like that. And off again.

I shivered, ashamed at myself for being so childish. But it taught one a lesson; it showed how even the simplest manifestation of such technology could distract a person; beguile them, fill their head up with clutter and an obsession with fripperies, drowning out the thin, quiet voice that is all we can hear of God. I looked furtively towards the hall again. Mr Warriston was still talking. I put down my cup and went to inspect the CD.

The case was disappointing, but the rainbow-silver disc inside looked interesting.

'Wonderful little things, aren't they?' Mr W said, coming back into the room.

I nodded, gingerly handing the disc to him. It occurred to me to ask Mr Warriston whether he owned any CDs by my cousin Morag, the internationally acclaimed baryton soloist, but to have done so might have seemed like vicarious boasting, so I resisted that temptation.

'Amazing they manage to squeeze seventy minutes of music onto them,' he continued, bending to the hi-fi device. He switched it on and all sorts of lights came on; sharp points of bright red, green and yellow and whole softly lit fawn windows with sharp black lettering displayed in them. He pressed a button and a little drawer slid out of the machine. He put the disc inside, pressed the button again and the tray glided back in again 'Of course, some people say they sound sterile, but I think they—'

'Do you have to turn them over, like records?' I asked.

'What? No,' Mr Warriston said, straightening. He pressed another button and the music burst out suddenly on both sides of us. 'No, you only play one side.'

'Why?' I asked him.

He looked nonplussed, and then thoughtful. 'You know,' he said, 'I've no idea. I don't see why you couldn't make both sides playable and double the capacity . . .' He stared down at the machine. 'You could have two lasers, or just turn it over by hand . . . hmm.' He smiled at me. 'I might write to one of those Notes and Queries features about that. Yes, good point.' He nodded over at my wooden chair. 'Anyway. Come on; let's get you sitting in the best place for the stereo effect, eh?'

I smiled, pleased to have thought of a technical question Mr Warriston could not answer.

*

35

I listened to the CD then thanked Mr and Mrs Warriston for their hospitality, declined both lunch and a lift home in their car and set off back the way I had come. The day was warm and the clouds small and high in a luminously blue sky; near a small meadow by the side of Allan Water, I sat on a soft bank in leaf-dappled sunlight and ate the apple and the haggis pakora Sister Anne had thought to furnish me with earlier.

The broad river gurgled over its smooth rocky slabs, sparkling under my feet; a train clattered unseen on the far bank, hidden by the trees. I folded the pakora's greaseproof paper back into my pocket, went down to the river and drank some water from my cupped hands; it was clear and cool.

I was shaking my hands free of the droplets and looking round with an exultant heart, thinking how beautiful God had made so much of the world, when I recalled that this was the spot where, two years ago, some sad Unsaved had dragged me from the path and into the bushes.

His hand over my mouth had smelled of chip-fat and his breath stank of cigarettes.

It had taken a moment or two for my poor slow brain to register the fact that – in the words of Grandmother Yolanda – This Is Not A Drill.

Appropriately, of course, it was also Grandmother Yolanda who had organised those self-defence classes which had left me with (to ` adopt Yolanda's words again) the chance to set the agenda for my encounter with this scumbag.

I had waited until he'd stopped hauling me backwards and I found my footing (I think he tried to throw me down, but I was holding tightly onto his arm with both my hands), then I'd raked my foot smartly down his nearest shin – and was thankful for my heavy, farm-sensible boots – and stamped down on his instep with all my might and weight; I was surprised at how loud the snap was.

He dropped me and screamed; I did not even have to use the six-inch hat-pin which Yolanda herself had presented me with and which I carried in the lapel seam of my travelling jacket, only its little jet-beaded head showing.

The man lay curled up on the shaded brown earth; a skinny fellow with longish black hair, a shiny, synthetic black jacket sporting two white stripes, faded blue jeans and muddy black training shoes. He was clutching his foot and sobbing obscenities.

To my shame, I did not stay and try to reason with him; I did not tell him that for all his weakness and wickedness God still treasured him and – if he only chose to look for it – there was an intense, enhancing and unending love to be found in the adoration of the Divinity which would assuredly be infinitely more satisfying than some short physical spasm of pleasure, especially one achieved through the coercion and subjugation of a fellow human being and so entirely lacking in the glory of Love. Indeed what I thought of doing at the time was kicking his head very violently several times with my heavy, sensible boots while he lay there helpless on the ground. What I actually did was search for my hat (while keeping one eye on him as he crawled away, whimpering, further into the bushes) and then having found it and dusted it off, go down to the sunlit river and wash my face to get rid of the smell of chip fat and stale cigarette smoke.

'I shall tell the police!' I shouted loudly towards the wind-loud trees, from the path.

I did not, however, and so was left with a nagging feeling of guilt on several counts.

Well, that is water under the bridge, as they say, and I can only hope that the poor man attacked nobody else and found an un-depraved outlet for his love in the worship of our Maker.

I completed drying my hands on my jacket, and continued on my way.

*

I arrived back in High Easter Offerance to find disturbance and alarums, a disaster in the making and a War Council in progress.

CHAPTER
THREE

The next morning, while the dawn was still just a grey presence in the quiet mists above, I splashed into the waters of the river just downstream from the iron bridge, my feet squelching through the chill mud under the brown water. On the steep bank above, under the sombre canopy of the drooping trees, in a silent, massed presence, stood almost every adult of our Community.

I heaved myself up and into my rubber coracle while Sister Angela steadied the dark craft. Brother Robert handed her the old brown kit-bag from the shore and she passed it on to me; I placed it in my lap. My boots were hung round my neck on tied laces, my hat was slung over my back.

Brother Robert slid into the water too; he held my little boat and passed the trenching tool to Sister Angela, who delivered it into my hands; I unfolded it and locked the blade into place while she used the cold river water to clean my feet – which stuck out over the edge of the giant inner-tube – and then dried them slowly and reverently with a towel.

I looked up at the others, standing watching on the shore, their collective breath hanging in a cloud above their heads. Grandfather Salvador was in the midst of them, a white-robed focus within their darkly sober penumbra.

Sister Angela was passed my socks, which she carefully put on my feet. I gave her my boots and she laced those up too.

'Ready, my child?' our Founder said quietly from the shore.

'I am,' I said.

Sister Angela and Brother Robert were looking round at my Grandfather; he nodded, and they pushed me firmly away from the bank and out towards the centre of the river. 'Go with God!' Sister Angela whispered. Brother Robert nodded. The current caught my odd craft and started to turn it and draw me away downstream. I dipped the trenching tool into the

41

silky grey waters, paddling to keep my Brothers and Sisters in view.

'Go with God – with God – Go – God – Go with – God – with God – God – with – Go . . .' the others whispered, their mingled voices already half lost in the river's gurglings and the lowing of distant, awakening cattle.

Finally, just before the river bore me around the tight bend downstream and out of sight, I saw Grandfather Salvador raise his arm and heard his voice boom out over all the others; 'Go with God, Isis.'

Then the inner-tube entered an eddy and I was spun around, the world whirling about me. I paddled on the other side and looked back, but the river had swept me away from them, and all I could see were the reeds and bushes and the tall black trees, hanging over towards each other from each bank of the mist-wreathed river like monstrous, groping hands.

I set my mouth in a tight line and paddled away downstream, heading for the sea and the city of Edinburgh, where my mission would take me first to the home of Gertie Possil.

*

'What?' I asked, appalled.

'Your cousin Morag,' Grandfather Salvador told me, 'has written from England to say that not only is she not returning for the Festival at the end of the month, but she has found what she calls a Truer Way to God. She has sent back our latest monthly grant to her.'

'But that's terrible!' I cried. 'What false faith can have poisoned her mind?'

'We don't know,' Salvador snapped.

We were in the Community office across the mansion landing from Salvador's quarters; my Grandfather, my step-aunt Astar, Allan, Sister Erin, Sister Jess and I. I had just returned from Dunblane; I still held my travelling hat. I had been crossing the boundary back into our lands when I saw Brother Vitus running towards me along the old railway track; he stood, breathless, telling me I was required urgently at the house, then we ran back together.

'We must write to her,' I said. 'Explain to her the error of her thoughts. Have any of her previous letters given any hint of the exact nature of her delusion? Is she still living in London? Brother Zebediah is still there, I believe; could he not talk to her? Shall we call a Mass Prayer Session? Perhaps she has lost her copy of the Orthography; shall we send her another?'

Allan glanced at my Grandfather, then said, 'I think you are missing the point here a little, Is.' He sounded tired.

'What do you mean?' I asked. I put down my hat and took off my jacket.

'Sister Morag is important to us in many ways,' Astar said. Astar is forty-three, a year younger than her Sister Calli, and as lightly European looking as Calli is dark. Tall and sensuous, with long, glossy black hair braided to the small of her back and large eyes hooded by dark eyelids, she is the mother of Indra and Hymen. She dresses even more plainly than the rest of us, in long, simple smocks, but still manages to exude elegance and poise. 'She is most dear to all of us,' she said.

'The point is,' Salvador cut in – Astar's head dipped deferentially and her eyes half closed – 'that while I'm sure we care as much for Sister Morag's soul as for any of our number and so feel the grief of her apostasy most keenly, and would in any event do all we can to bring her back to the fold with all due speed, there is the more immediate result of Morag's desertion, namely, what do we do about the Festival?'

I hung my jacket on the back of a chair. Salvador was pacing up and down in front of the office's two tall windows; Sister Erin stood by the door near the small desk which supported the Remington typewriter, Allan – arms folded, head slightly bowed, face pale – stood by his desk, which took up a fair proportion of the other end of the room, in front of the fireplace.

'Beloved Grandfather, if I may . . . ?' Allan said. Salvador waved him on. 'Isis,' Allan said, spreading his hands, 'the point is, we've made quite a thing of Morag attending the Festival as Guest of Honour; we've been writing to the faithful all over the world

43

encouraging them to come to this Festival, citing Morag's fame and her continuing faith—'

I was shocked. 'But I didn't know anything of this!' We usually shunned anything that smacked of publicity; one-to-one conversions were more our style (though, in the right circumstances, we'd always felt there was a place for standing on street corners, shouting).

'Well,' Allan said, looking pained as well as pale. 'It was just an idea we had.' He glanced at Grandfather, who looked away, shaking his head.

'There was no particular need for you to know at this stage, Beloved Isis,' Erin said, though I wasn't sure she sounded convinced herself.

'The point is Morag's not coming to the damn *Festival*,' Salvador said before I could reply. He turned and paced past me. He wore a fresh set of the long creamy woollen robes – from our own flock, naturally – which he wore every day, but on this occasion he looked different somehow; agitated in a way I could not remember him being before.

Morag – beautiful, graceful, talented Morag – had always been a special favourite of my Grandfather's; I suspected that in a clean fight, as it were, without the special status as the Elect of God conferred upon me by the exact date of my birth, Morag, not I, would be the apple of our Founder's eye. I felt no bitterness or jealousy regarding this; she had been my best friend and she was still, even after all this time, probably now my second-best friend after Sophi Woodbean, and anyway I was as taken with my cousin as my Grandfather was; Morag is a hard woman not to like (we have a few like that in our extended family).

'When did we find all this out?' I asked.

'The letter arrived this morning,' Allan said. He nodded at a sheet of paper lying on the age-scuffed green leather surface of his desk.

I picked up the letter; Morag had been writing home for the last six years, ever since she had moved to London. Until now her letters had been the source of nothing but pride as she became more and more successful, and on the two occasions she had come back to see us since she had seemed like some fabulously exotic, almost alien creature; svelte and groomed and sleek and brimming with an effortless self-confidence.

I read the letter; it was typed, without corrections, as usual (Allan had told me he half suspected Morag used something called a word processor, which for a long and rather confused time I imagined must do to words what a food processor – a device whose activities I had once witnessed – does to food). Morag's signature was as big and bold as ever. The text itself was terse but then her communications had never been particularly wordy. I noticed she still used 'do'nt' instead of 'don't'. The letterhead address, of her flat in Finchley, had been scored out.

I mentioned this. 'Has she moved?' I asked.

'It looks like it,' Allan said. 'The last letter Sister Erin sent to Morag came back marked "Moved Away". Sister Morag's last letter before this one was on notepaper from the Royal Opera House, in London. We should perhaps have guessed that something was wrong then, but assumed that her busy schedule had led her to forget to keep us informed of what was happening.'

'Well, what are we to do?' I asked.

'I have called an extraordinary Service for this tea-time,' Salvador said, stopping pacing to look out of a window. 'We shall discuss the issue then.' He was silent a moment, then he turned to look levelly at me. 'But I'd be grateful if . . .' He broke off, then strode over, took me by the shoulders and stared into my eyes. His are deep brown, the colour of horse chestnuts. He is an inch shorter than I, but his presence is such he made me feel he towered over me. His grip was firm and his bushy beard and curled white hair shone in the sunlight like a halo around his head. 'Isis, girl,' he said quietly. 'We may have to ask you to go out amongst the Benighted.'

'Oh,' I said.

'You were Morag's friend,' he continued. 'You understand her. And you are the Elect; if anyone can persuade her to change her mind, it must be you.' He continued to look into my eyes.

'What of the alterations to the *Orthography*, Grandfather?' I asked.

'They can wait, if need be,' he said, frowning.

'Isis,' Allan said, walking closer to us. 'You're under no obligation to do this, and,' – he glanced uncertainly at Grandfather – 'there are good reasons why you should not go, too. If you have any doubts about such a mission, you must stay here, with us.'

Sister Erin cleared her throat. She looked regretful. 'It might be best,' she said, 'to assume that Morag won't be coming back, in which case perhaps the Beloved Isis could take her place in the Festival.'

Salvador frowned. Allan looked thoughtful. Astar just blinked. I gulped and tried not to look too shocked.

'Perhaps we'll come up with another idea at the meeting,' Astar suggested.

'We can only pray,' Allan said. Grandfather clapped him on the shoulder and turned back to look at me; they all did.

I realised they were waiting for me to say something. I shrugged. 'Of course,' I said. 'If I must go, I must go.'

*

The service was held in our meeting room, the old ballroom of the mansion house. Every adult was there. The elder children were looking after the youngsters across the lower hall from us, in the schoolroom.

The meeting room is a plain, simple room with tall windows, white walls and a knee-high podium at the far end. In one corner there is a small pipe organ; it stands about six feet high, has two keyboards and is worked by bellows. In a regular, celebratory service – for a full moon, or for a baptism or a marriage – I would be sitting there playing at this point, but on this occasion I was standing with everybody else in the body of the kirk.

At the front of the podium is a lectern adorned by two scented candles; Grandfather stood at the lectern while the rest of us sat on the wooden pews facing him from the floor. Against the rear wall stands the altar; a long table covered in a plain white woollen sheet and holding pots of our holy substances. The table was made from flotsam washed ashore at Luskentyre, while the cloth was made from wool gathered from our own flock at High Easter Offerance. In the centre of the table stands a small wooden box which contains a vial of our holiest substance, *zhlonjiz*, while behind it stands a tall Russian samovar on a battered silver tray; other boxes and small chests are scattered over the rest of the table's surface.

Salvador raised his arms above his head, the signal for talking to cease; the room fell silent.

The samovar had already been lit and the tea brewed; Sister Astar filled a large bowl with tea; she gave it to our Founder first, who sipped at it. Then she brought it to those of us sitting in the front pew. I drank next, then Calli, then Astar herself, then Allan and then so on through all the other adults. The tea was just ordinary tea, but tea has great symbolic value for us. The bowl came back from the rear of the room with a little cold tea in the bottom; Astar set it to one side on the altar.

Next came a plate containing a slab of common household lard; this too was passed round. We each rubbed a finger over the surface and licked the smear from our fingers. A large cloth followed, so that we could wipe our hands.

Salvador raised his arms again, closed his eyes and bowed his head. We did the same. Our OverSeer said a brief prayer, asking God to look upon us, guide our thoughts, and – if we were worthy, if we listened faithfully, if we held our souls open to God's word – talk to us. Our Founder bade us rise. We all stood.

Then we sang in tongues.

This is a regular part of our life and we pretty well take it for granted, but apparently it is utterly startling for the uninitiated. As Grandma Yolanda would say, You Had To Be There.

Salvador always starts, his fulsome, muscular voice booming out over us and providing a deep, luxuriant bass line to which we all gradually add our voices, a single flock following its leader, an orchestra obeying its conductor. It sounds like nonsense, like babble, and yet through this glorious chaos we communicate, singing solely as individuals and yet absolutely together. We follow no score or agreed-on script; nobody has any idea where our song will lead us when we start or at any point during it and yet we sing harmoniously, linked only through our faith.

Singing in tongues reminds us of our Founder's first and most glorious vision, during the night he lay near death, in a storm at Luskentyre, in a trance of understanding and transcendence, his lips speaking words no one could understand. Singing in tongues brings peace to our souls and a feeling of intense togetherness; we never know when it will stop, but eventually, somehow when the time just seems right, the sound dies away, and it is over. And so it was on this occasion.

The timeless interval of our singing had passed. We stood quietly, smiling and blinking, with the only echoes those resounding in our souls.

Salvador let us collect ourselves in silence for a while, then said another short prayer, thanking God for the gift of tongues, then smiled upon us and bade us sit down.

We did so. Salvador gripped the sides of the lectern and bowed his head again for a moment, then he looked up at us and began to talk about Morag, recalling her grace and her talent and her beauty and reminding us of the place she held in our missionary ambitions. He ended with the words, 'Unfortunately, there has been a development. Sister Erin?'

Sister Erin nodded, then rose and stood on the podium beside Salvador, explaining the situation as we understood it. When she sat down again, Allan took her place by the lectern and talked about potential solutions, including the possibility of sending somebody on a mission to find Morag and attempt to bring her back within the fold, though without mentioning me by name. Allan resumed his place on the front pew and then Salvador opened the discussion up to the floor.

Calli said we should not have allowed her to go in the first place (Salvador rolled his eyes), then said the same thing several more times in slightly different ways until she got onto the subject of pickles and condiments and the possibilities offered for spiritual propaganda by my grandmother Aasni and Great-aunt Zhobelia's recipes; why, if we sold those we could finance a whole orchestra on the profits (an old refrain). Astar was asked what she thought and circumlocuted with brief grace.

Malcolm, Calli's husband, a big, rough-looking but gentle man, suggested that as young people often needed something to rebel against, it might be best if we didn't rise to her bait; then she might come creeping back after having made her point. Perhaps we ought just to do nothing (glowered down by Grandfather).

Indra, our wiry, fidgety fixer of all things, offered to go and find her and tell her to pull herself together (muttered down by almost all).

Sister Jess, our doctor, a small delicate woman, pointed out that Morag was a grown woman and if she didn't want to come to the Festival then that was her decision (much in-drawing of breath and shaking of heads).

Brother Calum, our principal teacher, un-hunched himself long enough to stand up and suggest we might put an advertisement in a paper, or in the personal columns, asking her to contact us (more of the same).

Sister Fiona, wife of Brother Robert, wondered what the possibilities were of putting Brother Zebediah on the case (laughter from those who knew Zeb – he was generally regarded as something of a hopeless case, and it was known he hadn't gone to a single one of Morag's concerts in London).

Brother Jonathan said he thought we were missing something; why not just hire a private detective to look for her and possibly even kidnap her and bring her back? He was sure his father would put up the money. Come to think of it (he said, when this was met by shocked silence) he, Jonathan, had some money; a single call to his stockbroker, or his bank in the Cayman islands . . . What on earth was all the fuss about? (Brother Jonathan is young; his father is an underwriter at Lloyds. I didn't think he'd last long with us.)

Allan explained patiently, not for the first time, about the importance of the Sanctity of the Source when it came to money. No lucre was entirely unfilthy, but it was a matter of revelatory fact that funds earned through farming the land and fishing the sea were the least contaminated of all, followed by those made playing serious music – preferably serious *religious* music.

Jonathan stood up again and said, Well, he had a good and philanthropic friend who owned a recording studio in an old church . . . (Salvador himself scowled that one down. Like I say, I don't think Jonathan's really right for us.)

Eventually, Sister Erin said that there was a suggestion that I be dispatched to London to talk some sense back into Morag (most eyes turned to me; I looked about, smiling bravely, and tried not to blush too much). Sister Fiona B. stood up to say, Yes, it was about time we started talking about our errant Sister's spiritual state, not just the mechanics of getting her back here. This met with applause and Hallelujahs; Salvador and Allan both nodded slowly, frowning.

Sister Bernadette said that as the Elect of God I was far too precious to be risked in the Kingdom of the Wicked.

'Babylondon!' shouted Sister Angela, starting to shake and speak in tongues (Sister Angela is excitable and prone to do such things). Concerned Brothers and Sisters restrained her gently.

Brother Herb said he didn't think I should go either but if I did then my Anointed state made me all the more likely to be safer and more successful than anybody else.

There was much more talk; I was asked what I thought and said that all I could contribute was an expression of honest willingness to travel to London and remonstrate with Morag if that was what was decided upon. I sat down again.

Had we debated much longer we would have had to light the chapel lamps. Eventually Salvador announced that, reluctantly, he had to concede that the only thing to be done was to ask me to leave the Premises of the Just for the Cities of the Plain, charged with the mission of restoring Morag's faith. A further special service a week from now would provide a forum for the discussion of any fresh developments and offer a venue for the evaluation of any new ideas on the Community's plight. The main responsibility was mine, however, and we would have to trust that the Creator would protect and steer me on my embassy amongst the Unsaved.

Responding to my Grandfather's look, I stood and announced that I was honoured to accept my task in the wilderness humbly, and would leave as soon as practicable. Allan stood and announced that our OverSeer, himself, Calli, Astar, Malcolm, Calum and I would retire to consider our next move. I stood quickly and said that I would like Brother Indra to join us, and this was agreed.

The service broke up after a final prayer, and those on dinner duty went off to make a belated start on the evening meal, which included bridie samosa, channa neeps, black pudding bhaji and saag crowdie paneer.

*

The day brightened slowly around me. I paddled on through the swelling dawn chorus and beneath the drifting mists, between the mud and grass of the river banks where puzzled-looking cattle stared big-eyed at my passing. The great gentle beasts chewed the cud, sometimes stopping to low at me. 'Moo yourself,' I told them.

The kit-bag resting in my lap was getting in my way as I paddled; I pushed it further down, flattening it between my legs and into the well of the inner-tube where Indra's sheet of welded rubber was keeping my bottom from getting wet. The bag scrunched down and under until I was more or less sitting on it; paddling became easier.

The kit-bag contained a copy of the *Orthography* (with Salvador's most recent amendments hastily written in by myself from our notes), old, battered but beautiful leather-bound pocket editions of *The Pilgrim's Progress* by John Bunyan, *Waverley* by Walter Scott, *Paradise Lost* by John Milton and Maunder's *Treasury of Knowledge*, some vials of important substances (river mud, hearth ash, seaweed ointment), a travelling hammock, a bed roll, a compact Sitting Board, various maps, a miniature candle-lantern, a tiny can of wind- and water-proof matches, some envelopes, paper and stamps and a pencil, a penknife, a roll of twenty-nine one-pound notes, a parcel of food wrapped in greaseproof paper, a bottle of water, some toiletries and a change of clothes.

Our final sub-committee'd council of war had been to decide on my mode of transport to Edinburgh. I had already determined what this ought to be, and was able to argue my case over the objections of some of the others. Brother Indra agreed immediately to check

51

on and modify the inner-tube, and left to do just that. I had also formed an opinion on how to approach Gertie Possil's, based on the study of certain old maps, and had an idea how I might effect the much longer journey to the city of London, in the south-east of England. My arguments carried the day.

Before we go any further, I had best try to explain why – given that I am on a mission of such importance where time is potentially of the essence – I was not doing something more obviously expeditious, like catching an inter-city train straight to London or ordering a taxi to Glasgow or Edinburgh airport. This will require some theology.

*

God is both and neither male and female, and everything else as well.

God is always referred to as 'God' in the singular, but takes the third rather than the second person in the plural, to remind us of the mysterious and ultimately inexpressible nature of Their being.

God is omniscient, but only strategically concerning the far future, not tactically (otherwise time would be redundant).

They are also omnipotent, but having chosen to set up the experiment-cum-art-form that the Universe is, They are unlikely to intervene unless things go either apotheosistically well or apocalyptically badly.

To God, our Universe is as a snow-scene or the contents of a test-tube, and far from unique; They have many more, and although They care for us and love us, we are not the only apple of Their eye.

To God, Man is like a deformed child; They love him and would not deny him, but They cannot suppress Their regret that Their child is not perfect.

There is no Devil, only the Shadow caused by Man obscuring God's radiant splendour.

There is a fragment of God's spirit in Man, but while God might be said to be perfect, Their perfection comes from Their immense completeness, therefore Man lacks this aspect of God's qualities.

52

Man is the creature of God and made to serve Them and to Oversee the Universe, but in his closeness to the business of mundane existence he is corrupted by his own intelligence and ability to change what appears to be important but is not, rather than applying himself to the more difficult but ultimately far more rewarding task God has appointed him to, and in this respect is rather like a young child who has become skilled at just crawling very quickly, instead of standing up and learning to walk.

Man must learn to stand and walk with his spirit rather than crawl with his technology before he allows that technology – which is the physical expression of his spiritual Shadow – to destroy him.

God's ultimate aim for Man is not known and *not even knowable in our present state*; we must become spiritually adult before we can even discover what God holds in store for us as a spiritual species; all previous ideas of Heaven (or Hell) or Second Comings or Judgment Days are childish attempts to come to terms with our own ignorance. The perception of God's ultimate aim is one of the tasks of future prophets.

What awaits us individually when we die is reunion with the Godhead, but during this process we are relieved of our narrow and limiting individuality, becoming one with the Universe. New souls are drawn from the pool of spirit that is God in the Universe and sometimes a tiny fragment of memory from some previous existence will survive the twin disturbances of death and dissolving and birth and reforming; this accounts for the beguiling but ultimately appallingly vain and conceited concept of reincarnation.

The possibility exists that Man can achieve perfection in the sight of God because Man's nature is not immutable; just as it can alter through evolution, so it can be altered through listening to the voice of God, with the soul.

Your whole body is your soul (with the brain the most important part, like the cat's whisker in an old crystal radio). We do not yet understand exactly how it works, and may never be able to do so without the direct help of God Themself.

Physical love is the communing of souls, and therefore holy.

53

All Holy Books and all religions contain grains of truth broadcast from the mind of God, but politics and money corrupt the signal, and so the trick is to reduce the Clutter around oneself and listen calmly to the soul (which is one's God-given radio receiver).

At certain (seemingly but not really) random Psychological Moments you will hear or experience God talking to you; this means – for example – that when you see somebody standing in a field staring – apparently vacantly – into space, you should not disturb them (as a consequence, I might add, people of the Community are occasionally mistaken for scarecrows).

This is called Receiving.

Naturally, some people hear the Voice of God more clearly than others, and they are usually called prophets.

A prophet's first vision or revelation will tend to be the most intense but also the most debased by all that the prophet has experienced before. It follows that the first codification of that revelation will be the least perfect, the most contaminated by the prejudices and misunderstandings of the prophet. The full story, the real message only comes out gradually, over time, through revisions, glosses and apparent marginalia, all the result of God's persisting attempts to make Themself clear through the imperfect receiver that is the human soul.

Much of what other prophets have said, before all the above was made clear to our Founder, may be useful and true, but because their teachings have been corrupted by being institutionalised in the form of large religions, they will have lost much of their force.

The best strategy is to treat the revelations and teachings of others with cautious respect, but rely most fully on the teachings of our own OverSeer and listen to the Voice from inside all of us, the Voice from God.

Merit and calmness are to be found in the out-of-the-way, the byways of life; in the unnoticed, in the hidden and ignored, in the interstices; amongst the gaps between the slabs in the pavement of life (this is called the Principle of Indirectness, or the Principle of Interstitiality).

Therefore there is goodness and the potential for enlightenment in doing things differently, seemingly just for the sake of it.

The less conventional and normal one's life is, the less interference, the less jamming one will experience from the machinery of civilisation and the more receptive one will therefore be to God's signals.

Being born on the 29th of February is a good start.

*

Is it starting to become clear? The fact that I am not taking a train or a bus or even hitch-hiking to Edinburgh but instead am floating and paddling down this virtually untravelled stretch of twisty, muddy old river with the full intention of walking round half the city when I get there is because to do so is important for the holiness of my mission; to travel so is to sanctify the act of journeying itself and correspondingly increase my chances of success when I arrive at my eventual destination because I am travelling in the uncluttered sight of God, with a soul as uncontaminated by the fuss of Unsaved life as possible.

I paddled on into the misty, brightening morning, passing between more fields where cattle stood, coming within hearing of the main road, and seeing the roofs of a few farms and houses over the grassy river banks. I passed the remains of what must have been a small suspension foot-bridge in the shape of two obelisk-like concrete structures, standing facing each other across the brown waters. Near Craigforth House I had to negotiate a river-wide blockage of tangled tree-trunks and debris, and almost left my hat behind, snagged on a grey, weed-hung branch. I went under a pair of bridges and then swung round another bend to where the Forth is joined by the Teith. An army base lay to my right. The matt green aluminium hulls stacked on the grass were the only boats I had ever seen on the river upstream from this point.

I passed under the concrete expanse of the motorway; one lorry rumbled overhead in the sparkling mist. Immediately, the current increased as I approached some small low islands and passed two fishermen on the left bank, standing on the first sandy shore I had seen; then I heard the rush of water ahead, and knew the tidal weir lay before me.

The tide was in and the rapids negligible; my inner-tube craft bumped into a couple of submerged rocks and I'll own that my heart did beat a little faster as I was swept down the broad white slope of rushing water, but the total drop must have been less than two feet and I estimated that the worst I risked was a soaking. I got a few odd looks floating through Stirling, but you become used to stares when you're a Luskentyrian.

*

I had hardly slept that night. After our various councils of war and a long briefing session with my Grandfather in his sitting room, part of which Allan sat in on (during which, it must be said, Grandfather became gradually the worse for wear courtesy of a bottle of whisky), it had been late into the lamp-lit darkness when Brother Indra had reappeared from his workshop to declare himself satisfied with his alterations to the old black inner-tube. The inner-tube had been the largest of the inflatables the children had been using in the river during the previous summer; we had no paddle as such but Indra suggested the trenching tool. Sister Jess left for Gargunnock, the nearest village, where she would post a letter to my half-brother Zeb, in London, telling him to expect me within the next few days. On the way back she would call in at the Woodbeans' house and use their telephone to send a signal telling of my coming to the house of Gertie Possil (a process *much* more long-winded than the words I have just used to describe it).

Meanwhile I had been given the old kit-bag which had been in our Order almost since it was founded and which had something of the status of a holy relic with us, and chosen what I would put into it. Sister Erin handed me a thick roll of paper cash, bound with a rubber band and sealed inside a plastic bag. I had already thought about this, and thanked her and the others, but then sorted out the twenty-nine one-pound notes and handed the rest back.

My Grandfather watched as I did this; I saw tears in his eyes, and he came over and crushed me to him, hugging me fiercely and saying, 'Ah, God; Isis, child! Isis, Isis, child!' and slapping me vigorously on the back. Allan smiled tremulously at the two of us, his face still pale. Erin's jaw had the set that meant she was biting her tongue; she forced a smile.

'You will make sure you come back in time for the Festival, won't you, child?' Salvador said, pulling away from wetting my shirt collar with his tears. 'You have to be there; more than anybody, you must be there. You will be back?'

'Please God it won't take anything like that long to talk to Morag,' I told him, holding his fleshy forearms. 'I hope I shall be back for the Full Moon Service, in the middle of the month. But if it does take longer, I shall . . .' I took a deep breath. 'I shall return in any event, in good time for the Festival.'

'It's so important,' Grandfather said, nodding. He patted my cheek. 'So important. I may not see another.' He blinked rapidly.

'You will,' I told him, 'but anyway, don't worry. Everything will be all right.'

'Sweet child!' He hugged me again.

*

With the preparations complete, Grandfather called a short after-supper service to ask for the blessing of God on my mission.

I found a morsel of time, late on, to slip out and away across the dark bridge to the Woodbeans' house on the far bank, to tell Sophi that I had to leave and to say goodbye.

CHAPTER
FOUR

My thoughts that night – as I lay in my hammock in my room in the farmhouse – centred around the coming trip, and the possible reasons for my cousin Morag's apostasy. I knew that sleep was probably impossible and that if I did drift off it would probably be just before I was due to be awakened, leaving me feeling shaky and disoriented and tired for much of the day, but I was resigned to this, and it is anyway well known that in such waking tiredness one can often experience a trance-like state which opens one all the better to the voice of the Creator.

Morag and I had been close friends even though she was four years my senior – I had always mixed easily with Community children older than myself, my special status as the Elect conferring the equivalent of a handful of years added to my actual age. Morag and I got on especially well, despite the difference in our years, sharing an interest in music and, I suppose, a similar demeanour.

Morag is the daughter of my aunt Brigit, who left us six years ago. Aunt Brigit joined a Millennialist cult based in Idaho in the United States of America; one of those strange sects who appear to think salvation grows out of the barrel of a gun. She came back for the last Festival of Love, but spent most of her time trying to convert us to her new faith, although to no avail, of course (we are, arguably, far too tolerant sometimes). Aunt Brigit was never entirely sure who Morag's father was, which is a not uncommon result of the Community's informality, and one of those unfortunate trends which can help give credence to the more sensationalistic media reports about us. Certainly my Grandfather always treated her like a daughter, but then Salvador has always behaved as though all the Order children are his own, probably just to express his love for all the Saved, but perhaps just to be on the safe side.

Brigit's daughter is a tall, perfectly proportioned creature with bounteous brown-red hair and eyes deep and blue and big as an ocean; her saving flaw was a rather wide gap between her two front teeth, though – much to our disappointment – she'd had that seen to when she too came back to visit us four years ago.

I think that in any other upbringing Morag would never have developed the talent she had for music; she would have learned too early that her looks were a facile passport to whatever she might desire, and so have been spoiled, wasted, even as a person, fit only to hang on a rich man's arm, signalling his status by her pampered glamour and her over-priced clothes, and with nothing more to temper the vacuity of her existence than the prospect of bearing him children they could spoil together.

Instead, she grew up with us, in the Community, where plain clothes, no make-up, a practical hair-cut and just a general lack of concern with looks mitigates against such distraction, and so was given the time to discover that the greatest gift God had seen fit to bestow upon her was something less ephemeral than physical beauty. Morag learned to play the violin, then the cello, then later the viola da gamba, and eventually the baryton (a kind of viola da gamba with extra, resonating strings) not just with fluent, flawless technique but with an emotional intensity and an intuitive understanding for the music that at first belied her lack of years, and later continued to develop and mature. Though they are expressed with all due modesty, it is obvious from her letters that she, almost alone, has been responsible for the revival of interest in the baryton as an instrument, and through her appearances and recordings given pleasure to many thousands of people. I hope we are not guilty of vanity in feeling as proud of her as we do, and even in some small way partially responsible for her achievements.

The weather turned bright and sunny; I put on my hat to shield my head from the sun. I floated alongside acres of huge, windowless warehouses and passed Alloa with the ebbing tide, taking a rest from my paddling as I lunched on clapshot naan and ghobi stovies and drank some water from my bottle. During the afternoon the wind freshened from the west and helped drive me down river, past a huge power station and under Kincardine Bridge. I paddled with renewed vigour, hugging the southern shore with its gleaming mud-flats; to the north lay another gigantic generating station, while to my right the smokes, steams and flares of the Grangemouth oil refinery leaned away from the breeze, pointing the way towards Edinburgh.

I had been to Gertie Possil's in Edinburgh once before, when I was sixteen, so at least as far as there I knew where I was going. London was another matter. That city is almost as much a magnet for young Orderites as it is for the average youthful Scot, and as well as my cousin Morag and Brother Zeb, it had attracted various others from the Community, including, for a year, my brother Allan, who had also harboured some musical ambitions. He went to London with two friends he had made at the agricultural college in Cirencester where he'd been sent to study farm management. He has played the whole thing down since, but I got the impression he was sorely disappointed by his failure to make something of himself in the big city. I know that he joined a rock music ensemble while he was there and apparently played some form of portable electric organ, however it would seem that whatever visions of stardom he may have cherished came to nothing, and after what I suspect was a generally humiliating experience he returned, adamant both that his place and his work and his destiny were with us in the Order and that he would never again set foot in that vast inhuman fleshpot, epicentre of Clutter and scourge of dreams.

The day wore on; I paddled through the chopping water, taking rests when my arms grew too tired and sore and shifting my position as best I could to ease an ache in my back, which was wet from getting splashed by the waves. Ahead, perhaps ten miles in the distance, I could see the two great bridges over the river, and was heartened by the sight, knowing Edinburgh was not too far beyond. I took the trenching tool in my by now rather raw hands and paddled on.

If I was finding my journey tiring and painful, I reflected that it was as nothing compared to the seminal aquatic rebirth undergone by my Grandfather, four and half decades earlier.

*

63

The seeds of our sect were sown one wind-fierce night on the shores of the island of Harris, in the Outer Hebrides.

It was the last hour of the last day of September 1948 and in the first great storm of the season, the Atlantic wind threw the oceanic rollers at the fractured coast in waves of darkness edged by boiling foam; rain and salt-spray merged in the darkness of the storm to roll across the seaward land, bringing the taste of the sea miles inland, beyond even the thunderous hollow booming of the waves falling on the rocks and sands.

Two frightened Asian women sat huddled together around a single scented candle in an old van sheltering in the dunes behind a long dark beach, listening to the waves pound and the wind howl and the rain rattle on the wood and canvas roof of the ancient vehicle, which rocked and creaked on its leaf springs with each furious gust and seemed likely to tip over and crash into the sand at any moment.

The two women were sisters; their names were Aasni and Zhobelia Asis and they were outcasts, refugees. They were Khalmakistanis, daughters of the first family of Asians to settle in the Hebrides. Their family had established a business running a travelling shop round the islands and had become surprisingly well accepted for a place where hanging out washing on a Sunday is considered tantamount to blasphemy.

Khalmakistan is a mountainous region on the southern fringes of the Himalayas currently disputed by India and Pakistan; in this it is similar to Kashmir, though the inhabitants of each statelet share little else except a mutual contempt. Aasni and Zhobelia were the first of the family's second generation, and generally regarded as having had their heads turned by the bright lights of Stornoway; at any rate they were thought too head-strong and Westernised for their own good or that of the family. Had their family acted quickly enough they might have had the two girls successfully married off to suitable suitors summoned from the sub-continent before they got too used to making up their own minds, but as it was the Second World War intervened and almost seven years were to pass before an easing of both travelling and rationing restrictions created favourable conditions for a match to be arranged. By then, however, it was too late.

It was determined that the two sisters should be offered in marriage to two brothers from a family well known to their parents; certainly the brothers concerned were elderly, but their family was well off, known to be long-lived, and the menfolk in particular were notorious for being fecund well into their twilight years. Besides, as their father told them, he was sure they would be the first to admit that a steadying hand, even if it was wrinkled and a bit shaky, was exactly and manifestly what the two girls needed.

Perhaps infected by the spirit of independence sweeping the Raj itself, and catching something of the mood of female emancipation the war had helped to bring about by putting women into factories, uniforms, jobs and a degree of economic control – perhaps simply having seen one propaganda film too many about jolly Soviet crane drivers at the Stornoway Alhambra – the sisters refused point blank, and the eventual result was that they took the extraordinary step – in the eyes of both their original culture and that which they now found themselves part of – of estranging themselves completely from their family and going into competition with them.

They had some savings and they borrowed money from a sympathetic free-thinking farmer who was himself something of an outsider in that land of the Free Kirk. They bought an old van which had been used as a mobile library round the islands, and some stock; they sold the bacon, lard and beef that their family would not touch and for a few months they sold alcohol too until the excise men brought them to book and explained the niceties of the licensing system to them (luckily they were not also asked to produce a driving licence). They were barely making a living, they had to sleep in the back of the van, they were forever ordering far too much or much too little stock, they were constantly running foul of the rationing authorities and they were utterly miserable without their family but at least they were free, and that and each other's company was about all they had to hold on to.

That day, before the storm had darkened the horizon, they had washed their bedding on some stones in a river which decanted into Loch Laxdale and left it to dry while they went about their business in Lewis.

(Lewis and Harris are referred to as separate islands though in fact they are both thoroughly linked and decisively separated by a range of – by Himalayan standards – small but impressively craggy mountains. The Harris folk are generally smaller and darker than the people of Lewis, a phenomenon popular myth ascribes to the romantic efforts of hordes of swarthy Spaniards washed ashore after Armada ships were wrecked off the rock-ragged Harris coast but which is probably no more than the difference between Celtic and Norse ancestry.)

By the time the sisters had rushed back through the quickly steepening gloom of mid-afternoon the rain had already started, and when they got to where they had left their bedding the wind had flung most of it against a barbed-wire fence and thrown the rest of it into the swollen river. The rain was heavy and almost horizontal by then and the sheets and blankets on the fence could hardly have been wetter had they too been dumped in the river. The sisters salvaged their sodden bedding and retreated to their van, driving it to a hollow in the dunes nearby where they could shelter from the storm.

And so they sat in their coats, clutching each other while their little scented candle flickered in the draught, surrounded by tea chests and boxes full of lard – both symptoms of Aasni's inability either to resist a good deal or to remember how little storage space they had; meanwhile water from their sheets pooled about their feet and threatened to spoil the bags of sugar, flour and custard powder piled under the shelves.

Then there was a thump as something heavy hit the seaward side of the van. They both jumped. Outside, a male voice moaned, barely audible over the noise of the wind and the waves.

They had a lantern; they put the little scented candle inside and ventured out into the bellowing blackness of the drenching gale. Lying on the sandy grass by the side of the van was a young white man in a cheap two-piece suit; he had black hair and a terrible head wound in his upper forehead which oozed blood the beating rain washed away.

They dragged him towards the open rear door of the van; the man came to and moaned again and managed to stand up for a moment; he fell onto the vehicle's floor and they pulled him far enough inside – on a floor lubricated with water and now with blood – to close the banging, wind-blown door.

He looked deathly white, and shivered uncontrollably, still moaning all the while; blood dribbled from the wound in his forehead. They wrapped their coats around him but he wouldn't stop shivering; Aasni remembered that people who swam the English channel would cover themselves with grease, and so they broke out the lard (of which they had rather more than they needed, due to an irresistible grey-market deal with a man in Carloway who'd found several cases washed ashore) and – setting modesty aside – stripped the man to his sodden underpants and started to cover him in lard. He still shivered. Blood still trickled from his forehead; they cleaned the wound and dabbed some antiseptic on it. Aasni found a bandage.

Zhobelia opened the special chest her grandmother had sent her from Khalmakistan on her twentieth birthday and took out the bottle of cherished healing ointment called *zhlonjiz*, which she had been told to keep for extra special emergencies; she made a poultice and put it on the wound, binding his head with the bandage. The man still shivered. They didn't want to get their coats covered with lard, so they opened one of the chests of tea (the tea wasn't in the best of condition anyway, having been stored too long in a barn near Tarbert by a farmer who'd hoped to turn a profit on the wartime black market) and tipped the dark tea leaves over the man's quivering, white-larded form; it took two tea chests to cover him entirely; he seemed half unconscious, still moaning from within his covering of tea and lard, but at least and at last he appeared to have stopped shivering, and for a moment his eyes opened and he looked briefly around and into the eyes of the two sisters before falling back into unconsciousness.

They started the van with the intention of taking the man to the nearest doctor, but the grass in the little hollow they had parked in was so slippery from the rain they couldn't move the vehicle more than a few feet. Aasni put on her coat and went out into the storm to summon help from the nearest farm with a phone. Zhobelia was left in charge of their deathly white storm-waif.

She checked that he still breathed, that his poultice was in place and the bleeding had stopped, then she did her best to wring the water out of his clothes. He babbled, talking in a language that Zhobelia could not understand and suspected nobody else would be able to understand either. A couple of times, however, he mumbled the word, 'Salvador . . .'

The man, of course, was my Grandfather.

*

God spoke to Salvador. They were waiting, enthroned in and surrounded by glorious light, at the end of a dark tunnel which my Grandfather seemed to ascend to from the banal world. He assumed he was dying and this was the way to Heaven. God told him it was the way to Heaven but he was not going to die; instead he had to return to the earthly world with a message from Them to humanity.

Cynics might suggest that it had something to do with the poultice, the potent, exotic, unknown Khalmakistani herbs seeping from it to enter Salvador's bloodstream and poisoning his mind, producing something akin to a hallucinatory 'trip', but the small-(and fearful-) minded will always try to reduce everything to the triviality and mundanity which their stunted, de-spiritualised minds feel safe dealing with. The fact remains that our Founder woke a different man, and – for all that he had almost died from hypothermia aggravated by loss of blood – a better, more whole one; one with a mission, one with a message; a message God had been attempting to transmit complete to Man for a long time through the aggregating clutter of modern life and technology; a message that only somebody whose ambient mental activity had been reduced to something close to quietitude by the proximity of death would be capable of hearing. Possibly other men had heard God's message, but been too close to that edge of death, and slipped over it, unable to transmit the signal on to their fellow men; certainly there had been no shortage of death over the previous decade.

However that may have been, my Grandfather knew when he finally awoke – on a calm, milky-skyed day, with warm tea being poured down his throat by the two dark-skinned women he had assumed were figments of his imagination – that he was The One; the Enlightened, the OverSeer, to whom God had given the task of establishing an Order which would disseminate the Truth of Their message on earth.

Thereafter, then, whoever our Founder had been before, whatever had driven him to that place on that night, however he had made his way through the storm – out of the sea, off the land, or even falling from the sky – became unimportant. All that mattered was that Salvador awoke, remembering his vision and the task he had been charged with, and decided he had a purpose in life. He had work to do.

First, however, there was the matter of a canvas bag . . .

*

The last leg of my water-borne journey, in the early evening, seemed to take forever. I had passed beneath the bowed deck of the grey road bridge and the straight bed of the rail bridge fighting an incoming tide with only the wind at my back to aid me; once through the narrows between the Queensferries I could slacken my efforts a little, but every muscle in my upper body felt as if it were on fire.

Finding that the bottom of my small craft was sloshing with water which had splashed in during my battle with the tides, and fearful for the contents of my kit-bag, I stopped for a while and bailed out the water, using my handkerchief, then I paddled on, between golden sands and quiet wooded shores to my right, and two long, land-isolated jetties to my left, to each of which a huge oil tanker was tied up.

A motor boat left one of the jetties and swung round towards me. The boat proved to be full of surprised-looking workmen

69

in brightly coloured overalls. At first they seemed reluctant to believe that I was not in some difficulty, but then laughed and shook their heads and told me if I had any sense I'd head for shore and continue on foot. They called me 'hen', which I found mildly insulting, though I think it was meant congenially enough. I thanked them for their advice and they powered off, heading upstream.

I came ashore, at last, at Cramond, at the point where a line of tall obelisks strides out across the sands to a low island. Just before I touched the sands, I heaved my kit-bag out from under me – it was only a little damp – and dug out the vial of Forth mud to freshen up the mark on my forehead, which I suspected must have been washed off by a combination of spray and sweat. My strange craft bumped ashore onto grey-blond sands, and I got out. I had a little difficulty in standing, and then in straightening, but eventually did so, and luxuriated in a long if painful stretch, all under the quizzical gaze of numerous swans floating in the waters of the river Almond, and a few suspicious-looking youths standing on the promenade.

'Hey, mister; you ship-wrecked, aye?' one of them shouted.

'No,' I said, pulling my kit-bag out of the inner-tube and packing the folded trenching tool away. I left my craft lying on the sand by a small slipway and climbed up to the youths. 'And I am a Sister, not a mister,' I told them, drawing myself up.

They wore baggy clothes and long-sleeved T-shirts with hoods. Their short hair looked greasy. One of them looked down at the inner-tube. 'Zat big tyre goin' spare then, hen?'

'It's all yours,' I told them, and walked away.

I felt a kind of exhilaration then, having accomplished the first part of my journey. I strode out along the esplanade, munching on another naan with my kit-bag slung over my shoulder while my shadow lengthened in front of me. I consulted my map, negotiated a few roads and found the abandoned railway line – now a cycle-way – at Granton Road. Within a hundred yards I discovered a thin, straight, broken branch hanging off a tree by the trail; I tore it down and used my penknife to remove a few twigs, and soon had a serviceable staff to accompany me on my way. The old railway path took me almost three miles towards my destination, by turns under and over the evening traffic; the air was full of the smell of engine exhaust and the sky was lit with flagrant red clouds as I crossed to pick up the towpath of the Old Union Canal and then took the footpath skirting school playing grounds. The last part of my trip was as well accomplished in near darkness, given that it took me along a stretch of railway line which was still in occasional use. I hid in some bushes up the embankment as a loud diesel engine came swinging round the bend from the east, pulling a long train of open, double-deck wagons stacked with cars.

The red tail-light on the last wagon blinked fast as a racing heart as it disappeared round the turn in the cutting, and I sat there on my haunches for a moment or two, thinking.

After a moment I got up and continued along the track-side, passing through an abandoned station and then walking under a busy-sounding road junction until I came to within a couple of streets of the home of Gertie Possil, in the douce Edinburgh suburb of Morningside, and arrived there in time to take part in a ceremonial supper.

CHAPTER
FIVE

'lessed Isis! *Beloved* Isis! Oh! What an honour! We are so honoured! Oh! Oh!'

Sister Gertie Possil, tiny, white-haired, frail and easily old enough to be my grandmother, made the Sign, set the paraffin lamp she carried down on a narrow table and prostrated herself at my feet, then edged forward until she could touch my boots, which she patted as though they were tiny, delicate animals.

Gertie Possil was dressed in something oatmeal-coloured and flowing which settled around her on the black and white tiles of the hallway floor like a pool of porridge. Behind me, the stained-glass door swung shut.

'Thank you, Sister Gertie,' I said, making the Sign in return and feeling just a little embarrassed at having my boots petted. 'Please; do rise.'

'Welcome, welcome, to our humble, unworthy house!' she wailed, getting back up again. I helped her the last couple of feet, putting my hand to her elbow, and she stared open-mouthed at my hand and then at my face. 'Oh, *thank you*, Blessed Isis!' she said, and felt for the glasses that hung from a cord on her chest. She positioned them properly and sighed deeply, staring at me, seemingly lost for words. Behind her, in the dark hallway of the large, gloomy house, stood a tall, plump man with a large and mostly bald head. This was Gertie's son, Lucius. He wore a heavy purple dressing-gown over dark trousers and spatted shoes. A cravat was bunched awkwardly under his double chins. He beamed at me and rubbed his fat hands together nervously.

'Umm, umm, umm . . .' he said.

'Let Lucius take your bag, you wonderful child you,' Gertie Possil said to me, and then turned to her son. 'Lucius! The Anointed's bag; see? Here! You lump! What's the matter with you?' She *tsk*ed as she reverently took my staff and leaned it

75

against the coat stand. 'That boy of mine!' she muttered, sounding exasperated.

Lucius bumbled forward, bumping into things in the hallway. I handed him my kit-bag. He took it and smiled broadly, nodding, his Adam's apple bobbing up and down like a pigeon's head.

'Tell the Beloved you are honoured!' Gertie said, using the flat of her hand to hit her son in the stomach with surprising force.

'Honoured! Honoured!' Lucius gulped, still smiling broadly, nodding vigorously and swallowing powerfully. He swung the kit-bag over his shoulder and clunked the grandfather clock with it. He appeared not to notice. 'Honoured!' he said again.

'Brother Lucius,' I nodded as Gertie helped me off with my jacket.

'You must be exhausted!' Gertie said, carefully hanging my jacket on a padded hanger. 'I shall prepare some supper and Lucius will run you a bath. You are hungry, aren't you? You haven't eaten? May I wash your feet? You poor child; you look tired. Are you weary?'

I glanced at my face in the mirror by the coat hooks, illuminated by the weak yellow light of the paraffin lamp. I thought I did look tired. Certainly I felt weary.

'It has been a long day,' I admitted as Gertie shooed her son ahead of her towards the stairs. 'I would love a cup of tea, Sister Gertrude, and something to eat. A bath would be pleasant, later.'

'Of course! And please, call me Gertie! Lucius, you lump; upstairs; the good bedroom!'

'Thank you,' I said as Lucius thumped up the stairs and his mother led me through to their candle-lit parlour. 'Firstly, however, I must use your telephone to tell the Community I have arrived safely.'

'Indeed! Of course! It is here . . .' She doubled back and flitted past me, opening the door to the cupboard under the stairs. She set down the paraffin lamp on a narrow shelf and showed me to a small wooden chair facing a tiny table which supported a large black bakelite phone with a twisted fabric cord. 'I shall leave you the lamp,' she announced. She turned to go, hesitated, gazed raptly at me, then held out her hands to one of mine and tremulously said, 'May I?'

I gave her my hand and she kissed it. Her thin, pale lips felt soft, and dry as paper. 'Beloved Isis, *Blessed* Isis!' she said, blinking quickly, and scurried away into the dim hall. I sat down and picked up the phone handset.

We do not, of course, have a telephone in the Community, and while there is a set in the Woodbeans' house we are allowed to use, we do not make or receive normal calls. There is a tradition in the Order that telephones must only be used for urgent messages, and then not in a way so trivial and facile as by simply lifting the receiver and talking.

I dialled the Woodbean's number. Above me, I could hear Lucius clumping around on the first floor. I let the phone ring twice, then put it down and dialled again, this time letting it ring nine times, then clicked the cradle buttons down once more before dialling a third time and allowing four more sets of trills to sound.

This was my special cipher; it had been agreed on the previous evening during our final council of war that no further coded signal would be required to let the Order know that I had arrived safely at the home of Gertie Possil. This was just as well; sending a long message in this manner – using our own form of Morse code – can take several hours, especially if one has to transmit one's own number to the person initially receiving the call and then has to leave gaps in one's transmission during which they may ring back to send signals containing questions, and never forgetting that there is a degree of inaccuracy inevitable to the whole process anyway, given that the rings heard at the source phone do not always tally exactly with those at the receiving machine (this, I am told, is why a caller can think that a phone they are calling into has been lifted before it has started ringing).

Of course, we do not ask the Woodbeans to sit by the phone all night noting down the sequence of rings; either a pre-agreed time is set up for a call during which an Orderite will be sitting with pencil and paper in the Woodbeans' front hall, or a special machine can be switched on, designed and built by Brother Indra, which records each trill the phone makes on a piece of paper wound round a metal drum and which is made from bits of an old tape-recorder, a clock and a barometer.

There was also, of course, a security aspect to all this; while my Grandfather no longer believed there was a special government department dedicated to the observation and harassment of our Order, and there seems to have been little recent interest from those peddlers of prurience, the popular press, it is always wise to keep up one's guard, for – as my Grandfather has pointed out – it is the surprise attack, the assault undertaken once the victim has been lulled into slackened discipline and sloppy vigilance, that is the most devastating. Some ungracious apostates have suggested that the whole ritual is motivated by a desire to economise on telephone bills, and it is true that the system does have the additional benefit of considerable frugality; however the sheer awkwardness of the whole business surely points to a holier, more pure purpose.

When I finished my call I joined Gertie in the kitchen, to find her preparing the supper. On the stove, a kettle sat surrounded by several cast-iron pots, all gradually coming to the boil and filling the room with mouth-watering aromas. 'Blessed Isis!' Gertie exclaimed, adding a dab of lard to each of three large white china plates on which tiny piles of tea already sat. 'You said you were hungry.'

'Indeed I am,' I conceded.

We ate in the dining room, round a long table of darkly gleaming polished wood whose centre was lined with tall candles, condiments, preserves, pickles and baskets of leavened and unleavened bread. The supper was conducted with all due solemnity. The presence of the lard and the tea on the side of the plate, as well as the incense candles and a dish as grand as venison tikka pasanda, marked this out as a special occasion. I said the blessing, I served the first piece of food from each dish, I read from the *Orthography* and marked both Gertie and Lucius's foreheads with the vial of mud from home; I even made polite conversation and brought the Possils up to date with the news from the Community; they had not visited for a year or so, and though they were hoping to be there for the

Festival of Love in four weeks' time, they were grateful for a briefing beforehand.

I accepted the offer of a bath, though I was already almost dead on my feet, and woke to find myself chin-deep in the tepid water, with Gertie banging as loud as deference would allow on the bathroom door. I assured her I was awake again, rinsed and dried and then made my way to my bedroom. It was the finest room in the house and it possessed a large Victorian four-poster bed which I remembered from my visit here three years earlier. This was ideal for my purposes as it meant I was able to sling my hammock between two of the sturdy posts, and even orient my hammock in a direction that ensured my head would be pointing towards the Community. I slept soundly, and dreamed of nothing I could recall.

*

It was while I was sorting out my kit-bag the following morning that I found, right at the bottom of it, something extra and very special; something I did not know I had. It came in the shape of a tiny vial wrapped in a scrap of paper and secured by a rubber band. '*In case. S.*,' said the words printed on the note. I opened the tiny glass jar with some difficulty and sniffed the dark, almost black ointment inside.

It was *zhlonjiz*; the priceless, irreplaceable unguent that is more precious and significant to us than gold, frankincense and myrrh to Christians . . . no; more precious yet; it is as though we possess our Grail, but it is still magically powerful, and consumable. I had heard of *zhlonjiz* since toddlerhood but only ever seen or smelled it once before, at my coming-of-age ceremony three years earlier. I knew that my Grandfather had only the tiniest amount of the treasured, mystical salve left after all these years. That he should honour me so by entrusting this substantial fragment of our holy of holies to my keeping was both a humbling tribute to the love he had for me and the faith he had in me, and a sobering reminder – had I needed one – of the importance of my mission.

79

I felt tears prick behind my eyes. I carefully resealed the vial, pressed its little bakelite cap to my forehead and whispered a blessing, then kissed the tiny glass jar and stowed it carefully, wrapped in my extra clothes, back in the bottom of my kit-bag.

*

Edinburgh has the merit as a city – by our beliefs – that it is at its centre erratic, convoluted and full of different levels and strange steep passageways (though by all accounts the old cities of the Holy Lands surpass it in this regard, and Tokyo, in Japan, is apparently quite creditably difficult to find one's way around). Edinburgh is still a city of course, and therefore to be avoided unless one has some pressing need to stay there – in Gertie Possil's case a nostalgic weakness for the marital memories associated with the house was what had persuaded her to remain – but as cities go it is neither overly regular in pattern (save in the New Town) nor too large to see out of, two criteria which have always seemed to me important. We have always held it to be a bad sign when navigating one's way round a city becomes a matter simply of knowing one's x-axis from one's y-axis, and we are I think rightly horrified at the prospect of discovering that the only direction to look in the hope of finding something natural to look at is up at the clouds (like as not polluted by the sight of aircraft and their vapour trails or, at night, by the reflected lights of the city itself).

I had still to decide how I was to make my journey to London with sanctity, but the relative speed of my progress the previous day – I had envisaged taking two days and having to find shelter somewhere ashore – together with the comparatively benign atmosphere of Edinburgh left me in no hurry to start travelling immediately when I woke up the next morning at a shamefully late hour; I decided I could take up to a day to rest and think.

Fêted at breakfast as much as at supper – there were rose-petals in my tea and I had to let Gertie Possil wash my feet – I told her and her son that I needed to reconnoitre various aspects of the city, and would return once I had completed my scouting expedition. I declined Gertie's offer of a guide in the shape of Lucius – he looked relieved too, behind an anxious smile – and assured her that I could look after myself. Gertie still looked worried, and so I mentioned that I felt doubly secure knowing that I had the jar of *zhlonjiz* upon my person; Sister Gertrude was suitably impressed that the semi-legendary salve had been entrusted to my care, but seemed satisfied that my safety was thereby guaranteed.

And so I went out amongst the Unsaved (also known as the Wretched, the Insane, the Norms, the Obtuse, the Reject, the Clinker, the Chaff, the Cluttered, the Rank, the Passives, the Benighted and the Asleep), uncomfortably conscious of the fact that I was walking away from the only other two people in the city who were numbered among the Saved (likewise the Enlightened, the Sane, the Preferred, the Acute, the Chosen, the Refined, the Engraced, the Clear, the Commissioned, the Active, the Dawned and the Awoken), my jacket pockets filled with the more precious items I had brought from the Community and a couple of cheese and mango pickle sandwiches prepared by Gertie.

The day was warm and I left my hat dangling down over the back of my jacket, which had been cleaned as best she could by Gertie overnight. The main thoroughfares of the city were choked with cars, the pavements aswarm with people. The air reeked of burned petrol; lurid advertisements and shop windows screamed for attention from every side. A few people looked at me oddly – I did not think that my monochrome garments were particularly different from those worn by many of the youths – of both sexes – whom I saw, and I observed a few people with hats, so perhaps it was the staff I carried which set me apart. I felt awkward and tense in the midst of so much strident clutter and so many people and after a while I took to the quieter streets, away from the stressing mass of humanity.

Some children in a school playground shouted through the railings at me, accusing me of being what they called a Loony, and asking for 'a shot of your stick. Does it turn into a power sword?'

I had been going to ignore them, but turned and approached instead; they shrank back initially, then – perhaps encouraged by their numbers and by the railings between us – they came back.

81

'What's a power sword?' I asked

'You know like in *Transforcers*; on Saturday mornings,' one of them said.

I thought for a moment. 'You mean on television?'

'Aye! Of course! Yeah! On the telly!' they choroused.

I shook my head. 'We don't have a television set in our house.'

'What? *No!* Yer kiddin'! Get outa here! You live in the loony bin, missus?'

'No, I live in the Community—'

This caused some mirth amongst a few of the older ones, one of whom – the one who'd talked first – asked, 'What's that on your forehead?'

'It's a mark of respect,' I told him, smiling. 'A mark of love, and faith . . . what's your name?'

'Mark,' he replied, to some giggles. He looked defiant. 'What's yours?'

'Well, I have a bit of a funny name,' I told them. 'I am The Blessed Very Reverend Gaia-Marie Isis Saraswati Minerva Mirza Whit of Luskentyre, Beloved Elect of God, III.'

More laughter. The bell rang then and they were called away by a teacher who looked at me suspiciously. I waved to the children and blessed them under my breath, then turned away, looking at the stave in my hand and thinking how slight are the signals by which we serve notice – inadvertently or not – that we are not part of the Bland world. It also struck me that such signs are often emblems of an unfamiliar practicality, and how misguided it is to believe that the greater world is somehow ultimately cosmopolitan and tolerant.

My own school days – not long over I suppose, judged against the scale of a full life, though they seem moderately distant to me now – were passed at the Gerhardt Academy. We have been sending our secondary school children as day pupils to the Academy – just outside the village of Killearn, on the western flank of the southern hills – for thirty years, ever since we'd had some trouble with the local authorities; they were and are happy with the standard of our primary teaching but demanded we put our elder children through more formal educational channels. The

Gerhardt Academy is a school for the children of parents who wish them to have an education that is officially recognised but less strictly structured than the state or private norm. It was still a long-term aim of my Grandfather to educate all Order children up to secondary standard and even to lay the foundations for a college some time in the future, but in the meantime the Academy provides a satisfactory secondary alternative.

I had both mostly enjoyed the experience at the time and felt afterwards that I had benefited from it. To this day whenever I see the younger Brothers and Sisters heading off to catch the bus in the morning, I still feel a smidgen of nostalgia for the days when I too carried a Sitting Board and a satchel over the bridge, past the Woodbeans' house and up the drive to the rusted gates (the satchels are self-explanatory; the boards were because the bus had padded seats which we were not allowed to use, so took our own hard wooden boards to sit on. Rebellion then consisted of sitting on the soft seats and using one's board with a roller skate underneath as a skate board).

The Academy, housed in a high and Gothic castle in the trees above Killearn village, is a good place to learn; I'm sure to some of the pupils and parents it seems a strange, spartan and even eccentric institution with its odd combination of archaic fixtures and traditions (I was given slates and chalk to work with during my first year), free-flowing curriculum, easy discipline and unconventional teachers, but to us Order children it tends to seem like a haven of luxury, order and common sense after the Community.

In addition to its formal scholastic role, the Academy has traditionally been the place where young Luskentyrians learn more about the non-academic world, mixing with Unsaved children and being exposed to the more common adolescent interests such as pop music, comics, the adulation of sporting and cultural heroes, the use of popular slang and so on. This can be a traumatic experience for a child of the Community, however we tend to arrive forewarned by those who have gone before us and in groups that can offer support to any individual in need of it, plus of course we have our Faith to comfort us through any teenage angst that

83

may result. Furthermore, possessing a generally superior (if usually only theoretical) knowledge regarding sex and drugs compared to our Unsaved peers – gained in the enlightened atmosphere of the Community – means that we can give as good as we get when it comes to peer-impressing.

So, I had enjoyed my school days and I suppose I could even be said to have shone academically, if that is not too immodest. Indeed, a few of my teachers had tried to persuade me to go on to university, either to read physics or English, however my Grandfather and I knew that I had been marked out for a more holy purpose, and that my rightful place was with – and in – the Community.

I turned and walked away from the school.

*

In the end it took me two days to get out of Edinburgh. I spent that day fruitlessly trying to work out how to stow away on a Motorail train at Waverley station, but it looked too difficult (to my surprise, I saw a notice that said the service would soon cease altogether). I could just have jumped on a London-bound train and trusted to my wits to keep away from a guard – we have our own nonsense language and a look of somehow foreign incomprehension perfected for when one is caught in such situations – or I might have tried a long-range variant of the technique we call Back Bussing. However it struck me that this would prove problematic over such a distance, and – more to the point – there was something insufficiently holy about this approach. We are not averse to travelling in trains – either sitting on the floor of the guard's van or using the wooden Sitting Boards we carry to avoid the luxury of soft furnishings – but my mission was so important I had to be rigorous in my piety, and there was something too beguilingly easy about simply avoiding paying my fare on an ordinary passenger train.

I retreated to Morningside, using as many out-of-the-way routes as I could, including one snicket, or footpath, charmingly called Lover's Loan. En route I saw several cars with signs in the back saying 'Child On Board', and was reminded, by now with more amusement than embarrassment, of my first trip to Edinburgh three years earlier, when I had proudly pointed out to Sister Jess – who was one of my attendants for that trip – that given the number of people so advertising the fact their offspring were not deigning to sit on soft automobile seats, our Order obviously had many converts in the city.

While taking tea at the Possils' that afternoon I heard the distant sound of a diesel locomotive, and was reminded of the train which had passed me the night before as I'd been travelling along the nearby cutting. Thereafter I went out and walked around, trying to recall exactly what the cars I had seen last night on the freight train had looked like. Happily, I have a good memory and the cars proved common. I went to the nearest car dealership and inquired about where Ford Escorts were constructed, then spent some considerable time in the area around the junction where Morningside Road and Comiston Road join, watching freight trains. The trains came from the west through the abandoned station immediately to the west of the bridge carrying the crossroads, or through the shallow, tree-lined cutting just to the east, which had been the point at which I'd struck out for Gertie Possil's the night before. The trains were few and far between, which made it easy to memorise their times via the old clock tower near the junction, but I became concerned that I might become conspicuous, and so returned to the Possils' and borrowed a wooden tray, a length of wallpaper which I tore into tray-sized rectangles, and a thick black crayon Gertie used to write messages for the milkman; thereafter I returned to the railway and the road junction, and made a series of sketches of the buildings while I watched for passing trains. I was relieved to see one pass westwards loaded with cars at approximately the same time as the one I had hidden from yesterday.

Finding no regularity in the trains' schedule from hour to hour, but having formulated a plan which might work if they kept to the same timetable on a day-to-day basis, I returned to the home of Gertie Possil and another ceremonial supper followed by a service, which I trust I conducted in a manner my Grandfather would have approved of. The service went well enough, I think (despite the fact that Lucius is profoundly tone deaf and when it comes to singing in tongues can only mumble in them).

Still thinking about my plan, and having come to the conclusion that it possessed the flaw of being difficult to carry out in daylight or even around dusk, I walked back to the road junction yet again, and was rewarded with the sight of a train that would suit me perfectly.

*

The following night found me crouched in some bushes on what had once been the platform of Morningside station, my jacket buttoned up so that no trace of my white shirt showed, my hat on so that my face was in shadow and my pale kit-bag concealed behind me. A light rain was falling from clouds smudged orange with the city's glare. I was getting wet. Above and behind me, late-night traffic roared and hissed on the road junction where I had spent so much time yesterday. I estimated that I had been waiting for almost half an hour, and was beginning to worry that somebody might already have noticed the large cardboard box I had thrown over the train signals further up the track near the next bridge to the east, where the railway passes under Braid Avenue.

The box had apparently once contained a washing machine; I had found it in a skip a couple of streets away, carried it to the cutting, made sure there was nobody about, thrown it over the jagged railings and climbed after it, then fought my way through brambles and bushes and heaved the box over the signals. I wondered how long it would take for somebody to spot this and report it to the relevant authorities. Luckily no trains had yet passed in the opposite direction whose drivers might have noticed, but I was becoming concerned.

I had bade the Possils farewell after another solemn supper and another reverential washing of my feet by Gertie. She gave me food and water for my journey; Lucius mumbled and spluttered until hit firmly on the back of the neck by his mother, whereupon he explained that the cravat he was holding out to me – and which I had been about to bless – was a present.

86

I accepted Gertie's food and Lucius's cravat and thanked them both. I had already packed the map of London I'd asked to borrow. I presented them with the drawings of the buildings around the road junction and told them they could keep the wooden staff. Lucius bubbled with gratitude; Gertie put her hand to her chest and seemed about to have a seizure. She thereupon fell at my feet, and so I exited the house, backwards, as I had entered it, with Sister Gertie patting my boots.

Walking through the drizzle to the railway track and the abandoned station had been oddly relieving.

I heard a train rumbling towards me along the cutting to the west. I gripped my kit-bag and flexed my legs, which had become stiff squatting in the same position for so long.

Small white lights appeared in the black cutting and the diesel noise swelled; the dark mass of the loco rumbled past; I could make out the driver, sitting staring ahead in the yellow-lit cab. The engine hauled empty open wagons similar to those I had seen the night before at around this time, and which I guessed I had seen twice before in addition, on each occasion loaded with new cars. The locomotive roared under the bridge supporting the road junction, its exhaust billowing around me, stinking. The train of wagons flowed clatteringly past, and for a second I thought my plan had foundered, then with a squeal and a cacophony of metallic shrieks the train began to slow.

I almost jumped up then, but waited for the wagons to draw to a stop before walking calmly out of the bushes to where the third-last wagon lay, stationary. I stepped onto it from the weed-strewn platform as easily as a fare-paying passenger into a normal carriage.

I squinted down the girdered length of the train towards the rear, then walked in that direction, jumping from one wagon to the next. On the final wagon there was a single automobile, sitting right at the rear. I went up to it. Its bodywork looked dull and mat, and felt as if it was covered in wax; there was a large, pale, chalky-looking 'X' scrawled on its bonnet and a sheaf of paperwork taped to the inside of the windscreen. I tried the passenger door and discovered it was unlocked.

I looked up into the drizzle. 'Praise be,' I said, smiling, and would have whooped for joy had I not been afraid of revealing my presence. 'Praise be indeed,' I said, laughing quietly, and jumped inside, my heart rejoicing.

A minute later, the train gave a series of jerks and started moving forward again, gathering speed and taking me away from Edinburgh, heading south.

CHAPTER
SIX

The day after the great storm, Aasni and Zhobelia scraped my Grandfather clean of tea and lard and took him to the farm of Mr Eoin McIlone, the free-thinker who had offered shelter to the sisters before. On this occasion he also offered succour to their storm-tossed foundling, for whom he made up the bed in what he called his spare room, though in truth it was more like a study or even a library; the walls were lined with mismatched bookcases and rickety shelving nailed to the wooden walls, all supporting Mr McIlone's considerable collection of books on philosophy, politics, theology and radical thought.

My Grandfather continued to drift in and out of something between a fever and a coma for most of the next few days, rambling incoherently and moaning. The local doctor had been summoned and had judged Grandfather too ill to move. He had taken the *zhlonjiz* poultice off my Grandfather's head and had applied a proper dressing, which Aasni had removed and replaced with a fresh poultice the instant she heard the doctor's car start up again. It took Grandfather some days to come fully round. The name of Mr McIlone's farm was Luskentyre.

When my Grandfather did eventually become entirely conscious and lucid and sat up in the bed in his book-lined room and was asked what his name was, he told his two dusky rescuers that he had been reborn, and so had no name. Hearing that he had muttered the name 'Salvador' during the first night, he suggested this was a sign from God to take that name, and asked his rescuers to address him so.

He then told the sisters of a canvas grip he had possessed which was all he wished to salvage from his past life. This canvas bag was most important to him, as was proved by the fact that while he could remember nothing else from the day of the storm, he knew that he had been carrying the canvas bag and that everything he valued had been inside it. He implored Aasni and Zhobelia to search the beaches and rocks around the place he had been found for the grip, and to bring it to him unopened if they did.

They duly searched, while my Grandfather recovered – often talking at some length about his revelations with Mr McIlone. Mr McIlone was an atheist, but he was still fascinated by my Grandfather's revelatory experience, even if he ascribed it to the effects of being near death, losing a lot of blood and possibly being affected by whatever strange herbs, liniments and potions were contained in the *zhlonjiz* poultice. Mr McIlone suggested that my Grandfather make use of the books on the shelves around him if he wanted to think further about his apparently religious experience, and this Salvador duly did, diffidently at first.

The sisters reported back to say they had found many things washed ashore, but no canvas grip. Before he was really well enough, Salvador struggled out of bed and joined them in the search, and the three of them scoured the beaches, coves, islets, inlets and rock pools of the coast. As the search went on, my Grandfather expounded upon his revelations with increasing force and conviction and in greater and greater detail. What the sisters understood, with their imperfect English and lack of a common cultural and religious background, they found both impressive and interesting.

Mr McIlone loaned Salvador an old army ridge-pole tent and he pitched it in the remains of an old seaweed processing factory a mile along the coast, not far from where Grandfather had been washed ashore. The tumbledown seaweed plant had become the centre of a highly complicated and acrimonious legal dispute before the war and so there was nobody to turn Grandfather and the sisters off the land; gradually they made the old factory their base and then their home. Meanwhile Aasni and Zhobelia continued to run their travelling shop business and Salvador roamed the shoreline further and further in each direction in the shortening daylight hours, still searching for the canvas grip. In the evenings, while the wind moaned through the old building and their paraffin lamps guttered in the draughts which swept the rooms they had refurbished in the factory offices, Salvador took to writing down the revelations the Creator had visited upon him and branded into his brain, while the livid mark on his forehead slowly faded to leave a V-shaped white indentation and his hair grew in prematurely white.

Often at his elbow were books borrowed from Mr McIlone's library, where he had begun his studies and was still welcome to pursue them. Grandfather had decided to work his way through every book and tract and pamphlet in Mr McIlone's spare room, a task he was accomplishing with voracious expedition as he used their insights and teachings to further refine his own.

Exactly when Grandfather and the Asis sisters embarked upon the more intimate aspect of their tripartite relationship is not recorded; Grandmother Aasni and Great-aunt Zhobelia were always coy about the details concerning which one took him to their bosom first, or whether they shared him from the start. Whether there was any acrimony over this (especially by the professed standard of the time) unorthodox sexual arrangement was not something they ever talked about. For his part, when asked about such matters Salvador has always assumed an air of regretful silence, implying that while of course he believes in openness and in the unashamed, celebrative sanctity of the bodily communing that is physical love, he is first and foremost a gentleman, and so forsworn from confiding anything on the subject without the express permission of both sisters (which, given that my grandmother Aasni died some years ago, is unlikely to be given unless it is at least partially from beyond the grave).

Salvador found manual work on Mr McIlone's farm to help himself and the sisters through the next year; meanwhile he continued to search and to write, with gradually less and more conviction respectively as time went by.

*

It took me some time to fall asleep after the car-wagon train restarted its journey; I suppose I was still excited after the whole business of stopping the train and boarding it.

The car I was in smelled strongly of plastic; the dashboard and much of the other trim was plastic and there were transparent plastic covers over the seats. I had taken out my compact Sitting

Board in case I wanted to sit rather than lie down, then stowed my kit-bag in the front footwell and got into the back seat where there was more room. Judging that it might be rather noisy if I was trying to sleep, I had taken the plastic cover off the back seat and left it folded on the driver's seat, then I'd settled down for the night, but had not been able to sleep.

I felt uncomfortable just being in the car at all; it smelled so new and seemed somehow designed to be so archetypically bland that a true Luskentyrian could hardly feel otherwise. However my delight at having secured such an Interstitial mode of transport helped to ameliorate the effects of the car's toxic banality.

While I was still lying there trying to sleep, I thought of my cousin Morag, the apostate, and recalled once sitting with her on the platform of the Deivoxiphone, in the warm sunlight of a summer four years ago, when she was the age I am now and I was fifteen.

The Deivoxiphone was a piece of army surplus which was there at the farm before the Order took up residence; Mrs Woodbean – the lady who gifted the estate to us – had had a brother who collected strange vehicles and pieces of equipment and stored them at the farm (he was killed at a meeting of like-minded enthusiasts in Perthshire when a jeep he was driving too exuberantly turned over). One of the things he collected was a bizarre-looking device on a trailer which had been used briefly during the Blitz at the start of the Second World War. The instrument consisted of what appeared to be a number of gigantic fluted listening trumpets. Appearances in this case were not deceptive, for that was exactly what the apparatus was: a huge artificial ear for pointing at the skies and trying to hear German bombers before they arrived overhead. A sort of poor-man's radar, in other words, and from the little I have heard concerning their efficacy, about as useful as one might imagine.

When I was nine I thought this piece of junk was just the most wonderful mechanism on God's earth, and somehow got it into my head that it was important to rescue the thing from the paddock where it was being slowly submerged in weeds, and set it up somewhere. My Grandfather had been dubious, thinking the device had too much of an aura of clutter about it, but he could refuse me nothing, and so he'd had the thing taken off its trailer and hoisted up onto a wooden platform built especially on top of the old circular barn at the back of the farm. Grandfather named it the Deivoxiphone.

I did not, of course, believe that we would literally be able to hear the voice of God any better using this extraordinary contraption, but as a *symbol* of our ideals I thought it was powerful and important (I was going through a serious stage at that age and objects and stories which seemed symbolic meant a lot to me).

Of course, as soon as the instrument had been raised to its position of prominence I lost all interest in it, but there it sat, perched on its octagonal wooden rostrum to the south of the farm, aimed at the heavens like an olive-green multi-barrel blunderbuss. There was enough space on the decking around it for sunbathing or just sitting looking out over the gardens, woods and distant hills, and that was where I'd sat, legs dangling over the platform edge, arms flat on the platform's lower rail, four years earlier, talking to Morag.

'The Pendicles of Collymoon,' she said.

'What?'

'The Pendicles of Collymoon,' she repeated. 'It's a place. I saw it on the map.'

'Oh, Collymoon,' I said, placing the name. 'Yes; up near Buchlyvie.' Buchlyvie is a wee village about a dozen miles west from the Community, due south of Scotland's only lake, the Lake of Menteith. In between is Collymoon, a scatter of houses on the north shore of the Forth east of Flanders Moss. I'd noticed it on a map too, and had passed it once, on one of my long-range walks a couple of years earlier. It was a pleasant enough situation, but nothing special.

Morag lay back in the sunlight, gazing up at the sky, or perhaps the Deivoxiphone's preposterous trumpets. 'Don't you think that's the most wonderful name, though? Don't you think that's just the most romantic name you ever heard?' (I shrugged.) 'I think it is,' she said, nodding emphatically. 'The Pendicles of Collymoon,' she said once more, with languorous grace. 'It sounds like a romantic novel, doesn't it?'

'Probably a hopelessly slushy one,' I said.

'Oh, you're so unromantic,' Morag said, slapping my hip.

'I'm not,' I protested awkwardly, 'I just have a higher threshold of . . . romanticism, that's all.' I lay down on my side, one arm supporting my head, facing her. I envied Morag her shiningly auburn hair; it was a billowed halo on the sun-bleached planks around her head; a wild red river sparkling in the sun. 'It takes more than a few words on a map to make *me* go all gooey.'

'Who's all gooey? I didn't say I was all gooey.'

'I bet you imagined some dishy guy coming from the Pendicles of Collymoon—'

'*Dishy?*' Morag said, her face screwing up as she started giggling. '*Dishy?*' she laughed. Her breasts shook under her T-shirt as she chortled. I felt my face go red.

'Well, *hunky*, then,' I said, pinching her arm to no effect. 'Sorry if I'm not up with the latest slang; we live a sheltered life here.' I pinched harder.

'Aow!' she said, and slapped my hand away. She raised her head up, turning on her side to face me. 'Anyway,' she smiled, 'what does make you romantic?' She made a show of looking about. 'Any of the guys here?'

I looked away; now it was my turn to lie down on my back and stare up at the sky.

'Not really,' I admitted, frowning.

She was silent for a while, then she tapped me on the nose with one finger. 'Maybe you should get out more, cuz.'

I took her finger in my hand and held it and turned to look at her, my heart suddenly beating wildly. She looked puzzled for a moment, as I gently squeezed her finger and gazed into her eyes, then gave a small, perhaps regretful smile. She took her finger gently from my grasp and said, 'Oooh . . .' very softly, nodding. 'Really?'

I looked away, crossing my arms across my chest. 'Oh, I don't know,' I said miserably. I felt like crying all of a sudden, but refused to. 'I have so many feelings, so much . . . *passion* inside me, but it never really seems to come out the way it should. It's like . . .' I sighed, struggling to find the right words. 'It's like I feel I *ought* to be interested in boys, or if not in boys then in girls, but I almost have to force myself to feel anything. Sometimes I think I do feel *something*, like I'm normal, but then . . .' I shook my head. 'I do the laying on of hands, and it's like all that passion is . . . earthed then, like lightning.' I looked imploringly at her. 'Please don't say anything to anybody.'

'Don't worry,' she said, and winked. 'You'd be amazed at just how discreet I am. But listen; love is all that matters. That's what I think. Love and romance. People get all worked up about things they think are unnatural or perverted, but the only thing that's really unnatural and perverted is thinking there's something wrong with people loving each other.' She patted my shoulder again. 'You do what you think's right, Is; it's your life.'

I turned and looked at her. I still hadn't cried, but I had to sniff a bit, and blink to clear my eyes. I cleared my throat. 'It doesn't always feel that way,' I told her.

'Well, look, whatever it is you feel, if it doesn't feel like sex, then it isn't. All right, you're feeling *something*, and maybe it is to do with love, but I don't think it's necessarily got that much to do with sex. If that's the way it is, don't try to make it into something it isn't just because you feel it's expected of you.'

I thought about this, then said, 'Yes, but what about the Festival and everything?'

She frowned, and for a while I was able to look into her handsome, firm face. Then she said, 'Oh,' and took a deep breath and lay back beside me, looking up at the strange device above us. 'Oh, yes, the Festival, and everything,' she said. 'There's that.'

'There certainly is,' I said unhappily, lying back.

*

I sat in the plastic-fragranced car and watched the yellow lights of towns roll past in the distance; suddenly bright white lights strobing through the carriages ahead announced a train passing in the opposite direction. I ducked down to lie on the seat while the locomotive thundered past, then sat up again when the train had disappeared up the track heading north.

A moment's dizziness afflicted me as I sat back up, the immediate memory of the white lights flickering through the sides of the wagons ahead seeming to reflect and multiply inside my mind as though my brain was transparent and my skull a mirror; my heart raced and my mouth tasted of something metallic.

The moment passed and I returned to my thoughts of my cousin, realising, as though to sum up, that I had another reason for wanting Morag to come back to us; if she did not return and be our Guest of Honour at the Festival then I might be expected to step into the breach (not to mention having somebody step into mine, so to speak).

That was not a prospect I relished.

Sleep finally claimed me around the border, I would guess, and I dreamed of High Easter Offerance and our Community, and in my dream I was a ghost, floating through the farm's busy courtyard, calling to everybody I knew, but unheeded, unheard, somehow exiled.

*

I awoke with the dawn. I yawned and stretched, then peeked over the top of the windowsill. The train was passing through damp, flat countryside which I guessed was in the middle of England. I took a drink of water then snoozed some more. Later I sat up and watched the view while eating a light breakfast of cheese and pickle sandwiches and consulting my map of London.

I detrained at a red signal north of Hornsey, climbed a low embankment, relieved myself behind a bush, then scrambled over a brick wall by a bridge and dropped onto a pavement in front of a surprised-looking Indian lady. I tipped my hat to her and strolled away, feeling distinctly pleased with myself at getting to London in such a sanctified but relatively effortless manner. I took it as a good omen that the first person I should encounter down south had been another person of sub-continental origin.

It was mid-morning; half past eight according to the clock displayed in the corner of a programme playing multitudinously in a TV-shop window. Time for some Back Bussing.

Back Bussing is a way of minimising travel expenditure which we have used on buses for decades and which can occasionally be employed on other forms of transport. It consists of getting on the bus and asking the conductor – preferably in a strange, alien accent – for a ticket for a stop in the opposite direction one is travelling in. On being informed one is heading the wrong way, it is vital to look most confused and be extremely apologetic. Usually one will then be allowed to get off (almost invariably without paying) at the next stop along the route, from where one may begin to repeat the process until one arrives at one's destination.

I waited at a bus stop on High Road, Wood Green, having selected a stop which served the route numbers I required. The kit-bag was over my shoulder, my Sitting Board was in my hand. I got onto the first bus that came along. It had folding doors at the front and the driver seemed to double as the conductor; this threw me somewhat. I mumbled unintelligibly and got off again, blushing. The next few buses were all of the same sort. I stood looking at the traffic, which was slow and noisy, and at the buildings, which were low and undistinguished. After a while, and a few more one-person operated buses, I gave up and walked south, which was roughly the right direction for Kilburn, where my half-brother Zeb lived (I read my map as I walked and decided I would take the A503 south-west when I came upon it). Eventually, however, I was passed by an old-fashioned bus with an open rear platform heading in the right direction. I found the next bus stop with the relevant route-number and waited.

*

99

A bus came; I jumped on and went upstairs. Unfortunately, the four front seats were already taken. I chose the next row back, put my wooden Sitting Board down, and sat. While still in the car on the train I had peeled the top four pounds off my roll of cash and stuck the notes in my jacket's inside pocket; when the conductor came I held out a pound note and said, 'A ticket to Enfield, plis.'

'What's this, then?' the conductor asked, taking the note and looking at it.

I glared at him; he was a small, grey man with thick glasses. 'It is beink vun off your pounds,' I told him, in a foreign-sounding accent.

'Not one of ours, mate.'

'I think it is.'

'Na, this is toytown money this is.'

'It is note of the realm, I think.'

'You what?' He held it up to the light. 'Na, look; it's Scottish, innit? This here's some old Scottish one-spot. Where'd you get that, then? You been savin' them or sumfink? Na, mate,' he said, handing the note back to me. 'Come on; I 'aven't got all day; where'd you say you was going?'

'Enfield, plis.'

'Enfield?' he exclaimed, laughing. 'Blimey, you are in a state, aren't you? You're goin' in the wrong direction, chum . . . Oh, sorry, miss, is it? Sorry; couldn't see for the 'at. Should have known you was a girl from you wearing an 'at inside, shouldn't I? Anyway, like I say – you're going in the wrong direction, love.'

'Excuse, plis?' I said, looking confused.

'YOU ARE GOING-GIH IN THE WRONG-GIH DOI-RECT-SHUN,' he said loudly. 'You want to get off at the next stop and – look; here we go. You get up . . . come with me; get up; yes; you . . . that's it.' I stood up and let the man usher me downstairs to the platform as the bus slowed. 'We'll put you off 'ere . . . See that stop over there? Na, na; other side of the street, love. Yeah. That's the stop for the bus to Enfield, right? You catch bus there; it go Enfield, yeah? There you go, then. Mind out. Bye now!' He rang the bell and disappeared back upstairs, shaking his head as the bus moved off.

100

I stayed where I was, grinning, and waited for the next bus.

*

Over the next two hours I moved a shorter distance than I could had I walked. On two occasions, even though it was a couple of minutes before the conductor came to take my money, I still got off nearer to the stop I'd got on than to the next one down the route, due to the abominably clotted traffic. Eventually I got onto a bus and met the same conductor I'd encountered originally.

'Bleedin' 'ell, darlin'; you still lost?'

I looked at him blankly, desperately trying to think what to say. Finally I managed, 'This is Enfield, plis?'

He took me across the road himself and left me at the bus stop.

I admitted defeat and walked south to the Grand Union Canal. I hiked along the towpath to Maida Vale, then headed north-west to the house where my half-brother Zeb lived, on Brondesbury Road.

The basement and the ground storey of the three-storey end-of-terrace house were boarded up and I had to go round the back and pull corrugated iron sheeting aside to gain entry to the rear garden. I banged on the back door. Eventually a voice rang out above.

'Yeah?'

I stepped back and looked up at a female face. The sides of her head were shaved; long fair lengths of hair like skinny pigtails hung down from the back of her head. She appeared to have several rings piercing her nostrils. 'Good morning,' I said. 'I'm looking for Zebediah Whit. Is he here?'

'Zeb? Dunno. Who're you?'

'Isis.'

'Isis?'

'Yes.'

'Nice name.'

'Thank you. Most people call me Is. I'm a relation of Zebediah's. Tell him I'm here, if you can find him.'

'Right. Hang on.'

101

The door opened a minute later, and Brother Zebediah stood there, bare-footed, stuffing a crumpled shirt into tattered jeans.

'Wow. Is. Jeez. Shit. Brilliant. Wow.' Zeb is two years older than me; he was even skinnier than I recalled, and his black hair both longer and much more tangled. His face looked spottier, where it was visible between little tufts of black facial hair that probably signalled he was trying to grow a beard.

I made the Sign and held out my hand to him. Zeb looked confusedly at it for a moment, then said, 'Oh. Wow. Yeah. Sorry. 'Course. Like. Yeah,' and took my hand. He kissed it and went down on one knee. 'Yeah. Like. Wow. Beloved. Blessed? Beloved. Isis. Welcome. Cool. Yeah.'

The girl I'd talked to first stood in the hallway behind. She stared open-mouthed at my half-brother, then at me.

'Brother Zebediah,' I said. 'I am pleased to see you. Please – arise.'

He did so, grinning broadly. He attempted to comb his fingers through his extravagantly untidy locks, but didn't get terribly far. I handed him my kit-bag. He took it, and – following my gaze – turned to the girl with the half-shaved, half-pigtailed hair. 'Oh. Yeah. Yeah. Ah. Beloved Is: Roadkill. Roadkill: the Beloved Is. Yeah.' He nodded with his whole body and grinned, then made the Sign, and bowed, ushering me forward.

I entered the house, taking off my hat and handing it to Zeb. The girl was still staring at me. I nodded gravely at her. 'Charmed,' I said.

C H A P T E R
S E V E N

B rother Zebediah had not received the letter informing him of my imminent arrival; the squat – for such the house he lived in was – had at best an erratic postal service which seemingly depended largely on the sympathy or otherwise of the post-person on whose round it was. The household did not possess a telephone, so the letter had been our only means of communication. Accordingly, no preparations had been made for my arrival. Zebediah did the best he could however, considering. He was all set to give me his room which he shared with Roadkill, his girlfriend, while they decanted to the loft, but on viewing the room and the state of the plaster on the walls, I suggested that the loft might be more suitable for me, as I could rig my hammock safely between two of the roof trusses. Roadkill looked relieved at this.

The loft was haphazardly floored with old doors and random bits of wood; I had Zeb rearrange these and take away the single electric light bulb which hung from the roof; I would use a candle for light. (In fact I had been hoping that the squat might be entirely free of electricity, and I had been disappointed to find that it was not.) In addition, Zeb generously donated a rug and a small table from his room to make the place look more welcoming.

I stuck my head out of the skylight to check which direction was nor-nor-west, then instructed Zeb – who had found a hammer and two six-inch nails – where to rig my hammock. With it in place, we repaired to the kitchen, where Zeb lit the stubs of some scented Order candles and ceremonially washed my feet in a small plastic basin while Roadkill prepared food in the form of some type of pastie or samosa; I handed her some blessed tea and a tiny amount of lard. She looked at the two little twists of greaseproof paper oddly, then looked inside, sniffing.

'This smells like tea,' she said. She had a pleasant accent I was unable to locate anywhere more exactly than south-east England.

'It is,' I told her.

'Eeurgh; this one smells of animal.'

'That is lard,' I said, and looked severely at Zeb, who was cleaning between two of my toes with his little finger. He looked guilty, as well he might; it was obvious that Brother Zeb had not been performing certain of our dietary rituals.

'What, like from pigs?' Roadkill asked.

'That is correct,' I told her.

'Can't handle that, man,' Roadkill said, taking the tiny package in two fingers and dropping it on the Formica-topped table near me.

'Roadkill's a veggie,' Zeb said apologetically.

'That is quite all right,' I said, and smiled at the lass. 'I understand. As you no doubt know, our own Faith forbids eating some meat too, in the form of that from anything with two legs, like birds for example.' I saw Roadkill and Zebediah exchange an odd look at this point, and surmised that Zeb had been corrupted by the city to the point where he had eaten fowl. My mission down here might have to include bringing Brother Zebediah back onto the straight and narrow too, I suspected (if there was time). Appearing not to notice their guilty glance, I went on, 'If you'd just put a little of the tea into whatever you are making for me, I'd be most grateful.'

'What, tea leafs, in the patties?' she asked.

'Just the merest sprinkle,' I told her. 'As if it were salt or pepper. It's not for taste; it has symbolic value only.'

'Right,' she said. 'Symbolic value. Sure.' She turned away, shaking her head.

I retrieved the little twist of lard and pocketed it; I would anoint the food with it myself just before eating.

There was a bang from the hallway, footsteps, and a large young white man with very short hair and wearing a grubby anorak with colourful badges on it entered the kitchen. He stopped and looked down at Zeb, who was still washing my feet. I smiled up at him.

'Chroist,' he said in an Irish accent, and grinned.

'Close,' Zeb said, sighing.

*

'You've got a step-sister called *what*?'

'Hagar,' I confirmed, nodding.

'But that's a guy's name, innit, Zeb?'

Zeb looked vague, and shrugged.

'Yeah,' Roadkill said. 'Like that strip in the *Sun*.'

For a moment I wondered what possible relevance removing one's clothes in daylight had before I recalled there was a popular newspaper called the *Sun*. 'Well, as I understand it,' I said, 'Hagar is a biblical name, a Hebrew name; that of Abraham's wife's maid; her slave.'

'Cool.'

It was early evening and we were walking back from an off-licence on Kilburn High Road, through the roar and stench of the rush-hour traffic; I had volunteered to help Zeb and Roadkill fetch some celebratory alcohol for the squat's evening meal; I rang my 2-9-4 code back to the Woodbeans' house from a nearby call-box while they were actually buying the drink. This turned out to come in the shape of garishly labelled plastic bottles full of something called Litening Stryke, a form of cider.

I thought some more. 'And I have a step-brother called Hymen.'

'*Hymen*?' Roadkill said. 'Like in virginity; like in maidenhead?'

'That's right.'

'A step-*brother*?'

'Yes.'

'Weird. Does he really use that name?'

'Regrettably, no; Brother Hymen is an apostate, and—'

'A what?'

'An apostate; one who has renounced his or her faith.'

'Oh.'

'I'm afraid so. Apparently he makes a living diving for golf balls in lakes on American golf courses, and goes under a new name now.'

'Don't blame him; I mean, *Hymen*.'

'It is a male name, you know,' I said. 'Hymen was a Greek deity; the son of Apollo.'

'Wow,' Roadkill said admiringly. 'You know a lot about this holy stuff, don't you?'

107

I smiled. 'Well, you might say it's my job.' (Zeb guffawed, then looked a little fearfully at me, but I just smiled.)

'What exactly *are* you supposed to be?' Roadkill asked.

'I am the Elect of God,' I told her. 'The third generation of our family born on the twenty-ninth of February.'

'Wow.'

'In my case, I was born on the twenty-ninth of February nineteen seventy-six. Officially, if you were to ask me what age I am, I would have to say that I am four and three-quarters.'

'Shit.' Roadkill laughed.

'Not four and three-quarter *years* of course; four and three-quarter quadquennia. I am nineteen years old.'

'Hmm.' Roadkill looked thoughtful. 'So what sign does that make you?'

'Astrologically? It is our belief that the Elect have no sign. It is one aspect of our holy separateness.'

'Freaky.' She shook her head. 'Shit, you must have to have a hell of a birthday party if it only comes round every four years.'

'We try to make it special,' I agreed.

'Tell Roadkill about the Festival, Is,' Zeb suggested, putting together the first real sentence I'd heard him utter since I'd arrived.

'You mean you haven't, Brother?' I asked.

'He ain't told me nothin' about this sect of yours,' Roadkill said, hitting Zeb on the forearm with her free hand.

'Well. Shit. You know. Complicated,' Zeb said, reverting. Actually I was glad he hadn't. While any festival is by its very nature not something one can really keep secret, Salvador did prefer us not to bruit the details of ours about too much, for the media-sensitive reasons I have already gone into. However, I judged that telling Roadkill was probably a reasonable course of action.

'It happens at the end of May every year before a leap year,' I told her. 'We ask those wishing to participate to perform the act of love without contraception as frequently as possible around that date, to increase the chances of another Elect being born.'

'Fuck,' Roadkill said after a moment's thought. 'An orgy?'

108

'Well, that's a pejorative term, isn't it?' I said. 'No; that implies exclusively group sex, I believe, whereas the Festival is concerned to promote all forms of potentially procreative activity. Really, it's just a huge celebration; the public side of it wouldn't embarrass the most prudish soul. What goes on behind closed doors afterwards is up to the individuals concerned.'

'Oh yeah?' Roadkill said.

'Well then, why not come and visit us?' I suggested. 'You and Zeb would be very welcome at any time, of course, but especially so if you came for the Festival,' I said to her.

Roadkill glanced at Zeb, who frowned down at the pavement. 'I dunno,' she said. 'He hasn't said nothin' about it.'

Zeb glanced at me and I frowned at him.

'Well, you should come,' I told Roadkill. 'Not necessarily to take part in the procreative side of the Festival, but just because it's such an enjoyable time; we have music and dancing and feasts and the children stage little plays . . . It's a time of celebration, of rejoicing,' I told her. I laughed. 'There is absolutely no compulsion to engage in constant sex if you don't want to, believe me.'

'Hmm; right,' Roadkill said, noncommittally.

As I'd spoken the words, though, I'd wondered who I was trying to convince. As far as I was concerned there was indeed a degree, if not of compulsion then certainly of expectation that I would be taking a full part in this Festival, even if Morag did show up (I recalled that remark of Grandfather's to the effect that I was looking 'healthy' and telling me I had a duty to enjoy myself, just a couple of days ago). The pressure I'd be under if my cousin didn't come to the Festival hardly bore thinking about. Great things – it seemed to me – might be expected of my ovaries.

Roadkill had obviously been thinking along the same lines. 'So,' she said, smiling at me and flexing one pink-rinsed eyebrow. 'Were you under-age last time, or is this your big . . . you know; big occasion? This Festival.'

I smiled as confidently as I could. 'Well, yes, it's possible that I might be expected to be one of the centres of attention, this time round.'

109

'Wow,' Roadkill said. 'You got anybody lined up yet, as a father I mean?'

I shrugged. 'I'm still thinking it over,' I said, which contained an amount of truth.

'So do you have to get married first or anything?'

'No. We regard marriage as optional to love and procreation; some people actually treat their partners better without that form of commitment, and some people are better as single parents, especially in our Community, where child care can be shared. But if I did want to marry, I could. In fact, I could marry myself,' I told Roadkill, who looked a little dubious at this. I explained. 'As an officer of the Luskentyrian Sect I'm empowered to officiate at all religious ceremonies including marriages, and there is a precedent for the officiating cleric himself – or herself – being one of the parties to the marriage.'

'Freaky,' Roadkill said.

'Hmm,' I said. 'Ah.' I nodded at the lane that led round to the back of the squat. 'Here we are.'

*

In February 1949 my Grandfather decided to marry Aasni and Zhobelia Asis; he had – not just with God's permission but indeed at Their insistence – bestowed upon himself the title Very Reverend, which meant that he could carry out religious ceremonies. The sisters agreed that their *ménage à trois* ought to be regularised, and a ceremony was duly held in the specially decorated hall of the old seaweed factory. The only witness was Eoin McIlone, the farmer who had given the sisters and later Grandfather shelter and succour. He and Salvador had taken to playing draughts several evenings a week in the spare room-cum-study at Luskentyre Farm, a couple of miles along the road from the seaweed factory. They argued incessantly each evening, and with increasing vehemence as they gradually drank more and more of Mr McIlone's whisky, but – partly because they both enjoyed arguing and partly because neither could ever remember what they had been arguing about when they woke up the following morning (Mr McIlone alone in his narrow bunk set into the wall of his old farm house, Grandfather in between the two Asis sisters in his bed on the floor of the old factory office) – they both entirely looked forward to their draughts games, whisky and arguments.

Salvador and his two brides spent their wedding night in the seaweed factory as usual, but the sisters had redecorated a different room in the offices and moved the bed – two mattresses covered with bedding – through to their candle-lit marital suite. That night, a rat ran across the bed, terrifying the two sisters and rather spoiling the whole event, and the next day Salvador constructed a kind of huge, three-person hammock out of various lengths of rope, stout wooden battens and a large piece of sailcloth, all of which he'd found washed ashore over the previous few months while he'd been scouring the shores for the lost canvas grip.

Slung from the iron roof-beams of the old factory office in their giant hammock, the sisters felt much safer, and when the factory and almost everything in it were burned a few months later by a crowd of indignant locals with flaming torches and Grandfather and his two wives moved into a barn at Mr McIlone's farm, the one thing the girls had rescued from the fire and bundled into the back of the van – apart of course from Great-aunt Zhobelia's special chest sent to her from Khalmakistan by her grandmother, and repository of the *zhlonjiz* – had been the giant hammock.

Actually I strongly suspect, from hints dropped by Calli and Astar, who heard the original story from Aasni and Zhobelia, that it was a very small crowd of indignant locals, and I know that it was late one Friday night, and that drink had been taken, and the men concerned had probably heard some grotesque exaggeration of Grandfather and the sisters' marital arrangements, and they probably didn't mean to torch the factory, they were just looking for Salvador to give him a good hiding. He was, however, already hiding, having taken refuge in the sisters' van which was outside; they had concealed him beneath some bolts of reject tartan they'd picked up for a song from a fire-sale in Portree, but being drunk and clumsy one of the men fell and smashed his lantern and the fire started and the rest ran away while Grandfather cooried deeper under the bales of tartan and the sisters at first tried to put the fire out and then just saved what they could. But the way Grandfather tells it is better.

At any rate, although the original monumental hammock was left behind in Luskentyre when the Community moved to High Easter Offerance, and Salvador and the sisters thereupon enjoyed more normal sleeping arrangements in the shape of a couple of beds shoved together, that is why hammocks are sacred to us and why an Elect is expected to sleep in one at least every now and again, and whenever they are away from the Community (and preferably with their head pointed towards the Community, to show their thoughts lie in that direction). Personally I've always liked hammocks and never really felt comfortable in ordinary beds, so I rarely sleep in anything else.

*

I lay in my hammock. The loft was spinning. I suspected I had put away too much of the Litening Stryke cider over the course of the evening. At home, when we wish to partake of alcohol we almost invariably drink our own ales, produced in the brew house at the farm. There are certain ceremonies in which small amounts of a special Holy Ale are used, and generally the fact that fermented or distilled fluids have a certain effect on the human brain is taken as being at best a benediction and a gift from God, and at worst an example of Their irritatingly inventive sense of humour which it would be dangerously unwise as well as distinctly unsporting not to be a willing party to. At the same time, however, while a degree of tipsiness is welcomed and indeed even encouraged at certain social events in the Order, extreme inebriation and loss of control of one's mental and bodily functions is very much frowned upon.

Community beers tend to be relatively heavily flavoured but mild in strength, whereas the cider we had consumed with the evening meal had been just the opposite, and I was suffering the effects of having treated one like the other.

The evening had passed very pleasantly; the others in the squat were Dec, the Irishman who'd walked in as Brother Zebediah had been washing my feet; Boz, a most sizable and lustrously black Jamaican man with a fabulously deep, slow voice; Scarpa, his interestingly pale south London girlfriend; and Wince, a smaller version of Boz but, confusingly, with an Irish accent.

They had been a little wary of me at first, but things had gradually become more convivial, first over the meal of vegetable curry, sweet potatoes and chicken (the last of which I couldn't eat, of course, and was glad to see Brother Zebediah passed on as well) and later while watching a videotaped film in the squat's living room, which was bare but functional and – in terms of new-looking electrical entertainment equipment – surprisingly well-equipped. I was, especially initially, distinctly uncomfortable sitting in the presence of all this cluttering technology, but felt that it was my duty to be sociable; I was, after all, the ambassador for my Faith amongst these people, as well as owing them the normal courtesies a guest owes hosts.

Partly, no doubt, the feeling of relaxation I experienced was due to the effects of the Litening Stryke as well as the 'blow' drug cigarettes they smoked, but partly too it was thanks to my somewhat playing the holy fool, regaling them with tales of our life at High Easter Offerance, our history, Revealed truths, commandments and rituals.

They all appeared to find this most entertaining, and there was much laughter and giggling. Dec wiped tears from his eyes at one point and asked me, 'Jayzus, Is, what are you *on*?'

'A mission,' I informed him, to further hilarity.

I think Zeb was a little embarrassed in places, but I counted it no disgrace for our Order to be the cause of such enjoyment in others, and it is anyway the case that what one initially laughs at and finds quite ridiculous can often, on more sober reflection, come to seem quite sensible and latterly even wise. There are more ways than one in which to spread the good word!

I had managed to have a quiet word with Zeb at one point, helping him to do the dishes after the meal. I briefly explained the nature of my mission and told him I expected his full cooperation in the search for our cousin Morag, which would start promptly on the morrow.

'Well, I. Never heard. Her. Being. Internationally famous,' Zeb muttered towards the suds.

'Well, she is, Brother Zeb,' I told him. 'Are you in the habit of attending classical concerts or mixing in that sort of circle?'

'No. But.'

'Well, then,' I said, emphatically.

Brother Zebediah looked as though he was going to argue about this, but I looked sternly at him, and he smiled meekly and looked down, nodding.

We were watching one of the videotaped films – it appeared to consist largely of cars chasing each other, lots of large colourful explosions and American men becoming angry and sweeping coffee tables, mantelpieces and so on clear of breakables – when I realised I was getting overly intoxicated. I stood and made my goodnights, requesting only a pint glass of water to take to my hammock-side. I tried to read a few passages from the *Orthography* by candlelight but confess that my vision, even with one eye determinedly closed, was not really up to the task. I closed the word of the Creator and vowed to read twice as much the following evening; I disrobed to my underwear and climbed into the hammock with a practised ease that even my sobriety-compromised state could not endanger.

It occurred to me, as I lay there, swinging in my hammock and trying to ignore the pressure in my bladder, that we were all abbreviated: I from Isis to Is, Zebediah to Zeb, Declan to Dec, Winston to Wince . . . I wasn't sure about Boz or Scarpa but one certainly *sounded* contracted, though both could have been nicknames.

I got up to relieve myself, donning my jacket for modesty. As I left the toilet, I heard somebody say something like, '—got the bucket!' and Brother Zebediah barged out of his and Roadkill's room wearing only his trousers and an amulet, dashed past me holding his mouth and was sick in the still-flushing toilet. I hesitated, looking from the toilet to the wooden ladder which led to the loft, uncertain whether to offer to help my half-brother or not.

Zeb came out of the toilet a few moments later, sighing and smiling.

'Are you all right, Brother Zebediah?' I asked.

'Yeah,' he said, and smiled broadly. 'Yeah,' he nodded, and took me by the shoulders and then hugged me. 'You're beautiful, Is,' he said, and sighed again, then walked off, smiling, back to his room.

I climbed back to my hammock in the loft, somewhat bemused, but thankful that Zeb seemed able to shrug off minor maladies with such alacrity.

CHAPTER
EIGHT

'What about kangaroos?'

'Kangaroos?' I said, wondering what Brother Zebediah was talking about.

'Kangaroos,' he confirmed as we boarded the Underground train at Kilburn Park. There were seats free and I thought I detected Zeb making to head for one and sit, despite the fact he did not have his Sitting Board with him. He coughed and made a show of walking past the first free seat to look at a newspaper lying on a more distant seat, then came back to where I was standing near the doors, which closed. The train moved off.

'Kangaroos?' I reminded him.

'Oh. Yeah,' he said. He shrugged in a quizzical manner. 'Eat them?'

'I see,' I said, and thought. The train charged through the dark tunnel, shaking and rattling.

It was mid-morning. It had taken an unconscionably long time to rouse my half-brother from his slumbers but I had been loathe to embark upon such a crucial part of my mission alone. I had been happy with my navigation through London the previous day; considering that I had not visited the British state's capital before, and while admitting the relative failure of my Back Bussing ploy, I thought I had done reasonably well in coping with a city of such – in my own experience – unprecedented size. Nevertheless, I did not imagine myself to be 'streetwise' and – suspecting that today's expedition would be more complicated in nature – I believed that I would therefore benefit from having Zeb's considerable local knowledge, built up over a number of years of capital living and the subject of obvious if quiet pride in his all-too-occasional letters home.

Extracting Zeb from his room or even his bed at a decent hour that morning had proved to be by far the most demanding and frustrating task of my mission so far; my gentle cajolings, offered

119

cups of coffee, eulogies on the beauty of the day, waftings of toast under the nose, admittedly jocular threats of excommunication, and even an invigorating reading from a particularly stimulating passage of the *Orthography* all failed to elicit more than low groans from the narrow crease in the covers that was all I could see of my brother in faith. (Zeb was alone in bed at this point, Roadkill having already left.)

Finally, it took a graduated series of containers – a thimble, an egg cup, a tea cup, a pint glass and a bucket – to convince him that I was serious and that he was getting no more sleep that day, no matter how much he was 'hurting'. People usually give in after having the thimble of water poured over them but Zeb held out until the tea cup, which indicated either a remarkably violent hang-over or admirably steely determination. I knew which one I'd have put my money on (if we were allowed to do such things).

He certainly didn't look well, and seemed to have developed a cold overnight; he spent so long in the toilet I suspected he was trying to indulge in some more sleep, though when I banged on the door he sounded already awake. He did eventually succeed in what he colourfully described as 'getting his shit together' and we finally left the house at the disgracefully late hour of ten o'clock.

Zeb wore grubby training shoes with no socks, the same flayed jeans he'd worn the night before, a shirt, a holed jumper and an old parka. I looked through one of the holes in his jumper as we walked to the Underground railway station. 'Brother Zebediah,' I asked suspiciously, 'is that shirt reverse-buttoned?'

'Aw,' he said. 'Shit. Is. Please. Look. Christ. Come on.'

'Brother Zebediah, this back-sliding has to stop. Come on; off with the jumper.'

'Aw. Fuck. Shit. Come on. No. Is . . .'

I stood in front of him and helped him off with his jacket, then pulled the jumper over his head.

'Christ. I don't. I mean. This. Fuck. Unreal.' We were outside a newsagent's, and I did not wonder at the looks we were getting, what with this stream of profanity. Zeb held his parka and jumper while I undid his shirt buttons one by one and did them up properly.

'Fuck. Is. What. I mean. Roadkill. I mean, she. We. Share. Both. Fuck. Whatever's. You know. Lying about.'

' "Reverse-button your shirts, that the Saved shall know each other." ' I quoted him.

'Yeah. But. Fuck.'

Reverse-buttoning apparently started because Salvador was ashamed of having mismatched buttons on his shirt one time when he had to go to Stornoway. It became one of our rituals when it was realised that it could be a way of recognising other Orderites, as well as acting as a constant reminder that we are Different. Reverse-buttoning consists simply of pushing a shirt button through from the outside of the button-hole, so that the button is hidden, and faces in towards the skin. 'There,' I said, pushing Zeb's shirt back into his jeans and patting his concave belly. 'Heavens, Brother Zebediah, there's nothing of you.'

Zeb sighed and put his jumper back on, then shrugged his jacket over his narrow shoulders. He made to move off. 'Ah!' I said, and pointed at his forehead.

'Jeez. Is. Fuck. Hell.'

'I don't expect you have any of the blessed mud,' I told him, 'but you may use mine this once, and luckily I have brought some spare vials from the Community, one of which I can leave with you.'

'Shit,' Zeb said, but let me make the little V on his forehead with the mud-ointment. I pocketed my jar. 'There,' I told him, taking his arm and continuing towards the station. 'Now we are indeed ready to face whatever the city will throw at us.'

Zeb had gone very quiet after that and only spoke again once we had our tickets, when he asked about eating kangaroos.

'Tricky one,' I admitted. 'Could kangaroos' fore-legs really be said to be legs at all, given that they seem to be used more as arms?'

'Yeah,' Zeb said. 'See? 'Zactly.'

'Could go either way,' I said, nodding grimly. 'Sort of thing one might have to ask the Founder.'

'My pal,' Zeb said. 'Ozzie. Had some. Said. Like. Great. Best meat. Ever. tasted. Lean. Delicious. Totally. Brutal. Brilliant. Really.'

121

'Hmm,' I said. 'In that case I'd probably err on the side of generosity; I have always been of the opinion that God does not normally make things appetising for no good reason.'

'Right. Good. Thought so. Yeah.' Zeb looked relieved for a moment and then oddly thoughtful, as though some aberrant brain-state had succeeded in troubling him.

'Orwell?' he said, tentatively.

'Orwell?' I echoed, puzzled.

He shrugged. 'Four legs good.'

I stared nonplussed at him for a moment, then understood. 'Ah!' I exclaimed, clapping him on the back and causing him to stagger. 'Two legs bad!' I laughed. 'That's quite funny, Brother Zebediah.'

He still looked confused.

Our train terminated at Baker Street. We returned almost to the surface; I stood to one side while Zeb queued at the ticket office, it being a frustrating property of the London Underground system that the techniques of Back Bussing cannot be applied.

I looked around. Such crowds of people! I was conscious of the complete reversal of the situation one experienced living in the Community, where for days, weeks, and even in certain cases months at a time one would know, and know fairly well, every single person one came into contact with; to see a stranger was an event. Here the opposite was the case; one assumed that everybody one bumped into was a stranger, and meeting a familiar face was generally a cause for joy and celebration.

'Excuse me. Can I help you?' said a quiet spoken, middle-aged man in a grey coat. He put one hand gently on my elbow. His other hand held a black briefcase. 'Are you lost?' he asked me.

'Far from it,' I told him, looking down at his hand. 'I am one of the Found. I suspect it is you who are one of the Lost, sir.'

'What?' he said, looking confused.

'Friend, you see before you one of the most fortunate and favoured people to walk the sorry soil of earth, for I walk in the sight of God. I have the joyful honour of—'

'Oi,' Zeb said, walking smartly up to us.

122

The man muttered something vaguely apologetic and moved away into the crowd, head down.

'Brother Zebediah, I was engaged in missionary work just there,' I rebuked him as we returned to the train tunnels.

'Like. Shit. Fuckin'. Pervert. More like. Got. Be careful.'

'Zeb, I am not totally naive concerning the ways of the world and the vices of the city,' I told him. 'Quite possibly that gentleman did have some nefarious and even sexually predatory motive in talking to me, but I ask you: what other sort of soul is more in need of being saved? I have a duty as an Officer of the True Church and especially as the Elect to spread the good word wherever and whenever possible. I am grateful for your concern but you must not assume that I am being gulled when in fact I am evangelising. I am perfectly capable of requesting help should I happen to need it.'

This seemed to send Zeb into something of a huff, and I reflected that perhaps it was as well that I hadn't gone on to point out that, as I was an inch or so taller than he, not to mention better and more sturdily built, his intervention in such circumstances might not always be as decisive as he seemed to imagine. Zeb's pique continued onto the train, and even my attempt to jolly him out of the mood by suggesting that we repair to the buffet car for a cheering cup of tea was met with a roll of the eyes and a 'Huh!'

Still, I hoped I had proved something regarding my resource-fulness and general urbanity just by revealing that I knew of the existence of such civilisational complexities as buffet cars on trains.

Our next change of line came at Green Park station, where we ascended to buy tickets for Covent Garden.

'Are you sure this is the quickest way to travel?' I asked my half-brother as – clutching another couple of tickets – we descended underground once more.

'Buses,' Zeb explained. 'Slower.'

'Yes, but it seems wasteful to have to keep buying separate tickets for each leg of the journey; all this extra to-ing and fro-ing from platforms to ticket office and back cannot be efficient.'

'Yeah,' Zeb sighed. 'Crazy, innit?'

Once we had established ourselves on the correct platform for

Covent Garden, I stared suspiciously at an illuminated sign which read, 'Jubilee Line Southbound'.

'Hmm,' I said.

*

Yet another change of line, and a concomitant return to the surface for another pair of tickets at Finsbury Park station took us at last to Finchley; it was a short walk from the station to the block of flats off Nether Street which had been my cousin Morag's last address. I was unprepared for the opulence of the building; I suppose I have always associated flats with council dwellings and even slums, and had rather assumed that to her credit Morag was putting up with cramped conditions during her stay in London so that she could save money. However, from the size of the cars parked in the block's car park and the general look of the place, this was no rookery for the poor.

Marble steps led to glass double doors revealing a foyer lined by sofas and pot-plants. I shook the door handles but the doors appeared to be locked.

'Riff raff,' Brother Zebediah said. 'Keeps out.' He was looking at a sort of grid in the marble wall composed of small boxes with buttons and little illuminated labels. There was a grille to one side. 'Number?' he asked.

'Thirty-five,' I told him. He ran his finger down the little plastic windows. His fingernails were long and soiled. However, I thought the better of saying anything.

'Here,' he said. 'Thirty. Five. Says. Mr. Mrs. Coyle.' He pressed the button.

' . . . Yes?' a female voice said from the grille after a short delay.

'Excuse me, Brother,' I said to Zeb, taking his place. 'Good morning, madam,' I said into the grille. 'I am sorry to disturb you but I am looking for Ms Morag Whit, the internationally renowned baryton soloist.'

'. . .Excuse me?'

'Morag Whit, the internationally renowned baryton soloist,' I repeated. 'She is my cousin. Does she still live here? This is the last address we have for her.'

'No. I'm sorry. The lady who used to live here left a couple of months ago.'

'I see. It's just that I'm her cousin, you see, and my family are rather anxious to trace her. Did she leave a forwarding address?'

'Not really. Might I ask who that other gentleman is there with you?'

I straightened and looked, with a degree of consternation, I'll admit, at Zeb. He nodded over our heads to a small box just inside glass doors.

'Camera,' he said.

'Good grief!' I said. 'Are we on television?'

'Closed circuit,' Zeb said.

'Lordy!' I gulped. 'Is that a much-watched show?' My mouth had gone a little dry.

('. . . Hello?' said the small voice from the grille.)

Zeb stared at me, frowning with incomprehension. Then he grimaced. 'Not *broadcast*,' he said, sounding exasperated. 'Security. For flats. Private.'

I thought I understood and quickly turned back to the grille, blushing and flustered. 'I do beg your pardon, madam. I misunderstood. This is my half-brother, Brother Zebediah, another Luskentyrian.'

'I'm sorry?' said the female voice. Zeb sighed behind me and I caught him shaking his head out of the corner of my eye. 'Another what?

'Another Luskentyrian,' I replied, feeling my face colour again. Explaining these things to Blands could be time-consuming. 'It's complicated.'

'I'm sure. Well,' the voice said with an unmistakable note of finality, 'I'm very sorry I can't help you.'

'She left no forwarding address?' I said desperately. 'We just want to make sure she's all right.'

'Well . . .'

'Please.'

'. . . She did leave the address of her agent, or . . . manager or something, for anything urgent. But just the address, not phone or fax.'

'That would be wonderful!' I said. 'Oh, thank you!'

'Well, just hold on; I'll go get it.' There was a click.

I turned, feeling relieved, to Zeb, who was looking vaguely out at the trees between us and the road. 'There we are!' I said, and clapped him enthusiastically on the back. He stumbled forward, coughing, and had to jump down a couple of steps before he could regain his balance. He glared back at me.

'. . . Hello?' said the metallic voice from the wall.

*

Our journey from Finchley was relatively simple, taking the Northern Line south to Tottenham Court Road and then walking along Oxford Street and down Dean Street to Brewer Street.

The premises corresponding to the address we had been given for Cousin Morag's agent – a Mr Francis Leopold – did not look very encouraging.

'Dirty books?' Zeb said, and made another forlorn attempt to pull his hand through the topological – and trichological – nightmare that was his hair. We stood on the pavement looking at the oddly blank window of something calling itself an Adult Book Shop.

'Well,' I said, looking to one side. 'The number may refer to this establishment.'

Zeb glanced. 'Porn cinema.'

'Or here?'

Zeb stuck his head into the doorway. 'Peep show. Downstairs. Upstairs. Models. Girls.'

I must have looked blank.

'Prostitutes,' he said, sighing.

'Ah,' I said. 'Well, where shall we inquire first?'

Zeb's narrow face managed to display a breadth of dubiety. 'Inquire? Really? Wise?'

'Brother Zebediah,' I said, shocked. 'You're not embarrassed, are you?' I waved at the varied sexual emporia in front of us.

126

'Such places are stigmatised by a hypocritical society which is still frightened by the power of sexuality; nevertheless in their own admittedly somewhat sordid and avaricious way such places celebrate the physical communion of souls.'

(Actually, even as I was saying all this, I was feeling a bit dubious about it, but I was more or less quoting a certain Brother Jamie, a convert from Inverness who'd gone to Stirling University, the campus of which was only a few miles from the Community; for some reason this had all sounded more plausible when he'd said it. Now that I was actually confronted with the establishments he had been talking about, they didn't look celebratory at all. However, I'd launched into this mini-sermon so I supposed I'd better round it off, false signal or not.)

'Why,' I exclaimed, 'by our doctrine they ought to be accorded the status of churches!'

Brother Zebediah looked levelly at me through hooded eyes for a moment. He took a deep breath, then nodded slowly. 'Churches. Right. Yeah. Way. Go. Okay. Cool. Uh.' He nodded at the nearest door. 'After.'

*

Our inquiries at the various facilities of dubious repute met with no success. 'What's this abaht?', 'Who're you from?', 'Never 'erd of 'im.', 'Never 'erd of 'ur, neevir.', 'Look, I got a business to run, inn-I?' and 'Fack orf'. comprised the more helpful of the various replies we received. My attempts in the cramped foyer of the erotic picture house to explain that – despite the obvious squalidness of the surroundings and the primarily financial motive behind the pornographic concerns we found ourselves in the midst of – there was still a degree of common cause between such grubbily commercial exploitations of humanity's most holy instinct and the pure, sanctified expression of that urge to be discovered through our Holy Order was met initially with glazed incomprehension.

Then, quickly thereafter, the back of my jacket and shirt collar were gripped extremely firmly by the heavily ringed hand of a very large crop-haired gentleman in a suit – pushing my hat down over my eyes so that I could hardly see where I was going – and Zeb and I were given an undignifiedly rough escort past a variety of lurid posters to the doors, where we were ejected into the street outside with such force that I almost lost my footing and came within inches of colliding with a person on a motorcycle. This person then skidded to a stop, pushed up his helmet visor and informed me in no uncertain terms of my sexual activity, mental acuity and physical size, characterised me correctly by my genitals, then changed tack and insinuated that my hat was supported by a – presumably grossly enlarged – male sexual organ, and finally that my parents' union had not been sanctioned either by the state or an established church.

I tipped my hat and begged his pardon. He roared away, shaking his crash helmet.

Zeb joined me on the far pavement; his collar had been in the other fist of the man who had seen us off (who was now standing with his arms massively crossed, filling the doorway to the cinema). A few people in the crowded street were looking at us.

'Okay?' Zeb asked.

'Dignity a little tarnished,' I told him, adjusting the lapels of my jacket. 'Otherwise, uninjured. And you?'

'Fine,' Zeb said, shrugging his shoulders forward and pulling down on his jumper.

'Good,' I said, adjusting my hat properly. 'Time for a cup of tea, I think; what do you say?'

'Tea. Yeah. Right. Café. There.'

*

The Royal Opera House, Covent Garden, proved no more able to offer help, if rather more polite and stately in the manner of not providing it.

'Well, obviously, we are not really the sort of venue one would find a soloist *at*,' said the young man who had been summoned by the box office to talk to us. He seemed quite pleasant and well dressed, though he appeared to be troubled by his hair, a length of which over his right temple continually fell over his right eye and had to be swept back into place. I was surprised to find somebody working for an Opera House who did not appear to open his teeth or make more than the most cursory of movements with his lips when he spoke.

'I see,' I said. Our surroundings now were rather at the other end of the scale from the pornographic picture house only a fraction of a mile away, though the amount of gilt and deep, vibrant colours gave the magnificent foyer a similar if more monumental feel. 'But you have heard of her; Morag Whit, the internationally renowned baryton soloist?'

'Baryton,' the young man said, sweeping his blond hair back and staring at the central chandelier high above us. 'Baryton . . .' He pursed his lips. 'Isn't that in Ireland somewhere?'

'It is a form of viola da gamba,' I said frostily. 'With extra resonating strings.'

'Yes,' the young man said, drawing the word out as though it was an extrusion. 'Yes.' He nodded. 'You know, I think I did *see* something about a concert once . . .'

'It would probably be my cousin who was soloist,' I told him.

'Hmm,' he said, crossing his arms and putting one hand up to his mouth. 'Apart from that, I really can't help you, I'm afraid. I can't imagine what your cousin was doing writing to you on our headed notepaper, but then I imagine it isn't something we keep under lock and key, exactly, and of course with photocopiers and so on these days, well . . .' He smiled, tipping his head to one side. His hair fell over his eye again; he swept it back once more.

'I see,' I said. 'Oh well, thank you anyway.' I fished in one of my jacket pockets.

'My pleasure,' he said, smiling. He turned to go, his hair falling over his eye again as he did so.

'Please; with my compliments.' I handed him a Kirbigrip.

*

129

'Well,' I said, 'this is all most odd.' Brother Zebediah and I stood on the terrace of the Royal Festival Hall in a mild, blustery river wind, looking across the broad, grey-brown back of the River Thames. Pleasure boats crisscrossed before us, sunlight glinting on their windows as they rocked across the waves and slapped through the scissoring wakes of their fellow craft.

'Yep.'

I turned to face Zeb, arms folded, my back against the railings. Zeb's face looked pinched and jerky somehow. 'But I have seen the poster!' I protested.

'Yep.'

The Royal Festival Hall claimed never to have heard of Cousin Morag; they certainly had not hosted a concert by her at eight o'clock on Tuesday, the 16th of February, 1993, which was – unless my normally accurate and reliable memory was failing me – the date and time detailed on the poster which hung in the hall of the mansion house back in High Easter Offerance and which my Grandfather was so proud of.

The eventually helpful lady member of staff we had been referred to was adamant that no person of that name was known to her, and that indeed there had never been a solo baryton concert in the South Bank complex (at least when I mentioned the instrument itself she had heard of that; I was beginning to wonder if it existed). She was slim, cardiganed and well-spoken and her hair was neatly bunned. I suspected at the time – from her confident manner and general bearing – that I had met a memory as retentive as my own, but knew that one of us must be wrong, and so implored her to check. She invited us to take a seat in the coffee bar and disappeared back into the administrative offices of the building, to reappear with a large, battered-looking thing she called a print-out and which detailed all the events in the various parts of the complex over the year 1993.

'If there had been such a concert it would probably have been more suited to the Purcell Room . . .' she told us, leafing through the broad, green-lined pages.

'Could the poster have got the year wrong?' I asked.

She looked sour and took off her glasses. 'Well, it certainly didn't happen last year; I'd remember, but if you really want I can check 'ninety-two.'

'I'd be terribly grateful,' I said in a small voice, taking off my hat and trying to look waif-like.

She sighed. 'All right.'

I watched her go. 'Brother Zebediah,' I said to him. He looked startled, as if he had been falling asleep in his seat. 'I think we ought to get the lady a cup of coffee, don't you?'

He looked at me. I nodded towards the serving counter. He looked cross for a moment. 'Me,' he said. 'Always. Me. Paying. Not,' he waved one hand at me. 'Turn?' (I glared at him.) 'No?' he said, faltering.

'Brother Zebediah,' I said, drawing myself up and putting my hat back on. 'I am on a highly important mission with the blessing of and instructions directly from our Founder himself; I do have some emergency funds but otherwise I am relying on the support of the Blessed, whether they adhere strictly to our code or not. I hope you are not already forgetting the gravity of this matter; Morag has been central to our missionary plans for some time now, quite apart from being especially favoured by our dear Founder and due to take centre-stage at the quadrennial Festival. We all have to make sacrifices at such a time, Brother Zebediah, and I am shocked that you should—'

'Right! Okay! Right! All right! I'm going!' he said, interrupting me before I had really had a chance to make my point. He loped off to the counter.

The lady did not want any coffee, which put me at a disadvantage with Brother Zebediah for the rest of the meeting, during which I became convinced that Cousin Morag had indeed never played on the South Bank. I thanked her as she rose to leave and then I sat back, thinking. Zeb drank the cup of cooling coffee with a smug expression and an unnecessary amount of noise.

'No forwarding address, no agent, no concerts; nobody has heard of her!' I exclaimed. 'And her a soloist of international repute!'

'Yup. Weird.'

In such a situation the average person might start to doubt their sanity. However, Luskentyrians have it drummed into them from a very early age that it is the outside world, the world of the billions of Blands, that is obviously, demonstrably, utterly and (in the short term) irredeemably insane, while they themselves have had the immense good luck (or karma, if you like, there's a fine and still debatable theological point at issue here) to be born into the one True Church with a decent grasp of reality and a plausible explanation for everything.

I did not, therefore, even begin to question whether I was in full possession of my faculties (with the singular and brief exception of my memory, as mentioned above), though I was well aware something was seriously out of kilter somewhere, and that as a result my mission was rapidly taking on a degree of complexity and difficulty neither I nor my fellow Officers back at the Community had bargained for.

Urgent action was obviously called for.

What I really needed to do was talk to God.

CHAPTER
NINE

I think my Grandfather still holds that one of the greatest achievements of his ministry was the conversion of Mr McIlone to the set of beliefs which at the time our Founder was still in the act of formulating. If I say that I suspect it was also an accomplishment my Grandfather found extremely enjoyable and hence craved to repeat, I think I am paying our Founder a compliment, given the intrinsic goodness and holiness of the act concerned.

Mr McIlone was a kindly, generous man, but a free-thinker; an atheist of long standing who had had the strength of will and character – however fundamentally misguided and wrong-headed – to maintain and preserve his sinful belief in the face of the opprobrium and isolationary contempt of a conservative and even self-righteous community of the sort that tends to get called 'close-knit' by those not inclined to search overly long for their images of social cohesion.

While by our creed we must count the dour Presbyterians of the Western Isles, with their cruelly humourless, fear-demanding and vindictive-sounding idea of God, our allies (whether they like it or not), and the humanely compassionate Mr McIlones of this world our evangelical prey at best and outright opponents at worst, and it is undeniably more effective preaching to the already half converted than attempting to plant the seeds of faith in souls hardened by a history of material Falseness, there is nevertheless often more common cause spiritually to be found with those who are naturally generous, sharing, wise and enlightened (but by chance brought up out-with the sight and hearing of God) than with those who – while part of a community or faith whose beliefs are in some strategic sense more in keeping with our own – are by the very strictness and severity of that persuasion individually far less happily unrestricted in the joy of their worship of God and the appreciation of the beauty of the

135

Universe, the World and the Human, in both its spiritual and its physical form.

I think myself that by the sound of it Mr McIlone was one of those sensitive souls prone rather to Despair. He was like my Grandfather in seeing little but cruel idiocy in the actions of his fellow humans, but different from him in choosing for his response the easy, easeful option of simply condemning everybody and turning his back on the world.

From what I have read – and I think I may fairly claim to have read a fair amount, for my age – I think it must have seemed a world worth turning one's back on; the most destructive war in all history was finally over, but only at the cost of ushering in – with those two diabolic nuclear dawns over Japan – an age which seemed to have finally brought the epoch of Apocalypse to earth. The thunderous, earth-shaking power to annihilate whole cities in an instant that Humanity had habitually ascribed to its gods was now at Man's own beck and call, and no god ever seemed so fearful and capricious as the new possessor of that power.

Humanity had thought itself progressing, after that earlier war to end wars, only to discover, once the dust and soot had settled, that one of the world's most civilised and sophisticated nations had found no better outlet for its ingenuity than to attempt to annihilate industrially an ancient people who had probably contributed more to the world's store of learning than any other single group (and perhaps knew, too, that their own nations had colluded in the prelude to that terminal obscenity).

And what future beckoned, after this spasm of destruction and the death of any idea that Humanity was in some way rational, that Humanity, indeed, was reliably humane?

Why, only the continuation of war in another, colder form, with weapons fit for the end of the world; Allies becoming enemies and the real victors of the European war turning upon themselves and their new conquests with redoubled savagery, as though their twenty million dead had only given the apparatus a taste for it. (Meanwhile Mr Orwell, on another Hebridean island, near the whirlpool, wrote what he almost called *1948*.)

This was Mr McIlone's world, then, as was the pallid, washed-out Britain of the still-rationed late 'forties, and for all that the semi-independent croft and fishing economy of the Western Isles softened the blow of some of the shortages most keenly felt in cities on the mainland, it was still a hard, cold, windswept place, where a man lived close to land or sea with only his God, family and friends and sometimes the drink to sustain him and provide a little comfort.

Perhaps it is not so surprising, then, that Mr McIlone, brought into contact with my Grandfather's messianic, blazing certainty and the unconventional but obvious love he shared with his two exotically foreign beauties, should feel that he was missing out somewhere, that there was another retort to the world's absurdities and viciousness besides hermetic, hermit-like withdrawal.

Whatever factors, emotional, personal or philosophical, eventually produced this holy sea-change in Mr McIlone, by the end of 1949 it was complete, and our Founder had his first real convert (I don't think he ever felt his wives fully Believed, though they gave every appearance of Behaving).

He also had the run of the farm at Luskentyre, the continuing opportunity to study in its library, the use of its buildings, access to whatever funds and produce it gave rise to, and an eventually decisive say in its running. And so it was there that our sect, the True Church of Luskentyre, made its first home, from 1949 until 1954, when Mrs Woodbean gifted us the estate at High Easter Offerance, on the green and ancient flood plain of the river Forth, far to the south-east of those wild isles.

*

'Well, it smells like that liniment stuff me mother used to slap on us soon as we coughed out of turn,' Dec said, flopping into a huge cushion on the floor beside me.

I had partaken of the precious *zhlonjiz* unguent some hours earlier, in my loft bedroom, shortly after Zeb and I had made our way back to Kilburn from the South Bank (happily this required no changes of Underground train line). I had pulled up the loft ladder and closed the loft door, placing the ladder on top of it. I removed all my clothes save for my knickers and sat in the lotus position, meditating for some time beforehand. A cup of water I'd brought from the bathroom sat to one side, a scented Order candle to the other.

I struggled to open the tiny jar; the cap gave an audible crack when it finally turned. The sharp, spicy salve inside was black in the candlelight. I took a little of the thick dark cream on my little finger and placed some on my forehead, some behind my ears and some on my belly-button. I slipped the rest into my mouth, scraping it off against the back of my teeth and quickly swallowing it. I washed it down with the cup of water; the gritty black cream burned my tongue and the roof of my mouth as it slid down my throat.

I coughed and my nose ran and the fierce dark smell of the stuff seemed to surround me, fiery and raw and dissolving, reeking of a mountainous, half-mythical East. I sniffed back, breathing deeply to suffuse my being with the magical balm, relaxing and trying to let my soul open to the voice of the Creator, attempting both to ignore the vast city and its millions of Cluttered, Unsaved souls, and at the same time to use their untapped, ignorant capacity for Receiving to focus the signals of God upon myself.

In short, it did not work. I waited for the blink of an eye and the life of an old God, I waited until the next heart beat and the next Ice Age, I waited for the merest whisper of murmured acknowledgement and the erupting scream of God at last losing patience with us all; I waited long enough for the candle to flicker and go out, my legs to grow sore and my skin to prickle with goose-bumps.

Eventually I opened my eyes and stared into the darkness, aware of an edge of light round the sides of the loft door and the vague buzz of voices and smell of food drifting up from downstairs. I lowered my head and might have wept, until I rebuked myself for such self-pity, and told myself that – if fault there was – it was my own, and I had nobody else to blame. I sniffed, rose stiffly and dressed, tidied things up and lowered the wooden ladder through the opened loft door.

'What liniment?' I asked Declan.

'I dunno,' he said, lighting a small roll-up cigarette. 'Some stuff. She just called it "Di lineament" and dabbed the damn stuff on us at every opportunity; worst was when you had the toothache; stung like hell; worse than the toothache.'

'I thought it smelled like coriander,' said Roadkill, who was rolling one of their drug cigarettes. We were all – save for Scarpa – in the living room, listening to some modern CD music on the hi-fi. I had eaten after the others, having missed the main meal while I was attempting to Receive. I had, perhaps misguidedly, attempted to explain to the others what I had been trying to do in the loft; probably I ought not to have mentioned the *zhlonjiz* at all. Roadkill at least seemed sympathetic. Brother Zeb, also now rolling what they called a 'number', seemed to be ignoring me.

'Dec,' Boz said, stretching his hand across me to offer Declan the drug cigarette which was currently in circulation.

Dec seemed to hesitate, and Boz offered the long white tube to me. 'Hey, Isis, child; you want to try the holy ganja instead?'

I looked at it. 'I'd probably just cough,' I told him, though I was thinking about it. Our creed holds no thing wrong just because the Blands say it is, and from what I had heard both at school and from various people at the Commune, cannabis was a benign, if befuddlingly distracting drug. Indeed, I felt much more discomfited by the presence of all the electrical activity around me than I did by the haze of smoke that hung in the room.

'Ah, go on with ye,' Declan said.

'Very well,' I said, and exhaled to the bottom of my lungs. I reached out for the drug cigarette, but Boz moved it away out of reach.

'Hey, don't take too much there, Isis; you'll give youself a coughing fit, sure enough. You just breathe in gentle-like.'

I breathed in, looking up at Boz, who was sitting on another giant cushion. (I, of course, was on the wooden floorboards). I took the long cigarette and sucked on it, not too hard.

'. . . Easy now, Isis,' Boz said, as I gulped and tried not to cough, and handed the thing quickly on to Declan. I exhaled and took another few deep breaths, cooling my fiery throat (at least the cannabis had that in common with the *zhlonjiz*). 'You all right

139

now, Isis?' Boz asked, looking at me. I nodded. I rather liked the way Boz said 'I-sis'; slowly and deeply with the emphasis on the 'sis'.

'Fine,' I said, with only the smallest of coughs.

My head started to spin; alcohol never acted as rapidly. I passed on the next 'spliff' and went for another cup of water, but took some of the next drug cigarette, and the next.

There was much talk and laughter, and at one point I found myself trying to explain to Roadkill that in a sense everything was action at a distance and that this was the most important thing in the world, even though as I told her this I knew I was talking complete nonsense. I told her this too and she just laughed. Some people I didn't know came in and Boz went through to the kitchen with them. When I went there for more water later on I saw him sitting at the table using a knife and a pair of scales to measure out small pieces of black stuff which he then wrapped and gave to the strangers. Boz smiled at me. I felt a little faint at the time so I just smiled back and went through to the living room again. I surmised, in a sort of hazy, dissociated way, that Boz must be cutting up weights to be distributed to small businesses in the area so that their scales were all properly calibrated.

To my shame it was at least a good quarter-hour before I saw Declan rolling another joint with the same black stuff – made crumbly by having been heated with a cigarette lighter – and realised what Boz was actually doing; this led me into a fit of the giggles so intense that at one point I almost lost control of my bladder. Once I had calmed down I explained the cause of my confusion to the others, whereupon several of them started laughing too, causing me to relapse into hysteria.

A little later I dried my eyes, excused myself and bade them all goodnight. I negotiated my way carefully and deliberately to my lofty boudoir, taking great care always to have three points of contact as I climbed the ladder, and – leaving the loft trap-door open to light my way – taking equal care to tread only on the doors providing the loft's flooring, and even more extra special care when, having partially disrobed, I swung myself into my hammock.

My head was spinning, the loft-space was spinning, and I had the distinct impression that they were in contra-rotation to each other. I closed my eyes but this only made the sensation worse. I thought it not impossible that with my senses so unusually disrupted I might be able to open my soul to God and so receive Their word, but not until I could both stop the room spinning and prevent occasional after-shocks of giggles afflicting my body.

I took several deep breaths and tried to compose myself by thinking of our family history, a subject which requires considerable concentration and an alert, retentive and – some might argue – an open mind.

*

Salvador Whit and Aasni Whit née Asis begat two daughters, Brigit and Rhea, and a son, Christopher, who was Salvador's first boy-child and born on the 29th of February 1952, and so was known as the Elect of God, and given a long, impressive name which ended in the Roman numerals II because he was a second-generation Leapyearian. Salvador Whit and Zhobelia Whit née Asis begat two daughters, Calli and Astar, and a son, Mohammed.

Christopher Whit and Alice Whit née Cristofiori begat a son, Allan, and a daughter, Isis, who was born on the 29th of February 1976, and whose name was suffixed with the numerals III because she was a third-generation Leapyearian. Brigit and anon begat a daughter, Morag, but Brigit later became apostate and moved to Idaho in the United States of America and reputedly is to this day without further issue. Rhea became apostate early on, allegedly married an insurance salesman and moved to Basingstoke in England and we know of no children from her loins. Mohammed lives in Yorkshire in England and is childless. Calli and James Tillemont begat a daughter, Cassiopeia, a son, Paul, and another daughter, Hagar. Astar and Malcolm Redpath begat two sons, Hymen and Indra, and Malcolm Redpath and Matilda Blohm begat a son, Zebediah, and Astar and Johann Meitner begat a son, Pan.

Erin Peniakov and Salvador Whit begat a son, Topec, and possibly a daughter, Iris. Jessica Burrman and Salvador Whit probably begat a daughter, Helen. Fiona Galland and Salvador Whit probably begat a daughter, Heather. Gay Sumner and Salvador Whit may have begat a daughter, Clio.

After that it gets complicated.

The room was still spinning.

I imagined I was in a porcelain-hulled boat, drifting silently upstream to the Pendicles of Collymoon with my cousin Morag at my side; she was slowly bowing the throaty, many-voiced baryton and somehow that was our means of propulsion; I was floating in a silvery spaceship, its rocket tubes like organ pipes; I was lying under the Deivoxiphone listening to the Voice of God but we had a crossed line and all I could hear was opera; I lay on the floor in Sophi's room in the little turreted house across the half-ruined bridge, talking about playing the organ in the cathedral while she lay on the bed, leafing through magazines, but my words were coming out of my mouth as literal bubbles with little fat naked men and women in them, performing strange and unlikely sexual acts in each one; I sat at the Flentrop organ, but the keys just snarled at me and became a piano with the top down and locked and all I could hear was the sound of a dwarf running up and down inside, stamping out some stupid, monotonous tune, and swearing loudly but muffledly; I lay in the moonlit clouds of my Grandfather's beard, listening to the clustered stars sing overhead; the northern lights curved and twisted in great shawls of ghostly luminescence, like the flapping sails of some vast craft fit to sail between the galaxies.

I wondered hazily if this might be the start of a vision. It had been my ambition to start having visions and so to take over from my Grandfather and follow in his footsteps, as it were. But – despite a few promisingly unsettling sensations I had experienced over the years – I had never been privileged with such a visitation. My Grandfather had told me that there were different ways to hear the Voice of God; one could calm oneself, prepare one's mind, meditate and relax and eventually know what it was God had said to one – the way everybody else in our Order did – or one could – as he had, in the past at any rate – just suddenly find oneself dumped willy-nilly, effectively at random, into one of those fit-like visions over which he seemed to have no control. But that was God speaking to him too, so if what I was experiencing now was the start of a vision, I reasoned, then perhaps my attempt this evening had worked after all, albeit not quite as I had anticipated.

'Howyi, Isis; you all right there?' said a voice nearby, making me start. I must have closed my eyes. I opened them again. I had no idea how much time had passed.

There was somebody standing by the side of my hammock, a tall shadowy shape looking down at me. I'd recognised his voice. 'Declan,' I said, focusing with some difficulty. What was it he had asked? Then I remembered. 'Yes, I'm fine,' I said. 'How are you?'

'Ah, I just thought you might be feelin' a bit strange, you know?'

'Yes. No; I'm all right.'

'Right,' he said. He stood there for a moment, just visible in the light from the loft trap-door. 'You sure, now?' he asked, putting his hand out to my forehead and running his fingers through my hair. He stroked the back of my head. 'Ah, Jayzus, Isis; you're a beautiful kid, ye know that?'

'Really?' I said, which was probably the wrong thing.

'Chroist, *yes*. Anyone ever tell you you look like Dolores O'Riordan?' he said, bending closer.

'Who?'

'The Cranberries.'

'Who?' I repeated, confused. Actually his hand was producing quite a pleasant sensation at the back of my head, but I knew that, as a man, Declan would be unlikely to regard that as an end in itself.

'Ye mean ye've never heard of the Cranberries?' He laughed gently, bringing his face nearer to mine. 'By God, ye have led a sheltered life, haven't you?'

'I suppose so. Look, Declan—'

'Ah, ye're glorious, so ye are, Isis,' he said, and used his hand at the back of my head to lift my face up to his as he bent further forward.

143

I put my hands up to his chest and pushed. 'Declan,' I said, turning my face away to avoid his lips and getting an earful of wet tongue. 'You're very nice and I like you, but—'

'Ah, Isis, come on . . .' he said, putting one arm round my hammock and pulling me to him, his lips seeking mine. I pushed harder and he let me go, leaving me swinging to and fro between my roof beams. He sighed, then said, 'Ah, Isis, what's the matter? Will ye not even—' as he leant forward and reached out again.

I extended my hands to push him away, but he stumbled, I think, and next thing I knew he was falling forward on top of me, forcing the wind out of me. Declan went, 'Whoo!' Our combined weight swung the hammock out away from over the doors forming the floor; there was a creaking noise from somewhere beyond my feet, then a jerk, and in a moment of helpless horror I knew what was going to happen next.

'Oh, *no!*' I shouted.

The nail Brother Zebediah had bashed into the roof truss to take the foot of my hammock sprang out of the wood and sent Declan and me tumbling forward into the darkness under the slope of the roof. Had Declan not had both arms around me, my hammock and sleeping roll, and had I not had my arms trapped for that same reason, one of us might have been able to save one or both of us, but instead the second nail at the head of my hammock gave way too and sent us crashing lengthwise to land neatly between two rafters onto the rough, grimily ridged surface of the plaster. It broke like puddle-ice and we fell through into light, surrounded by dust and brittle shards of plaster with me screaming and Declan shouting, and somebody else screaming too.

We must have twisted in mid-air as we fell because I landed beside Declan with only his head thumping onto my midriff. We landed half on the floor of the room below – which proved to be Boz's – and half on the double mattress which was Boz's bed and on which he was lying at the time, propped up by a couple of cushions and watching a video; we must have just missed landing on his feet.

He gave a surprisingly high shriek and pulled the bed sheet quickly up over himself as Declan and I bounced once and lay stunned under a rain of dust and more lumps of plaster. I'd got just the vaguest glimpse of something black and purple Boz had been holding as we crashed down onto the bed in front of him. I moved an arm to shift some plaster off Declan's head and my hip and caught a glimpse of Boz's video, being shown on another remarkably new-looking television set on the other side of the room. I saw a woman sucking – in a somehow exaggerated way, and from a distinctly unnatural-looking angle – a man's erect penis. I stared at this. Two in one batch of seconds. Life was strange. Declan moaned and looked up, instantly aged thirty years by the grey dust coating his face and hair. He looked at me and then at Boz. He coughed. 'Oops,' he said.

I hardly heard. I was staring with my mouth open and my eyes boggling almost out of their sockets at the screen of the television set. The girl in the erotic video was now lying on her back by a sun-lit swimming pool while the man did something to her one could not see; her face contorted with what was probably meant to be ecstasy.

I couldn't believe it. I pointed with one shaking hand at the television. Declan followed my gaze to where the woman pouted and grimaced on the screen.

'That,' I exclaimed loudly, 'is my cousin Morag, the internationally famous soloist on the baryton!'

Declan watched the screen for a moment, looked back round at me, glanced at Boz – who still seemed stunned into wide-eyed silence – then shook his head, releasing a cloud of dust. 'Yer arse!' he laughed. 'That's Fusillada DeBauch, the porn queen, and the only thing she's renowned for is playing the pink piccolo, pal.'

CHAPTER
TEN

T he next morning, in the living room, I studied the videotape Boz had been watching.

Boz had recovered his cool and then started laughing at us while the dust was still settling around his bedroom. Declan apologised – to Boz first, I noticed, but then afterwards to me. He repaired the roof as best he could with a couple of posters over the hole in the ceiling and one of the loft's door floor-boards on the other side. Boz slipped into a pair of boxer shorts; he and I cleaned up the plaster. My head was still spinning but I felt somewhat more sober for the experience.

Of the others, only Roadkill seemed to have either heard anything or thought there was aught untoward about what they had heard. I told her Zeb's handiwork had proved fragile, to the sound of Declan banging the hammock nails back into the roof trusses. I felt faint again and – waving away Dec's apologies – climbed back up to the loft, taking my hammock and bedroll with me. I shook it free of dust and re-hung it, then collapsed into it and was asleep within minutes.

Next morning, with a head that felt stuffed with cotton wool and a cough that made me think I was coming down with the cold, I politely asked Boz for the videotape. (We will pass over my attempt by the laying on of hands to cure the sore knee which Declan woke up with and which was probably a delayed result of our fall, but what better proof is needed that all this clutter robs the Saved of their Holiness?) Boz seemed unembarrassed at my request, which was a relief, and went upstairs to get the video cassette. He showed me how to work the videotape player then went to make some breakfast.

The sensation of so deliberately using the video player, the television and their remote control devices – not just sitting in the same room to be sociable while they were used – made my teeth ache. Our rules concerning such matters take the form of

149

disciplines rather than outright prohibitions, and I did experience a kind of excitement in taking command of this seductive, blackly buttoned technology, however my principal emotion was one of tense, fractious unease, and I grew extremely frustrated when the machines did not seem to obey the remote controls. I muttered at the machinery and felt like throwing the remote controls across the room.

Suddenly it occurred to me that this must be how Blands feel all the time. I calmed myself and persevered and before too long everything behaved. The videotape began to play.

The woman was definitely Morag. Her voice sounded Euro-American somehow, but I could hear the Scottish accent coming through every now and again. From what I saw, the video itself had a semblance of a plot but it was patently used merely to provide punctuation for the various unlikely sexual exploits the heroine – Morag, Fusillada – indulged in with both sexes. As for the video's effect, well, I had a chance as never before to admire my cousin's bounteously sleek physique, and cannot say I was left unmoved by the theatrical but obviously unfaked copulatory shenanigans displayed, though quite why the video's makers thought that it was always necessary to show the men ejaculating each time was a mystery to me; the sight, which I had not witnessed before, hardly seemed to warrant the amount of time devoted to it and made me feel slightly queasy.

Nevertheless, all in all, I admit I felt quite hot and bothered as I sat there, and viewed rather more of the production than strictly required to establish Morag's identity. I handed back the tape to Boz over breakfast. He asked did I really know Fusillada DeBauch? I replied that I did and asked him what he was doing that day.

*

Soho again. Suddenly the location we had been sent to the previous day seemed less like a complete red herring. The revelation that my cousin had – at the very least – a sideline as a worker in the sex industry suddenly made looking for her agent in this area seem quite reasonable, and so we had returned to try again to find Mr Francis Leopold.

Brother Zeb had put his hair into a bushily disorderly ponytail as a disguise; he and Boz – who seemed unduly impressed that Fusillada was my cousin, and, I suspect, hoped we might bump into her – together distracted the large man with the much-be-ringed hands in the foyer of the erotic cinema while I slipped up the stairs between the picture house and the entrance to the Adult Book Shop. The stairs were narrow and steep. Three doors led off the landing at the top, which was lit by one grubby, dirt-streaked window whose outlook was anyway largely obscured by the façade advertising the cinema next door. Round a turn in the landing, another flight of stairs led to the next storey. I peered at the doors. Each had a little sign on it: Kelly Silk, Madame Charlotte, and Eva (S&M).

I ascended to the next floor, where the landing was marginally better lit. Vixen, Cimmeria, FL Enterprises. Ah ha!

I knocked on the door. There was no reply. After half a minute I tried the handle but the door was locked. A siren – ever the chorus to the city's songs – sounded somewhere nearby. I knocked again and rattled the door.

The door to the left, marked Cimmeria, cracked open and a sliver of dark face looked out. I smiled and tipped my hat.

'Good morning,' I said.

'Yeah?'

'Oh, indeed, it is!' I said, gesturing to the window. I glanced back at the door to FL Enterprises. 'I'm, ah, looking for Mr Leopold; is this his office?'

'Yeah.'

I could still only see about two inches of the black face looking at me through the gap between door and jamb. I cleared my throat. 'Ah. Good. Only he doesn't seem to be in.'

'Yeah?'

'Do you know when he might be expected to return?'

'No.'

'Oh dear,' I said, and took off my hat, looking dejected.

The one eye of the Negress I could see moved, her gaze taking

151

in my hair, my face and then torso. 'What you want anyway?' she asked, opening the door a fraction wider.

'I'm trying to trace my cousin, Morag Whit . . . I think she might be better known as, ah, Fusillada DeBauch.'

The single eye widened. The door closed and it occurred to me that perhaps I had said something wrong. Well, this wasn't proving too fruitful, I thought, gripping my hat to replace it on my head. A chain rattled behind Cimmeria's door, and it swung open. The woman came out onto the landing, glancing around, then stood with her back to her door, her arms crossed. She was small and very black, with tied-back hair. She wore a black kimono which looked like silk. Her head tossed up once, like a horse's.

'What you looking for her for? You really her cousin?'

'Oh, I'm her cousin, certainly; her mother was my father's sister. We're from Scotland.'

'Never have guessed.'

'Really? I thought perhaps my accent would rather give—'

'That was irony, child,' the woman said, looking away for a moment with widened eyes.

'Oh. I beg your pardon,' I said, blushing. I felt awkward, but for some reason I trusted this woman. I decided to trust my instincts. 'Anyway, to answer your first question, I'm looking for Morag because . . . well, it's complicated, but we – I mean, her family – are concerned about her.'

'Are you now?'

'Yes. Also,' I hesitated, then sighed. 'May I be frank with you, Miss . . . Cimmeria?' (She nodded.)

'Well,' I said, fingering the rim of my hat. 'The plain fact is Morag is, or was, a member of our church, back home, and we are concerned that she has lost her faith. Of most immediate concern is the matter of a festival that we are to hold at the end of the month – a very important festival, one that only takes place every four years. Cousin Morag was to be our Guest of Honour at that, and now, well, we don't know what to do. The festival is important, as I say, but her soul is more important, and personally I am worried that my cousin has fallen under the spell of some religious charlatan, and judge that ultimately to be the more important business, but

I'm afraid it is the question of her attendance at the festival which presents us with the most immediate predicament.'

Cimmeria looked through narrowed eyes, face turned slightly. 'What church is this?'

'Oh,' I said, 'it's the True Church of Luskentyre; the Luskentyrians, as we're usually known. I don't expect you've heard of us. We're a small but active Faith based in Scotland; we have a . . . oh, I suppose you could call it sort of an ashram, a commune, near Stirling. We believe in—'

Cimmeria held up one hand. 'Okay, okay,' she said, smiling. 'You people Christians?'

'Strictly speaking, no; we regard Christ as one prophet amongst many and the Bible as one holy book amongst many; we believe there is merit and wisdom to be found in all holy teachings. We do believe in love and forgiveness and the renunciation of excess materiality and—'

'Fine. Spare me,' Cimmeria said, holding up her hand again. She nodded at the door. 'So you're looking for Frank?'

I explained about visiting Morag's old apartment block in Finchley the day before. '*Is* Mr Leopold her agent?' I asked.

Cimmeria shrugged. 'Agent, manager; whatever.'

'Phew!' I said, grinning. 'On the right track at last!' I hit my thigh with my hat. I can be quite shameless.

Cimmeria laughed and pushed her door open. 'Come on in. You'll have to excuse the mess; this is early for me.'

'I doubt it can match the mess created last night in the squat where I am staying while in London . . .' I said, accepting her invitation.

*

Twenty minutes later I joined Boz and Zeb in the same café Zeb and I had retreated to a day earlier. They both appeared unharmed and in good spirits.

'All right, chaps?'

'Yeah. Fine. Cool. You?'

'We're okay, I-sis.'

153

I sat down between them, getting Brother Zebediah to move over. 'I had tea,' I told them, 'with a very nice lady called Cimmeria whose real name is Gladys; she told me that Mr Leopold is indeed Morag's – Fusillada's – agent and manager, and that he was here just yesterday, but that he has had problems with . . . Vat?' I said, looking inquiringly from one to the other.

'VAT.' Boz nodded slowly, then sipped carefully at his coffee. 'Value Added Tax, I-sis.' He tutted and shook his head, seemingly unimpressed with the concept.

'Indeed,' I said. 'Well, apparently Mr Leopold has been experiencing difficulties with this VAT for some time now and is currently helping Customs and Excise with their inquiries.'

'Huh. Well. So,' Zeb said.

'So,' I said, 'Cimmeria – Gladys – told me that she thought Mr Leopold lives in the county of Essex, in a village called Gittering, near Badleigh, and thinks that that was where he took a number of the papers and files he previously kept in the office. She suggests we try there. What do you say?'

'*Essex?*' Zeb said, with an expression on his face which, given we were sitting in a café in central London, might have been better suited to accompanying the word '*Mongolia?*' delivered in the same tone of voice.

'I-sis; you think your cousin might be there?'

'Well,' I said, 'apparently some of the scenes for certain of Fusillada's videotape productions were shot in Mr Leopold's home there, which is called La Mancha. Cimmeria – Gladys – knows this because some of her friends have been there to take part in them. So, as Morag is no longer living at the flat in Finchley, I suppose it is not impossible she is there, though we have no guarantee, of course.'

Boz thought about this. He looked very big and bulky in baggy black trousers and an expensive-looking black leather jacket. He wore a black peaked cap; it was back to front so that people behind him could read the white letter X. 'What the hell,' he said. 'I wasn't doin' nuthin' much today anyway. And I heard about Essex girls, eh?' He delivered what looked like the gentlest of pulled punches past me to Brother Zebediah's arm; Zeb rocked in his stool and looked pained. He forced a smile while he rubbed his arm.

'Suppose. Yeah. Shit. Essex. Shit.'

'Let's make tracks!' I said, jumping off my stool and unable to resist nudging Zeb in the elbow. He looked startled and stared concernedly at his elbow. Boz slurped on his coffee.

*

We took a bus to Liverpool Street station and a train from there to Badleigh. Not having anticipated a journey outside the capital, I had not brought my Sitting Board, so Zeb and I stood in the aisle by Boz's seat. Boz read a paper called the *Mirror*. I whiled away the time for Zeb by reading him parts of passages from the *Orthography* and asking him to recall what words came next. He was shockingly poor at this, though that may have been because completing the pieces of text would have required talking in sentences of more than one word and he had obviously quite got out of that particular habit.

At one point, when Boz had gone to the toilet for 'a quick toke' (which I took to be Jamaican slang for a bowel movement, given the amount of time he was away), I asked Zeb, 'Why does Boz wear his cap back to front?'

Zeb looked at me as though I had asked him why Boz wore his shoes on his feet. 'It's. Like. Baseball cap,' he said scornfully.

I thought about this. 'Ah,' I said, really none the wiser.

The city went on and on; every time I thought we had finally left the metropolis behind, the patch of greenery I'd based this assumption on would turn out to be a park or an area of waste ground. Eventually, however, while I was engrossed in the *Orthography* (Zeb had gone off to the toilet some time earlier) the city gave way to countryside, and when I next looked up we were sliding through a level landscape of fields and narrow lanes, dotted with buildings, villages and towns, all sliding quickly past under a sky of small clouds. I felt some relief at having left the vast busyness of the city behind, as though my clutter-smothered soul was finally drawing something like a clear and unobstructed breath again.

155

Badleigh proved to be a flat town with a split personality: a village-like old town with low, erratically streeted buildings to one side of the railway line, and a cubical landscape of medium-rise brick and concrete on the other. One building I thought at first must still be under construction proved on closer inspection – as the train slowed and we got ready to get off – to be a multi-layered car park.

*

'He says it's three miles, I-sis,' Boz told us, after talking to the man in the ticket office.

'Good!' I said. 'A stroll.'

'No way, man,' Boz said, grinning from behind dark sunglasses. 'I call us a taxi.' He loped off to the exit.

'For a mere three miles?' I said, aghast, to Zeb.

'City,' Zeb said, shrugging, then appeared to think. His face brightened briefly. 'Lanes,' he said, with a hint of pride, I thought. He nodded happily. 'Lanes,' he said again, and sounded pleased with himself.

'Lanes?' I asked.

'Lanes. Narrow. No pavements. Cars. Speeding. Walking. Dangerous.' He shrugged. 'Lanes.' He turned and walked to the doors, beyond which Boz could be seen getting into a car.

'Lanes,' I muttered to myself, feeling obliged to join my two comrades.

*

'Well, I'm sorry, dear, but you can't kneel on the seats.'

'But I could put the belt round me!' I said, struggling to pull the restraining seat-belt out far enough.

'That's not the point though, love, is it? The regulations say that my fares have to be seated. If you're kneeling you're not seated, are you?'

'Could I sit on the floor?' I asked.

'No, I don't think so.'

156

'But I'd be seated!'

'Yeah, but not on a seat; you wouldn't be seated on a seat, know what I mean? There something wrong with her, mate?'

'The child's eccentric, man; she's from Scot-lan'. I'm sorry. Hey, I-sis; you got the man here thinkin' he got some sort of lunatic in the back of his car here—'

'Well, I meant like piles or sumfing, actually . . .'

'—he goin' to be askin' us to get out an' walk if you don't settle down. Sorry, man; you just start the meter rollin' now; we get this sorted.'

'Look,' I said, 'haven't you got some sort of board or something hard I could sit on?'

The taxi driver looked round at me. He was a hunched little chap with alarmingly thick glasses. 'Sumfing hard to sit on?' he said, then glanced at Boz. 'See; told you.'

He reached down the side of his seat and handed me a large book. 'Here we go; the *A to Z*; will that do?'

I tested it; the battered hardback flexed a little. 'It will suffice. Thank you, sir.'

'All part of the service,' he said, turning back. 'Nuffink to be embarrassed about. Had the same problem myself once, 'cept you don't usually see people young as you wif it, do you?'

'No,' I agreed as we started off and I belted myself in, too flustered to follow what he was talking about.

The car smelled powerfully of a cheap, sharp perfume. We passed the three miles to Gittering being regaled with graphic tales of our driver's multiple hospitalisations and various operations.

*

'Attractive. Ranch style,' Zeb said, staring with admiration at the large house beyond the gate separating road from driveway. At the far end of the drive, La Mancha was a white bungalow complex with roofs at various angles and large windows backed by closed curtains. The gardens looked well tended, although somebody had abandoned a gaily painted horsecart in the centre of the lawn, there was a new-looking plough standing on a strip of grass across the drive from the lawn, and a brightly decorated cartwheel lay against the side of the house. It looked terribly clean and tidy to be a working farm.

There were various signs on the shoulder-high white wooden gate; one said, 'La Mancha', another said, 'Private Property – Keep Out', and another said, 'Beware Of The Dog', and had a colour picture of the head of a very large dog on it, just in case the reader was under any illusion concerning what dogs looked like.

'This is it,' I said, looking through the bars of the gate for a slide or staple that would allow us to open it.

'Whoa,' Zeb said, tapping the 'Beware Of The Dog' sign.

I slid the gate's bolt and started to push it open. 'What?' I said. 'Oh, don't worry about that; they probably don't have any dogs. Besides,' I told my two uncertain-looking companions as I held the gate open for them, 'I have a way with animals, especially dogs.' I closed the gate after us, then took the lead and headed for the house.

We were halfway down the drive when we heard the deep-throated barking. We all stopped. A huge hound came running round the side of the building, looking very much like the one on the sign at the gate; it was brown-black, its head was huge and there was spittle already flying from its jowls as it came powering towards us. It looked about the size of a foal.

'Jeez!'

'Run! I-sis; *run!*'

I glanced back to see Zeb and Boz – who was still looking back at me – heading smartly for the gate.

I felt calm. I had faith. And I really did have a way with animals. I thought for a moment, weighing up the situation. Behind me, the dog barked again; it sounded like a dinosaur with a bad cough. I started to run.

*

A way with animals does run in our family; when my Grandfather persuaded Mr McIlone to become his first apostle and moved in to the farm of Luskentyre, he discovered a gift for working with cattle and horses; he was always able to calm them when they were distressed and often able to tell what was wrong with them even before the vet arrived.

My father inherited the same talent, and was largely in charge of the sheep and cows at High Easter Offerance even before he left school, though our Founder thought that animal husbandry was beneath an Elect. Still, Salvador could refuse his son nothing, a trait that seems to have been made transferable to other Elects and become an article of faith, I'm glad to say (certainly I have benefited from it), and so my father was allowed to indulge his vocation for farming to his soul's content.

*

I do not share my father's love of animals, though I like them well enough and have inherited both a modicum of the facility for empathising and working with them to which he fell heir from my Grandfather, plus an ability to Heal them.

When I was happy that Zeb and especially Boz were convinced I was following them as they sprinted for the gate, I stopped, spun round onto the grass and went down on all fours with my forearms extended in front of me. I crouched there on the grass, looking up at the giant dog as it bore down on me; I sort of flopped forward a little, bouncing up and then down, arms still extended, backside up in the air. The dog looked confused, and slowed as it approached; I repeated the movement and to my enormous relief the beast dropped back to a walk and made snuffing, huffing noises. I repeated the gesture once more. The dog hesitated, looked around and then padded forward. I made the same movement – it's dog for Let's Play – and lowered my eyes when it growled at me. When I looked up again its tail was wagging. It came up to sniff me.

I have, as I have said, a gift. If a large dog comes running at most people, running smartly away is probably by far the best idea.

159

Whatever; a minute later I was squatting on the grass, patting my new slobbering, panting friend and looking at Zeb and Boz, who were on the far side of the gate, staring at me.

'Y'all right there with that thing, I-sis?'

'So far,' I called. 'I wouldn't come in just now though; I'll see if it's happy with me standing up, then I'll head for the front door.'

The beast growled when I made to rise; I could have sworn the ground shook. I decided that dignity must bow to expediency, and so crossed to the front door on all fours, with the huge dog padding contentedly at my side. I reached up and rang the doorbell. The hound barked loudly, its voice echoing in the open porch, and then it ran away back the way it had come, disappearing round the side of the house. I stood up.

It was some time before the door was half opened, by a tall young man with streaked blond hair whom I immediately guessed was not Mr Leopold; somehow the way Cimmeria had talked about him, and even the place where he had his office, did not tally with the bronzed, fit-looking fellow standing in front of me; from the vertical half of him I could see he was wearing a peaked cap (like Boz's, worn the wrong way round), a T-shirt and jeans.

'Yeah? What you want?'

'Ah; good afternoon. My name is Isis Whit.' I put out my hand. The young man looked me in the eyes, his brows furrowed. 'Pleased to meet you,' I said, taking off my hat with my other hand and smiling. I used my eyes to indicate my hand, and cleared my throat delicately. The young man went on scowling at me; my hand went unclasped. 'Excuse me, sir; I am offering to shake hands. I had been given to understand that good manners extended to this part of the country.'

He frowned even more deeply. 'Wot?'

'Sir,' I said sharply, presenting my hand almost in front of his face.

Perhaps it is simply that persistence pays with such people; he looked at my proffered hand as though seeing one for the first time and finally, tentatively, put out his own hand and shook it.

'There, that wasn't so difficult now, was it?' I said, setting my hat back on my head at a jaunty angle. The young man's frown had lifted a little. 'I'm very sorry to disturb you and your fine dog, but I'm looking for a young—'

'Where's Tyson?' he demanded, his frown deepening again.

'I beg your pardon?'

'Tyson,' he said. He looked over my head to the lawn, eyes swivelling. I hazarded a guess at who Tyson was.

'The dog? He's fine, and in good voice.'

'Where is he, then?'

'He escorted me here to the door and then ran back round the side there when the bell went.'

'Wot you want?' he asked suspiciously, letting the door swing further open to reveal that he was holding a long, polished wooden stick.

'Gosh,' I said. 'What's that?'

He gave me a look not dissimilar to the one I'd received from Zeb on the train when I inquired about the directional orientation of Boz's cap. 'It's a baseball bat, innit?' he told me.

It crossed my mind to ask whether he was holding it the right way round, but I just nodded appreciatively. 'Is it really?' I said. 'Well, as I was saying, my name is Isis Whit; I'm really looking for my cousin, Morag Whit. I was told that Mr Francis Leopold is her manager and that he lives here, so I'm sort of looking for him. It's just that my family is rather worried about Morag and I'd really like to—'

'Spain,' the young man said suddenly.

'Spine?' I asked, mishearing.

'Spain,' he repeated. 'You know; the country.'

'Mr Leopold is in Spain?'

The fellow looked troubled. 'Well, no.'

'He's not in Spain.'

'No; we was supposed to go, like, but . . .' His voice trailed away and his gaze wandered over my head somewhere.

'Customs and Excise?' I ventured chirpily.

'How you know about that?' he asked, scowling as he focused on me again.

'Ah, bad news travels fast, doesn't it?'

He was looking over my head again. He nodded. 'Who's that, then?' He hefted the baseball bat.

I looked round to see Boz and Zeb in the driveway, advancing tentatively. Zeb waved. 'The skinny white one is my cousin, Zebediah,' I told the young man. 'The big black one is our friend Boz.'

'What they want, then?' the fellow said, slapping the baseball bat into the palm of his hand. At that point I heard Tyson barking. Zeb and Boz promptly turned tail again and ran for the road; Tyson appeared, racing after them, but broke off the chase halfway up the drive as the men scrambled over the gate. The dog barked in a perfunctory manner, then came swaggering across the lawn towards us, pausing only to collect a small rubber ball which at first I thought he'd swallowed but which proved to be lodged wetly between his massive jaws. He joined us in the porch and dropped the ball at my feet. I squatted on my haunches and Tyson let me chuckle him under his chin, snuffling.

'How you do that?' the young man asked, seemingly mystified.

'I have a way with animals,' I explained, stroking Tyson's back and smiling at the hound.

'You wot?' he said, his voice suddenly high.

'I have a way with animals,' I repeated, looking up at him.

'Oh,' he said. He gave what could well have been a laugh. 'Right.' He patted Tyson on the head; the beast growled. 'Anyway,' he said. 'She's not here.'

'Who? Morag?' I asked, rising carefully and keeping one hand on Tyson's back; I could feel the animal vibrating but there was no audible growl.

'Yeah; she's not here.'

'Oh dear. Where— ?'

'She's gone.'

'Gone. Really? Well, she would be, wouldn't she? I suppose . . . Wh— ?'

'To an elf farm.'

'Ha-ha; I didn't quite catch that . . . ?'

'She's gone to—'

At that point a telephone rang somewhere behind him. He

looked back into the hall, then at me, then at Tyson. 'Telephone,' he said, and swung the door until it was almost closed. I heard him say, "'Ullo?' then, 'Yeah, 'ullo, Mo,' and for a second I was filled with confusion, wondering what my Uncle Mo was doing phoning here, before I realised; it was probably Morag!

I glanced down at Tyson and smiled. The dog growled. I put one finger to the edge of the door and pushed very gently so that it appeared the door was being blown open by the breeze. The young man was a couple of yards inside the hall, by a small table on which the telephone sat. He still held the baseball bat. He frowned at me. I grinned vacuously, then stooped and picked up Tyson's rubber ball. The ball was old and worn and porous; the beast's saliva felt cold and slimy as it oozed to the surface of the rubber toy. I threw the ball out onto the lawn. Tyson took off after it.

'Yeah, got it,' the young man was saying into the phone, and glanced down at a little cube of paper notelets by the side of the telephone. 'Fine. No. Yeah. Na, no word,' he said, turning so that he had his back to me. He lowered his voice. 'Yeah, actually there's somebody here just now, askin' for you . . .' I heard him say, as a panting noise and a hefty thud on the outside of my left thigh announced Tyson's return. I kept my eyes on the young man as I went down on my haunches and retrieved the sodden ball.

'Can't . . .' the young man said. He turned back to look at me. 'What you say your name was again?'

'Isis,' I said.

He turned back, hunching slightly. 'Isis,' I heard him say. Next second he jerked straight. '*Wot?*' he barked, sounding angry. 'You mean it's *this* one? You mean it's this bastard 'ere; this one?'

I didn't like the look or the sound of this. A plan I had been turning over tentatively at the back of my mind suddenly thrust itself to the fore and demanded an immediate Yes or No.

I didn't really have to think about it. I decided the answer was Yes, and threw the soggy rubber ball into the hall.

The ball squelched on the carpet just behind the young man and bounced past him further down the hall; Tyson pounced in after it and shouldered the fellow out of the way, making him bang his leg into the telephone table.

'Aow, *fack!*' the young man said. He recovered his balance by clunking the baseball bat against the wall.

The saliva-saturated ball rolled into a distant room; Tyson thundered after it. 'Call yer back!' the young man said, and threw down the phone. Tyson skidded and disappeared from view. There was an expensive-sounding crash from the room. 'Tyson!' the young man yelled, sprinting after the hound.

'Tyson! You *cant!*' he screamed, charging into the room and disappearing from view. I slipped in through the door as more crashes and oaths resounded from the room concerned. I had been hoping the young fellow would just put down the phone, thus giving me a chance to talk to Morag, assuming that had indeed been her calling, but the handset was back in its cradle. I picked it up anyway, but heard only the dialling tone.

'You facker; come 'ere!' The hall floorboards shook to the sound of something like a sideboard falling over. I looked at the little cube of notelets by the side of the phone, the one the young man had glanced at when he'd said, 'Yeah, got it', a minute or so earlier. There was a telephone number written there.

I glanced down the hall, just as the young man appeared in the doorway, holding Tyson by his studded collar and waving the baseball bat at me. His face looked somewhat florid. Tyson had the ball clamped in his teeth and seemed pleased with himself. '*Right!*' the young man yelled, jabbing the bat towards me. '*You*; Ice, or whatever your fackin' name is; aht the ahse, *now!*'

I was already retreating. Then the fellow added, 'And Mo says to stop boverin' her, or else, *right*? You'll get a *slap*, you will.' He glanced down at Tyson, who seemed to have become vicariously upset as well by now and was glowering at me, growling sonorously. The young man let go the beast's collar. 'Get the bint, my son.'

Bothering her? I was thinking as Tyson dropped the ball and leaped towards me with a furious snarl.

Somehow I didn't think that my way with animals was going to prove effective this time. I stepped back into the porch and swung the front door closed behind me. Then I turned and ran.

I cut across the lawn to the drive; I heard the door open behind me and the young man yelling something; then all I could hear was barking. Boz and Zeb stood at the gate, eyes wide; I got the impression as I raced up the drive that the two men were getting ready to help me over the gate. 'Out the way!' I yelled, waving one arm. Thankfully, they moved, one to each side. I got to the gate a second before Tyson and vaulted it cleanly, staggering as I landed but not falling. Tyson could probably have jumped it too, but contented himself with slamming into the woodwork and making it shudder; he continued barking furiously. The young man was charging up the drive, shouting and waving his baseball bat.

I gathered myself, looked from Zeb to Boz and nodded down the road. 'Race you to the station,' I panted.

CHAPTER
ELEVEN

We stopped running after a bend a hundred or so yards up the lane; when we lost sight of him, the young man was standing on the road outside the opened gate, holding the howling, bellowing Tyson by the collar with some difficulty and still shouting and waving the bat.

We slowed to a trot as we entered the small village of Gittering itself; a quiet-looking place with a village green and a single public house. Boz chuckled. 'Hoo-ee!' he said. 'That was some big mean muthafucka of a dog!'

'Shit,' Zeb gasped, 'less.' He looked pale and sweaty.

'Sorry about that, chaps,' I said.

'Hey, you're an athlete, I-sis,' Boz said admiringly.

'Thank you.'

'But you're crazy; what the hell you doin' stayin' back when that hound of the fuckin' Baskervilles come at us like that?'

'I told you,' I told him, 'I have a way with animals.'

'You're crazy,' Boz laughed.

'According to my maternal grandmother Yolanda,' I told him, setting my hat straight upon my head again and trying not to let my heart swell too much with pride and vanity, 'I am a tough cookie.'

'Yeah,' he said, 'sounds like your maternal grandmother Yolanda ain't no fool neither.' He nodded at a telephone box on the far side of the village green. 'Let's call a taxi.'

Zeb and I watched for pursuit while Boz rang a number on a card inside the telephone box, but neither Tyson nor his blond handler appeared. Boz came out of the telephone box. 'It's the same guy; he's on his way; says he'll bring the book for you.'

'How kind,' I said. 'Excuse me, would you?' I took a deep breath, gritted my teeth and stepped into the telephone box. I studied the instructions, then stuck my head and one arm out. 'Zeb; some change, please.'

169

Zeb gave me his long-suffering look but coughed up a half-pound piece. 'God, forgive me,' I whispered as I inserted the coin and buttoned the number that had been on the pad by the telephone in La Mancha. Boz and Zeb looked quizzically in through the glass.

'Good morning,' said a pleasant female voice. I was startled, even though I was prepared to be spoken to; after years spent using telephones as telegraphs, it was slightly shocking to hear a human voice rather than the ringing tone. 'Clissold's Health Farm and Country Club,' the warm, welcoming voice said. 'How may I help you?'

Bothering her, I thought, and reluctantly restrained myself from asking to speak to Morag. 'I'm sorry?' I said.

'This is Clissold's Health Farm and Country Club. May I help you?' the lady said again, with a little less warmth. Her accent was definitely English, though I couldn't place it more accurately.

'Oh; I was trying to reach, ah, Scotland,' I said, sounding flustered.

'I *think* you have the wrong number,' the lady said, sounding amused. 'Wrong code, really. This is Somerset.'

'Oh,' I said, brightly. 'What part? I know Somerset quite well,' I lied.

'Dudgeon Magna; we're near Wells.'

'Oooh, heavens, yes,' I said, with such shamelessly specious conviction I almost had myself persuaded. 'Know it well. I – oh, bother; there goes my money.' I clicked the handset back onto its rest.

Zeb looked suspicious. He glared at the telephone in the box. 'I thought you weren't—' he began.

'Somerset,' I announced to him and Boz as the same taxi that had brought us here swung into sight on the far side of the green.

*

Perversely enough, it was probably the burning down of the old seaweed factory that ensured our Faith became more than just an eccentricity shared by a handful of people. My Grandfather just wanted to forget about the whole incident, but the lawyers who had charge of the disputed estate to which the old factory had belonged were not so understanding. Several of the men responsible for the conflagration were apprehended and charged, and when the matter came to trial in Stornoway, Salvador, Aasni and Zhobelia had no choice but to appear as witnesses.

My Grandfather had taken to dressing entirely in black by then and whenever he left the farm at Luskentyre he wore a black, wide-brimmed hat. With him dressed so, and boasting long (and now entirely white) hair and bushy white beard, and the two sisters clad in their best, most colourful saris, they must have presented a singular sight as they attended the court. There was some press interest; our Founder abhorred such attention, but there was little he could do about it, and of course the fact that he refused to talk to people on the *Stornoway Gazette* or a journalist sent from Glasgow from the *Daily Dispatch* only piqued their interest (and given the rumours about our Founder and his two dusky consorts, they were already pretty piqued).

My Grandfather managed to avoid most of the publicity and discovered that a wide-brimmed hat was particularly effective at shielding him from photographs – especially as the cameras of the time were bulky, awkward items which are hard to handle while trying to take a snap of somebody striding purposefully down a narrow street, usually in the rain. Nevertheless, while he managed to avoid claiming to be married to the two sisters, and succeeded in side-stepping insinuations about the exact nature of his relationship with the women, he was less reluctant to express himself when it came to his new-found faith, and some of the things he said – helpfully enhanced by the mysterious process of metamorphosis that tends to occur between reality and newsprint – must have struck a chord with a couple in Edinburgh called Cecil and Gertrude Possil, though of course my Grandfather didn't know this at the time.

Aasni and Zhobelia were called as witnesses but were unable (unwilling, actually) to provide any help; their English and Gaelic

171

– both of which they were reasonably at home in – seemed to deteriorate to the point of almost total incomprehensibility the instant they crossed the threshold of the Court. When an interpreter was called for, the only people capable of helping proved to be other members of the Asis family, which might or might not have been acceptable to the defence, but in the end didn't matter because the family simply refused to speak or listen to the two brazenly shameless, marriage-wrecking hussies who had once been their daughters, and no threat of being charged with contempt of court was going to change their minds.

Faced with such intransigence in a case which was, in the end, only concerned with the destruction of a factory nobody who mattered had really cared about, the exasperated sheriff thought the better of pressing the point; Aasni and Zhobelia were excused from providing evidence.

Salvador, who had never met the rest of the Asis family, took its rejection of its daughters more personally than they did themselves, and swore never to enter the store they had opened in Stornoway or, later, the branch in Tarbert. Somehow this ban became an article of faith and extended – as the Asis family's commercial interests expanded and shops opened in Portree, Oban and Inverness – to all retail premises, presumably just to be on the safe side.

The trial ended; the cowed, murmuring, Sunday-best-dressed men accused of the dastardly drunken factory incendiarism were found neither guilty nor innocent but were told that the charges against them had been found Not Proven, a uniquely Scottish verdict that has exactly the same legal force as Not Guilty but is often popularly taken to mean, We think you did it but we're not certain, and which has the twin merits both of introducing into the usually monochrome guilty/innocent, decent folk/criminal classes, good/bad world of the law the concept of quantum uncertainty, and leaving a lingering cloud of public dubiety and suspicion over the accused just so they didn't get too cocky in future.

Grandfather and the sisters returned to the farm at Luskentyre, Salvador to work alongside Mr McIlone with the animals on the farm and continue reading, studying and writing the *Orthography*,

172

and the sisters to continue driving round the isles in their converted library van, making bad deals and not much of a living. Come the first summer my Grandfather spent on the islands, that of 1949, the two sisters found themselves doing something else together, as their bellies started to swell. Salvador – while suffused with virile pride, of course – was already wondering how they were going to cope with two extra mouths to feed when the Possils arrived.

Cecil (pronounced See-sill, apparently) and Gertie Possil were an eccentric couple of independent means who wiled away their otherwise relatively pointless lives by joining different sects, cults and churches as though they were trying to collect the set. Cecil was a tall, awkward man who had been unable to take part in the War because he only possessed one eye, the other one having been hooked out when he was a child when his father – a keen angler – was teaching him to cast; a traumatic incident one might have thought would put the young Cecil off fishing, and possibly fish, for life, but which in fact had had exactly the opposite effect. When Cecil disappeared on one of his frequent fishing trips in the Highlands or to the chalk streams of southern England, Gertie would spend the time attending séances and talking to mystics.

They had read something about Grandfather and his strange new faith – including his emphasis on the importance of the 29th of February – in their daily newspaper on the first of March that year, and realised that *that was the day that would have been the 29th of February had 1949 been a leap year*. Convinced that this meant something entirely profound, they had determined to make a pilgrimage to Luskentyre later that year. (Though it has to be said that Cecil later confessed he had also been thinking of the opportunities for sporting fishing to be had in the Hebrides, had he and his wife proved unwelcome at or been disillusioned with Grandfather's proto-church.)

Salvador was wary of the Possils at first, though Mr McIlone seemed happy to have them stay, and the sisters appeared politely indifferent. Cecil and Gertie arrived on Harris in a large pre-war shooting break (a kind of estate car or station wagon which

173

Sister Jess assures me a lady called Everidge once memorably termed a half-timbered car) packed with Mesopotamian scatter cushions, Afghan rugs, Ceylonese onyx incense holders and all the other essentials required for prolonged survival on a modest island farm.

They also brought with them at least twenty different types of tea, which they kept in airtight Javanese cinerary urns. This greatly endeared them to my Grandfather, and was probably the difference between them being trusted and accepted when they first appeared or being treated with such suspicion they felt obliged to leave. Blithely bestowing the Luskentyre farm with batiks, lacquer screens and silver candelabra, the Possils were able to bring an air of luxury to the place that at first appealed to all concerned, including my Grandfather. Until then the farm had been a place of creaking iron beds, smoky paraffin lamps and bare floorboards relieved by off-cuts of linoleum. By the time the Possils were finished all of those were still there but by all accounts they didn't seem to define the place any more.

The Possils stayed initially for two months, providing the farm with its veneer of opulence, Grandfather with all the speciality teas, pens and paper he desired, and the locals with both a rich new vein of gossip and a lurid new example to brandish in front of children and weak-minded adults whenever a paradigm of hedonistic immorality and heathen decadence was required.

I think they also gave our Founder something else: an outside perspective, a calibratory check, a chance to measure his revelations, thoughts, insights and future teachings against the experience of people who'd pretty well played the field as far as odd new sects were concerned, and quite assuredly knew their way round a decent cult when they saw one.

Cecil and Gertie became converts. Something about Salvador's new religion seemed to chime with them; it was, if you like, both backward and forward looking, and they found elements in each direction that agreed with them. They had, years earlier, decided against having their house in Edinburgh's Morningside connected to the electricity mains and were already curiously hermetic in their private lives. Trying to keep up with all the services and meetings of so many splintered faiths left them little or no time to socialise with the real faithful afterwards, and each had few acquaintances outside respectively game fishing and séance attending, and no real friends at all. I think even Salvador's patently scandalous relationship with the two sisters seemed a breath of fresh air to them after the small-minded and hysterical attitude to sexuality the other sects and faiths they had paid court to tended to display, and in both that and a desire to live frugally and unfussily out-with conventional society, with a respect for the wisdom of the past, for nature and for all mystic faiths, it might be true that my Grandfather was one of the first hippies.

Cecil and Gertie left at the end of that first summer, as Aasni and Zhobelia bloomed bigger, and shortly after Gertie discovered, to her alloyed joy, that she too had fallen pregnant (this was the lump that would turn out to be Lucius). They swore that they would return, and that they would spread the good tidings of the new Faith's birth, both by word of mouth and by financing the publication of the *Orthography* once Salvador had completed it. They took all their exotic trappings with them, stowing them in the back of the shooting break without a thought for the finer sensibilities of the pregnant sisters, who to their dismay suddenly found themselves dumped back into the world of creaking iron beds and curling lino after a heady existence amongst the luxuries of perfume-saturated cloth-of-gold cushions and silk rugs of fabulous design.

I think that was when Salvador, who bore the brunt of the sisters' complaints in this matter, finally turned his back on extravagance and luxury and made simplicity an article of faith.

The Possils kept up an almost daily correspondence with the farm at Luskentyre, telling of their mission amongst the heathen folk of Edinburgh and their efforts at spreading the good word amongst those who sought game fish in still pools and those who angled after the words, warnings and entreaties of the dear-departed.

Meanwhile Aasni and Zhobelia each grew big with child, and jointly developed a passion at a certain point in their confinement for the pungent pickles and condiments they remembered from

175

their childhood. Forbidden from contacting their parents, having no wish to do so anyway and knowing of no other nearby source of spiciness, they started to make their own, ordering supplies of the rarer raw ingredients – chillis, coriander, cardamom, etc. – by mail from an Indian grocer in Edinburgh whom Gertie had put them in touch with.

Their experiments with the likes of chilli and garlic sauce, lime and brinjal pickle, apple and ginger chutney and so on did not always meet with complete success, but they persisted, and Salvador – discovering along with Mr McIlone a liking for the sisters' fiery concoctions which might not have been totally unconnected with the commonality of effect produced in the mouth by both cheap whisky and any chilli-laced comestible – happily encouraged these fragrant forays into the Epicurean realm.

Aasni and Zhobelia's original cravings proved to be the pump-priming inspiration for an avocation that lasted decades, and after a long period of initial reluctance which persisted well beyond the time when Aasni had been delivered of Brigit and Zhobelia of Calli and the sisters again fitted comfortably behind the counter of their converted library van, their chutneys and pickles eventually became their most successful line in the travelling shop, giving the more broad-minded citizens of Lewis and Harris a taste for palate-scalding sub-continental condiments that has persisted to this day.

*

The train carrying Zeb, Boz and me back to London broke down just outside the town of Brentwood and limped into the station at little more than walking pace. We detrained, and encountered some confusion amongst the railway staff on the subject of a relief service, but the consensus seemed to be that we might have an hour or so to wait.

'Fuck. Shit. Man. Trains. Fuck.'

'How annoying.'

'Hey, maybe we should get somethin' to eat, yeah?' Boz suggested.

We headed off to find a public house. Outside the station on the street we passed four men with very short hair dressed in large boots, short jeans, and shiny green blouse-style jackets; they seemed to be selling papers. I don't think I'd have noticed them further but for the fact they started to make a sort of 'Oo-oo oo-oo-oo' noise as we passed by. One of them spat on the pavement in front of Boz, who just lifted his head a little and strolled serenely on.

'Who are they?' I asked Zeb, who was at my side. 'Do they know Boz?'

'Na. Fascists,' Zeb said. 'BNP. Bad fucks.'

I looked back at the men, who were still staring after us. One of them threw something yellow; I reached up and caught a half-eaten banana that might have been aimed at Boz, who was a little in front of us. I stopped.

'Fuck. Sake. Just. Walk,' Zeb said tersely, pulling on my sleeve. I slid my arm free and walked back to the group of men.

'Good afternoon,' I said to them as they came forward. I held up the half-eaten banana. 'Why did you throw this?'

'It's for the coon, dear,' said the tallest and blondest of them. 'You give it to your black monkey,' he told me. The others sniggered.

I stared at them; probably my mouth was hanging open. 'Good heavens,' I said. 'Are you people racists?'

'Yeah.'

'Yeah. Want to buy a fucking newspaper, darlin'?' One of them shook a tight bundle of newspapers in my face; the headline said something about Enough being Enough and Paki Death Gangs.

'Yeah, we're fucking racist; we believe in white rights,' said the tall blond one. 'What do you believe in, apart from associatin' wif niggers?'

'Well, I'm sorry,' I said, 'but I believe in love and understanding and the worship of the Creator through the—'

'Worshipping nigger cock more like.'

'Yeah; you let him fuck you up the bum, do you?'

'Look at 'im; back there, fucking shittin' himself 'e is; look at 'im; 'im an' the little cunt; fuckin' shittin' themselves, they are!'

177

one of the others said, then shouted over my head, 'Yeah? Yeah? Yeah? You want some? I said do you fucking *want some?*'

'Excuse me,' I said, tapping that one on the shiny shoulder of his jacket. 'There's no need for that sort of thing.'

He looked down at his shoulder and then turned on me. The tall blond one stepped between us and said, 'Look, just fuck off back to your nigger friend, all right?'

I looked into his eyes. I turned to go, then swivelled back again. 'Could I have one of your newspapers?' I asked. 'I'm just interested in what you think.'

The tall blond one sneered, then pulled a newspaper from the pile he held. He held it in front of me. I reached out to take it but he lifted it beyond my reach. 'Fifty pence,' he said.

'I do beg your pardon,' I said. 'I haven't any money, but it occurred to me that if you believe in the justice of what you say, you might let me have it free.'

'We'll fuckin' let you have it, Jock tart,' the tall blond one said, bending very close to me. He slapped my face with the paper then shoved it into my chest, pushing me backwards; I dropped the half-eaten banana, grabbed the paper with both hands and took another step to the rear.

'Fuck off,' the man said again, pointing at me. 'I'm not fuckin' telling you again.'

I nodded and touched my hat. 'Okay. Thanks for the paper,' I said.

I walked away to jeers and sudden laughter. The banana went sailing over my head and landed at the feet of Boz and Zeb, who were standing ten metres away at a street corner, looking distinctly anxious.

'I-sis,' Boz said once we were out of sight. 'You got to stop doin' that sorta thing. I think I walk behind you from now on; you always turnin' back into danger. Those guys are more dangerous than that damn Baskerville dog.'

'Hmm,' I said.

'Jeez. Fuck. Christ. Shit. God . . .'

'. . . Language, Brother Zebediah,' I said absently, leafing through the newspaper as we walked. '. . . Good grief!'

We ate lunch in a pub. I read the paper, half-page by half-page, keeping it tightly folded at Boz's request so that it was hard to tell from any distance what I was reading. I asked a few questions of Zeb and Boz regarding what I was reading, and can only assume they answered truthfully.

We spent half an hour or so eating lunch (I stood leaning against a wooden partition while Boz and Zeb sat). The sandwich I ate looked attractive but was damp and almost totally lacking in flavour. I drank a pint of beer which tasted rather of chemicals, and may also have led to what happened next.

'They prob'ly gone from there by now,' Boz said confidently. We were approaching the corner where he and Zeb had waited for me while I'd talked to the four young men. I looked in a shop window and saw their black-green reflections; they were just where we'd encountered them earlier.

'Yes, I'm sure they have,' I said, slowing and looking round. We were passing an interesting-looking shop called a Delicatessen. 'Boz,' I said brightly, halting and causing the other two to stop. 'I would like to contribute to the meal this evening. Unfortunately I am not allowed to enter retail premises; would you mind going into this shop here and purchasing an ingredient or two?'

'No problem, I-sis; what you want?'

'I have some money,' I said, pulling out a couple of one-pound notes.

Boz looked at the notes and laughed. 'I'll stand you it, I-sis. Just tell me what you wantin'.'

'Some fresh coriander, please,' I said.

'Comin' right up.'

Boz disappeared into the shop. I handed the two one-pound notes to Zeb. 'There was a toy shop back there,' I said. 'Could you get me a couple of water pistols?'

Zeb looked blank, an expression that I confess I thought suited him. 'Please,' I said. 'They're a present.'

Zeb walked back to the toy shop, still looking blank. Boz reappeared from the Delicatessen shop. 'Oh,' I said, touching my forehead. 'And a couple of bottles of that red pepper sauce; what's it called?'

179

'Tabasco?' Boz said, handing me the clump of fresh coriander. I stuffed it in a pocket and nodded. 'That's it.'

Boz grinned. 'That's strong stuff, I-sis. You sure you need two bottles?'

I considered. 'No,' I said. 'Make it four.'

*

I approached the group of shiny-green-jacketed men. They formed a line in front of me. I walked with my head bowed and my hands pressed in front of me in a gesture of supplication.

The fascists towered in front of me; a wall of crew-cut, black denim and green shiningness plinthed by bulbous brown leather boots. I bowed my head further and let my hands drop to my sides. I hoped my pockets weren't dripping.

'Sirs,' I said, smiling. 'I have read your publication. I have read of your hatred and despite of people different from you . . .'

'Yeah?'

'Fuck, really?'

'Despite wot?'

'You just don't fuckin' listen, do you?'

'. . . And I would like you to know that I feel exactly the same way as you do.'

'Wot?'

'Oh yeah?'

'Yes; I feel exactly the same way about people like you.'

'What— ?'

'Right—'

'God, forgive me,' I muttered, taking the little water pistols from my jacket pockets, one in each hand, and firing them in the faces of the green-jacketed men, straight into their eyes.

*

'Somerset,' Boz said, on the train into Liverpool Street.

'Apparently,' I confirmed, still carefully cleaning the watery red liquid off my hands with damp toilet paper. I had been thinking, trying to work out what Morag could have meant by talking about me bothering her. I still had no idea. It was troubling. 'I shall leave tomorrow,' I told Boz and Zeb.

Zeb stood with his arms crossed, staring at me. 'Mad.'

*

Boz kissed me hard on the lips when we got into the squat. 'Don't mean nuthin' by it, you understand, I-sis,' he said, still holding my shoulders. We looked at each other for a moment or two. 'But,' he said. '. . . well . . .' He patted me on one shoulder and walked off.

'Mad.' Zeb stood there in the hall, shaking his head. He grinned. 'Tough,' he said.

'Cookie,' I agreed, and patted Zeb on the shoulder, as though passing it on.

CHAPTER
TWELVE

I think it was my friend Mr Warriston of Dunblane who observed that the ridicule of fools is the surest sign of genius, and the scorn of political or religious leaders one of the least ambiguous signals that the object of their venom is espousing something threateningly close to the truth.

To this I would only add that as most of us are only too willing to define a fool precisely as a person who disagrees with us, a degree of self-fulfilment is inevitably introduced to the process which – while smacking of a kind of facile elegance – robs the observation of much of its utility.

Either way, it has always seemed to me that the average person has no difficulty weighing their own desires, prejudices and bigotries against the totality of the world's most sophisticated philosophies and every moral lesson such systems have ever given rise to, and judging their selfishness to be the more worthy of action.

As a Luskentyrian, of course, I am far from being an average person, and as a third-generation Leapyearian (indeed, the only one), I have privilege heaped upon exclusivity, with all the responsibility and freight of consideration that entails. Perhaps, therefore, it is not really my place to judge my fellows too harshly when what we share is debatably of less importance than that which divides and distinguishes us, which made me no better than the four men I'd left on their knees wheezing and cursing outside the station the previous day. Nevertheless, whether it was good for my soul or not, I was still relishing the memory the following morning while I stood at a motorway on-ramp in Gunnersbury, being occasionally jeered at from passing cars and vans – perhaps on account of my gender, perhaps due to my hat – and, as a rule, insulted by the drivers whose offers of a lift I declined because their automobiles seemed somehow too Blandly conventional.

This was part of my strategy for shaking the faith-corroding

185

influence of the big city off my feet. I had grown too used to the electric light of the squat (which had confused me, once I'd stopped to think about it, but had been explained to me as simply the result of the electricity company not caring whether the building was legally occupied or not as long as the bills were paid). I had considered taking more of the cannabis cigarettes last night while Boz – with backing in mono by Zeb – detailed my exploits of the day to the others and I glowed with pride in spite of myself, regardless of an outward show of modesty. In the end I had not indulged.

I had a word with Zeb, telling him that I thought it best that I continued to search for Morag in the hope that my mission might be successful before I – or anybody else – reported back the bad news concerning our cousin's double life. Zeb did not demur. Then I had said my goodnights and goodbyes at a still respectable hour and gone to my hammock, pleased at not having given in to temptation. Next morning, however, I had found myself thinking about hopping on a bus or taking a tube, while I walked from Kilburn to here in the breaking dawn. Again, I had resisted, but all these urges and hankerings were signs that I was becoming infected with the thoughts and habits of the Unsaved.

There is a perhaps perverse pleasure to be had from not taking the obvious course bred into all Luskentyrians and diligently developed all our lives; the longer I stood on the slip road leading to the motorway and turned down the offers of lifts – sometimes successfully waving on one of the other people hitch-hiking there to take the vehicle instead – the better I felt about this latest leg of my mission. I was experiencing an odd mix of emotions; elation at my feats of guile and arms the day before, relief at leaving the big city, a nagging homesickness and general feeling of missing everybody at the Community, disquiet that – unless either I or the young man at La Mancha had entirely got hold of the wrong end of the stick – my cousin Morag seemed to have developed an antipathy towards me and might even be avoiding me, and an undercurrent of paranoia that one or more of the men I'd attacked with the pepper sauce yesterday might for some reason drive past while I was standing here and jump out and attack me.

186

I kept telling myself there were getting on for seven million people in London alone and Brentwood was really quite far away and almost directly opposite from the direction I'd be travelling in, but I think it was that fear that finally overcame the prideful feeling of blessed righteousness I was experiencing by turning down all those offered rides and made me accept a lift from a nice young couple in a small, old and rather tinny French car. They were only going as far as Slough, but it got me started. They commented on my Sitting Board; I started explaining about Luskentyrianism and our ascetic tendencies. They looked glad to get rid of me.

I estimated it took me ninety minutes or more first to make my way out of Slough and then to get another lift, this time in the back of a builder's pick-up whose cab was crammed with three young men in what looked like football strips. They took me as far as Reading; cement dust flew up in the slipstream and stung my eyes.

I spent about an hour by the side of the A4 on the outskirts of Reading – mostly spent studying my map and brushing cement dust off my jacket and trousers – then accepted a ride from a well-groomed but casually dressed chap heading for an amateur cricket match in Newbury. He asked about the Sitting Board too; I told him it was a kind of prayer mat, which I think just confused him. I studied the book of maps in his car and decided against the obvious course of being dropped at the junction with the motorway to continue along the M4, accepting it as more blessed to stay with the byways. I stuck with the man – a sales rep for a pharmaceutical company, though obviously off-duty, as it were – all the way to Newbury and chatted easily enough to him. I suspect that I was being flirted with but I'm really a novice in such matters so perhaps he was just being friendly. While walking out of Newbury I ate the sandwiches Roadkill had given me the previous evening.

In succession, my next hitches took me to Burbage (with a chain smoker; more eye watering), Marlborough (courtesy of a youngish off-duty soldier who kept brushing my thigh and hip with his hand when he changed gear, until I ostentatiously extracted the six-inch hat-pin from my lapel and started picking my teeth with it), Calne (a kindly greying fellow on his way back from what sounded like

187

an assignation), Chippenham (in a delivery lorry with a sorry soul who was to become a father for the first time later that month, and due to hear the following morning whether he had lost his job in something ominous called a rationalisation) and finally, with the light fading fast, to a village called Kelston with another couple. They were rather older and even more chatty than the two who'd begun the day. They commented on my Sitting Board, too; I told them it was to combat a back problem. They invited me to stay at their house in Kelston. I declined politely, though I availed myself of a look at their road atlas. I slung my hammock in a wood on the village outskirts. It rained for a while during the night; I used my kit-bag as an extra covering, but still got wet.

I woke feeling damp and stiff and cold shortly after dawn and washed my face in the heavy dew that lay upon the grass, then climbed the most scalable-looking tall tree I could find, partly for the exercise and partly so that I would warm up.

Above the tree tops, the sky looked worryingly red, but beautiful all the same, and I sat there, wedged in amongst the branches for a while just watching the soft clouds move and listening to the birds sing, and praising God and Their Creation with a song of my own, sung silently in my soul.

*

I walked through Bath's outskirts to the A39 and after about an hour's walk started hitching just past a large roundabout. The traffic seemed much busier than the day before, and it was only as I stood at the side of the road trying to account for this that I realised today was Monday and yesterday had been Sunday; I cursed myself for a fool, not having realised this the day before. It made no difference to my journey or quest for Morag, but I had been slow not to ask myself why so few of the people who'd given me lifts the day before had been working.

It was not unusual for Luskentyrians to lose track of the days – we work on the natural cycles of lunar month and year, not artificial divisions like weeks – but I had thought that living in the midst of the Norms I would naturally fall into their ways;

I suppose the squat in Kilburn had been less than archetypically Bland. I thought of home again, and everybody there. I hoped Mr Warriston wouldn't be too worried when I didn't turn up to play the Flentrop. For a while, as the traffic roared past on its way back in towards Bath, I wallowed in a sweet, lost feeling of self-pity, imagining what everyone back home would be doing now, and hoping some of them were missing me.

I shook off the mood and concentrated on feeling positive and looking pleasant and eager, but not seductive. Within a few more minutes I got a lift from a baker returning home after a night shift; I walked from a village called Hallatrow to one called Farrington Gurney and – courtesy of a commuting office manager – was in Wells before the shops were open.

Wells possesses an attractive cathedral and seemed altogether quite a pleasant, holy place. I felt a certain pleasing fitness that I had ended up here this morning when normally I would have been visiting Dunblane, and was tempted to stay and take a look around, but decided to press on. A traffic warden gave me directions for Clissold's Health Farm and Country Club, which was less than ten miles away, near the village called Dudgeon Magna. I started walking west and kept my thumb out as I left the small town behind; a strange-looking van stopped within a minute, barely a furlong beyond the speed-limit sign.

The van's bodywork appeared at first sight to be constructed of bricks. The back door opened to reveal a group of motley-dressed young people sitting on sleeping bags, rucksacks and bed-rolls.

'Headin' for the gig?' one called.

'No, a place called Dudgeon Magna,' I said. There was some muttering amongst the young people. Finally somebody up front looked at a map and the message came back to hop in. I sat on the ridged metal floor

'Yeah, 'pparently it used to belong to a company that sold stone cladding and wall coverings and stuff,' said the lass I was sitting next to, who was about my age. I'd commented on the van's odd appearance.

The old vehicle had sheets of artificial brick stuck to the inside as well as the outside. The ten young people it contained were on their way to some sort of party in a field near Glastonbury.

I thought back to the map I'd looked at the night before. 'Isn't this a rather strange route to take to Glastonbury?' I asked.

''Voiding the filth,' the chap at the wheel called back cheerfully.

I nodded as though I knew what he was talking about.

'What's in Dudgeon Magna?' one of the others asked.

'My cousin,' I told her. She was dressed like the others, in layers of holed, ragged but colourful clothes; she wore sensible-looking boots that had obviously seen a few fields in their time. The six young men all had dreadlocks – I'd asked Roadkill what they were called – and the four young women all had part or all of their heads shaved. I wondered if perhaps they were part of some Order.

'Shouldn't that be Dudgeon Alto or something?' another lass asked, passing me a can of cider.

I smiled. 'I suppose it should be really, shouldn't it?' I said, tasting the drink in the can.

'Oh fuck,' said our driver. 'What are they doing *here*?'

'Roadblock,' the fellow in the passenger seat said. 'Bastards.' Various of the others got up and crowded round the area just behind the seats, making noises of disappointment and annoyance.

'It's the pigs,' somebody muttered back to those of us still sitting as the van slowed to a stop. The girl across from me, who'd passed me the cider, rolled her eyes and sighed loudly. The driver wound down his window.

'What's the matter?'

'. . . reason to believe . . .' I heard a deep male voice say; the others started speaking and I only caught snatches of the rest.

'But—'

'. . . way to a trespassory assembly . . .'

'Aw, come on, man—'

'. . . serious disruption to a community . . .'

'. . . not *doing* anything, we're not *harming* anybody.'

'. . . justice act that you may be . . .'

'. . . mean, what're we supposed to have *done*?'

190

'Why aren't you out catching rapists or something?'

'. . . back the way you came . . .'

'Look, we're just going to visit friends, for fuck's sake!'

'. . . hereby deemed to be . . .'

'. . . unfair; I mean, it's just so un*fair*.'

At that point the van's back doors were hauled open by two policemen wearing overalls and crash helmets carrying long batons. 'Right, come on; out!' one of them said.

I got out with the others, amongst much complaining.

'What appears to be the problem, officer?' I asked one of the men.

'Stand over there,' we were told.

Ahead on the road was a police van with blue lights flashing; we had been pulled in to a lay-by where other worn-looking vans, a couple of old cars and a decrepit coach had also been stopped. There were more police vans and cars perched on verges nearby and lots of police moving around, some dressed in ordinary uniforms, some in overalls.

We stood on a grass verge while the van was briefly searched and the police checked its tyres and lights; our driver had to show some documents. Some of the vans and cars which had been stopped were made to turn round and head back the way they had come. Others seemed to be the objects of disputes between their occupants and the police; a few small groups of people, some of them in tears, tramped back up the road carrying sleeping bags, back packs and plastic bags. Meanwhile another tired-looking old minibus was stopped and more people forced to get out and stand on the grass. Smartish looking cars and other types of traffic were allowed to carry on past the roadblock.

'Right; back the way you came,' we were told by a policeman after the police left our van and went on to the minibus.

'But look,' the man who'd been driving protested. 'We're just—'

'You've got one very borderline tyre, son,' the policeman interrupted, pointing his finger in the young man's face. 'Want us to check the spare? If it's there? You got a jack? Yes? No? Want us to check that tyre again? Very borderline, it was. You understand what I'm saying?'

191

'Look—'

'Fuckin' police state,' somebody muttered.

'Get in the van, get out of here, get out of Avon. Understand?' the policeman said, poking the driver in the chest. 'And if I see you again, you're nicked.' He turned and walked away. 'This one's goin' back, Harry!' he shouted to another policeman, who nodded and then read the van's licence number into a hand-held radio.

'Shit,' somebody said as we trooped back to the van.

'I'm still going; we're still going, aren't we?'

''Snot far.'

'Fuckin' is! Good ten miles.'

'Bastards.'

'Na; we'll get a bit closer. Cross the fields job.'

I got my kit-bag out of the back of the van. 'Why exactly are they stopping everybody?' I asked.

'They're the fucking pigs, man; it's their fucking job.'

'The fucking Fascist Anti-Fun Police.'

'Bastards!' somebody said from inside the van. 'They've spilled all the drink.' There were groans as people watched rivulets of pale yellow liquid trickle out the rear doors.

'You not coming with us?' the girl who'd given me the cider asked.

'Dudgeon Magna,' I said, pointing.

'You'll be lucky,' one of the young men said.

'Thank you. Go with God,' I said. They closed the doors. The van started up and turned round, heading back towards Wells. I waved to the people looking out the back windows and set my face to the west again.

'And where do you think you're going?' asked an overalled, crash-helmeted police officer, standing directly in front of me.

'The village of Dudgeon Magna,' I said. 'To see my cousin Morag Whit at Clissold's Health Farm and Country Club.'

The officer looked me down and up. 'No you're not,' he said.

'Yes I am,' I said, trying not to sound too indignant.

'No,' he said, pressing me in the chest with his truncheon, 'you're not.'

I looked down at the truncheon and put one of my feet out

behind the other so I could better control my centre of balance. I leaned into the truncheon. 'Where I come from,' I said slowly, 'we treat guests with a little more courtesy than this.'

'You're not a guest, love; you're just a fucking nuisance as far as we're concerned. Now fuck off back to Scotland or wherever it is you come from.' He pushed at me with the truncheon. My chest was hurting where he was pushing, but I was standing my ground.

'Sir,' I said, looking him in the eyes beneath the pushed-up visor of the crash helmet. 'I'm not entirely clear why you're intercepting all these young people, but whatever it is you think they are going to do, I am not interested in it. I am going to visit my cousin at Clissold's Health Farm and Country Club.'

The officer took the weight off the truncheon, then started tapping me in the chest with it in time to his words. 'And, I, just, told, you, you're, not,' he said, finally pushing me hard and forcing me to take a step backwards. 'Now do you want to turn round and fuck off or do you want to get into serious fucking trouble? Because I've just about fucking had it with you people.'

I glared at him through narrowed eyes. I raised my head. 'I want to speak to your superior officer,' I said frostily.

He looked at me for a moment. 'Right,' he said, standing to one side and motioning with his baton. 'This way.'

'Thank you,' I said, taking a step past him.

I think he tripped me to get me off balance; the next thing I knew he had me on the ground, my cheek ground into the damp, gritty tarmac of the lay-by, his knee in the small of my back and one of my arms pushed so far up my back I let out an involuntary shriek of pain; it felt like my arm was going to break. 'All right!' I screamed.

'Dave,' he said calmly. 'Search this bag, will you?'

I saw boots appear to one side and my kit-bag, lying on the ground beside me, was wrenched from my hand.

'You're going to break my arm!' I shouted. The pressure eased a little until it was merely very uncomfortable. I felt my face flush as I realised how easily I'd been first fooled and then brought down. Any self-satisfaction I'd felt at my

exploits in Essex two days earlier was being wrung out of
me now.

'What's that?' my attacker asked.

'What?' the other one said.

'That there. What's that?'

'Bottle of something.'

'Yeah; and that?'

'Yeah . . . could be something, couldn't it?'

The pressure came back on my arm again and I sucked in breath,
trying not to cry out. I sensed the policeman who was pinning me
down lower his head to mine, then felt his breath on my neck.
'I think we've found a suspicious substance here, young lady,'
he said.

'What are you talking about?' I gasped.

I was dragged upright and held, still painfully, in front of the
one who'd brought me down as the second policeman held two
of my vials in front of me. I could feel my hat, crushed between
my back and the policeman's chest.

'What're these, then?' the other one asked.

I grimaced. 'That on the left's hearth ash!' I said. I was having
to work hard at not appending 'you oaf!' or 'you idiot!' to a lot
of these utterances. The contents of my kit-bag had been strewn
over the tarmac. The bag itself had been turned inside-out.

'Harthash?' said the one holding the vial.

'You mean hashish?' the one behind me said.

'No! Ash from a hearth,' I said, seeing some other policemen
walking over towards us. 'It's for a ceremony. The other jar's for
my mark. The mark on my forehead. Can't you see it? These are
religious substances; holy sacraments!'

The second officer was taking the top off the ash vial. 'Sacrilege!'
I yelled. The second officer sniffed at the ash, then dipped a moistened finger in. 'Desecration!' I screamed, as the other policemen
came up towards us. I struggled; the grip on my arm tightened as
I was lifted onto my tiptoes. Pain surged through my arm and I
shrieked again.

'Steady on, Bill,' one of the other officers said quietly. 'We've
got a telly crew back there.'

'Right, sarge,' the one behind me said. The pain eased again and I gulped some deep breaths.

'Now then, young lady; what's all this about?'

'I am *trying*,' I said through clenched teeth, 'to make my lawful and peaceable way to visit my cousin Morag Whit in Clissold's Health Farm and Country Club, in Dudgeon Magna. This ... person behind me was *most* insulting and when I asked to speak to his superior officer to report his unmannerliness he tricked me and attacked me.'

'Suspicious-looking substance, sarge,' the one with the vial said, presenting it to the older man, who frowned and also sniffed it.

'That is *gross* irreverence!' I yelled.

'Hmm,' he said. He looked at the kit-bag's contents on the ground. 'Anything else?'

'Other jars and stuff here, sir,' one of the others said, squatting and picking up the vial of dried river mud. A crunch sounded from under his foot as he rose. He looked down and moved something sideways with the edge of his shoe. I saw the remains of the tiny *zhlonjiz* jar.

'My *God*! What have you *done*?' I screamed.

'Now now,' somebody said.

'Heresy! Impiety! Desecration! May God have mercy on your Unsaved souls, you wretches!'

'This could be something, too,' the desecrator said, rubbing the dust between his fingers.

'Are you people *listening*?' I shouted. 'I am the Elect of God, you buffoons!'

'Put her in the wagon,' the sergeant said, nodding his head. 'Sounds like she might have escaped from somewhere.'

'What? How *dare* you!'

'And get this stuff bagged for checking out,' the sergeant said, tapping the vial of hearth ash and turning over the limp kit-bag with his foot as he turned away.

'Let me go! I am an officer of the True Church! I am the Elect of God! I am on a sacred mission! You heathens! By God, you will answer to a higher court than you have ever glimpsed for this insult, you ruffians! Let me go!'

195

I might have saved my breath. I was marched off past numerous other vehicles, groups of people, white lights and flashing blue lights and bundled into a police van some way up the road, still protesting furiously.

In the police van I was handcuffed to a seat and told to shut up. A burly policeman in overalls and crash helmet sat at the far end of the passenger compartment, twirling a baton in his hands and whistling. The only other people in the van were a sorry-looking young couple who smiled at me nervously and then went back to holding each other tight.

The van smelled of antiseptic. I found myself breathing quickly and shallowly. There was a queasiness in my stomach.

I flexed my wrists and scowled at the officer, then closed my eyes and arranged my limbs as comfortably as I could. I attempted to do some deep breathing, and might have succeeded had we not shortly been joined by some loudly protesting youths who were bundled into the van by a clutch of overalled, crash-helmeted policemen.

Shortly thereafter we were driven off at high speed.

*

The True Church of Luskentyre underwent something of a schism – albeit an amicable one – in 1954, when we were gifted the estate at High Easter Offerance on the flood-plain of the river Forth by Mrs Woodbean, who had become a convert three years earlier. Mrs W was about the dozenth full convert, lured to the now quietly flourishing farm/community at Luskentyre by my Grandfather's reputation for holiness and lack of interest in taking money off even the richest of his followers (an aspect of his renown which he had realised early on only made people all the more generous; another example of the Contrariness of life).

It was, sadly, a tragedy which spurred Mrs W to act. The Woodbeans had a son called David, their only child. Mrs W had been told after his birth that she could not bear another baby, and so the boy was all the more precious to them, and was kept cosseted and pampered. In 1954, when he was seven, he walked through a glass door in a shop in Stirling. He wasn't mortally wounded but he lost a lot of blood and an ambulance was called to take him to hospital; it crashed en route and the boy was killed. Mrs Woodbean took this as a sign that the modern world was too saturated with technology and cleverness for its – or her family's – own good, and decided to renounce the majority of her worldly goods and devote her life to Faith (and allegedly to having another child at all costs, an ambition which was fulfilled years later, when she gave birth to Sophi at the age of forty-three, though at the cost of her own life).

Mrs W's extraordinary act of charity was unique in its scale, but converts were bountiful in smaller ways all the time, though by all accounts Salvador produced a great show of grumpy reluctance when accepting a gift, and made sure the donor always knew that he was doing it for the good of their soul (on the grounds that it was indeed more blessed to give than to receive, and Salvador's soul was already doing quite well, thank you, and so could afford to be generous when it came to accepting tribute).

People heard about our Order through the media (very occasionally), sometimes through the warnings of sincere but misguided priests and ministers who had not heard the adage concerning the non-existence of bad publicity, but most often just by word of mouth (it has to be admitted that no attempt to spread the word through the commercial distribution of the *Orthography* has ever been successful). As I have said, there is a sense in which we were the first Hippies, the first Greens, the first New Agers, and so a few brave souls who were in the vanguard of social change, and at least twenty years ahead of their time, were sure to be attracted to a cause that would shake the world in various guises a few decades later.

In the years following the establishment of our Order, my Grandfather gradually stopped looking for the – by now almost mythic – canvas bag, and settled down to the life of what we now call a guru, dispensing wisdom, experiencing visions which helped guide our Faith and providing a living example of peaceful holiness. The sisters continued to share my Grandfather and have his children – most notably and wonderfully my father, born on the 29th of February 1952 – and, with gaps for pregnancies, continued with their mobile shop business until the year of the schism.

Mr McIlone elected to remain at Luskentyre, which was, after all, his, though he insisted that Salvador accept his entire library as his parting gift. By this time there were five full converts, that is, people who had come to stay at Luskentyre, to work the land and fish the sea and be on hand to listen to our Founder's teachings. There were perhaps another dozen followers like the Possils, who would come to stay (usually providing their own keep in some form or another) for a few weeks or months at a time. Two of the more ascetic full converts – apostles, as they called themselves by now – decided to stay at the farm on Harris after the gifting of High Easter Offerance and Grandfather, doubtless wisely, put no pressure on anybody to go or to stay.

Grandfather and the sisters had seen many photographs of High Easter Offerance and some silent ciné film too, projected onto a sheet in the parlour of our only other sympathiser local to Harris, whose house happened to have electric power. Still, it must have been an adventure for them when, in the spring of 1954, they finally packed all their belongings in the ex-mobile library – now ex-mobile shop – and drove to Stornoway, where the van was driven onto a huge net on the quay side and then winched aboard the ferry for the long, rolling journey to Kyle of Lochalsh. From there they headed slowly south on the narrow, winding roads of the day, away from the fractured geometries of the storm-flayed western isles to the comparatively balmy climes of central Scotland, and the abundant expanses of smooth-sloped hills, coiled river, breeze-rustled forests and sunny pastures of the Forth's broad run.

Mr and Mrs Woodbean had already moved out to the little turreted house over the iron bridge from the main farm. My Grandfather, the sisters, their children and assorted followers – including the Possils, who had come along to help with the move – held a service and then a party to celebrate the relocation, installed themselves and their modest possessions in the mansion house and old farm, added Mr McIlone's library to the already impressive if under-used one which existed in the mansion house and in the weeks, months and years that followed, got down to the business of renovating the farm buildings and restoring the neglected fields to productivity.

Mrs Woodbean's brother had made a fortune after the War dealing in scrap and army surplus; he toyed with the idea of becoming a convert for a while and during this period either generously donated to the Order several pieces of potentially valuable ex-service equipment which would in many cases later be pressed into previously unthought-of practical applications, or used the farm as a dump for useless junk on which there was no quick profit to be made (depending who you listen to).

The only things he did provide which really were useful – I suppose the Deivoxiphone doesn't count – were a couple of short-wave radio sets mounted on sturdy, if wheel-less, army trailers. Mr McIlone was persuaded to accept one, and both were eventually persuaded to work, powered by wind generators. The radios provided a link between the two outposts of our Faith which was both fairly reliable and relatively secure (my Grandfather was starting to worry about the attentions of the government, and at one stage appeared to be convinced there was an entire Whitehall agency called the Department Of Religious Affairs, or DORA for short, which had been set up specifically to spy upon us and disrupt our every dealing, though he laughingly dismisses this as an exaggeration nowadays; a parable taken literally).

Of course, the radios had a very definite air of clutter and newfanglehood about them, but – perhaps because the radio provided such a perfect image of the human soul – Grandfather had always had a soft spot for the device, and was more inclined to suffer the presence of one of them than any other symptom of the material age.

The radio also provided a new aspect of – one might even say weapon for – our Faith when Grandfather awoke one morning from an obviously Divinely inspired dream with the idea of Radiomancy, whereby one tunes the radio at random, then turns it on, and uses the first words one hears – either immediately or as a result of sweeping gradually further and further along

199

the frequencies to either side – as a means of prediction and divination.

So we were not so remote from our original home, but more importantly, with our relocation to this leafy arable alcove just off the central industrial belt, it was easier for potential converts to visit and make up their minds whether they wanted to Believe, or even to come and stay and Work and Believe. A slow trickle of people, young and old, mostly British but with the occasional foreigner, paid court to my Grandfather, listened to his teachings, read his *Orthography*, conversed with him and thought about their own lives, and – in some cases – decided that he had found the Truth, and so became Saved.

Grandfather thought up the Festival of Love in 1955. It occurred to him that it might not be wise to rely entirely on providence to provide Leapyearians, who were now seen very much as prophets and perhaps potential Messiahs. Indeed it might even be seen as impious to expect the Creator to ensure a child was born on any given 29th of February; it could be thought of as taking God for granted, which did not sound like a good idea.

Grandfather's Faith had embraced something very like the idea of free love from the start, thanks to Aasni and Zhobelia's generosity, and he had had revelations which certainly appeared to sanction the extension of his physical communing beyond the two sisters, and to allow his followers the same leeway with their partners, providing those concerned were agreeable and sufficiently enlightened to reject possessiveness and unreasoning, unholy jealousy (which had been Revealed to be a sin against God's bountiful and forgiving nature).

So, if the Order was to give nature a gentle helping hand with producing a child at the end of February in a leap year, it obviously made sense to encourage those ready, willing and able to assist in this matter to enjoy themselves as much as possible nine months earlier. Our Founder therefore decreed that the end of May before a leap year should be the time for a Festival; a Festival of Love in all its forms, including the holy communing of souls through the blessed glory of sexual congress. The month before should be a time of abstinence, when the Believers ought to deny themselves

200

the most intense of pleasures in order to prepare for – and fully appreciate the advent of – the Festival itself.

Of course, the cynics, apostates and heretics – and those sad souls who hold it an article of their own perverted faiths that everybody else's motives can never be any better than their own – will point to the presence of several attractive young women amongst Grandfather's followers at this time as some sort of reason for our Founder's idea concerning the Festival. Well, we have grown to expect such shameful drivel from the ranks of the profoundly Unsaved, but it has been pointed out by no less than Salvador himself that even if the beauty he saw around him at that time did somehow lead his thoughts towards such a happy and Festive conclusion, what was that but an example of God using the Fair to inspire the Wise?

Not coincidentally, I think the first real attempt by the press to sabotage our cause occurred around this time, and confirmed to our OverSeer that he was right to shun publicity and refuse cameras access to the estate.

Aasni and Zhobelia seem not to have been discomfited by the concept of the Festival; they apparently felt secure in their joint relationship with Salvador and had devoted themselves both to the upbringing of their children and the upgrading of their home. They had, also, made friends with Mr and Mrs Woodbean and seemed to draw comfort from that as well. The sisters had not ceased to develop their culinary and condimentary skills; now that they were free of the need to travel the islands peddling their wares in the ancient van, they could devote even more time to the expansion and refinement of their range of sauces, pickles and chutneys.

At about this time, too, they began to experiment with other more substantial dishes, and made their first tentative excursions into the strange and exciting new world of cross-cultural cuisine-combining, as though through such provisional promiscuity and the amalgamation of the Scottish and the sub-continental, they could participate in their own terms in the freshly formulated Festivities. It was then that the process really began that would lead to such dishes as lorne sausage shami kebab, rabbit masala, fruit pudding chaat, skink aloo, porridge tarka, shell pie aloo gobi, kipper bhoona, chips pea pulao, whelk poori and marmalade kulfi, and I think the world is a better place for all of them.

CHAPTER
THIRTEEN

B riefly I spent the night in the cells, in a police station in Bristol. The police seemed suspicious that I had no way of proving my identity, but amused at my name and my protestations of innocence and outrage, at least until they got upset with my persistence and told me – very rudely, I thought – to shut up.

The following morning I was told I was free to go, and that there was somebody to see me.

I was too surprised to say anything; I was led down a corridor between the cell doors towards the desk at the front of the station, trying to work out who could possibly be waiting there for me. Not just that; how could they have found me?

It must, I supposed, be Morag. My heart lifted at the thought, but somehow, nevertheless, I suspected I was wrong.

A few steps before I entered the office, I knew I was.

'God*dammit*!' a strident female voice rang out ahead of me. 'Call yourselves policemen; you haven't even got any goddamn *guns*!'

I felt my eyes widen.

'*Grandmother*?' I said, incredulous.

My maternal grandmother, Mrs Yolanda Cristofiori, five foot nothing of bleached blonde, leather-skinned Texan, flanked by two tall but cowed-looking men in suits carrying briefcases, turned from berating the duty sergeant and fixed a dramatic smile on me.

'Isis, honey!' she exclaimed. She strode over. 'Oh, my, look at *you*!' she squealed. She threw her arms around me, lifting me off my feet as I struggled to respond, hugging her in return.

'Grandmother . . .' I said, feeling dizzy, almost overcome by surprise and Yolanda's perfume. I was so astonished I hadn't even remembered to make the Sign.

'Oh, it's so good to *see* you! How you doin'? Are you okay? I mean have these bozos treated you good?' She waved at the two men in suits she'd been standing between at the counter. 'I brought

205

some lawyers. Do you want to file a complaint or anything?' She put me down.

'I – well, no; I'm, ah—' I said, somewhat lost for words. My grandmother Yolanda's face was less lined than I remembered; it was still painted with make-up. Her hair looked like spun gold, except harder. She was dressed in highly decorated alligator-hide cowboy boots, embroidered jeans, a silk shirt in what looked like bar-code tartan and a little suede waistcoat studded with pearls. Yolanda's two lawyers looked on, smiling insincerely; the duty sergeant she'd been talking to seemed exasperated.

'Right,' he said. 'You two belong to each other?' He didn't wait for an answer. He pointed to the door with one hand and with the other reached down, produced my kit-bag and plonked it on the counter. 'Out,' he said.

Yolanda took my hand firmly in hers. 'Come on, honey; we'll discuss filing a suit against these jerks over a margarita or two. They fed you yet? You had breakfast? We'll go to my hotel; get them to fix you something.' She marched me to the door, glancing back at the lawyers. 'Get the child's bag, would you, George?'

*

Grandmother Yolanda originally came to High Easter Offerance in the summer of 1954 with her first husband, Jerome. She was eighteen; he was sixty-two and suffering from cancer. He had just sold some sort of oil company (mud logging, whatever that is), and had decided to spend some of his millions travelling the world, investigating cancer clinics and indulging a recently developed interest in sects and cults in general (I suppose technically we're a cult, though at the time some people still considered us to be a Christian sect; it took a while to get that misunderstanding cleared up). When Yolanda and Jerome left after a few weeks, Yolanda was pregnant. She came back to the Community with another husband, Francis, and her first child, Alice, in 1959, for the second Festival of Love (the first had failed to produce any Leapyearians, but had otherwise been acclaimed a success by all concerned) and continued to visit us every few years, often in May, for the Festival when there was one and in any event usually with a new husband in tow.

Yolanda's second husband, whom she divorced after a couple of years, was called Michael. She once told me Michael had made a fortune in malls and then lost it all in Las Vegas and ended up valet parking in LA. For four years, between two of her visits, I had assumed she meant gangsters' molls and that valet parking was a specialised form of landscape gardening, so had formed entirely the wrong impression of the man.

Her third husband was Steve, who was much younger than her and something called a garage software wizard; apparently he became a multi-millionaire overnight while back-packing in Europe. He died in the Andes three years ago, while attempting to develop the sport of avalanche surfing, which seemingly – and obviously, I suppose – is every bit as dangerous as it sounds.

Yolanda has inherited at least two fortunes, then, and leads what sounds like an energetic and restless existence; I think her daughter and her visits to High Easter Offerance were almost the only two things that introduced any stability into her antsy life.

Due to those visits, my mother and father knew each other as children, though they used to meet only every four years. My father, Christopher, was the Elect of God, of course; the first Leapyearian to be born after the founding of our Faith, he was used to being spoiled. I'm told that Alice, my mother, grew up teasing him terribly and making fun of the arguably excessively reverent treatment he had become used to receiving from those around him in the Community. Alice was three years younger than my father, but I imagine that her US-based but globe-trotting life made her seem at least as old as he. They became sweethearts when she was fourteen and wrote lots of letters while she was alternately travelling the world with her mother and attending school in Dallas. They were married by Salvador himself in 1973, and obviously wasted no time, for Allan arrived later that year and I was born, to Order-wide rejoicing, by all accounts, on the 29th of February 1976.

*

'Television?' I said, slightly shocked.

'Checked in, turned on to see what miserable handful of channels you had over here these days and almost the first thing I saw was you, being strong-armed into a paddy wagon shouting imprecations.'

'Good heavens,' I said. I thought about it, taking time off from tearing into my breakfast. 'Well, I suppose the Creator can use the works of the Benighted to tip the hand of Providence should They so desire; who are we to question?' I shrugged and tucked back into my smoked salmon and scrambled eggs, pancakes and syrup.

We were in Grandmother Yolanda's suite on the top floor of her hotel, a Sybaritically luxurious former mansion on a hill overlooking the city. I had just stepped out of the shower in the marble and mahogany bathroom and now sat on the floor of the sitting room, wrapped in a huge white fluffy robe, my back resting against a beautiful floral-patterned couch. Yolanda had dried my hair and then wrapped the towel round my head. In front of me on the coffee table sat a huge silver tray loaded with food. I slurped coffee and chomped salmon, looking out over Bath, visible beyond the tall windows and between the sweeping vertical folds of sumptuous green velvet curtains. I felt clean, fresh, wickedly perfumed from the soap in the shower and just generally submerged in heady opulence; meanwhile my stomach gradually filled with food. It will not have escaped the more alert reader that my maternal grandmother has never really gone wholeheartedly for the more ascetic aspects of our faith and probably never will, even if – in her own words – we show her a hair-shirt designed by Gootchy.

I will confess to feeling a little awkward, surrounded by all this luxury, but reckoned that it merely balanced out the effects of my night sleeping rough and my night in the cells, not to mention my unseemly treatment at the hands of the police.

Yolanda had flown into Glasgow on the Friday, hired a car and driven straight to High Easter Offerance on her way to Gleneagles. She had been told I was staying with Brother Zebediah in London and so drove to Edinburgh and flew from there to Heathrow and hired another car, been unable to work out where the squat was

208

so flagged down a taxi and followed it to the address in Kilburn, where Zeb told her I had left for Dudgeon Magna. Yesterday she had taken a train from London to Bath and hired yet another car – 'Scorpion or something; looks more like a dead cod. Why can't you people *build* cars? Supposed to be big but it feels more like a sub-compact to me . . .' – and driven to Dudgeon Magna.

I now silently cursed myself for not telling Zeb exactly where I'd been heading; whatever instinct had led me not to mention Clissold's Health Farm and Country Club to him had obviously been a product of Unsaved contamination polluting my soul. Anyway, Yolanda had turned up no sign of me in Dudgeon Magna, and so had returned to her hotel to work out what to do next when she'd seen me being unjustly apprehended on the local television news; it had taken until this morning to find out where I was and to hire some lawyers with whom to browbeat the police.

After dismissing the lawyers and lambasting them for not accepting payment by American Express card on the spot, she'd spent the blurringly fast drive from Bristol to Bath regaling me with what she'd been up to since I'd seen her last. An athletic young swimming pool cleaner from Los Angeles called Gerald seemed to figure rather prominently, as did a running battle with whatever authority supervises the waiting list for rafting expeditions down the Colorado River through the Grand Canyon; Grandmother seemed to find the idea of a five-year queue for anything in the United States to be not just criminally obscene but tantamount to treason to the American Dream; a hanging matter ('I mean, are these people *communists*, for God's sakes?'). With that out of her system she was then free to concentrate on giving me her itinerary over the last few days with particular attention to detailed critical notes on the various institutional inefficiencies and organisational absurdities she had encountered along the way while trying to catch up with me ('You can't even make a right – well, a left – on a red light here; I did it this morning and the goddamn attorneys nearly bailed out on me. What's *wrong* with you people?').

While my grandmother held forth I checked my kit-bag to make sure everything was there ('My vials have been interfered with!' I'd wailed. 'Great. We'll sue their asses!' Yolanda had said, flinging the car into another distinctly adventurous overtaking manoeuvre).

'Are you in a rush, then, Granny?' I asked, wiping the plate with a pancake.

'Child,' Yolanda said throatily, putting one hand heavy with precious metals and stones onto my towellinged shoulder, *'never call me your "Granny".'*

'Sorry, Grandmother,' I said, twisting my head to grin cheekily up at her. This is something of a ritual with us, each time we meet. I went back to my pancakes and syrup.

'As it happens, yes, I am,' Yolanda said, crossing her legs and resting her alligator-hide boots on the coffee table. 'Leaving for Prague on Wednesday to look at a red diamond. Heard there's one there might be for sale.'

'A red diamond,' I said, in a pause that seemed to require some response.

'Yep; ordinary diamonds are common as cow-shit, just DeBeers keeps the prices artificially high; anybody who buys an ordinary diamond is a damned fool, but red diamonds are scarcer than honest politicians; only about six in the whole damn world and I want at least to see one of them and hold it in my hand, just once, even if I don't get to buy it.'

'Blimey,' I said. 'Prague.'

'Prague, Chekland, or whatever the hell they call it these days. You wanna come?'

'I can't; I have to look for my cousin Morag.'

'Yeah, what *is* all this shit about her? Your grandaddy gone soft on her or somethin'? What's goin' on up there anyway? They seemed real frosty to me when I was there. You done something wrong? They angry with you?'

'What? Eh?' I said, turning to frown up at her.

'No shittin', honey,' she said. 'I didn't get to see the Dear Leader but I talked to your brother Allan and Erin; they acted like Salvador was angry with you or somethin'.'

'*Angry* with me?' I gasped, wiping my fingers on a starched white napkin and sitting up on the couch with my grandmother. I was so shocked it was some minutes before I realised I hadn't used my Sitting Board. I think the carpet had been so soft there was little sensation of change. 'What are they angry about?'

'Beats me,' Yolanda said. 'I asked but I wasn't told.'

'There must be some mistake,' I said, feeling funny in my insides all of a sudden. 'I haven't done anything wrong. My mission was going fine until yesterday; I was very pleased with it . . .'

'Well, hey, maybe I picked them up wrong,' Yolanda said, drawing her feet up underneath her, turning to me and starting to towel my hair again. 'Don't you listen to your crazy old grandma.'

I stared towards the window. 'But what can have happened?' I could hear my own voice faltering.

'Maybe nuthin'. Don't worry about it. Hey, come on; what's happenin' with Morag?'

I explained about my cousin's importance to the Community's missionary work and her letter informing us she was leaving our Faith and would not be returning to us for the Festival.

'Okay, so you haven't been able to find her,' Yolanda said. 'We'll hire a detective.'

'I'm not sure that would really be appropriate, Grandmother,' I said, sighing. 'I was personally charged with the task.'

'Does it matter, as long as you find her?'

'I suspect so, yes.'

Yolanda shook her head. 'Boy, you people,' she breathed.

'There is another problem,' I said.

'Yeah?'

I explained about the video and my discovery Morag worked under the name Fusillada DeBauch as a pornographic film artiste.

'*What?*' Yolanda yelled. 'You're shittin' me!' She slapped both her designer-jeaned thighs at once. I think that had she been wearing a Stetson or a ten-gallon hat or something she'd have thrown it in the air. 'Whoo; that girl! Oh boy.' She laughed towards the ceiling.

'You don't think Salvador could have found out about Morag being Fusillada from Zeb or somebody, do you?' I asked, wondering if that might account for his displeasure.

'No,' Yolanda said. 'It didn't seem like it was anything to do with her.'

'Hmm. Oh dear,' I said, frowning and putting my hands to my lips.

'Don't worry about it, honey,' my grandmother said. 'You going to keep looking for Morag?'

'Yes, of course,' I said.

'Okay. So, am I allowed to help you?'

'Oh, I'd think so,' I said.

'Good. We'll see what we can do together. Maybe Morag will turn up yet.' She sat forward, reaching for the telephone on the coffee table. 'Let's have a margarita.'

'Yes,' I said absently, still troubled by what might be wrong at High Easter Offerance. 'God has a way of providing when one most needs.'

'Yeah, hi; I need a pitcher of margarita and two glasses. And don't forget the salt, okay? In a saucer, or whatever. That's right. And a fresh, repeat, *fresh* lime and a sharp knife. That's all. Thank you.' She put down the telephone.

'You really didn't get any idea what might be wrong at the Community?' I asked my grandmother.

'None at all, honey. I just thought they seemed a bit pissed at you.' She held my hand. 'But I could have been wrong.'

'Oh dear,' I said, biting my lip.

Yolanda hugged me. 'Don't you worry now. Hey, come on; what do you want to do? Want me to call this health farm place and get . . . Fusillada?' she said, grinning and wiggling her head from side to side.

'I don't know,' I said, playing with the cord of my dressing-gown. 'I got the impression she might be trying to avoid me. Maybe . . . oh, goodness knows!' I threw up my hands and then stuffed them under my armpits.

'Well, let's just head on down there, what do you say?'

'What, now?'

'Soon as we've had our margaritas; and soon as we can find some clothes for you; suppose it'll take the hotel laundry at least overnight to clean that stuff of yours.'

I had already used my one change of clothes – things seem to get dirty very fast in London – and had not managed to get the

212

others washed. I thought there was still a couple of days' wear in what I'd been wearing but my grandmother disagreed, and is not the sort of person to argue with in such circumstances. So I needed new clothes. Yolanda's method of shopping was to bring the shop to us; she rang a clothes boutique in town and ordered them to bring the articles I'd asked for; socks, undergarments, white shirts, black trousers and black jackets (my hat, though battered, would do as it was). As I wasn't sure what size I was, she made them bring a selection.

An hour or two later, my head buzzing slightly from the three margaritas I'd had, I was dressed. I don't think either of us were really happy; I felt the clothes were too fine and dressy while my grandmother thought they were far too severe on the grounds of colour alone.

'The boots, then,' she said, tramping through the piles of dis-carded clothes, boxes and voluminous wrapping material strewn about the floor as she looked me up and down. The shop assistant she'd had come out to us kneeled on the floor looking tired. 'Don't you think those boots are just awful, Sam?' Yolanda asked the assistant.

'They are a bit sort of . . .'

'Agricultural,' Yolanda supplied.

'Yah. Agricultural. Yah.'

'I count that as praise,' I said.

'Ain't meant as such, honey,' Yolanda said, shaking her head. 'Why don't we find somewhere that does proper boots; like these!' She lifted up one foot to show me her alligator hides.

'*Cowboy* boots?' I exclaimed. (Even Sam looked shocked, I thought.)

'Well, sure!' Yolanda said. 'Real boots; with a heel. I don't know how you can wear those things; must feel like you're walking uphill all the time.'

'Excuse me,' I said primly. 'These boots are fine. These boots and I are used to each other. I will not part with them.'

'Stubborn child. Sure you won't try on the red velvet jacket?'

'Positive.'

'The black skirt?'

213

'Certainly not.'
'The Gaultier dress.'
'It's horrible.'
'It's black.'
'It's black and horrible.'
'It's black and beautiful.'
'Nonsense.'
'It is too, and he's a lovely guy. I've met him; Jean-Paul; a cuddly bear. You'd like him. Wears a kilt.'
'I don't care.'
'The leather trousers then.'
'Oh . . . !' I said, exasperated.
'Go on; just try them. They're *you*, honey; really.'
'Well . . .'

*

'These trousers *creak*,' I said, shifting my bottom on the Sitting Board. We were in Yolanda's latest hire car, heading south for Dudgeon Magna at high speed.

'They're fine; you look great in them. Hell, you *smell* great in them, honey!'

We hurtled round a corner. The car lurched and I had a strange sense that it was pivoting. Yolanda swore and chuckled at the same time and did something fancy with the steering wheel.

'What was that?' I asked, glancing at her.

'Bad camber, tightening bend,' she said tersely. 'When will you people learn to build *roads* properly?'

'At least,' I said, 'these trousers don't let me slip around so much on the Sitting Board when you go round corners.'

'Yeah,' my grandmother chuckled, sounding like she was enjoying herself, 'keep those buns well anchored. Haw haw haw.'

I gripped the sides of the seat as we went round another bend. I looked down. 'What are these buttons for?'

Yolanda glanced over. 'Seat adjustment. Electric.'

I nodded, impressed that disabled people were so well catered for in ordinary automobiles. I grabbed the sides of the seat again

214

for the next bend, and duly found myself rising and tipping back in my seat. I giggled, then gasped as we just missed an oncoming car.

'Ah; this bit isn't dual carriageway, Grandma.'

'I know that! ... Why are these people flashing their lights at me?'

'Well, I don't think it's because they know you.'

'Wimps!'

*

The big, dark blue car swept into the drive of Clissold's Health Farm and Country Club. We had encountered a few police vehicles, and passed a lay-by where they were checking an old, decrepit-looking coach, but we hadn't been stopped.

The Health Farm and Country Club proved to be a mansion with what looked like a giant conservatory tacked onto the back. I suppose I had been expecting something more farm-like. The mansion's grounds looked old, neat and manicured, just like the receptionist.

'I'm afraid Miss Whit checked out this morning.'

'Oh drat.'

'Shit!'

'Did she say where she was going?' I asked.

'Well, I wouldn't be able to tell you if she had, but—'

'Oh for God's sakes; this is her cousin; and she's my—' Yolanda broke off and looked at me, frowning. 'Hell, what *is* Morag to me?'

I shrugged. 'Great-niece? Grand-niece?'

Yolanda turned back to the receptionist. 'Yeah, whatever,' she said, with convincing decisiveness.

'Well, she didn't, anyway. Sorry.' The receptionist smiled. She didn't look very sorry.

'Was she due to check out today?' I asked, trying to look sweet and reasonable and in need of help.

'Let me see,' the receptionist said, lifting a pair of glasses from round her neck and placing them on her nose. She keyed something

215

into her computer, then consulted the screen. 'No; she was due to
stay until the end of the week.'

'Damn!'

'Hmm,' I said.

'Oh, I remember,' the lady said, replacing her glasses on her
cardigan. 'I do believe she said she'd changed her plans because
of something she'd seen on the local news last night.'

Yolanda and I looked at each other.

CHAPTER
FOURTEEN

'I know you think I'm just a complaining old woman, Isis—'

'Not at—'

'—and I know you don't drive, but you must see what I mean.'

'Well—'

'I mean, it stands to reason; you go into a gas station and you get gas. You get served; somebody fills your tank, maybe gets their hands dirty, checks your oil, washes the bugs off your windshield, kicks the tyres, whatever; you pay the bill, and that's all very fine ... but you pull into a gas station, you serve *yourself*, you get your *own* hands dirty, maybe break a nail, for God's sakes; no oil check, no windshield wash unless you do it yourself; and you pay the *same amount of money*! Now, really, I mean, come on; does that seem reasonable to *you*? Do you think that's *right*?'

'Put like that—'

'I'm only asking you because maybe you can be objective because you don't drive and maybe you haven't ever thought about all this, maybe you've never noticed all this. I mean, you've never bin to the States, have you?'

'No.'

'No; exactly. So you don't expect service pumps and self-serve pumps, and because you're a good little Orderite you've never even seen movies about the States either, right?'

'Right.'

'Right; unusual in this day and age, believe you me. So you—'

'Grandma?'

'What, honey?'

I laughed. 'Is all this important? I mean to say, does it really matter?'

'Well hell *yes*! Service matters. This country used to be cute and quaint and kinda socialist; it's got a bit better now since your Mrs Thatcher; people are more polite, they know their jobs are on the

219

line and there are other people who'll do them, they know there are other corporations who'll do the same thing for less money or just plain better, so you're sort of on the way, you know? But you still got a long way to go. And you lost a lot of the cuteness along the way, believe me. You abandon cuteness, you better make damn sure you're pretty goddamn efficient or you're down the tubes, baby. And all this ye olde fuckin' heritage shit ain't gonna fool people forever.'

'. . . Is that a blue flashing light behind us?'

'Say what? Ah, shee-it . . .'

*

' . . Now, you see? That was a case in point; if you had on-the-spot fines those traffic cops could have taken me for a couple of hundred bucks; help pay for that fancy bear-mobile there. Instead, what do I get? A ticking-off. I mean, that's sad.'

'I think being American helped,' I said, watching the needle swing back up across the speedometer. 'Are American miles really shorter than British ones?'

'I think so, aren't they? Same with gallons, I think . . .' Yolanda waved one hand dismissively. 'What the hell; it worked. They let us go; probably thought of all the paperwork involved.'

'Hmm. Anyway . . .' (I'd been thinking.) '. . . is efficiency really the best way to measure this sort of thing?'

'What?'

'Well, if you can do a job more efficiently with fewer people, that's all very well for that one particular company, but if you all still have to live in the same society, does it matter? We could probably do a lot of things more efficiently with fewer people at the Community, but that would just leave the people put out of work hanging around feeling useless. What's the point in that? You can't throw people off the farm or lock them up or kill them, so why not let them all have a job, even if that's less efficient?'

Yolanda was shaking her head. 'Honey, that's what the communists used to do, and look what happened to them.'

'Well, perhaps that happened for other reasons. What I'm saying is that efficiency is a strange way to evaluate how a society is doing. After all, the most *efficient* thing to do might be to kill everybody as soon as they grow old, so they won't be a burden, but you can't do that either because—'

'The Eskimos; the goddamn Inuit; they used to do exactly that,' Yolanda said. 'But it wasn't when you got to a certain numerical age, it was once you couldn't pull your weight. If you looked after yourself you could go on a long time.'

'Maybe they had no choice. But my point is that morality outranks efficiency. And, anyway, extreme efficiency would dictate less choice in the end; the most efficient thing would be for everybody to drive the same sort of car due to the economies of scale. Or for there not to be any private cars at all. You wouldn't like that, would you?'

Yolanda grinned and shook her head. 'You don't really understand Capitalism, do you, Isis?'

'From what I've heard, the best economists in the world don't understand Capitalism either, or do they all agree nowadays, and there are no more booms and slumps, just a steadily rising growth rate?'

'Child, no system is perfect, but this one's the best we got, that's the point.'

'Well, I think our system works better,' I said, settling myself primly in my seat with my hands clasped in my lap. 'The High Easter Offerance estate is a model of archaic working practices, inefficiency, over-manning and job-duplication, and everybody is extremely happy.'

Yolanda laughed. 'Well, good for you guys, Isis, but I don't know that would scale up too successfully.'

'Perhaps not, but it is my belief that contentment speaks for itself and has no need to worship at the altar of monetary efficiency's false and brazen idol.'

'Whoa,' Yolanda said, glancing over at me with narrowed eyes. 'You speaking ex-cathedra there, oh Elect one?'

'Let's just say that when the Community passes into my charge, as it sadly must one day, there will be no change in the way the farm and the Order is run.'

'Good for you, honey; you do it your way. Don't let me persuade you no different.'

'Whatever you say,' I said.

*

We had returned to Bath from Dudgeon Magna to discuss what to do next. We had another margarita. We suspected that Morag might have returned to La Mancha, Mr Leopold's home in Essex; Yolanda attempted to call the house, but the number was ex-directory and I had not thought to look for the number when I'd had the chance, in the hallway by the phone when Tyson was distracting the young man.

'How far's Essex?' Yolanda asked.

'A hundred and . . . fifty miles?' I hazarded. 'Beyond London.'

'Wanna go, or d'you want to head north now?'

'I don't know,' I confessed, pacing up and down the sitting room of Grandmother Yolanda's suite, my hands clasped behind my back. I was in a quandary. I really didn't like the sound of the way things were going back at High Easter Offerance, and my first instinct was to return there as quickly as possible to discover what was going on and do whatever sorting out might be required. Nevertheless, I was here on an important mission, and Morag/Fusillada's trail had not yet gone totally cold. My duty remained as it had been: to attempt to track and intercept my cousin and reason with her. I continued pacing. My new leather trousers creaked and squeaked, and I kept wanting to giggle at this. Which reminded me. I stopped and looked Yolanda in the eye. 'Are you fit to drive, Grandma?'

Yolanda raised her glass. 'Almost up to operating level.'

'Maybe we should get the train.'

'Nonsense. But where are we going?'

'Essex,' I decided. I stuck my hands in the pockets of my fancy trousers. 'Do you think my old clothes are ready yet?'

*

222

La Mancha was dark, silent and locked. It was evening by the time we got there and we'd have seen any lights on inside. There was no sign of Tyson or the young man or anybody else.

We stood on the back lawn, looking into a smoked-glass conservatory which held a huge round bath. The light faded slowly from the skies above.

'They're outa town, we're outa luck,' Yolanda growled.

'Oh dear.'

We stepped back and walked round the side of the house. A small bright light came on under the eaves. 'Ah-ha!' I said.

'Ah-ha nuthin',' Yolanda said, shaking her head. 'Those are security lights, child; automatic. Must of just got dark enough.'

'Oh.'

We returned to the car, past the painted plough, cartwheel and buggy, which I realised now were just ornamental. The gate had been padlocked so we had to get back over as we'd got in, over the top.

'Well, *hell*,' Grandma Yolanda said, settling into the driver's seat of the hired car, 'we'll just be forced to go into London, stay at the Dorchester, eat at Le Gavroche, catch a show and party the night away in some grotesquely expensive club drinking vintage champagne.' She made a clicking noise with her mouth and fired up the car. 'I *hate* it when that happens.'

*

'How's your head?'

'It feels like the china shop just after the bull's paid a visit.'

'What, full of bull shit? Haw haw haw.'

I opened my eyes and gave my grandmother what was supposed to be a withering look. She glanced at me over the top of her *Wall Street Journal* and winked. The grey-suited chauffeur slid the car – a 'Jag-waar' according to Yolanda – into a gap in the mid-morning traffic near Harrods. We were heading for Heathrow Airport. I shifted on my Sitting Board, making the leather trousers squeak. I'd had little choice over what to put on that morning; the hotel in Bath had not been able to extricate my old clothes from the laundry

223

in time for us leaving for London. We had left the Order's address and been assured they would be forwarded, but it meant I had to wear the gear my grandmother had bought for me, which didn't seem altogether suitable for a return to the Community. However, I was in no state to try to find different clothes. Yolanda wore boots, dark blue culottes and a short matching jacket.

'. . . Oh dear,' I said. 'I think I'm going to—'

'You know how to open the window?' Yolanda said urgently. 'It's this button here—'

'Oh,' I said, farting audibly inside my leather trousers. 'Sorry,' I said sheepishly.

Grandma Yolanda sniffed the air. She shook her head, then buried it in the newspaper.

'Hell, child; smells like a skunk crawled up your ass an' *died*.'

*

As I've indicated, our Faith is happy with tipsiness but frowns upon drunkenness taken to the point of incapacity, inarticulacy and insensibility. Nevertheless, it is recognised that people who normally only ever get slightly intoxicated may occasionally become utterly inebriate, and that one state can lead to the other. Unless this starts to happen rather too frequently, the hang-over will itself be seen as quite sufficient punishment for the transgression, and nothing will be said.

Occasionally, when a Luskentyrian has a bad hang-over, they are inclined to wish that Salvador had been instructed to ban the use of alcohol entirely when he was being given the rules which would govern our Faith. In fact, right at the start, that is exactly what did happen; for a whole week, as my Grandfather scribbled down the results of his having tuned in to God's frequency, there was a commandment – there is no other word for it – written on page two of Salvador's original notes which stated that strong liquor had to be avoided, strenuously. It was crossed out during week two of our Founder's revelations, around the time when Mr McIlone started giving my Grandfather medicinal measures of whisky, reminding Salvador that there was a place for such things and causing him to realise that what he'd heard when he thought he was being told to prohibit drink was in fact a false signal.

Before I'd left High Easter Offerance I'd been helping my Grandfather with his latest revisions to the *Orthography*, our holy book and repository of all Salvador's wisdom and insights. Part of this process had comprised weeding out false signals, the results of Dispatches our Founder had been the medium for which had turned out not fully to represent God's message. I regard it as a sign of strength and the influence of a higher Truth that our OverSeer is happy to look back and admit that some of his pronouncements were flawed, or at least capable of improvement. Of course, this wasn't really his fault; he has consistently tried to report the Voice which he hears as accurately and faithfully as possible, but he is only human, and to be human is to err. But to be human is also to be flexible and adaptable, and – if the individual does not succumb to the terrible influence of Pride – it is also to be capable of admitting one has been wrong, and to try to make corrections.

So, having originally held that God was male, our Founder later realised that the Voice he had heard had only sounded male because he himself was male; he had been expecting a male voice, he had grown up in a Christian society which took it as read that God was male and always depicted God as a man, and so it was understandable that while undergoing the revelatory whirlwind which had swept through him, my Grandfather had missed the fact that God was not as he'd been brought up to believe.

It is true that we can only take so much revelation at one time, only bring on board a certain amount of change; otherwise we simply become confused and start to lose context. We must have some sort of framework to understand ideas within, and when the ideas you are using are so powerful and so important that they threaten to change the nature of that framework itself, you have to be careful to change only a little at a time, or you risk losing the pattern for the whole

225

fragile artifice that is human understanding. So it might even be, Grandfather has hinted, that God deliberately misled him, or at least made no attempt to correct him when it became clear that he was making such mistakes, because to have done so would effectively have been saying, *Everything* you have believed until now has been false, which, if it had not caused my Grandfather to doubt his very sanity, might well have caused him to take the easier course of ignoring what God was telling him, dismissing the Voice as some aberration, just some banal medical condition, not a profound paradigm-shift in the spiritual history of the world and the birth of a fresh and vital new religion.

However it may have been, it is the case that having put in place the skeleton of Salvador's faith, God later fleshed out this new creation, and gradually revealed to our Founder the tripartite nature of Their being: both male and female and sexless (this was what God had been saying to Christians, but they had misinterpreted it as Father, Son and Holy Ghost because of the nature of society of the time, which was profoundly patriarchal).

Similarly, Salvador originally thought that there was a Devil – old Redtop as he sometimes referred to him – and that there was a Hell, too, a place submerged in eternal darkness whose walls were made of glass, where tormented souls burned like a billion scattered embers on a million blackly towering levels, forever sliced and cut by the razor-sharp edges of their frozen prison.

Later, he was able to separate this fevered, fearful vision from the quiet, calm articulation of perfection that is the true Voice of God, and realise that – again – what he had been experiencing was something from inside himself. These were his visions, not God's; they were the result of the fear and terror and guilty dread that exist in everyone and which certain faiths, especially Christianity, prey upon and exaggerate the better to control their flocks. My Grandfather was a new voice bringing glad tidings of joyful, ultimate hope and a whole new way of looking at both the world and God, but he still had to speak in the tongue he'd been taught as a child and which other people understood, and that language itself carried with it a host of assumptions and prejudices, telling its own old stories even as Salvador was using it to reveal his brand-new one.

The idea that there is a Devil is obviously a powerful one, and common to many different cultures, but I think our Founder is right in emphasising the Satan-free nature of our Faith. We have no need of bogeymen to frighten our children with, and do not believe in giving adults any excuse for their own faults; ours is a modern faith, born after the War's great blood-letting in the midst of our century of pain, when humanity finally revealed itself as the ultimate devil. Just as there is both fear and comfort to be drawn from devils – the fear speaks for itself, the comfort comes from being able to absolve oneself of responsibility for one's actions – so there is, inversely, both comfort and fear to be drawn from the realisation that there are no such things after all.

Of course, this means that we must shoulder more responsibility for our lives than other religions would allow, and one of the other errors in this area my Grandfather has cleared up over the years includes the Heresy of Prudishness.

The Heresy of Prudishness was a result of Grandfather originally teaching that while it was wrong to restrict sexual relations between people of the same generation, it was right to do so *between* generations. He later amended this to specify that only if one full generation lay between the two people concerned should their love be forbidden. Again, I think one can see the divinely inspired but still humanly limited prophet struggling to hear the Creator's voice above the clutter of a hypocritical and morally constipated society whose restrictive teachings still echoed in his ears. Let cynics find their own shortcomings and denied desires in what they blame our Founder for; I believe he has only ever tried to tell the truth as best he can, and if the truth leads him – as *our* leader – to a better, fuller personal life then we ought all to be grateful, both for him and for ourselves.

227

There is an afterlife, and our Faith's ideas on that too have evolved over the years. Originally, incorporating the idea of Heaven and Hell, it was fairly conventional and recognisably Christian in inspiration. However, as Grandfather has tuned in more and more accurately to what God is saying, the afterlife, in the shape of the all-absorbing Godhead, has become more complicated and more sophisticated. Indeed it might almost be more true to say that what we live in is the pre-life; a sort of minor overture to the grandly symphonic opera that follows; a scrawny solo before the richly glorious massed choir. Most religions have some sort of angle on the truth in this regard, but I think it obvious that Luskentyrianism, with elements of almost all of them, decisively out-does the lot.

*

I did not enjoy my flight from London to Edinburgh, which was the first I had ever made. For one thing, I did not feel well, and the various movements and changes of pressure involved in flight seemed almost designed to introduce a feeling of discomfort even without the effects of far too much alcohol the night before. In addition, though, there are various mistakes and errors of practice and etiquette one can make when travelling by aircraft, and I think I made all of them.

Grandmother Yolanda found my gaffs most amusing; the business-suited fellow sitting to my other side was less impressed. My first mistake was to tell him – in a spirit of vigilant and caring friend-liness and general camaraderie – to study his safety instructions when the conductress told him to; he looked at me as if I was quite mad. My final mistake – on the plane itself, anyway – was a result of trying to show off (how often is that the case!).

The cup of tea I asked for after my miniaturised meal was a little hot, and I'd noticed that above each seat was a small swivelling nozzle which dispensed cold air. I decided to redeem myself in the eyes of the businessman at my side by using the stream of air to lower the temperature of my tea. This was a fine idea in theory and would undoubtably have worked perfectly well if I hadn't

228

ostentatiously held my cup right up to the nozzle and twisted it fully on, producing a fierce and highly directed pulse of air which displaced the tea in the cup and showered it over the businessman and the person in the seat behind him. Yolanda found the whole episode quite hilarious, and even stopped complaining about the lack of First Class for a few moments.

Yolanda's good mood evaporated rapidly when we got to Edinburgh Airport and she couldn't remember where she'd left her hire car.

'Thought it'd be quicker just leaving it here instead of turning it in and having to hire another one,' she said, stamping down another row of cars.

I followed, pushing a trolley. 'What sort of car was it?' I asked. Not that it would make much difference to me; cars are cars.

'Don't know,' Yolanda said. 'Small. Well, smallish.'

'Doesn't the car key tell you something?'

'I left the keys inside the exhaust pipe,' she said, with a hint of embarrassment. 'Saves carrying zillions of keys around.'

I'd noticed that some cars had stickers in the back window identifying hire companies.

'Can you remember what company it belonged to?'

'No.'

'They've got these letters on posts all over the car park; was it near— ?'

'Can't remember. I was in a hurry.'

'What colour was the car?'

'Red. No; blue. . . . Shit.' Yolanda looked frustrated.

'Can you remember what cars it was parked between?'

'Get real, Isis.'

'Oh. Yes, I suppose they might have moved. But maybe they're still here!'

'Range Rover. One was a Range Rover. One of those tall things.'

We checked all the Range Rovers in the car park before Yolanda thought to check her credit card slips. There was no sign of a car hire from Glasgow Airport.

'Probably left it in the car,' she admitted. '. . . Oh, the hell with this. Let's hire another one.'

'What about the one that's here?'

'Fuck it. They'll find it eventually.'

'Won't you get charged?'

'Let them sue. That's what lawyers are for.'

*

If our Faith had a Golden Age it was probably between the years 1955 to 1979; that was when our Order grew from just a few people, many of them related in one way or another, to a fully functioning religion with a complete theology, an established base (indeed, *two* established bases, the original at Mr McIlone's farm at Luskentyre and the new one at High Easter Offerance), a settled succession of Leapyearians – through my father, Christopher, and then myself – and a steadily growing number of converts, some of whom came to stay and work at the Community and some of whom were happier in the outside world, though remaining committed to the Order and pledged both to come to its aid if required and to act as our missionaries to the Unsaved.

Then, in 1979, two disasters befell us, one affecting each of our two spiritual and physical homes. On Harris in April, Mr Eoin McIlone died. To our astonishment – and it has to be said, to our Founder's fury – he died intestate, and his farm was inherited by an Unsaved: Mr McIlone's vile step-brother from the town of Banff, who was interested only in selling the place as quickly as possible and making as much money as he could. He had no sympathy with our Faith, and as soon as he took possession of the property he turned out the Brothers and Sisters who lived and worked there. Some of those people had been there for thirty years, working the land and maintaining the fabric of the buildings, putting three decades of sweat and toil into the place for no more reward than a roof over their heads and food in their bellies, but they were ejected without a thought, without as much as a Thank you or a By-your-leave, as though they were criminals. We were told that Mr McIlone's step-brother went to church every Sunday, but by

God there was little Christian charity in the man. If his Hell was true he'd rot in it.

Of the five Brothers and Sisters who were living at Luskentyre when Mr McIlone passed on, two came to us at the Community, one stayed in the islands to work on another farm, one remained there to fish, and one returned to her original family in England. Our world was suddenly smaller, and for all that High Easter Offerance was a fine, productive place, and far more balmily easeful than Luskentyre, still we felt, I think, the loss of our original home as though we had lost an old friend. Of course, I was barely three when this happened and can remember little or nothing of the time, but I'm sure I must have been affected by the mood of the people around me and surely joined in the mourning in my own childish way.

Luskentyre remained and remains a holy place for our Order, and many of us have been on pilgrimage to the area – I myself travelled there last year, attended by Sisters Fiona and Cassie – though we are denied access to the farm itself by its current owners and must content ourselves with staying in local Bed and Breakfasts, wandering the coastline and the dunes and surveying the remnants of the ruined seaweed factory.

Our grief at losing Luskentyre proved to be only a presentiment of what was to come, however, at the other end of the year.

*

'I have to be in Prague tomorrow,' Yolanda said as we finally made the motorway that would take us to within a few miles of High Easter Offerance. 'Sure you don't want to come?'

'Grandma, apart from anything else, I don't have a passport.'

'Shame. You should get one. *I'll* get you one.'

'I think it causes problems when we apply for passports.'

'I'll bet. What do you expect from a country where they not only won't let you bring a gun into the country but won't even let you buy one when you *get* here?' She shook her head.

'Will you be coming straight back?'

'Nope; then I head for Venice, Italy.'

I thought about this. 'I thought your other house was in Venice, California.'

Yolanda nodded. 'I've a house there, and an apartment in the original Venice.'

'Doesn't that get confusing?'

'Does for the IRS,' Yolanda said, glancing over at me and grinning.

I was shocked. 'Aren't they some sort of terrorist organisation?'

Grandmother Yolanda had a good laugh at that. 'Kind of,' she agreed. 'Come to think of it, now that Russia's opened up, I might buy places in both Georgias. That would confuse the hell out of them, too.'

'Do you think you'll *ever* settle down, Grandmother?'

'Not even in an urn, child; I want to have my ashes scattered to the four winds.' She glanced at me. 'You could do that for me, maybe. If I left you instructions in my will, would you?'

'Um,' I said, 'well, I . . . I suppose so.'

'Don't look upset; I might change my mind, anyway; get myself frozen instead. They can do that nowadays, you know.'

'Really?' I had no idea what she was talking about.

'Anyway,' Yolanda said. 'Prague, Venice, then Scotland again.' (She pronounces it Skatlind.) 'I'm goin' to try and get back for the end of the month.'

'Oh, for the Festival.'

'Well, no, not specifically, but what is happening with that? For you personally, I mean.'

I shifted uncomfortably in my seat and looked at the scenery of fields and hills. 'How do you— ?'

'You know what I mean, Isis,' she said, not unkindly.

I knew what she meant. I knew so well that I had been trying hard not to think about it for some long time by then, and this whole excursion to look for Morag had itself provided a way of not thinking about it. But now that Morag's trail had finally gone cold and there seemed to be some sort of problem requiring my presence at the Community, I had no choice but to confront the question: what to do?

232

'Isis. Are you happy taking this part in this Love-Fest or not?'

'It's my duty,' I said lamely.

'Bullshit.'

'But it is,' I said. 'I'm the Elect of God.'

'You're a free woman, Isis. You can do what you please.'

'Not really. There are expectations.'

'Fooey.'

'I am the third generation; there's nobody else. As far as Leapyearians go, I'm it,' I said. 'I mean, anybody can be a Leapyearian; it doesn't have to be somebody in the family or even somebody in the Community, just somebody in the Order, but it would be . . . neater if it was kept in the family. Grandfather hoped it might be Morag who provided the next generation, but if she's not even part of our Faith any more . . .'

'That doesn't mean *you* have to try to produce the next generation now if you don't want to.' My grandmother looked over at me. 'Do you, Is? *Do* you want to be a mother now? Well?'

I had the sinking feeling that Yolanda wasn't going to look back at the road until I answered her. 'I don't know,' I said, looking away and watching the spire of Linlithgow Palace appear round the side of a low hill to my left. 'I really can't decide what to do.'

'Isis, don't let them put pressure on you. If you don't want to have a child yet, just tell them. Hell, I know that old tyrant; I know he wants another 'Elect' to keep this . . . well, to keep the Order going, but you're just young; there's still plenty of time; there's always the next goddamn Festival. And if you decide it's never going to be the right time, then—'

'But by the next Festival the pressure will be even worse!' I cried.

'Well then—' Yolanda began, then glanced at me, frowning. 'Wait a minute; you sure 2000 *is* a leap year?'

'Yes, of course.'

'I thought if the year's divisible by four it's a leap year, unless it's divisible by four hundred, when it isn't a leap year.'

'No,' I said wearily (we had all this drummed into us pre-school at the Community). 'It's not a leap year if it's divisible

233

by *one* hundred. But if it's divisible by *four* hundred, it is a leap year.'

'Oh.'

'Anyway,' I said. 'I don't think Salvador believes he'll see 2000.'

'Let's cut to the chase here, Is. The question is, are you ready to be a mother or not? That's what they expect of you, isn't it?'

'Yes,' I said, miserably. 'That's what they want.'

'Well, *are* you ready?'

'I don't know!' I said, louder than I meant, and looked away, chewing on a knuckle.

We drove on in silence for a while. The smokes and steams of Grangemouth oil refinery swung past to our right.

'You seeing anybody, Isis?' Yolanda asked gently. 'You got anybody special?'

I swallowed, then shook my head. 'No. Not really.'

'You had *any* boyfriends yet?'

'No,' I confessed.

'Isis, I know you seem to develop slower out here, but shit, you're nineteen; don't you *like* boys?'

'I like them fine, I just don't . . .' My voice trailed off as I wondered how to put it.

'You don't want to fuck them?'

'Well,' I said, blushing, 'I don't think so.'

'What about *girls*?' Yolanda sounded a little surprised but mostly just very interested.

'No, not really.' I leaned forward, elbows on thighs, chin in hands, staring glumly at the cars and trucks ahead of us on the motorway. 'I don't know what I want. I don't know who I want. I don't know *that* I want.'

'Well then, God's sakes, Isis!' Yolanda said, waving one hand around. 'All the more reason to tell Salvador to take a hike! Christ almighty; get yourself sorted out first. No one who loves you is going to give a damn if you're gay or want to stay celibate, but don't get pregnant on the off chance you'll drop on the twenty-ninth of February just to keep that old letch happy!'

'Grandmother!' I said, genuinely shocked. 'You mean Salvador?'

234

'Who the hell else?'

'He is our Founder! You can't talk about him like that!'

'Isis, child,' Yolanda said, shaking her head. 'You know I love you, and God help me I even have a lot of time for that old rogue because I think basically he's a good man, but he is a *man*; I mean, he's human and he's very male, you know what I'm saying? I don't really know that he's anything holy at all; I'm sorry to say that because I know it hurts you, but—'

'Grandmother!'

'Now! Just hear me out, child. I've seen just about every damn cult and faith and sect and religion and pseudo-religion the world has to offer in my time, and it seems to me maybe in some sense your Grandfather is right about one thing: they are all searching for the truth, but they never find it, not all of it, not any of them, and that includes you people; you're no more right than anybody else.'

I was sitting with my mouth hanging open, appalled by what I was hearing. I'd always known Grandmother Yolanda wasn't the strictest adherent of our Order, but I'd like to think that somewhere underneath all this restless, rootless, wasteful consumerism there was still a core of Faith.

'And you know what I think? I think it's all a load of crap. I don't doubt there is a God, although maybe even that's more habit than true faith, God knows, but I don't think anybody in any religion has ever said one damn useful thing about Him or Her or It. You never noticed religions always seem to get invented by men? When you ever hear of a cult or a sect started by a woman? Hardly ever. Women have the power of creation in them; men have to fantasise about it, create Creation itself, just to compensate; ovary envy. That's all it is.' Yolanda nodded with self-certitude while I looked on. 'Know what decided me on all this?'

She looked at me. I shrugged, too choked to speak.

'Koresh,' she said. 'Remember him?'

'I don't think so.'

'What? WACO: We Ain't Comin' Out? Were you on the moon or something? You must have seen . . .' Yolanda rolled her eyes. 'No, I guess you didn't.'

235

'Wait,' I said. 'Yes; I think my friend Mr Warriston might have told me something about it. Wasn't that in Texas?'

'Town called Waco,' my grandmother confirmed. 'About a hundred miles south from Dallas. Drove down there the day it happened. Day it ended. Saw the embers. Made me mad as hell, goddamn government doing that . . . not that it was right to bomb Oklahoma City, mind . . . But the point was Koresh,' she said, wagging one finger at me. 'They showed film of him from before, holding a Bible and leading his followers in some marathon worship session and said he wanted to be a rock star; tried to be one, in fact, but didn't get anywhere. Became a prophet instead. And how did he end up living? Worshipped, that's how, in a place where he could have any woman he wanted and smoke dope and drink all night with his buddies. Hog heaven. He got the rock-star life without having to become one; he got what he really wanted: sex and drugs and worship. He was no more holy than, I don't know, Frank Zappa or somebody, but he got to pretend he was, got his own farm, all the guns he could play with and at the end he even got to become some sort of dumb martyr, thanks to the Feds and that fat dick Clinton. Frankly I didn't care Koresh died, or care very much that his followers did, though I probably should; you like to think they knew the choice they were making and were just plain stupid, and if you'd somehow gotten into the same situation you'd have been smarter . . . No, it was the children that made me cry, Isis; it was knowing they died, knowing they suffered, and weren't old enough to have made up their own minds about whatever insane fucking power-trip that egotistical asshole Koresh was taking his people on.'

I stared at my grandmother. She nodded as she looked ahead. 'That's my thoughts on the subject, Grand-daughter. Seems to me women have been falling for this holy-man shit down through all the centuries and we ain't stopped falling for it yet. Jesus. The KKK: Koresh, Khomeini, Kahane; well, to hell with the lot of them, all the fundamentalists, and that Aum Shitface gang from Japan, too.' Yolanda shook her head angrily. 'World's more like a goddamn comic-book every fuckin' day.'

I nodded, and thought the better of asking my grandmother

exactly what she was talking about. She took a deep breath and seemed to calm herself somewhat. She smiled briefly at me. 'All I'm saying is, Isis, don't be in too big a hurry to join up too. You get your head sorted out, but remember: men are a bit crazy and a bit dangerous, and they're jealous as hell, too. Don't sacrifice yourself for them, because they sure as shit won't do it for you; fact is they'll try and sacrifice *you*.'

I watched her drive for a while. Eventually I said, 'So, are you apostate too, Grandmother?'

'Hell,' Yolanda said, looking annoyed. 'I was never really part of your Order in the first place, Is. I just went along with it. Jerome was interested in trying to save his soul. I found Salvador . . . charismatic at first, then later I just got to know all the people at the farm, and then Alice married Christopher; that tied me in tight.' She glanced over at me again. 'Then you came along.' She shrugged, looked back at the road. 'I'd have taken you from them if I could, Is.' She looked at me again, and for the first time ever, I thought, she looked uncertain. 'If you hadn't been born the day you were . . . well, I might have been allowed to take you; they might have let me, after the fire. However.' She shrugged once more and concentrated on the road again.

I turned to watch the road unwind towards us, the traffic like little purposeful packets of metal, glass and rubber, containing their fragile cargoes of humanity.

237

CHAPTER FIFTEEN

H igh Easter Offerance was beautiful that day; the breeze
was warm, the air was clear and filled with the sound of
fresh young leaves rustling; sunlight made each leaf a green
mirror. We parked the car at the semicircle of pitted, weed-strewn
tarmac in front of the rusted gates. Sophi's Morris was not there so
I guessed she was at work. Yolanda and I walked down the curving
drive, its crumbling, mossy surface a long carpet of shadow and
restless, flickering light beneath the over-arching trees. My leather
trousers squeaked. The long black jacket Yolanda had bought me
felt light and elegant, especially over the silk shirt. The closer to the
farm I got the more overdressed I felt, and the more contaminated
by the Sybaritic antics of the previous night. I fingered the little
black bead that was the head of the hat-pin Yolanda had given me
years before and which I had remembered to remove from my old
jacket and insert into the lapel of my new one (I had taken great
delight in the fact that the police had not discovered it). I rubbed its
smooth black head between my fingers like something talismanic.
I briefly considered dirtying my jacket, but that would have been
ridiculous. I was glad I'd kept my old boots, though I was starting
to regret I'd cleaned both them and my old hat.

'Jeez; you make all your roads so *narrow*,' Yolanda said,
stepping round a bramble bush that pushed itself out into the
middle of the road.

'It's just overgrown,' I told her, shifting my kit-bag over my other
shoulder. I felt a mix of emotions: elation at returning home and
trepidation at the prospect of what Yolanda had hinted might be
a frosty welcome.

'Yeah, but you do, anyway,' Yolanda insisted. 'Some of those
roads up north . . . I mean, don't you *like* tarmacadam? I thought
the Scots invented the damn stuff.'

The Woodbeans' house stood sentinel at the steep river bank,
in front of the old iron bridge. I looked up at the quiet house,

241

Yolanda stood shaking her head at the holes in the bridge's deck and the narrow pathway of odd assorted planks that led across it. Thirty feet below, the river swirled slowly.

'Hold my hand,' she said, putting her hand out behind her. I stepped forward and took her hand as she set one tentative foot on the first of the planks. 'Gettin' so you have to be Indiana fuckin' Jones just to *git* to your place . . .'

*

The drive left the trees and rose a little, heading between the wall of the apple orchard to the left and the lawn in front of the greenhouses to the right. A couple of the goats looked up from their tethered munching on the lawn to watch us approach. We saw the primary children, filing out of the greenhouse in an orderly fashion; one of them noticed Grandma Yolanda and me, and shouted. In a moment they had broken ranks and started running towards us. Brother Calum appeared at the end of the line of running children, looking at first concerned, then pleased, then concerned again.

Yolanda and I were surrounded by a small field of crop-headed children, all jabbering and smiling and raising up their arms to be lifted and held, while others pinched and stroked my leather trousers, and made ooing and ahing noises over my jacket and shirt. Calum stood by the open door of the greenhouse, waved once and nodded cautiously, then disappeared through the gateway into the farm courtyard. Yolanda and I followed, each holding hands with half a dozen children and trying to answer a whirlwind of questions.

We met Brother Pablo as we entered the courtyard, standing holding the bridle of Otie, the donkey, while sister Cassie brushed her. Several of the children left our sides to go and pat and stroke the donkey, which blinked placidly.

'Sister Isis,' Pablo said, lowering his eyes as he returned my Sign. Pablo is a couple of years younger than me, a tall, stooped, quietly spoken Spaniard who has been with us for a year. He usually had a smile for me, but not today, it seemed.

'Hi, Isis,' Sister Cassie said, nodding. She left the brush hanging in Otie's coat and let her hands rest on the heads of a couple of the children. 'Hey; you look . . . really elegant.'

'Thanks, Cassie,' I said, then introduced Yolanda and Pablo.

'We met, honey; last week,' Yolanda told me.

'Oh, yes; sorry,' I said, as more people appeared in the courtyard from the buildings; I waved and returned various greetings. Allan appeared from the mansion house and hurried through the crowd; Brother Calum exited shortly afterwards and followed him.

'Sister Yolanda, Sister Isis,' Allan said, smiling, and took our hands. 'Welcome back. Pablo; please take Sister Isis's bag and follow us.'

Yolanda, Allan, Pablo and I walked over to the mansion house; everybody else stayed outside. 'How are you, Sister Yolanda?' Allan asked as we climbed the steps. I looked at the poster advertising my cousin Morag's fictitious concert at the Royal Festival Hall.

'Felt better, felt worse,' Yolanda told him.

When we got to the landing between the Order office and Salvador's quarters, Allan hesitated, a finger tapping at his lips. 'Grandmother,' he said, smiling, 'Salvador said he was sorry he missed you the other day and he would love to see you now; would you like a chat?' He motioned towards Grandfather's quarters.

Yolanda put her head back a little and looked at my brother through narrowed eyes. 'You don't say.'

'Yes,' Allan said. He put one hand to the small of Yolanda's back. 'We'll just have a word with Isis; sort of a debriefing.' He nodded at the office doors. 'We'll just be in here.'

'Does—' I began, and had been about to say Doesn't Grandfather want to hear what I have to say? but Yolanda was there before me.

'Fine; I'll sit in,' she said.

'Oh?' Allan said, looking awkward. 'Well, I think Salvador's expecting you . . .'

'He's waited two years; he can wait another few minutes, I think.' Yolanda smiled narrowly.

'Well . . .' Allan began.

'Come on; faster we are, less time we keep him waiting,' my grandmother said, stepping towards the office doors. I saw Allan's jaw set in a tense line as we followed.

Sister Erin stood up from her desk as we entered the office. 'Sister Isis. Sister Yolanda.'

'Hello, Erin.'

'How ya doin'?'

'Thank you, Pablo,' Allan said, taking my bag from him and putting it down by the secretary's desk. Pablo nodded and left, closing the door behind him.

Yolanda and I sat in front of Allan's desk; he brought a chair over from beside the smaller desk. Erin remained there, behind us. 'So, Isis,' Allan said, sitting back in his seat. 'How have you been?'

'I'm well,' I said, though in fact I still felt hung-over and was starting to wonder if I had a cold coming on. 'However, I have to report that my mission to find Sister Morag has not been successful.'

'Oh,' Allan said, looking sad.

I started to detail my journey, turning round once out of politeness to include Sister Erin in my audience, only to discover that she must have slipped out of the office. I hesitated, then went on. As I told Allan of my adventures – and he took notes, leaning forward over a pad on his desk – I realised that my kit-bag had vanished too; Allan had left it lying at the side of the other desk, but it wasn't there any more.

'A *porn* star?' Allan coughed, calm demeanour and voice cracking at once.

'Fusillada DeBauch,' I confirmed.

'Good grief.' He made a note. 'How do you spell that?'

I explained about my visits to Mr Leopold's office, La Mancha in Gittering, Clissold's Health Farm and Country Club, and my return to La Mancha. Yolanda nodded now and again and grunted when I got to the bits that included her. I left out falling through ceilings, attacks on racialists and visits to night clubs.

Unfortunately I couldn't easily evade being arrested or being seen on television. I mentioned attempting to use the *zhlonjiz* to ask God what to do, and taking the cannabis cigarette for the same

244

reason when the *zhlonjiz* didn't work. Allan looked awkward, and stopped writing.

'Ah,' he said, looking pained. 'Yes, we heard from the Possils about the *zhlonjiz*. Why— ?' His voice cut off as his gaze flicked behind me, towards the door.

Yolanda glanced round, then swivelled in her seat. She cleared her throat.

I turned round to see my Grandfather standing in the open doorway; Erin stood behind him. Salvador was dressed in his usual white robes. His face, surrounded with white hair, looked red.

'Grandfather . . .' I said, rising from my seat. Yolanda turned round in hers but stayed sitting. My Grandfather strode into the room straight up to me. He did not return the Sign. He held something small in his hand. He leaned past me and slapped whatever it was on the desk in front of my seat.

'And *what*,' he hissed, 'is *that*?'

I looked at the tiny piece of bakelite. 'The top of the *zhlonjiz* vial, Grandfather,' I said, perplexed. 'I'm sorry; it's all I got back from the police. I used a little—'

My Grandfather slapped my cheek, banging my upper and lower teeth against each other.

I stared, shocked, into his furious, livid face. My cheek burned, like some fleshly mirror of his rage. I was aware of my grandmother standing quickly at my side, shouting something, but gradually the view narrowed down to my Grandfather's enraged face while everything else seemed to darken and evaporate away at the edges, until even the angry crimson of Salvador's face appeared to go grey, and the various voices I could hear dissolved into their own audible greyness, roaring incoherently like a waterfall.

I felt hands on my shoulders and then the firm wood of the seat beneath me. I shook my head, feeling as if I was underwater and everything was happening very slowly.

'—the hell gives you the right— ?'

'—*mine*; my flesh and blood!'

'Salvador . . .'

'Yeah, she's mine too, so fuckin' what?'

'She doesn't belong to you! She is *ours*! You don't understand what she's—'

'Ah, you always were a goddamn bully!'

'Grandmother, if you—'

'And you always were a bloody interferer, woman! Look at the way you've got her dressed, like some city hoor!'

'Salvador . . .'

'*What*? Hell, *you* got no right to talk about whores, you old fraud!'

'*WHAT*?'

'Grandmother, if you could please—'

'*What* did you— ?'

'Stop it! Stop it stop it stop it!' I shouted, struggling to my feet and having to hold onto the front of the desk to stop myself falling. I turned to Grandfather, involuntarily putting my hand to my cheek. 'Why did you *do* that? What have I *done*?'

'By God!' Salvador bellowed. 'I'll—' He stepped forward, raising his hand, but Erin held it while Yolanda stepped in between us.

'What have I *done*?' I shouted, almost screaming.

Salvador roared and lunged forward, reaching and picking up the cap from the *zhlonjiz* jar. '*This* is what you've done, ye stupid wee bitch!' He flourished the fragment of cap in my face, then threw it at my feet and pushed past me and Yolanda. He stopped at the doors and pointed back at us. 'You've no right being here,' he told Yolanda.

'Well, fuck you,' Grandmother said in a reasonable voice.

'And *you*,' he said, pointing at me. 'You can dress properly and think about coming on your knees as a penitent, if you can find some excuse for your treachery!' He walked out. I caught a glimpse of Sister Jess in the hall outside, then the door slammed shut, the noise echoing round the wood panelling of the room.

I turned to Yolanda, then Erin and then Allan, tears welling up in my eyes. 'What *is* all this?' I said, trying not to wail but failing.

Erin sighed, stooped and picked up the cap of the *zhlonjiz* vial. She shook her head. 'Why did you do it, Isis?' she asked.

'What?' I said. 'Take the *zhlonjiz*?'

'Yes!' Erin said, tears in her eyes now.

'That's what it was there for!' I exclaimed. 'I thought that's what I was supposed to do with it!'

'Oh, Isis,' Allan said heavily, and sat down in his chair.

'Did you think you heard God *tell* you to?' Erin said, as though confused.

'No,' I said. 'It was my decision.'

'Then *why?*' Erin implored.

'Because it seemed like the right thing to do. What else was I supposed— ?'

'But that wasn't up to you to decide!'

'Why not? Who on earth could I ask? Zeb?'

'Zeb?' Erin looked confused. 'No; your Grandfather, of course!'

'How was I supposed to ask him?' I yelled, simply not under-standing what she was talking about.

'Hey,' Yolanda began. 'I think you two are—'

'What do you mean, how?' Erin shouted. 'To his face, of course!'

'I was in London; how could I— ?'

'London?' Erin said. 'What are you talking about?'

'I'm talking,' I said, slowing and trying to keep my temper, 'about taking the *zhlonjiz* in London. How was I supposed to— ?'

'Well I'm talking about taking it from *here*,' Erin said. 'How *could* you? How could you just *take* it? How could you steal it from us?'

'. . . ah,' I heard Allan say.

'Jeez,' Yolanda said, shaking her head and sitting on the edge of the desk.

'I—' I began, then stopped. 'What?' I asked. 'Steal? What are you talking about?'

'Isis,' Erin said. A wisp of greying brown hair had dissociated itself from her bun; she blew it away with the side of her mouth. 'What we all want to know,' she said, glancing at Allan, who nodded wearily, 'is why you took the *zhlonjiz* in the first place.'

I stared at her for a moment, and it was as though the floor beneath me tipped somehow; I thought the room itself, the mansion

247

house and whole Community suddenly creaked and leaned to one side; my legs almost buckled and I had to hold onto the edge of the desk again. I felt Grandma Yolanda's hand on my arm, steadying me.

'I didn't take it,' I said. The note. I had lost the note. 'I didn't take it,' I repeated, shaking my head, feeling the blood leave my face as I looked from Erin to Allan and then to Yolanda. 'I was given it. It was in my bag. My kit-bag. I found it. In there. I found it. Really . . .'

I sat down again, my legs wobbly.

'Oh dear,' Allan said, running fingers through his hair.

Erin put her hand over her eyes, shaking her head. 'Isis, Isis,' she said, looking away.

'What is this stuff?' Yolanda said. 'This one of Salvador's holy ointments?'

'It's *the* holy ointment,' Allan said, sounding tired. He looked at Yolanda for a moment then gave a shrug. 'What it actually *does* . . .' he said awkwardly. '. . . I mean, it's very old . . . it's probably . . . The point is,' he said, leaning forward over the desk, 'Grandfather believes . . . he regards . . . he knows, in his own heart, that it is . . . effective.' Allan glanced at me. He hit his chest with his fist. 'In here, Salvador knows that it works. We respect that.' He glanced at me. 'We all respect that.'

'I didn't take it,' I said. 'It was in my bag. I found it. There was a note.'

'What?' Erin said. Allan just closed his eyes.

'A note,' I said. 'A note from Salvador.'

'A note?' Erin said. I could see the disbelief in her eyes, hear it in her voice.

'Yes,' I said. 'Well . . . it was signed with an "S".'

Allan and Erin exchanged looks. 'What did this note say?' Erin sighed.

'It just said, "In case you need it",' I told them. 'Then an "S".'

They exchanged looks again. 'It did!' I said. 'I think. Something like that. I think those were the words . . . or it was, "Just in case, S." Something . . . something similar . . .'

'Do you have this note?' Erin asked.

I shook my head. 'No,' I admitted. 'No. It disappeared. I think the police—'

'Don't, Isis,' Erin said, shaking her head and walking away with her hand over her eyes again. 'Don't. Please don't do this. Don't make it worse . . .'

Allan muttered something and shook his head.

'But it's true!' I said, looking from Erin to Yolanda, who patted my hand.

'I know, I know, honey; I believe you.'

'Isis,' Erin said, coming back over to me and taking one of my hands in hers. 'I really think you'd be better off just admitting you took the—'

'Look,' Yolanda said, 'if she says she didn't take the goddamn ointment, she didn't, okay?'

'Sister Yolanda,—'

'And I ain't your goddamn sister.'

'Isis,' Erin said earnestly, turning from my grandmother to me and taking both my hands in hers. 'Don't do this. Your Grandfather's *terribly* upset. If you just confess—'

'What, are you fucking Catholics now?'

'Isis!' Erin said, ignoring my grandmother. I had looked at Yolanda and now Erin jerked my hands, turning me back to her. 'Isis; make a clean breast of it; just say you took it on impulse; say you thought it was something else; say you—'

'But none of that's true!' I protested. 'I found the vial in my bag, with a note tied to it. Well, not tied to it; it was a rubber band—'

'Isis!' Erin said, shaking me again. 'Stop! You're only digging yourself in deeper!'

'No I'm not! I'm telling the truth! I'm not going to lie!'

Erin threw my hands down and walked off to the smaller desk. She stood there, one of her hands up at her face, her shoulders shaking.

Yolanda patted my arm again. 'You just tell it like it is, kid. You just tell the truth and the hell with them all.'

'Isis,' Allan said leadenly. I turned to him, still with a sense that things were happening in some strange, slowing fluid that was all around me. 'I can't . . .' He took a deep breath. 'Look,' he said. 'I'll,' he glanced at the doors, 'I'll have a word with Salvador, okay? Perhaps he'll have calmed down a bit, later. Then maybe you and he could . . . you know, talk. You have to decide what you're going to say. I can't tell you what to say, but he is really really upset and . . . Well, you just have to decide what's best. I . . .' He shook his head, stared down at his hands clasped on the desk. 'I don't know what to make of all this, it's just . . . it's like everything's . . .' He gave a small, despairing laugh. 'We must all just pray, and to trust to God. Listen to Them, Isis. Listen to what They say.'

'Yes,' I said, drying my eyes with my sleeve, and then with a handkerchief Yolanda produced. I straightened. 'Yes, of course.'

Allan glanced at the office clock, high on one wall. 'We'd better give him till this evening. Will you be in your room?' he asked.

I nodded. 'I may go for a walk first, but, later, yes.'

'Okay.' He raised his flat hands from the desk's surface and let them fall back again. 'We'll see what we can do.'

'Thank you,' I said, sniffing and handing my grandmother back her handkerchief. I nodded to her and we turned to go.

Erin was still standing staring down at the desk by the door. I paused, dug into my jacket pocket and took out a roll of pound notes bound with a little rubber band. I placed the roll on the desk and added two one-pence pieces from a trouser pocket. Erin looked at the money.

'Twenty-seven pounds, two pence,' I said.

'Well done,' Erin said flatly. Yolanda and I left the room.

*

'I guess a lawyer wouldn't be appropriate,' Yolanda said as we went downstairs.

'I don't think so, Grandma.'

'Well, first thing we should do is drive to the hotel, or into Stirling at any rate, and have us some lunch. I need a margarita.'

'Thanks, Grandma,' I said, stopping to face her as we got to the bottom of the stairs. I squeezed her hand. 'But I think I'd just like to . . . you know, be by myself for a bit.'

She looked hurt. 'You want me to go, is that it?'

I tried to work out how to say what it was I wanted to say. 'I need to think, Yolanda. I need . . .' I breathed in hard, gaze flickering over the walls, the ceiling and back down the stairs again until I looked at my grandmother again. 'I need to think myself back into the person I am when I'm here, do you know what I mean?'

She nodded. 'I guess so.'

'You've done so much for me,' I told her. 'I hate—'

'Forget it. You sure you don't want me to stick around?'

'Really, no.' I gave a brave smile. 'You go and see Prague; go and see your red diamond.'

'Fuck the diamond. And Prague will still be there.'

'Honestly; it'd be better. I won't feel I've disrupted your life totally too.' I gave a small laugh and looked around with an expression that spoke of an optimism I didn't feel. 'This'll all get sorted out. Just one of those daft things that comes along in a place like this where everybody lives on top of each other all the time; storm in a tea cup. Storm in a thimble.' I fashioned what I hoped was a cheeky grin.

Yolanda looked serious. 'You just look out, Isis,' she told me, putting her hand on my shoulder and lowering her head a little as she fixed her gaze upon me. It was a curiously affecting gesture. 'It ain't never been all sweetness and light here, honey,' she told me. 'You've always seen the best of it, and it's only now you're getting the shitty end of the stick. But it's always been there.' She patted my shoulder. 'You watch out for Salvador. Old Zhobelia once told me . . .' She hesitated. 'Well, I don't rightly know exactly what it was she was trying to hint at, to tell the truth, but it was something, for sure. Something your Grandfather had to hide; something she knew about him.'

'They were . . . they were married,' I said, falteringly. 'The three of them were married. I imagine that they had lots of little secrets between them . . .'

'Hmm,' Yolanda said, obviously not convinced. 'Well, I always

251

wondered about her heading off, just disappearing like that after the fire; seemed kind of suspicious. You sure she is alive?'

'Pretty sure. Calli and Astar seem still to be in touch. I can't imagine they'd . . . lie.'

'Okay, well, look; I'm just saying there might be more than one hidden agenda here. You will take care now, won't you?'

'I will. I swear. And you mustn't worry; I'll be fine. You come back in a week or two. Come back for the Festival and I'll have everything running back on track again. I'll sort it out. Promise.'

'There was a deal to get sorted, Isis, even before this, like we were talking about in the car today.'

'I know,' I told her, hugging her. 'Just have faith.'

'That's your department, honey, but I'll take your word for it.'

*

One night in November 1979 a fire destroyed half the mansion house; it killed my mother Alice and father Christopher and Grandmother Aasni and it might have killed me too if my father hadn't thrown me out of the window into the garden fishpond. He might have saved himself then, too, but he went back to look for my mother; they were eventually found huddled together in the room I had shared with Allan, overcome by smoke. Allan had escaped on his own.

Grandmother Aasni died in her kitchen in the house, seemingly the victim of her own culinary experimentation.

The fire engine called from Stirling that night could not be taken across the already holed and tumbledown bridge by the Woodbeans' home; the Community put out the fire itself, mostly, with some help later on from a portable pump brought over the bridge by the fire brigade. My Grandfather had always known that, with the number of candles and paraffin lamps we used, especially in winter, the risk of fire at the farm was high; accordingly he had always treated fire prevention with the utmost seriousness, had bought an old but serviceable hand-powered pump from another farm, and ensured that there were lots of buckets of water and sand stationed at various points throughout the farm, as well as carrying out regular drills so that everybody knew what to do in the event that a fire did break out.

Fire officers came the next day to survey the gutted wreckage of the mansion house and to attempt to discover how the fire had started. They determined that the seat of the fire had been the kitchen stove, and that it looked very much as though a pressure cooker had exploded, showering the room with burning oil. Aasni had probably been knocked unconscious in the initial blast. Zhobelia – distraught, weeping, incoherent, hair-tearing Zhobelia – left off her wailing just long enough to confirm that her sister had been trying to develop a new type of pressure-cooked pickle whose ingredients included ghee and a variety of other oils.

I don't remember the fire. I don't remember smoke and flames and being thrown from the window into the ornamental fish pond; I don't remember my father's touch or my mother's voice at all. I don't remember a funeral or a memorial service. All I remember – with a strange, static, photographic clarity – is the burned-out shell of the mansion house, days or weeks or months later, its soot-shadowed stones and few remaining roof beams stark black against the cold blue winter skies.

I think Allan felt my parents' loss more; he was old enough to know that he would never see them again whereas I could not really understand this idea, and just kept waiting for them to come back from wherever it was they had gone. I suppose the nature of the Community itself made the blow less keenly felt than it might have been in Benighted society; Allan and I would have been brought up much the way we were even if our parents had not perished, our care, upbringing and education spread out amongst the many faithful of the Community rather than left solely to one binary nuclear family.

I believe it dawned on me that my parents weren't coming back only as the burned-out mansion house was rebuilt during the following year, as though while the building's shell was still open to the weather and the skies my mother and father could somehow find a way to return . . . but as the roof was rebuilt and the new beams and rafters hoisted into place, the roof boards laid and the slates nailed down, that possibility was gradually but irrevocably removed, as though the wood and planks and nails and metal fittings that went to complete the house were not making a new place for people to live, but making instead a huge, too-lately-made mausoleum my mysteriously vanished parents ought somehow to inhabit, yet were forever excluded from.

I have a vague, contrary recollection of thinking then that my parents were still there somehow, hanging around in a sort of ghostly, spectral way, snagged there, caught by all those fresh floorboards and shining nails, but even that feeling gradually slipped away over time, and the completed, refurbished house became just another part of the Community.

I suppose, according to the more facile schools of psychology, I ought to have resented the mansion house, and especially the library, which survived undamaged but which for many, many years thereafter had about it the lingering odour of smoke, but if anything the effect was quite to the contrary, and I came to love the library and its books and its old, musty, smoky scent, as though through that faint aroma of the past I soaked up more than just the knowledge contained in the books as I sat there reading and studying, and so was still in touch with my parents and our happy past before the fire.

I think that for my Grandfather the loss of his son was probably the worst thing that ever happened to him. It was as if there was a God of the sort he did not believe in: a cruel, capricious, closely involved God who did not just speak from some great, passionless distance, but moved people and events around like pieces in a game; a greedy, spiteful, manipulative, hands-on God who took as much as He gave, and – provoked, or simply to prove His power – fell upon the lives and fates of men like an eagle upon a mouse. If my Grandfather's faith was shaken by his son's death, he gave no sign at the time, but I know that to this day he still grieves for him, and still wakes himself from sleep every few months with nightmares of burning buildings and shouts and screams inside rolling flame-lit billows of black smoke.

Things never were quite the same again; they are still good, and we thrive (or I thought we did), but they are good in a way that must be quite different from the way they would have been good had Alice and Chris survived, and Aasni and Zhobelia grown old together with Salvador. Instead, three of them died, and Zhobelia at first withdrew within the Community, and then withdrew from it.

My great-aunt mourned prodigiously, extravagantly, epically; she tore her hair out by the roots, which you hear about people doing but I'll bet you never actually saw. Neither have I, but I have seen the evidence and it was not pretty.

Zhobelia stopped eating, stopped cooking, stopped getting out of bed. She blamed herself for the fire; she had gone to bed that night instead of staying up with Aasni to carry on with their pressurised pickling experiment, and anyway felt that the accident would not have happened if she had ensured the pressure cooker had been properly cleaned; both she and Aasni knew that some of their earlier experiments had blocked the safety valves and caused dangerous pressure build-ups in the cooker. Zhobelia had been more concerned than her sister had appeared over the safety implications of this development, and blamed herself for not staying to make sure that Aasni did not put herself in danger.

Zhobelia recovered, slowly. She started to get up and to eat, though she never again cooked; not even as much as a popadum. Calli and Astar, Zhobelia's daughters, moved smoothly and quietly into the gap left by their aunt's death and their mother's domestic secession, jointly taking over the mistresship of the kitchen and the stewardship of the Whit family. Zhobelia entered a kind of self-imposed exile within her own home, having nothing to do with its running and taking little apparent interest in its welfare; she existed there, but she seemed to have little to say to anybody, and nothing that she wanted to do. A year to the day after the fire she left High Easter Offerance without warning.

We found a note from her saying that she had gone to visit her old family – who were now based in Glasgow – in the hope of effecting a reconciliation. We later heard that some form of rapprochement had been arrived at, but that Zhobelia had been looking for forgiveness and understanding only, and not a new home; she left there too, and, well, there seems to be some confusion over where she ended up after that. Astar, Calli and Salvador all seem vaguely sure that she is still alive and being well cared for somewhere, but the two sisters become sadly uncommunicative if pressed on the details, while Grandfather just gets tetchy.

I think the fire changed my Grandfather. By all accounts the least important aspect of it was that he took to dressing in white, not black, but more importantly he seemed to lose some of his energy and enthusiasm; for a while, I'm told by those who were around at the time, our Faith seemed uncertain of its way, and a mood of despondency settled over the Community. Morale recovered eventually, and Grandfather rediscovered some of his drive and vitality, but, as I say, things were never the same again, though we have prospered well enough.

I know the fire changed me. My memories begin with that vision of aching, empty blueness, the smell of dampened smouldering and the sound of my great-aunt's grief; the Gift of Healing came upon me two years later.

CHAPTER
SIXTEEN

I have always had my secret places within and around the policies which form our lands; they are part of that private, internalised landscape every child imposes upon their surroundings, which sometimes survives into adulthood if we stay in the same place and the world does not change too much around us. Unlike the retreats of many children, mine had been havens almost for the sake of it, as I had had nothing at the Community to wish to escape from, unless it was too much loving attention.

As children both Allan and I were pampered by everybody around us; children have a pretty good life in the Community anyway, revered as the product of two souls' communing and respected for their unblemished new soul, but my brother and I were given a particularly easy ride because of the tragedy of our orphanhood. Being a Leapyearian and the Elect of God, I suppose I had one increment of indulgence more even than my brother, though such was the obvious determination by all around to recompense us for the sadness of our plight through diligent applications of love and the gratification of all but our most outrageous wishes, that I doubt Allan ever suffered because of my superior rank, unless it was the self-inflicted pain we call jealousy.

I think all this would have applied to any Community children who had lost their parents when they were so young, but certainly it can have done us no harm that we were grandchildren of the Founder, and that he transferred so much of his love for his son and his son's wife onto us, and took such an interest in our upbringing that any kindness extended to us was almost as good as a tribute paid directly to Salvador himself (in one way it was actually better as it did not smack of sycophancy).

All this is not to say that any child may simply run riot within the Community; far from it, but providing you are not seen as exploiting your privileged position with too ruthless a degree of opportunism

259

and do not directly challenge adult authority, it is possible to live so well as a child at High Easter Offerance that when an adult tells you these are the best years of your life, you can almost believe them.

*

I sat on the rusted wreck of an old truck, its russet body lying perforated and submerged by grasses and weeds, surrounded by gently swaying young pine trees a couple of miles west of the the farm. I was sitting on the old lorry's roof, gazing out over the brown, glinting back of the gently flowing river. On the far bank, beyond the weeds and nettles, a herd of Friesians cropped the green quilt of the field, moving slowly across my field of vision from left to right, images of unthinking contentment engrossed in their methodical absorption.

I had seen Grandma Yolanda back to her car, still making reassuring noises and gently refusing her offers of further help. She hugged and kissed me and told me that she would be staying in Stirling that night, to be nearby in case I needed her. I assured her I wouldn't and told her to do whatever she had been going to do. She insisted this had been her plan all along, and that she would drive the few miles into the town, check in and then phone to leave the name of the hotel with the Woodbeans. I had not the heart to refuse her, so agreed that this was a good and helpful idea. She left with only a few tears. I waved her away and then returned to the farm.

I went up to my room in the farmhouse. It is a small room with a single dormer window and sloping ceilings. It contained a hammock, a small wooden desk and chair, one chest of drawers with a paraffin lamp on it, and an old wardrobe sitting – slightly lopsidedly on the old, uneven floorboards – in one corner. Aside from these things, there were a few clothes (*very* few, as those being sent from Bath hadn't turned up yet) and one or two small souvenirs of my modest travels. That was more or less it.

How little I had to show for my life, looked at from this perspective, I thought. And yet how rich I had always felt it was! All my life, all my worth and being were invested in the rest of the

Community, in the people and the lands and the buildings and the continuance of our life here. That was what and where you had to look to find the measure of me; not at these few paltry personal comforts.

It was a while, thinking about all this, before I realised that I hadn't got my kit-bag back; it had been left over in the mansion house. Well, there was nothing in it I needed immediately. I changed into a coarse white cotton shirt with a collar and cuffs that had seen better days and donned my one other jacket, an old tweed thing with worn leather elbow patches. It had probably been a fisherman's; when it had been brought back from the charity shop in Stirling for me there was a small fishing fly lodged deep in the corner of one pocket. I kept the leather trousers on; I only possessed the two pairs I'd taken with me on my journey and they were both – with luck – still en route from the hotel in Bath. I re-straightened the brim of my travelling hat and hung it up behind the wardrobe door. Then I went for a walk and ended up sitting on the roof of the old truck, a few miles up the river bank.

I suppose you could label what passed there as meditation, but that might be to dignify it over much. Really I was just letting everything that had happened recently wash through me and from me, imagining that the river I gazed at was the stream of events I had been submerged in for the last nine days, and it was all now flowing away, leaving no more than a thin deposit of memory behind like a skin of river mud.

I wanted to feel washed clean, absolved of whatever I had been accused of, before I went back to the farm and my Grandfather.

I could not understand what had happened. I had held the tiny *zhlonjiz* jar in my hand for the first time in the house of Gertie Possil; I knew I had not stolen it. I had read the note that the vial had come wrapped in, I could recall exactly the feel of its paper between my fingers, see the writing on it – enough like Salvador's for it certainly not to be in any way suspicious – and almost smell it.

I had thought the unction's inclusion in my kit-bag a gesture that was both practical and sweet; it had never occurred to me that it might be a trick.

261

I tried to think why it had been done, and by whom. I had to face the fact that there might be poisoned thoughts behind the smiling faces of my fellows in our Order. I was the privileged one, after all; brought to my exalted prominence by a simple accident of birth. Certainly I had the Gift of Healing to recommend me to my fellow faithfuls' favour, but that has always seemed extra, something that never sat entirely square with our Faith in its purest form. Part of our creed promoted the idea that those born on the 29th of February *became* different and better because they were led to realise how much this mattered and symbolised, rather than emerged already semi-divine from the womb (otherwise how does one account for the fact that those born on that date in the past have not been especially gifted or wise?). In a sense, it is just luck that determines who is born a Leapyearian, even though there is a hint in the *Orthography* that God has a fingertip on the scales if not a hand in the whole business. So might not one – or even some – of my fellows feel aggrieved at my rank and suspicious of my uncanny power, convinced in their own minds that they were both more deserving, and more pure? In theory they ought to feel glad for me, support me and – if not actually worship me – honour and venerate me, and accept that God would be unlikely to have let somebody utterly lacking in worth be born into my position or receive my gift, but I cannot deceive myself that in such matters theory always carries the day in the depths of the human soul, or that our followers are somehow immune from irrationality, jealousy and even hate.

I found it hard even to imagine that my Grandfather himself could be behind this; perhaps only the memory of that sudden, shocking slap to my face made it remotely thinkable. Could Salvador himself feel envious of me? It hardly made sense; his whole life – since his rebirth on the storm-scoured Harrisian beach that night – had led towards the exalted state that first his son Christopher and now I occupied and would, perhaps, pass on to my offspring (not that it *had* to be me; a Luskentyrian Leapyearian is a Luskentyrian Leapyearian, after all, but we had made it a direct, in-family line so far and such seeming coincidences tend to develop a momentum and a tradition – even a theology – of their own), but who was to say how rational he was being, as he came to appreciate the imminence of his own death?

Allan was another man with cause to resent me; under a different system, all the Community and Order might fall to him on Grandfather's death (though how did one take account of Brigit and Rhea and Calli and Astar, and even uncle Mo? After all, neither of Salvador's original two marriages had been sanctioned by the state or established church). But what could he stand to gain? Nothing could alter the fact of my birth-date – the event had been observed by half the women of the Order – or shake what was one of the central tenets of our Faith; what were we if we did not believe in the interstitial, out-of-the-way nature of blessedness, exemplified by that one day in one thousand four hundred and sixty-one? Allan already controlled much of the day-to-day running of the Order; he had more power than I could imagine wanting for myself and we had never really disagreed over the way we saw the Order going when the sad time came that meant my accession. To attack me was to attack the Order itself and the very Faith through which Allan drew his influence, threatening everything.

Calli? Astar? Together or alone they might see me as a threat to their authority, but they too stood to lose much more than they could possibly gain. Erin? Jess? Somebody else who somehow felt confident of producing a Leapyearian next year, and wanted me out of the way, or at least compromised, beforehand?

None of these possibilities seemed to make much sense.

As for how it had been done, getting the vial itself would have been easy; it normally resided in the unlocked box on the altar in the meeting hall, which itself was always open. Getting it into my kit-bag would hardly have been more difficult; I recalled packing the bag in my room and leaving it there while I met with my Grandfather, Allan and Erin again. Later I went across the courtyard to brother Indra's workshop to see how the inner-tube boat was progressing, and then returned to my room to fetch the bag and leave it outside the meeting hall in the mansion house while we all convened again to pray and sing.

Anybody could have slipped up to my room, or dropped the vial into my bag while it was outside the meeting room; there was no lock on my room door – I don't think there is a functioning lock anywhere in the farmhouse – and we are anyway simply unused to guarding property or caring much about chattels; there is no culture of watchfulness or wariness in our Order that would raise suspicions in the first place.

The last opportunity somebody would have had to put the vial in my bag would have been that morning, as I was getting into the inner-tube boat; who had carried my bag from the farm? How many people had handled it before it was delivered into my hands?

I recalled that I'd found the *zhlonjiz* vial at the bottom of my kit-bag, implying that it had been hidden by somebody with plenty of time to place it there rather than having been simply dropped into my bag, but the jar had been tiny and – jiggled and bounced around as I'd walked from the coast into Edinburgh – it would have had plenty of time to work its way down from the top to the bottom of the kit-bag. I'd opened the bag twice after I'd packed it in my room, I thought, for food and for the vial of river mud, so maybe I would have seen the little vial sitting on top of the other things packed in there, but – again due to its size – maybe not.

I was a very poor investigator, I thought. I had failed to confront Morag and now I was failing to work out when, how and why somebody had made it look as if I was a common thief.

I shook my head at my own dreadful incompetence, and rose with creaking trousers if not joints to dust myself down, bid farewell to the river and return to whatever it was I had to face at the Community.

*

I returned to the mansion house at about six; in the office, Allan said that Salvador had eaten early and was having a nap; he'd call me if and when Grandfather wanted to see me. I went to the farmhouse for the evening meal, eaten in the kitchen with various Brothers and Sisters in an unusual and strained atmosphere which was only relieved by the children being barely less boisterous and loud than normal. Sister Calli, who was supervising the kitchen that evening, did not speak to me, and made a point of not serving me my food. Astar was kinder if still as quiet as ever, just coming up to me and standing by me, patting me on the shoulder. A few of the younger ones tried to ask me questions but were hushed by Calli or Calum.

I went back over to the mansion house. I told Sister Erin I would be in the library, and sat in there trying to read passages from the previous edition of the *Orthography* in a restless, unsettled manner until I gave up and just sat, looking round those thousands of books and wondering how many I had read and how many more I still had to read.

I picked up *The Prince* and read a few of my favourite passages, then I returned to Erin and said I'd be in the meeting room – the mansion house's old ballroom, where the organ was.

I sat there at the old organ, playing it silently save for the click and clack of my fingers on the keys and my feet on the pedals, pulling out stops and sweeping my hands over the keyboard, caressing it and pummelling it, humming and hissing to myself on occasion, but mostly just hearing the music in my head, its flowing, pulsing power and body-shaking reverberations existing only between my ears. I played until my fingers hurt, and then Sister Jess came to fetch me.

Jess left me in the sitting room of Grandfather's quarters while she checked he was quite ready to see me. She reappeared from the bedroom, closing the door on the dark space behind. 'He's having another bath,' she said, sounding exasperated. 'He's in a funny mood today. Do you mind waiting?'

'No,' I said.

Jess smiled. 'He said to break out the drinks; shall we?'

'Why not?' I said, smiling.

Sister Jess opened the drinks cabinet; I declined a whisky, having not long since got rid of my hang-over from the previous night, and settled for a glass of wine. Sister Jess chose the whisky, well watered.

We settled down on a couple of seat-boarded but otherwise quite plumply luxurious couches and talked for a while. Sister Jess is a doctor; she is slim and has long black hair she wears in a single long plait. She is about forty and has been with us for nearly fourteen years. Her daughter Helen is thirteen and Salvador may or may not be the child's father.

I have always got on fairly well with Jess, though I sometimes wonder to what extent she feels that I usurp some of her powers with my ability to Heal.

I told her of my trip down south; she said that at the time she'd thought I was mad to travel to Edinburgh by inner-tube, but congratulated me on getting there. She took a dimmer view of interfering with train signalling systems, but let it pass. There was no embargo I had been told of regarding the things I had found out in England, so, while I did swear her to secrecy until we both knew how widely Salvador wanted such facts to be disseminated, I felt free to tell her about Morag's alter ego, Fusillada. She blinked rapidly at that point, and almost choked on her whisky.

'You *saw* one of these videos?' she asked.

'By sheer luck, yes.'

She glanced at the closed door to Salvador's bedroom. 'Hmm; I wonder what he feels about *that*?'

'I take it Allan's told him all this?'

She leaned over towards me, with another glance at the door. 'I think he overheard quite a bit from outside the office door,' she said quietly.

'Oh,' I said.

'Let's have another drink,' she said. 'About time the lamps were lit, too.'

We lit the lamps and recharged our glasses.

'How is Salvador?' I asked her. 'Has he been keeping all right?'

She laughed quietly. 'Strong as an ox,' she said. 'He's fine. Been tiring himself out a bit recently and drinking too much whisky, but I think that's just all this revising he's doing.'

'Oh,' I said. 'He's managing all right with that himself?'

'Allan's been helping him; him and Erin, sometimes.'

'Oh. Well, that's good.'

'It's keeping him busy,' she said, glancing at the door again. 'I think he's getting impatient for the Festival.'

'I suppose everybody is, a bit.'

'Some with better reason than him,' she said quietly, leaning forward and with a conspiratorial grin. I did my best to reciprocate the expression. 'But, anyway,' she said, sitting back, 'what happened after you were arrested?' She held her hand up over her mouth, giggling.

I regaled her with the rest of my story, settling into the swing of its telling with, by now, practised ease. Grandma Yolanda was about to make her appearance – and Jess was still laughing at the thought of me being arrested and being televised in the process – when we realised our glasses were empty again. Jess listened quietly at the bedroom door, then tiptoed away with her finger to her lips and whispered, 'Singing. Still in the bath,' as she made her way to the drinks cabinet.

'Thanks,' I said, accepting my refilled glass.

'Cheers.'

'Mud in your eye.'

'You *have* been with Yolanda, haven't you?'

'She does rather rub off on you,' I admitted as we resumed our seats. I took up the threads of my story. I had almost finished when there was a ringing sound; the spring-hung bell up in one corniced corner of the room went on jangling as Jess straightened her plain grey shift and went to the bedroom door. I undid the laces on my boots.

She stuck her head round, I heard Grandfather's voice, then Jess turned and nodded to me. I drained my glass and ascended into the bedroom.

The door closed behind me.

Grandfather sat at one end of the room, against a huge pile of cushions. Candles burned on the shelf that ran all around the dark space, filling it with their soft yellow light and the heady fumes of their scent. Joss-sticks were fanned out in a small brass holder on the shelf near Salvador. My Grandfather was plump, pale, voluminously robed and his face was surrounded with fluffily dry white curly hair. He looked like a cross between Buddha and Santa Claus. He sat looking at me.

I made the Sign and bowed slowly to him; the bed moved gently

267

underneath my sock-clad feet, like a gentle oceanic swell. Salvador nodded briefly when I straightened. He pointed to a place close in front of him to his left.

By his right hand would have been better, but probably too much to hope for. I sat where he had indicated, cross-legged. Grandfather's room-size bed was the one place one was allowed to sit without a Sitting Board; the softness was oddly unsettling when one's buttocks were habituated to the hardness of wood.

He reached under one of the giant cushions at his back and produced a bottle and two chunky cut glasses. He handed one glass to me, set the other on the shelf near him and poured us both some whisky. More drink, I thought. Ah well.

He raised his glass to me, though his expression remained serious. We drank. The whisky was smooth and I didn't cough.

He gave a great long sigh and sat back amongst the pillows. He looked at his glass and then, slowly, to me.

'So, Isis: do you want to tell me why?' he asked; his deep, luxuriant voice sounded thick, half choked.

'Grandfather,' I said, 'I did not take the vial. It was in my kit-bag. I didn't know it was there until I found it when I was at Gertie Possil's.'

He looked into my eyes for a long time. I returned his gaze. He shook his head and looked across the room.

'So you had no hand in this at all; no idea it had been put there?'

'None.'

'Well then, who do you want to accuse, Isis?'

'I don't want to accuse anybody. I've thought about who could have done this, and it could have been anybody. I have no idea who.'

'I've been told that you claim there was a . . . note,' he said, pronouncing the last word with the effect of somebody picking something distasteful up by the corner between thumb and forefinger.

'It said, "In case you need it", or something similar; I can't remember the exact words. It was signed with an "S".'

'But this has disappeared, of course.'

'Yes.'

'Weren't you even slightly suspicious?' he asked, a sour look on his face. 'Didn't it seem odd to you that I might have given you our most precious substance, our last link with Luskentyre, to take into the midst of the Unsaved?'

I looked down at my glass. 'I took it as a compliment,' I said. My face felt warm. 'I was surprised and I was flattered, but it never crossed my mind to be suspicious; I thought that you were giving me your blessing and trying to ensure the success of my mission by giving me something which would both succour me and be of practical value.'

'And was it? Of practical value, I mean.'

'No.'

'You took some.'

'I did. It . . . I was not able to make use of it. I don't know why. I hoped to hear more clearly the Voice of God, but . . .'

'So you then tried one of the Unsaved's illegal drugs.'

'I did.'

'Which didn't work either.'

'It did not.'

He shook his head and drank the rest of the whisky in his glass. He looked at my glass as he reached for the bottle. I finished my drink too. He refilled both glasses. I cleared my throat, eyes watering.

'And am I to understand, Isis, that our Sister Morag's fame does not come from . . . holy music, or even music in any form, after all, but from performing the sexual act to be recorded on film and sold to whosoever of the Benighted might wish to purchase such a thing?'

'It would seem so.'

'You're sure?'

'Quite positive. There was one close-up of her face in quite bright sunshine; she was sucking—'

'Yes. Well, we'll believe you, on this, for now, Isis, but I dare say we shall have to confirm this for ourselves, unpleasant though the task might be.'

'That may be possible without having to harbour a television

269

set amongst us; one of Brother Zeb's colleagues called Boz was sure that he had seen a pornographic magazine which featured Morag.'

Grandfather was shaking his head sadly.

'I think it's worth mentioning,' I said, 'that while I was unable to discover any evidence that Morag still plays music in public, it is still not impossible that she does so, though—'

'Oh, enough,' he said angrily.

'Well, it could still be—'

'What difference would it make, anyway?' he said loudly. He gulped at his whisky.

I sipped mine. 'It could still be seen as holy work in a sense, Grandfather,' I said. 'Certainly it is done for profit and involves the means of the dissemination of lies and Clutter, but still the act itself is a holy one, and—'

'Oh,' he said, sneering at me over his glass. 'And what would you know about that, Isis?'

I felt my face colour again, but I did not let my gaze fall from his. 'What I know is what you have told me; what you have told us all, in your teachings!' I said.

He looked away. 'Teachings change,' he said, his voice rumbling like thunder from those dense clouds of hair.

I stared at him. He was looking into his glass.

I swallowed. 'They surely cannot change to the extent that we join the Benighted in their fear of love!' I cried.

'No,' he told me. 'That's not what I meant.' He sighed, then nodded at my glass. 'Drink up; we'll find the truth of this yet.'

I drank, gulping the whisky down and almost gagging. Was this some strange new ceremony? Did we now believe that one could find the truth at the bottom of a bottle? What was going on? What was he talking about? He refilled our glasses again. He set the bottle down with a thump on the shelf between two heavy, flickering candles.

'Isis,' he said, and his voice was suddenly small and almost plaintive. His eyes glittered. 'Isis; is *any* of this true?'

'All of it, Grandfather!' I said, leaning forward. He reached out and took my free hand, holding it.

270

He shook his head in an angry, frustrated way, gulped some whisky down and said, 'I don't know, Isis; I don't know.' There were tears in his eyes. 'I'm told one thing, I'm told another thing; I don't know who to believe, who's telling the truth.' He drank some more. 'I know I'm old; I'm not young any more, but I'm not confused; I'm made confused, you see? I hear people say things and I wonder if they can be true, and I listen to the Voice of God and I wonder sometimes if what They say can be right, though I know it must, so I wonder is it something in me? But I know it can't be; after all these years . . . I just know, you see. *Do* you see, child?'

'I think so, Grandfather.'

He squeezed my hand, which he still held, on the covers.

'Good girl. Good girl.' He drained his glass, shook his head and gave a watery smile. 'You and me, Isis; we're the ones, aren't we? You are my grandchild, but you are the Elect, special like me; aren't you?'

I nodded hesitantly. 'By the grace of God and by your teaching, yes, I believe so, of course.'

'You believe in God, you believe in the Voice?' he said anxiously, urgently, squeezing my hand even tighter. It was starting to hurt.

'Yes,' I said. 'Yes, of course.'

'You believe in what is said, what is heard, what I am told?'

'With all my heart and soul,' I assured him, trying to flex the hand he gripped.

'Then *why are you lying to me?*' he roared, throwing his glass to one side and throwing himself at me. I fell back, toppling over as he thumped into me and pushed me down, pinning me down by the shoulders, my still-crossed legs pressed up into my chest by his belly; I had to put my hand holding the whisky glass out to one side to avoid spilling it, while my other hand lay on my chest, clutching involuntarily at the neck of my shirt. I stared up at my Grandfather's furiously livid face.

'I'm not lying!' I cried.

'You are, child! Admit you are! Open your soul! Let out this poison!' His body pressed down on mine, forcing my knees into my chest. He shook me by the shoulders; I felt whisky slop out of my glass onto my hand, chilling it. I felt around, trying to find

271

anywhere I could leave the glass without it tipping over and spilling its contents, so I could have two hands free, but all I could feel was rumpled bedclothes, nowhere firm.

'What poison?' I gasped, breathless from the pressure on my chest. 'There is no poison! My conscience is clear!'

'Don't lie to me, Isis!'

'I'm not lying!' I shouted again. 'It is all true!'

'Why persist?' he roared, shaking me again. 'Why add to your sin?' His breath was warm and smelled of whisky.

'I am not! There is no sin to add to!'

'You took that sacrament! You stole it!'

'No! No! Why should I?'

'Because you hate me!' he yelled.

'I don't!' I gasped painfully. 'I don't; I love you! Grandfather, why are you doing this? *Please* get off me!'

He slid off me to one side, falling against the bottom of the tumbled slope of pillows and cushions, lying on his side next to me, staring at me, eyes still wet with tears. 'You don't love me,' he said, his voice hoarse. 'You want me dead, out of the way. You want everything for yourself now.'

I struggled upright onto my knees, put the whisky glass on the shelf at last and kneeled by him, my hand on his shoulder as he lay there, wheezing, staring away at the far wall.

'Don't love me,' he mumbled. 'You don't love me . . .'

'Grandfather, I love you for yourself, for all you've done for me, the way you've looked after Allan and me as though we were your own children, but I love you doubly; I love you as our Faith's Founder, too. I can't imagine ever loving anybody half as much, not ever; not a quarter as much!' I lowered my face until it was beside his. 'Please; you must believe me. You're the most important person there will ever be in my life! No matter what happens! I love you beyond . . . everything!'

He turned his face from me, into the bedclothes. 'No,' he said, his voice muffled but steady and calm. 'No, I don't believe that is so; I have listened to God's Voice and They have given me the measure of your love for me. It has been beyond everything but it is not now . . . though I think it is beyond you, indeed.'

I didn't understand. 'Grandfather; you are everything to all of us. You are our light, our guide, our OverSeer! We rely on you. Without you we shall all be orphans, but with your teachings, with your *Orthography* and your example we shall at least have hope, no matter what the future holds. I know I can never be you and never equal you; I would never even attempt to do so, but perhaps, as the Elect, and as your son's daughter, I can reflect some part of your glory without disgracing it, and, with your teachings as my guide, eventually grow to be a fit leader of the Order. That is my—'

He turned his head to look at me, eyes bright with tears in the soft yellow candlelight. 'These are fine words, Isis, but you have known an easy life. We have kept you away from the harshness of it, from sacrifice and doubt and pain.'

'I am ready for all of them, for my Faith!'

His eyes searched mine. 'I doubt it,' he said, giving the smallest shake of his head. 'You say so, but . . . I doubt it. You only think you have faith.'

'I do have faith!'

'Untested, Isis. Mine has been tested, yours—'

'Test mine, then!'

'I cannot,' he said. 'God can, and would do, through me, but I'd risk losing you.'

'What?' I cried, pressing closer to him. 'What have They said?'

He looked away again, face in the bedclothes. 'Do you trust me?'

'With my life!' I said, hugging him fiercely.

He turned to me again. '*Do* you trust me?'

'I do.'

His gaze shifted across my eyes. 'Isis,' he said. He seemed to hesitate.

'What?' I said, hugging him.

'Will you trust me?' he whispered.

'I will trust you.'

'Will you believe me?'

'I will believe you.'

He gave a deep, deep sigh, and rose slowly, almost painfully up

273

from the bed covers. I helped him up and he nodded in thanks. He stood facing the shelf where the whisky bottle sat between the scented candles and the joss-sticks burned in their brassy holders. Standing there on that unsteady, shifting surface with him, my head was filled with the intoxicating warmth of the perfumed room. He took a step forward and blew out several candles, leaving one burning by the whisky bottle. He stepped to one side, and blew out more of the candles, dimming the room. He went along the wall, blowing out all but one other candle, then started blowing out the candles on the shelf beside the door to the sitting room beyond. I turned, watching him, wondering. He blew out all but two candles on the far wall, beneath the heavily curtained windows. By the door to the bathroom, he paused, his back to me. 'We must disrobe,' he said.

'Disrobe?' I asked.

He nodded. 'Disrobe,' he said, and leaning forward, blew out another candle.

I swallowed. I could barely think. What else was I to do? I had said I believed, I had said that I trusted. I did not know what it might be Grandfather had in mind, what he had been told to do by God, but I knew that it must be holy and blessed and – to my shame I thought of it, I confess – at least I knew that it could not be what the most prurient minds might imagine, for that was banned by the *Orthography*.

'Of course,' I said. I took off my jacket and placed it folded on the bed at my feet. I began to undo my shirt buttons. Grandfather took a deep breath and blew out another line of candles, not looking at me as I took off my shirt and then undid the button and zip on my leather trousers. He extinguished a last couple of candles. There were only half a dozen left burning round the walls of the whole large room now, their frugal light reducing everything, so that where there had been soft light there was now shadow, and where there had been shadows there was now darkness.

My mouth was dry as I slid my trousers off and placed them with my shirt and jacket. Grandfather faced away from me, turned towards the huge pile of pillows. He crossed his arms, reached down to his waist and with a grunt, and a slight stagger, pulled his robe up over his head. Underneath, he was quite naked. I had taken off my socks and now wore only my knickers. Seen from behind, Grandfather's body was bulky and solid; not as fat and soft as I'd thought. Certainly it was an old man's waist, bowing out, not narrowing, but there was a bull-like flatness across the small of his back that I doubted many men his age could boast. 'We must be quite naked,' he said quietly, still facing away from me, addressing the wall.

I felt my heart thud in my chest. My hands were shaking as I slipped off my undergarments.

He looked upwards, as if inspecting the room's ornate plaster frieze.

'The Creator's ways are many and strange,' he said, as though talking to the shelf. 'We question, we think, and we question our thinking, trying to determine what is right, what is true and what is false, what is given from above and beyond and what comes from within.' I saw him shake his head, slowly. 'We cannot ever know completely, and eventually we have to stop questioning.' He fell silent. He stood for a while, then nodded, again slowly. His shoulders quivered, and he put his hands up to his eyes. 'Oh, Isis,' he said, his voice breaking. 'Is God always right? I have always believed that They are, but . . .' His head bowed and his shoulders shook.

I stood and watched for a moment, then stepped forward, terribly aware of my nakedness, and stretched out my arms to put my hands on his shoulders. He clamped his hands on mine, then turned quickly and faced me, pulling me closer until his full belly touched my flat one. 'We are wisps, Isis,' he hissed, taking me by the shoulders and gripping me tightly. 'We are reeds caught in the storm, pulled away by the flood; who are we to stand in Their way?'

I shook my head, hoping that my eyes weren't too wide. 'I don't know,' I said, for want of anything better.

He looked down in between us and nodded vigorously. 'Let us sit, Isis,' he said.

We sat; I in the lotus position, he on his haunches with his arms resting on his knees. He looked me up and down, and I felt good and fine and pure and brazen at the same time, flushed with alcohol and God knows what. He shook his head. 'Ah, Isis; you are the very vision!' he breathed.

'I am God's image, as are we all, in our own fashion,' I replied, my voice shaking.

'No, no; more than that,' he said breathlessly, still staring at my body. 'What God has said . . .' He looked up into my eyes and slowly spread his arms wide. 'Isis,' he said thickly, 'come to me . . .'

I parted from my lotus position and kneeled forward, tentatively extending my arms. He took my hands in his and pulled me forward to him, enfolding me in his warmth and pushing my arms out above and to the side.

'Isis, Isis,' he said, burying his head between my breasts, breathing in hard.

'Grandfather,' I said into the clearing in the thicket of his hair that was his bald patch. '*What* has God said?'

'Isis!' he said again, raising his head to mine and hugging me tighter so that I could feel each fold and roll of fat on his torso as I was pulled into him. 'Isis!' he said, rubbing his head from side to side between my breasts. 'We are in Their power, under Their control! We must do as They say!'

His hands cupped my buttocks, kneading them. He raised his head and brought his face up to mine. 'We must join our souls, child. We must commune together!' He pushed his mouth towards mine.

'What?' I yelped, bringing my arms up to his shoulders to try and push him away. 'But, Grandfather!'

'I know!' he cried hoarsely, as his head turned this way and that, trying to bring our lips together. 'I know it seems wrong, but I hear Their voice!'

'But it's forbidden!' I said, straining at his shoulders, still trying to push him back. He was forcing me over and down now, onto the bed beneath. 'We are two generations apart!'

'It was forbidden; it isn't any more. That was a mistake. The Voice was clear about that.' He pushed me down so that my back thumped onto the bed; I managed to wriggle my legs to one side so that I was half on my side to him. He held me tightly round the waist, still trying to kiss me. 'Don't you see, Isis? This is meant. We are the Elect; the chosen ones. The rules are different for us. This is holy; this is ordained by God.'

'But you're my *Grandfather*!' I cried, bringing one hand up to my face to push his seeking, probing lips away. One of his hands was trying to push down to my belly; I held it with my other hand.

'Isis! We don't have to take any notice of the Unsaved's stupid rules! We're marked out, we're special, we can do what we want and what God decrees! What have their stupid rules and regulations got to do with our Holy Purpose?'

I was still wrestling with his hand as it tried to push down to my groin; his bearded face was panting and sweating above me; he kissed my lips for a moment but I twisted my head away.

'But I don't *want* to do this!' I wailed.

'*Want*?' he laughed bitterly. 'What has what either of us *want* got to do with this? We do what God tells us to do! We both have to submit to Their will, Isis! We both have to submit! We both have to trust; trust and believe! You promised to trust; you promised to trust and believe, remember?'

'But not this!'

'Is your love of God conditional then, Isis?' he asked breathlessly, still trying to work his sweat-slicked hand between my legs. His breathing was very quick and urgent now and his face was bright red. 'Do you only do what God insists you do when it suits you? Is that it? Is it?'

'No!' I spluttered, my own breathing becoming difficult as his weight bore down on me. 'But this must be a false signal! God would not demand this!'

'What? An act of love? What is that to demand? Did Buddha hesitate to renounce all his worldly goods? Did Mohammed hesitate to take up arms and make war? Did Abraham not take his son to the mountain to kill him, because God demanded it? Would he not have done so if God had not stopped him? All They demand here is an act of love, Isis; an act of love, to prove we are both true! We both must *submit*!' He gave a grunt and twisted his hand free of mine; it dived between my tightly clenched legs, trying to finger my sex; I heaved and wriggled out from underneath him, rolling away over the bed; he grabbed at me, catching my ankle as I tried to stand, bringing me down on all fours. 'Submit, Isis, submit! Prove your love for God!' He tried to mount me from behind but I wrestled him off.

'This is not you!' I shouted, and scuttled away, grabbing up my clothes as I stood on the bed's unsteady surface. 'God could not ask this!'

My Grandfather kneeled on the bed, his engorged manhood poking up at the underside of his belly like a supporting strut. His face set into an expression I had never seen before: a look of furious, seething loathing that produced a terrible feeling of emptiness and sickness in me.

'You would deny God then, Isis?' he said thickly. I backed into a closed door; it was the one to the bathroom, not the exit to the sitting room; he was between me and it. He spread his arms wide. 'You would deny the sacrament that is the holy joy of souls' communion?'

I leaned back against the door and pulled on one leg of my trousers. 'If God wanted this They would have spoken to me as well,' I said.

'They spoke to *me*!' he roared, thumping himself on his chest with one fist. He lunged at me as I stood on one leg to put my other leg in the trousers. I'd half expected he would, and so was ready for him. I jumped to one side and escaped him but dropped my jacket and socks onto the bed. I hopped across the bed, dragging on the trousers and pulling them up, my shirt wedged under one armpit. I had a clear run at the door to the outside now. I stood there, breathing hard and looking at him as he stood up by the bathroom door, a pale shadow in the flickering candlelight; his chest and belly heaved with every breath. His penis had gone limp now. He wiped his face with one hand.

'You Judas,' he breathed.

'Grandfather, please—' I began, pulling on my shirt.

'You *heathen*!' he rasped, a tiny fleck of spittle arcing through the air caught in the candlelight. 'Apostate! Infidel! Misbeliever! You Unsaved *wretch*!'

278

'This is not fair, Grandfather,' I said, my voice almost breaking.
I tucked in my shirt tails. 'You are—'

'Fair?' he said, grimacing, loading the word with sarcasm. 'What
is *fair*? God does not deal in *fairness*; God *commands*. You have
no right to deny Them.'

'I do not believe I am,' I said, trying not to cry.

'You do not believe *me*,' he whispered.

'I believe you have been . . . misled,' I said, biting my lip.

'Oh, *you* do, do you? You're barely more than a child; what do
you know of God's Word?'

'Enough to know They would not ask this, not without telling
me as well as you.'

'You vain child, Isis. You have sinned against God and against
your own Faith.' He shook his head and padded across the bed to
where his robe lay. While he slipped it on over his head I retrieved
my socks, knickers and jacket.

'I think we ought to forget this, Grandfather,' I said, putting
on my socks. He looked about, then picked up the glass he had
thrown across the bed. He poured himself another whisky.

'I can't forget this,' he said. 'God can't, either. I don't know if
this can ever be forgiven or forgotten.'

I put on my jacket. 'Well, I think it would be for the best if we
both forgot what's happened here.'

'You are a thief and a misbeliever, child,' he said calmly, not
looking at me but studying his whisky glass critically. 'It is not in
my power to forgive you.'

'I am *not* a thief; I am *not* a misbeliever,' I said, and then, despite
myself, started to weep. The tears stung my eyes and flowed down
my hot, flushed cheeks. I was furious at myself for behaving so
girlishly. '*You* are the one in the wrong; not me,' I said angrily,
speaking through my sobs. 'I have done *nothing*; nothing wrong.
I am falsely accused and all you can do is try to . . . to have your
way with your own grand-daughter!'

He gave a single scoffing laugh.

'You are the one who needs forgiveness, not me,' I told him,
sniffing back my tears and wiping my cheeks with my knickers.

He waved one hand dismissively, still not looking at me. 'You stupid, selfish ... foolish child,' he said, shaking his head. 'Get out of my sight. When I look on you again it will be to accept your confession and apology.'

I sucked in my breath. 'Grandfather!' I cried, despairing. 'What is wrong with you? What has changed you? Why are you *being* like this?'

'Isis, child, if you can accept your guilt and answer it in front of me, before the Festival, you may yet be able to take your proper part in that celebration,' he said, still studying his glass. He finished his whisky and then walked across the bed to the bathroom door; he opened it – golden lamp-light spilled from the open door – and closed it behind him. I stood there for a moment, then wept a little more. I stuffed the knickers in my pocket and left the room.

The sitting room beyond was unoccupied; one lamp shone on a desk by the drinks cabinet. I took my boots and ran out, sitting to do up my laces on the top step of the stairs, by the light of a wall candle. Sniffing and blinking, I walked down the stairs and out of the silent mansion house.

CHAPTER
SEVENTEEN

The sky over the courtyard was deep, deep blue, scattered with the brighter stars and enthroning a near-full moon. The monthly Service to mark the full moon would be only a few days away now.

Voices came from the lit windows of the farmhouse and the sound of muffled hammering from the workshop by the forge. Woodsmoke and cooking smells tugged at my attention, comforting and banal. I walked across the courtyard cobbles in a daze. My steps led to the archway facing the path that led to the river and the bridge. I stood beneath the archway, with the Community around and above and behind me, gazing out across the lawn and the curving path that sloped down towards the trees that marked the line of the river. Moonlight cast a faint shadow of the orchard wall across the path and reflected off the glass of the greenhouse on the other side. I looked up at the dark swell of the hills to the south, piled against the indigo of the sky like a huge wave.

I could hear singing and the sound of a guitar coming from behind me, and childish laughter, far away, quickly gone.

A wind rustled the tops of the trees. I walked down the path, not sure where I was really going or what I was meaning to do. The path was dark under the rustling trees; over the river it was a little lighter again, and the old bridge looked deceptively solid and whole, bowed over the dark waters. Beyond, a sliver of yellow electric light came from a curtained window of the Woodbeans' little turreted house.

I made my way to the middle of the bridge and then stepped gingerly across the holed timbers to its downstream edge. I stood at the centre there, just behind the rusted iron shield that held the indecipherable coat of arms, facing east. I put up my arms and held onto the rough, gritty-feeling surfaces of two girders, and watched the river. It seemed solid and unmoving in the darkness, only the

283

occasional muffled gurgle betraying its slow, untroubled current. After a while I thought I could make out the faintest of watery shadows on the waters, as the moon shone through the bridge in the increasing gloom. I could see it only when I looked away, and when I tried to see myself in that shadow – waving one arm slowly over my head – could not.

An owl hooted in the trees around the driveway and a car's engine sounded in the distance, the note faintly rising and falling as it passed unseen on the road. A couple of tiny, quick shapes flitted under the bridge, barely glimpsed, and must have been bats.

'Oh God,' I whispered. 'Help me.'

I closed my eyes and stood there in the darkness, listening with my soul, trying to call up the clear, calm voice of the Creator, abandoning myself to the silence so that I might hear Them. I heard: the river, like darkness liquefied, beneath me as it flowed; the owl, soft and distant and mysterious, a cry of hunting that sounded like longing; the susurrus of air shivering the branches, twigs and leaves; the far-away grumble of engine noise, dying on the wind. I heard my own heart beat, twin-pulsed: Is-is, Is-is, Is-is . . .

Images came, snatches of conversation, crowding, jostling their way to the front of my mind; Grandfather's body, Grandfather's voice. I shook my head slowly, heavily. My thoughts were still too noisy, drowning out anything else; I felt that God was there, that They were listening to me, but I could not hear Them. For all that there was quietness and peace around me – the slow river, the hushing breeze – there was a furious torrent and a shrieking gale in my mind, and I would hear no word of God until they abated.

I stepped carefully back to the wooden pathway that zig-zagged over the bridge's corrupted timbers and walked on to the drive in front of the Woodbeans' house. I looked up at the thin, toy-like house with its single small, cone-roofed turret. The light I had seen earlier came from the sitting room downstairs. I walked up to the door and knocked. I still didn't know whether I was going to try to contact Grandmother Yolanda or not.

Sophi opened the door, surrounded by light, holding a book, her long fawn hair spilling over her shoulders.

'Is!' she said, smiling. 'Hi. I heard you were . . . Are you all right?'

I could not speak; I tried to but I could not. Instead I started to cry again; soundlessly, hopelessly, helplessly. She pulled me to her, across that threshold, dropping the book from her hand and taking me in her arms.

'Isis, Isis, Isis!' she whispered.

*

Bonny, braw and big-boned, Sophi is my comfort and has been so for almost four years. One day, I know, she will find the good, kind man she yearns for and go off with him to be wifely and have babies. We shall be no more after that, and I hope that I am wise enough to accept this and make the most of the friendship we do have, for as long as we have it. I have asked myself if I love Sophi and I think the answer is yes, though it is genuinely the love of a sister, not a lover. I have asked her if she loves me and she has said she does, with all her heart, but it is a big heart, I think, and there will always be a place for others within it. Perhaps I'll never entirely vanish from that place, but I know that my position there will one day be overwhelmed by that good, kind man. I hope not to be jealous. I hope she finds him, but I hope she finds him later rather than sooner.

Mr Woodbean was out that night. I lay in Sophi's arms, on the couch in the sitting room, her blouse wet from my tears, her long hair curled across her breast, her blue-jeaned legs entwined with mine. Sophi has hair the colour of fresh straw. Her eyes are blue with brown flecks, like ocean worlds with islands scattered. She stroked my head, calmly and slowly, the way I imagined a mother would.

I had sobbed into her shoulder for a while after she had brought me into the sitting room, then she had sat me down on the couch and I had pulled myself together enough to tell her about my trip and my adventures – that alone had calmed me, and we even laughed a few times – then I'd come to the events of this evening, and I had broken down once more, throwing the story up as if it was sickness, spitting and hacking it out between great coughing sobs, until all that bile was finally out of me and I could wash it all away with tears.

'Oh, Isis,' she breathed when I was done. 'Are you sure you're all right?'

'Oh, far from it,' I said, sniffing. She handed me another tissue from the box she'd fetched when she'd realised that my tale would involve a lot of blubbing. 'But I'm unharmed, if you mean that.'

'He didn't hurt you?'

'No.' I coughed, then cleared my throat. I dried my eyes with the tissue. 'Except I feel like I've been . . . eviscerated, like everything's been pulled out of me, like there's just a huge space inside me where there used to be . . .' I shook my head. 'Everything. My life, my Faith, my family; the Community.'

'What are you going to do now?'

'I don't know. Part of me wants to go back right now and make my case before all of them; another part just wants to run away.'

'Stay here tonight, eh?' she said, raising my face to hers. She has a broad, tanned face, graced with soft brown freckles she pretends to hate.

'Is that all right?'

'''Course it is,' she said, hugging me.

I laid my head on her breast again. 'He said he wouldn't see me again unless it was to confess and apologise. But I can't.'

'You better not,' she growled, with mock severity, squeezing me.

'I don't know what he'll say to the others, what he'll tell them. I want to believe he'll come to his senses, realise that whatever he thought he heard was a false signal, that he will repent, and ask my forgiveness; that . . . Oh, Sophi; I don't know,' I said, lifting my head and staring into her eyes. 'Could he have put the vial in my bag, meaning to lead to this? Was that his purpose all along? I can't believe that, but what else is there? *Is* there a Devil, after all, and it's in him?'

'You're the theologian,' she said. 'Don't ask me. I think he's just a dirty old man.'

'But he's our Founder!' I protested, sitting up and taking her hands in mine. 'He's done everything for us; revealed so much truth, brought us the light. I still believe that. I still believe in our Faith. I still believe in him. I just can't believe this is really him; it *is* like he's possessed.'

'He's old though, Isis,' Sophi said softly. 'Maybe he's frightened of dying.'

'What?' I exclaimed. 'But he will be in Glory! An adventure awaits him on the other side that will make all this life look a small, insipid, selfish thing. Death holds no fear for us!'

'Even holy people have doubts,' Sophi said, squeezing my hand. 'Don't you ever wonder if you've got it wrong?'

'No!' I said. 'Well, yes, but only because we are told to think of such things by the *Orthography*; we must have faith, but not blind faith. But such theoretical doubt only strengthens our belief. How can Salvador himself really doubt what he's created?'

'Well,' Sophi said, crinkling her nose as she looked thoughtful, 'maybe that's it; you all have him to turn to but he only has God. You know; tough at the top, and all that. Buck stops with him, sort of thing.'

'He has *all* of us to turn to,' I said, though I saw what she meant.

'Anyway, holy men are still men. Perhaps he's just got used to having any of the women in the Order he wants.'

'But it's not like that!' I protested.

'Oh, come on, Isis. It's not far off it.'

'But there's never been any coercion. It's just natural; ours is a faith of love, in all its forms. We're not ashamed of that. And he is – has been . . . still is, I suppose – an attractive man; charismatic. Everybody finds him so; women have always been attracted to him. I mean, they still are,' I said. I ran my fingers through my hair. 'Lordy, he has no need of me.'

'Forbidden fruit, maybe?' Sophi suggested.

'Oh, I don't know!' I wailed, and fell upon her breast once more, clutching at her perfumed warmth. 'Morag avoiding me, Grandfather pursuing me; somebody traducing me . . .'

'Introducing you?' she said, sounding confused.

'Traducing me; defaming me. The whole thing with the *zhlonjiz*.'

'Oh.'

'What's *happening* to my life?' I said. 'What's going on?'

Sophi shrugged, and I could feel her shaking her head.

The telephone rang then, out in the hall. We listened to it. 'Not one of yours, then,' she said after the seventh ring. She patted my back. 'Better get it; might be Dad wanting a lift back . . .'

She went out to the hall.

'Hi?' Then a pause. 'Hello? . . . Hello?'

She put her head round the edge of the door, looking in at me and grinning, the telephone handset to one ear.

'Don't know what . . .' she said, then frowned. She shook her head, long hair making a sine wave in the air. 'I can hear music . . . Sounds like something sort of . . . something scrabbling around; clunking . . .' She made an odd expression, raising her eyebrows, turning down the corners of her mouth, the tendons on her neck standing out.

She held the phone out to me, and just as she did so I heard something clatter metallically from the handset and a tiny voice shout something. Sophi's expression changed to one of bemusement. She held the handset away from her and looked dubiously at it, then carefully brought it to her ear.

I got up from the couch. There had been something about the tone and cadence of that voice . . . Sophi held the phone away from her ear a little so that I could listen in, my cheek against hers.

'. . . dropping the damned thing,' said a miniaturised, mechanised voice. It sounded very odd, and both thick and slurred. 'I think this is right number . . . are you there?'

Sophi put her finger to her lips, looking amused.

'Ach; is the answer machine thing. I just . . .' There was some more clattering. 'That is . . .' The voice deteriorated into mumbling. 'That is right number, isn't it? Yes; yes, looks famil . . . familia . . . familiar . . . I'm sorry, very very, but bit . . . but bit . . . bit worse for wearing, you know. I am just call to say, I have got your message. And I am to be there tomorrow, is this all right? Well, be there, I will. I mean. You know this now. I . . . I am hoping . . . this will—' Silence, a muffled curse and another clatter.

Sophi put her hand over the mouthpiece. 'God,' she whispered, 'he sounds drunk, doesn't he?'

'Hmm,' I said. I was sure I recognised the man's voice.

We listened in again. There was a scuffling sort of noise; something redolent of fabric and friction. Then: '. . . bounced . . . under the flippink . . . sideboard this time; most vexing. I . . . I think I go now . . . Are you still . . . ? Well, I mean . . . oh . . . well, anyway. Tomorrow.' There was heavy breathing for a moment. 'Tomorrow. I come for her. Goodnight.' Then a clunk, and nothing.

Sophi and I looked into each others eyes.

'Weird, eh?' she said, laughing a little nervously.

I nodded. She leaned out into the hall, replacing the phone. 'Wrong number, I suppose,' she said.

I bit my lip, standing with my back to the edge of the doorway, arms crossed. Sophi put a hand on my shoulder. 'You all right?'

'I'm fine,' I said. 'But I think I know who that was.'

'You do?' Sophi laughed. 'Oh; should I have said something?'

'I don't know,' I admitted. And indeed I didn't. 'I think it was my uncle Mo,' I said to her.

'What, the one in Bradford, the actor?'

'Well, Spayedthwaite. But yes. Yes, that's the one.'

Sophi looked thoughtful. 'So who was he calling?'

'Who indeed?' I nodded. 'Who did he think he was calling, and who's this "her" he's coming for?'

Sophi leaned against the other edge of the doorway, also folding her arms and drawing one leg up under her backside. We looked at each other for a moment.

'You?' she said quietly, eyebrows flexing.

'Me,' I said, wondering.

289

CHAPTER
EIGHTEEN

I stayed with Sophi that night, lying chastely in her generous arms while she breathed slowly and made little shiftings and mutterings in her sleep. Her father returned about one in the morning; she stirred when she heard the door, woke and rose, padding downstairs. I heard their muffled voices and then she returned, giggling quietly as she took off her dressing-gown. 'Drunk as a monkey,' she whispered, slipping back in beside me. 'These golf club meetings . . .' she snuggled up to me. 'At least he gets a lift home . . .'

I stroked her hair as she fitted her chin into the angle of my neck and shoulder. She jerked a couple of times, apologised once, then went quiet again. I think she was asleep within the minute. I heard Mr Woodbean come up the stairs, and experienced the fluttering trepidation I'd always felt when I'd stayed over at Sophi's, frightened that he would burst in and discover us together, however innocently. As ever, his heavy tread creaked on past Sophi's door and along the landing to his own room, and I breathed easily again.

Sophi dreamed beside me, her hand clenching around mine, her breath hesitating, then speeding up a little, then dropping back.

I lay there, unable to sleep despite being deathly tired. I had been late to bed the previous night, had not so much slept then as fallen into an alcoholic stupor, and had subsequently undergone all the trials and tribulations that had overtaken me.

It already seemed like a week must have passed between sitting in the Jaguar car as it glided past Harrods department store in London and standing on the dark bridge watching the bats fly and hearing the owl call while I listened in vain for the Voice of my God.

Still, I could not sleep, but kept turning over and over in my head all the oddnesses of my recent life: Morag's apparent avoidance of me, the *zhlonjiz* business, my Grandfather's lecherous attention,

293

and now Uncle Mo, calling on the telephone, implicated and implicating, filthy drunk, seemingly thinking he was talking to a telephone answering machine when the Woodbeans had never had such a thing, and now presumably on his way, coming for somebody – me?

What was going on? What was happening to my life?

There had been enough untowardness and nonsense without Uncle Mo getting involved. Uncle Mohammed is the brother of Calli and Astar; a darkly handsome but prematurely aged early-forties actor who left the Community on his sixteenth birthday to seek fame and fortune in – where else? – London, and achieved a degree of fame before I was born when he landed a part in a Mancunian television soap opera. An unkind metropolitan newspaper critic, not remotely as impressed with Mo's talent as Mo was, once accused my uncle of putting the ham in Mohammed, which caused something of a fuss in the Moslem community – of which Mo, apostate, was now a part – and eventually required an apology and retraction. Mo was written out of the television story almost a decade ago and now exists in Spayedthwaite, near the northern city of Bradford, finding acting work very occasionally and – rumour has it – waiting on tables in an Indian restaurant the rest of the time, to make ends meet.

I think my Grandfather was more upset by Mo making his living on television than by his conversion to another faith, but I'm sure both hurt; the record of that first generation of those born into the Faith has not been a good one, with Brigit and Mo joining other religions and Rhea surrendering maritally to the cult of fundamentalist Blandness in Basingstoke. So much had depended on Calli and Astar and my father, and then he was taken from us by the fire; the full burden fell on my step-aunts, replacing him in some ways as well as their mother and aunt. I think it is fair to say that but for their dedication and sense of purpose our Order might have stumbled and fallen.

I had met Uncle Mo a few times and thought him a sad creature; we do not ban or banish people, even if they renounce

294

their Faith, so he was still welcome to visit us, and he has done so for each Festival. He had a surface presentability and heartiness which proved brittle and easily broken; underneath was desolation and loneliness. I think he might have rejoined us and even come back to stay in the Community, but he had too many ties in the north of England by then, and would have felt uprooted and alien wherever he went, and – by whatever algebra of longing and belonging he applied to his situation – had decided to remain with his chosen allegiance rather than his original persuasion.

The last time he had been here had been for the Festival of Love four years ago, when he had told me frankly he was looking for a wife (but did not find one). I'd assumed – indeed I'd been quite certain at the time – that he was joking when he'd asked me if I would marry him. We'd both laughed then, and I am still sure he was only kidding, but now he was on his way here, was he not? 'I come for her,' he'd said. For whom? For me? Morag, maybe? Somebody else? More to the point, why? And at whose behest?

I held Sophi like a drowning man holds a life-belt, so that I squeezed her and made her grunt and mutter. She stirred in my arms, not quite waking. I relaxed, content with the tactile reassurance that she was there. It seemed I could feel the world spinning around me, out of control, meaningless, mad and dangerous, and she was the only thing I had to hold on to.

The sound of the toilet flushing came from along the landing. I tried to turn the noise into a drain for my swirling thoughts, consigning my confusions, woes and fears to the same watery emptying and so leaving my head empty and ready for the sleep my body craved. But then the image struck me as absurd, and I found myself shaking my head in the darkness, chiding myself for such tortured foolishness. I was even able to raise the hint of a smile.

Sleep came for me eventually, after many more reviewings of the long, involved and fractious day, and many more attempts to stop thinking about all the mysteries surrounding me.

295

I dreamed of a wide, unsteady landscape of shaking bed clothes, and pursuit by something I could not see, forever just over the quivering horizon, but terrifyingly near and threatening. I was vaguely aware of disturbance and a warm kiss, but when I awoke properly Sophi was long gone and I was alone with an already half-aged day of brightness and showers.

*

Mr W had gone too. I used the Woodbeans' bath and made myself some toast and tea. I read the note – in Sophi's hand – that Grandmother Yolanda had left for me the previous day, giving me the number for her hotel in Stirling and telling me that she had booked a twin room so I was welcome to come and stay. She'd detailed her flight number and departure time today, too. I glanced at the clock on the mantelpiece; she would be at the airport by now.

I let a shower pass then walked back to the Community under dripping trees.

I nodded to a few Brothers and Sisters, who nodded back – warily, it seemed to me. I went straight to the office in the mansion house, where Sister Bernadette sat typing slowly at the desk by the door.

'Sister Isis!' she said, looking confused. She stood, smiling nervously.

'Sister Bernadette,' I said. 'Is Allan about?'

'He's with the Founder,' she said. 'Shall I ask him . . . ?'

'Please.'

She turned to go. 'Oh,' I said, 'and do you know where my kit-bag is?'

'I think Allan said . . . I'll look, Sister Isis,' she said, and went quickly out the door and across the hall.

I glanced at the letter she had been typing. It looked like a request for money; it was addressed to Aunt Brigit, the one in the Millennialist cult in Idaho. There was a pile of similar letters on one side of the typewriter, and a long list of names and addresses in an old school exercise book on the other, with ticks

296

down to Brigit's name. The list didn't seem to be alphabetical. I glanced up and down the list, then found Cousin Morag's name just as I heard footsteps out in the hall. Morag's old address in Finchley had been scored out, as had her old telephone number. La Mancha's full address had been added by hand. The footsteps were almost at the door. . . . And there was a telephone number, no; there were *three* telephone numbers beside the Essex address. I felt my jaw drop in astonishment.

I stepped away towards the windows a moment before Allan came into the room, carrying my kit-bag. He closed the door behind him, placing the kit-bag to one side. I tried to collect my scattered thoughts.

'Isis,' Allan said, putting the bag down by the door. He had abandoned his suit and was dressed in a robe not dissimilar to Salvador's. He indicated the seat in front of his desk. 'Please,' he said. He sat behind, in his swivel seat.

I stayed where I was, between the tall windows. A quick shower threw raindrops against the glass. I said, 'Good afternoon, Allan. I came to find out where I stand.'

'Ah,' he said, tenting his hands together and looking at them.

'What did Grandfather say about last night?' I asked.

'He . . . he seems to feel that you . . . need to confess,' Allan said, with what looked like a pained smile. 'That your soul is . . . muddied by . . . by something you've done.' He gave a great sigh. 'Salvador feels you've betrayed . . . well, yourself, certainly, but also him, and, I suppose, all of us, in a way. Do you see?'

'I didn't take the vial,' I said. 'And if anyone ought to feel betrayed after last night, it should be me.'

'What?' Allan looked genuinely puzzled, his fair, handsome face coated with a single layer of puzzlement. 'How do you mean?'

I looked at my boots. 'I can't tell you,' I told him. 'I'm sorry. That's up to Salvador.'

He shook his head. 'Well, I'm afraid he just doesn't want to see you until you apologise and admit you did wrong. He seems pretty determined about that; like a bear with a sore head this morning, believe me.'

'How are the revisions going?'

297

He looked startled, just for a moment. 'Oh,' he said, smoothly, shrugging. 'Well enough; you know.'

'Hmm,' I said, giving him time to say more if he wanted to. Apparently, he did not.

I said, 'I hope I'm not being kicked out or anything?'

'Oh, no!' Allan said, shaking his head. 'No. I think Salvador feels that . . . that a time of reflection and prayer may be called for. Retreat, even. You may want to contemplate things here, in your room, in the library . . .' He looked thoughtful for a moment, as though just having an idea. He raised his eyebrows. 'Perhaps a pilgrimage to Luskentyre, if you wanted to travel?'

'Perhaps. What about Cousin Morag?'

Allan exhaled loudly, putting his head to one side. 'Another sore point,' he admitted. 'Salvador feels . . . terribly deceived.' He shook his head. 'I don't know how he'll jump there. I'm not sure Morag will be welcome here for the Festival at all. She has made us look foolish.'

'But am I to stop looking for her?'

'I suppose so. You said the trail had gone cold, anyway.'

'All we'd need would be . . .' I shrugged '. . . a telephone number or something, and then I, or somebody, could . . .'

'Well,' Allan said, looking regretful. 'We had her number for her flat, but . . .' He held his open hands out to each side. 'She isn't there any more.'

'We've no other contact numbers for her?'

'No.'

'Hmm. What about her place in the Festival? It seemed very important a couple of weeks ago. Isn't it any more? Isn't anyone to try to find Morag?'

'Well,' Allan said, nodding with that pained expression on his face again. 'Perhaps, on reflection, we overreacted to the situation.'

'What?'

'It's just that,' he stood up, spread his arms wide, 'we've had time to think, review . . .' He came round from behind the desk. 'I think we all got a bit panicky that day, don't you?' He came up and stood before me, smiling. He looked fresh and clean and wholesome. 'The situation isn't quite as desperate as we thought back then,' he told me. 'Do you see what I mean?'

I nodded slowly. 'Yes, I think I do.'

'Anyway,' he said, gently taking my arm and walking us both towards the door. 'You don't need to worry about all that. You should get some . . . some time to think. Here's your bag; sorry about all that yesterday – you know how he can be. Get yourself unpacked and so on, give yourself some time to think, and if you do need to get any sort of message to him, just let me know; I'm . . . well, I'm desperate to help, Isis; really I am.'

He handed me my kit-bag, then leaned forward and kissed me on the cheek. 'See you soon, Isis, and don't worry.' He winked at me. 'Oh, and you can keep the kit-bag,' he said, and smiled.

'Thanks, Allan,' I said, and gave a brave smile. I went downstairs with the bag over my shoulder, thinking.

*

My instinct was to sit in my room meditating, or immerse myself in an improving book, or go for a long walk.

Instead I went round talking to other people, forcing myself to ignore the embarrassment both they and I felt, knowing that I had fallen into disfavour. I started by finding Brother Indra in his workshop and thanking him for the successful alterations he had carried out on the inner-tube which had borne me safely to Edinburgh. Indra is a quietly cheerful type, shorter than me and slim but muscled with a lot of his mother's appearance in him. He seemed a little wary of me at first but once we got talking about my trip to England he lost any reserve and we parted cheerfully.

I spoke to everybody I could find, just trying to remind them that I was who I was, not some demonised thief. I used my journey as the excuse.

Normally somebody coming back from such an important trip and with so much to tell would have been expected to stand up in front of a meeting of the whole Community and tell everybody at once, but it seemed I was not to be asked to do so on this occasion. (It had also not escaped my notice that there had been no ceremonial washing of my feet, which was positively insulting.) I went through my story, altering the weight given to each strand and detail according to whom I was talking; when I spoke with a frowning Calli and weary-looking Astar in the farm kitchen I dwelled shamelessly on Bland food, the encouraging prevalence of Asian people and businesses, and what people had been wearing in London; with my Sisters in general, when I came to the events of the previous evening, I did mention – sometimes with a little, perhaps regretful, smile – that Grandfather had been a little over-affectionate at one point last night, but left it at that, dismissing it with a shrug. If anybody wanted to know more about the *zhlonjiz*, I answered their questions honestly, only dissembling when asked if – assuming that I hadn't taken the vial – I had any theories on who might have done so.

In all this – and in something of a daze, for the full enormity of my predicament had not yet dawned upon me – I felt that I was somehow playing the part of the unjustly accused, even though that was exactly what I was. I wasn't sure why this should be, but the impression lingered, and was still there when I had finally talked to just about every adult – singly or in small, informal groups, often as they worked – in the Community. I didn't feel bad about this, but the feeling wouldn't go away. Still, I felt cheered as the evening approached. Indeed I was half looking forward to the evening meal, when I would be able – assuming I was asked the right questions – to continue pressing my case.

I had been hoping that out of all the people I spoke to there would be somebody who would ask me to perform the laying on of hands, to cure some ache or other condition that they or a child of theirs was suffering from, which they had been waiting on me to return to cure – I had never been away from the Community for more than a day without this happening – but nobody did. I suppose it was naive of me to expect anything else, but nevertheless I was at first surprised, then confused and finally saddened.

Then I heard through Sister Erin that Salvador intended to make one of his rare appearances at the evening meal, and would greatly prefer it if I was not there. I had no real choice, and so agreed to eat later, perhaps in my room, if Salvador got into story-telling mood after the meal proper was finished.

I decided to visit Sophi again, and walked in a light shower down to the bridge and across, but there was nobody home in the Woodbeans' house. A thought occurred to me, and so I walked on up the darkly dripping drive and discovered Sister Bernadette at the drive entrance, sitting on a section of broken wall beside the gates, looking out over the semicircle of weed-covered tarmac, holding a furled umbrella.

*

Sister Bernadette was wrapped up well but still looked cold. She was gazing the other way, at the road, as I approached.

'Sister Bernadette,' I said.

She jumped up, snagging the umbrella in overhead branches. 'Oh! Is. I didn't—' she said, sounding flustered. She looked up, then pulled down on the brolly, creating her own tiny but drenching rainstorm as the leaves and branches above dropped their load of moisture on her. She hauled again, but the entangled brolly was stuck fast and she tore its fabric. 'Oh! Bugger!' she said, then looked horrified. 'Oh, pardon.' She blushed, pushing a hand through her damp, disturbed red hair and then pulling again at the umbrella.

'Let me help you with that,' I said, and unhooked the offending implement from the branches.

She brushed some water off her face and head and nodded to me as she folded the umbrella. 'Thank you,' she said. She looked around. 'Wet, isn't it?'

'A bit showery,' I agreed. I looked at the sky. 'Seems to be going off now.' I sat down on the broken wall. She looked as though she was going to sit down too for a moment, but then didn't.

She took a deep breath, and moved her shoulders as though they were tired, staring down at me with a broad, false smile. 'Are you going for a walk?' she asked.

I shrugged. 'Just wandering,' I said, and sat back, drawing one

301

leg up until I could wedge my boot heel on the rock. Bernadette looked alarmed.

'Oh, I see,' she said.

'And you?' I asked.

'I'm waiting for the delivery van which is bringing the fireworks for the Festival,' she said quickly.

'Ah. I see.' I rested my back against the stones behind me. 'I'll give you a hand.'

'Oh, no!' she said, her voice high with stress but a smile still fixed on her face. 'No; no need for that,' she said, and then laughed. 'No; the van might be a long time yet; I'd rather do it myself, really I would.' She nodded emphatically, her rosy face shining with moisture. 'Actually, truth be told, Is, I'm quite enjoying the feeling of being alone. Gives you time to think. Gives you time to contemplate. Things. It does.'

'Oh,' I said, pleasantly. 'Would you rather I left?'

'Ah, Jesus, I'm – pardon me – I'm not saying that, Isis.'

'Good,' I smiled. 'So; Sister Bernadette. How have you been, anyway?'

'What?' she said, glancing wildly at the road as a truck went past heading west, and then staring back at me. 'Ah, sorry?'

'I was just asking you how you were.'

'Ah, fine. And yourself?'

'Well,' I said, crossing my arms. 'I was fine, too, really, until yesterday. Everything seemed to be going well, apart from the problem of finding Cousin Morag . . . ah, but I'm getting ahead of myself . . .' I said, smiling.

Bernadette's smile became even broader and even shallower than it had been. 'Ah,' she said. 'But you don't want to be bothering yourself telling—'

'. . . I got down to Edinburgh without any problems,' I said. 'The inner-tube worked very well, as I was telling Brother Indra earlier. The worst bit of the river journey was probably going down the weir, you know; the bit where the river becomes tidal . . .' I said, settling back even more comfortably.

I took my time. Bernadette stood looking at me with a smile so broad and stretched you could see right through it to the terror underneath, while her wide, round eyes moved desperately around like a pair of caged animals seeking escape. The sound of a larger vehicle approaching on the road brought an even tauter look to her face, and produced a sort of tic in her head as she tried to look at me and watch the road at the same time, while her gaze flicked back and forth with impressive speed, like somebody desperately trying to signal No with their eyes.

After a while, however, I think a degree of resignation crept in; a glazed expression settled over Sister Bernadette's face and I was left with the impression that her brain had stopped talking to her facial muscles, perhaps complaining of over-work. I had got to the flight north with Grandma Yolanda when the bus arrived. Bernadette was so far gone she didn't notice.

The bus drew away and Uncle Mo was standing there, looking small and dapper, a camel-hair coat draped over his shoulders and a leather bag in his hand.

It was only when I waved over to him that Bernadette seemed to come to. 'Oh look,' I said. 'There's Uncle Mo. Golly. What a surprise.'

'What?' she said, turning as I rose. I started off across the weedy tarmac towards Uncle Mo. Bernadette ran after me.

'Sisters! Niece!' Uncle Mo said, dropping his bag and holding out his arms as we approached. 'You shouldn't have come just to meet me!'

'We didn't, honest!' squawked Bernadette as I hugged and was hugged by Uncle Mo. He smelled strongly of cologne.

'Isis,' he said, beaming. He kissed my cheek. Since I had seen him last he had grown a little pencil moustache. And a little chubbier. 'So good to see you.'

'Hello, Uncle. This is most unexpected.'

'Ach, a whim, dear girl. To arrive early for the Festival. Ah; . . . Sister,' Mo said, shaking Bernadette's hand. 'Mary, isn't it?'

'Ah, no; Bernadette.'

Uncle Mo snapped his fingers. 'Bernadette, of course.' He tapped one temple then held out one hand and looked up at the sky. '*What* did I call you?' he asked.

'Mary,' she said.

303

'There you are. Meaning to say Bernadette, it comes out Mary. There you are. So. Now. Are you both well? How is everybody?'

'Fine,' Bernadette said as I picked up Uncle Mo's bag. Bernie looked annoyed, as though she should have thought of doing that.

'Niece,' Uncle Mo laughed, holding out both hands to the bag in my hands. 'Please; I am not yet so old as to be totally incapable.'

'Let me carry it, Uncle,' I said. 'It would be an honour.'

'Well. Well, if you . . . yes, well, there you are. Why indeed not?' He cleared his throat. 'So. Isis. I hear you've been on your travels.'

'Yes, Uncle. I saw the Possils in Edinburgh and Brother Zeb in London.'

'Zeb!' Uncle Mo said, nodding. 'Yes. Of course. I remember. Why, I haven't seen Zeb since he was this high.' He held out a hand at waist level. 'And so, how is Zeb?'

'Oh, he's just shooting up these days, Uncle,' I said.

'Excellent. Excellent. So; we are all well.'

'Yes, everybody's well, Uncle,' I told him as we walked towards the little gate. 'Though to be honest with you I'm having a few problems myself just at the moment, but I'm keeping well. How are you?'

'Most hale and hearty, thank you, Isis. But what are these problems you talk of?'

We were at the gate. 'Well, Uncle,' I said, holding the gate open for him. He stood to one side to motion that Bernadette should go first. She nodded and walked through. I let Uncle Mo follow, then with an expression of innocent surprise on my face said, 'Sister Bernadette?'

She looked at me. I looked back out at the road then back to her. 'What about the delivery van?'

She frowned. 'The— ?' She went crimson. 'Oh . . . I'll . . .' She looked back down the drive. 'It can . . . ah . . .'

'I know,' I said. 'I'll accompany Uncle Mo to the house; then, if you want, I'll come back and help you with the delivery.'

'Ah . . .' She shook her head in frustration. 'Oh, never mind it!' she said, and turned away. When she looked back she was

304

smiling desperately again. Uncle Mo and I looked at each other and exchanged that momentary lifting of the eyebrows that is the face's equivalent of a shrug. Somebody not quite knowing all the details of what was going on might have thought we were acknowledging that of the three of us there were only two half-decent liars and one total incompetent, and perhaps in a way that's just what we were doing.

'Let's both go, then,' I said.

'There you are. I shall have a beauty on both arms,' Uncle Mo said, with some satisfaction.

'This *is* a surprise, Uncle Mo,' I said emphatically as we walked.

'Yes,' he said. 'Yes; but there you are; the moment has always been my spur!'

'I bet that delivery comes later, anyway,' Bernadette blurted. 'I'll go back and get it later.'

'Good idea, Sister.'

'Quite so. There you are.'

And so with our various lies, we walked down the drive to the farm. I told Uncle Mo the quick version of my travels and explained about the *zhlonjiz*. I made an exception for him, despite the fact he was a man, by including the coy line about Grandfather becoming a little over-affectionate the previous night. He gave a small frown, then looked surprised, then finally seemed to dismiss it with a slightly puzzled smile, as though we obviously had misunderstood each other. Bernadette looked startled; she tripped on the drive's pitted surface, saving herself with the umbrella, which bent.

'I think your umbrella will have seen better days,' Uncle Mo said. She looked disconsolately at it and nodded.

Uncle Mo took a half-bottle-sized hip flask from a coat pocket and took a long drink as we approached the Community buildings. 'Medicine,' he explained to us.

He took his bag from my hand as we entered the farm courtyard; Bernadette seemed to want to head for the mansion house at first, but changed her mind. I saw her and Uncle Mo to the door of the kitchen, then wished him well.

'You're not coming in?' he asked, on the threshold. I could smell cooking and hear a babble of talk turning to a chorus of loud and friendly Hellos.

I lowered my head and smiled sadly. 'I've . . . been asked not to,' I admitted.

Uncle Mo put his hand on my elbow and squeezed. 'You poor child,' he said, looking and sounding most serious.

'Not to worry, Uncle,' I said. I brightened. 'Anyway; I'm sure there'll be a place free for you. Have a good meal; I'll see you later.'

'I'll see what I can do, Isis,' he said, projecting quietly.

'Thank you,' I whispered. I stepped back then turned and walked away. I kept my head down for a few smaller, slower than normal steps, then brought it proudly up as my stride lengthened and I pulled my shoulders back. How much of this little performance Uncle Mo was able to appreciate I really don't know, but I was reasonably pleased with it myself.

I heard a door close and then the sound of footsteps behind me as I got to the gateway. I looked back and saw Allan appear from the mansion house and hurry across the courtyard to the farm.

CHAPTER
NINETEEN

'So, Isis, it seemed to me that, all things being as they are, and with your best interests to heart, you might wish to come with me to stay in Spayedthwaite, just for a while. What do you think?'

'Hmm.' I crossed my legs and clasped my hands. We were in the office again, Allan, Erin, Uncle Mo and I. It was late, and the lamps were burning. I had been called here from my room by Sister Bernadette.

'Obviously you might want to think about this,' Allan said. 'But if you did want to take up Uncle Mo's offer, well, you could always return at any time. I'm sure we can stretch to a return ticket,' he smiled.

'Yes, I see,' I said.

I was only making the pretence of thinking about this. I'd guessed why Uncle Mo was here, conjectured upon what might be suggested, thought about what I ought to do and so already knew what I was going to say.

'There is a friend of mine in Spayedthwaite who has a theatre,' Uncle Mo said.

'Really?' I said. 'A theatre?'

'Indeed; a theatre,' Uncle Mo said. 'Well, it became a cinema, later.'

'Ah.'

'Mostly it is used for the playing of bingo, nowadays. Well, entirely, actually,' Uncle Mo admitted, but then brightened. 'However, it has an organ. A very splendid one, I might say, which rises from the beneath of the screen. I have heard that you are interested in playing the organ, Isis.'

I forbore to make any smart remarks about Morag, and just smiled and said, 'Hmm,' again.

Apparently thinking that he hadn't thrown enough organs into the battle to convince me to accompany him home, Uncle Mo

309

snapped his fingers and hoisted his eyebrows dramatically. 'I have another friend, a colleague, who also has an organ, in his home!' he said.

'Really?' I asked.

'Yes; it is free-standing, and has *two* keyboards.'

'Two? Good heavens.'

'Indeed.'

'Perhaps Isis would rather stay here,' Erin suggested, patting her bunned hair, as though a single filament would have dared stray.

'Well,' said Allan reasonably, 'yes, she could. Of course. Of course.' He tented his fingers, brought his forefingers up to his mouth and tapped them against his lips, nodding. 'Certainly.'

I had learned to appreciate the finer side of Allan's phrasing and body language many years before, and had rarely if ever heard him say No quite so decisively. It suddenly struck me that my brother could probably say Hello with a note of finality.

'That is true,' he said, holding out one hand to Erin. 'On the other hand,' he said, holding his other hand out flat in balance. 'Salvador does seem ... rather upset with Is. To the point of not wanting to see her, sad to say,' he said, looking at me sympathetically. 'Now, with him staying in his quarters so much of the time, this need not be such a terrible obstacle, but obviously when he does want to do something like lead a meeting or come along to break bread with us, there is a problem, and we have to ask Is to stay away, and he's aware that we have asked her to stay away, and that ... distresses him by itself. Similarly, he may even feel slightly trapped, one might say, in his quarters, as he doesn't want to leave on the off chance he might bump into Is, and so that too keeps what's happened at the front of his mind a lot of the time ... Obviously,' – another look at me – '*not* a good thing. So ...' Allan tented his fingers again and studied the ceiling. '... So there does certainly exist an argument that the best thing to do *would* be for Isis to depart briefly and let Salvador relax a little, maybe get this whole sorry thing sorted out, certainly let him think and, let us be frank,' – he looked from Erin to me and back – 'let us work on him, so that perhaps we can, well, finally get this ... sorted out,' he said

310

and coughed, as though using the sound as a way of covering up the repetition.

'I see,' I said.

'And it would be a holiday, as well!' Uncle Mo put in.

'Well, of course,' I said, agreeably.

'Still,' Erin said. 'Sister Isis has only just come back from her travels. Perhaps she is tired.' She smiled at me.

'Not in the least,' I said.

'Well, then,' Uncle Mo said, as though it was therefore all settled.

I nodded. 'Well, I can see it might be a good idea to go away for a while, but I'd like to think about it.'

Allan nodded. 'Good idea; sleep on it.'

'Jolly good!' Uncle Mo said.

Erin glanced at the clock on the mantelpiece behind Allan's desk. 'Well, it's late,' she said.

We all agreed it was late, and time for bed. As we left the room I took another look at the desk by the door where I'd seen the list of names and addresses earlier, but the desk had been tidied and was bare of paper,

After we'd all left the study, Allan locked the door behind us.

*

I lay in my hammock in my room in the farmhouse, my mouth dry, my hands sweating and my heart thumping. I had waited in a state of increasing dread and excitement for what I hoped was about two hours, but now I had to act, and I felt as nervous as I think I've ever felt in my life.

'God,' I whispered into the darkness. 'Forgive me and help me in what I'm going to do.'

I still had not heard the Voice. I knew that God was still there, still talking – or at least able to talk – to me if only I could calm my troubled soul. I was not sure there was any point in asking God for help – They do not tend to interfere at such a level of events – but if it kept Them trying to talk to me, perhaps I would hear something that might

311

help me over the course of the next hour or so. It could do no harm.

My Grandfather once compared the Voice of God speaking to a human soul to the reflection of the moon on water; if the water is perfectly calm, the moon is seen clearly, undistorted. If the waters of the soul are slightly disturbed, the moon will still be visible and recognisable, but it will seem to move and shiver and it may not be possible to make out any features upon it. If the waters of the soul are in torment, tossing stormily about, then the moon's single bright face will be broken into a million sparkling points of light, casting up a meaningless clutter of scattered light which an observer might not even be able to identify as moonlight.

Well, the surface of my soul just then was riven and agitated indeed, and I should not have been surprised that I could not detect the Voice. Still, I felt the loss keenly, and one petulant, childish part of me interpreted it as just another abandonment. I sighed.

'Here goes,' I whispered (though not, this time, really to the Creator), and got up.

I dressed, used my penknife to cut an inch of candle, then pocketed the knife, the stub of candle and a box of matches. I had a pencil and a sheet of paper in another pocket. I put on an old flat cap I hadn't worn since I was about fourteen – it was slightly too small for me but that meant it wasn't likely to fall off, and it did cover my fair hair quite effectively. I put my ear to the door, listening, but could hear nobody about. I left the room and went to the toilet; I had meant to, using the noise of the flush to cover my footsteps heading further along the corridor, but in the event I would have had to have gone anyway, so affected by my trepidation had my entire system become.

I knew from long experience where each and every loose floorboard was along the corridor, and could avoid them easily even in the total darkness. On the stairs I hugged the sides of the steps, and near the bottom – to avoid five noisy stairs without the noise created by jumping – I slid down the banister rail. The farm's back door is in the old kitchen, now used as a washroom; it has the quietest door. I closed it gently behind me, and was out into the cool night and the smell of freshly moist foliage, the south-facing greenhouse to one side. The sky was three-quarters clouded and the wind smelled damp, but the rain held off.

I kept near the wall as I crept away, heading north, clockwise round the buildings of the Community, round the outside of the orchard. I climbed over a wall into the formal garden behind the mansion house, glanced up at the sky and hid behind a bush. The moon came out from behind the clouds for a few moments and let me see the route ahead. As the darkness returned I padded along the grass beside the path until I got to the dark bulk of the house.

The blocks of sandstone which line each window space of the house have little horizontal notches cut into their top and bottom edges, creating a channel it is possible to wedge fingers and the welts of boots into. I climbed until I could reach the window-ledge of the storeroom behind the office, then hauled myself up and kneeled on the narrow shelf of stone, pulling out my penknife. I slid the blade up between the top and bottom parts of the sash and felt it connect with the window catch. Bless us for our happy indifference to security.

The bottom section of the window proved reluctant to move; the top slid down easily enough, however, and I stepped over and was inside. I pushed the window back up; it made a tiny squeak and a faint rumbling noise at the same time, but was probably not audible outside the room.

The storeroom's curtains hadn't been drawn, but the minuscule amount of light coming from outside wasn't enough to give me any idea of the room's layout, though I knew roughly where the door to the office must be and had the vaguest impression out of the corner of my eye of bulky, shadowy shapes. I crossed to the door, walking backwards, slowly. My left leg collided with something on my second step; I felt down and around and sidled past what felt like a desk. I bumped into another couple of obstacles with my calves, and hoped my shins were appreciating such thoughtfulness. Then my bottom connected softly with a shelf, which I felt wobble. There was a faint rattling sound from above and I grimaced, hunching instinctively and putting a hand over my cap, waiting for something to fall on my head. The rattling subsided; I relaxed and felt along to the door which led to the office.

313

I didn't imagine it would be locked like the door from the office to the corridor but it did occur to me it might be, and then what was I to do? I got down on all fours to look under the door and make sure there was no light coming from the office beyond. The door was not locked; it swung open. The office was even darker than the storeroom, the curtains drawn over the tall bay windows. I closed the storeroom door, took out my inch of candle and lit it, quickly waving the match out.

I went over to the desk by the door. The drawers were locked. I ground my teeth, screaming curses inside my head. I looked around the desk. There was a recessed handle above the top right-hand drawer; I pulled it out to reveal a shallow plastic tray whose various compartments held pencils, pens, paper-clips and rubber bands. In one small compartment there were two keys. I offered up a silent prayer of thanks, pointless or not.

Each key opened all the drawers on one side of the desk. There were various bundles of unused envelopes, a box of typing paper and a cardboard folder of carbon paper; in one deep drawer there were lots more cardboard folders, many of them stuffed with what looked like correspondence, and in another drawer there was a promising-looking bundle of loose papers. I set the candle on top of the typewriter case and started going through all the various papers and folders.

Footsteps. On the stairs, coming down.

I froze. Instantly, I realised I should have opened one drawer at a time, not left them all out and open. I started stuffing the folders and papers back into what I hoped were the right drawers in a frenzy of silent desperation, feeling my hands shake and my guts clench.

Somebody was at the door. I slid the drawers back in as quickly as I dared, once again howling imprecations at myself inside my head. One drawer stuck momentarily. I pulled it back out and slid it back in at a slightly different angle, my whole body quivering with fear.

I heard the sound of a key in the lock. I grabbed the candle stub off the top of the typewriter; the flame flickered and nearly went out. Hot wax spilled over my fingers. I almost cried out.

The door handle squeaked. I moved in two long strides to the nearest bay window and slipped behind the curtains, blowing out the candle as the door creaked open.

I put out my hand to stop the curtains waving from side to side and realised – as I saw light come into the office – that I'd left a small gap between the curtains as I'd moved between them. I stared in horror, not daring to close them properly for fear the movement would be seen by whoever was coming to investigate (Why had they come? Had I made a noise? Was there some silent alarm system I'd never heard about?). I held on to the curtain, the wax cooled and hardened on my fingers while my poor bowels felt they were doing exactly the opposite, as if in recompense.

Through the finger-wide gap between the curtains, I saw Allan come into the room, holding a small paraffin lamp. He wore the same simple robe he had on earlier, and carpet slippers. He locked the door behind him and went towards the desk, yawning. I relaxed a little; he didn't seem to be here because he'd heard something. I carefully let go of the curtain and stepped back, so that my face was further away from the lamp-light coming through the gap in the curtains. I felt the cool glass of the window behind me. I could still see Allan; he felt for the small chain round his neck, bringing it out and slipping it over his head, then held something small on the end of it and bent to the top drawer of his big desk in front of the fireplace. It must have been a key. He opened the drawer and brought out something that looked, I thought, like an electronic calculator or a remote control unit for a television set. He yawned again and moved towards the door to the storeroom I'd made my entrance through. Then he stopped, turned round and looked almost straight at me, a frown on his face. I thought I was going to faint. He sniffed the air.

The match! I thought. The match I'd used to light the candle; he could detect its treacherous, sulphurous smell! Ice water seemed to run in my veins. Allan sniffed the air again, glancing down at the fire, then the frown disappeared and he shook his head. He went into the storeroom, closing the door after him. I breathed out, half delirious with relief. And I'd even thought to close the window in the storeroom, too, though I hadn't locked it after me.

315

I waited, wiping sweat off my brow. My heart seemed to shake my whole torso. It felt like it was trying to escape from my chest. I wondered if nineteen was too young to die from a heart attack.

Several minutes passed; my heart slowed. I picked the solidified wax off my hand and put the bits in my pocket. I licked the smarting skin underneath, waving my hand about to cool the moistened area. Then I thought I heard a voice coming from the storeroom. Allan's voice. As though he was talking to somebody.

I hesitated. It would be madness to go and listen; I could never get back here in time when he returned to the study. It was obviously insane, and it would be tempting fate; I had only just managed to set the desk by the door back in order before Allan came into the room; I'd already used up all my luck. I ought to stay here, keep quiet, let Allan do whatever he was doing, let him leave and then continue with my search. I turned and looked away from the room, out into the darkness where the courtyard and the farm buildings were, invisible in the night. Of course it would be stupid – idiotic – to go over to the storeroom door.

I don't know what made me do just that, but I did; I left the comparative safety of the curtains and – with a clear image in my mind of how the room had looked while illuminated with the glow from Allan's paraffin lamp – stepped smartly across the floor and through the darkness to listen at the door to the storeroom.

'. . . told you, she's obsessed,' I heard Allan say. Then, 'I know, I know . . . Why, have you had any more letters? . . . No, no, she doesn't, ah . . . didn't find out. No, you're all right there. . . . Well, I don't know how, but she, ah, she didn't . . . well, she didn't say anything. No, wouldn't be like her. . . . I don't know. . . . You did? Yes, so did that old bat Yolanda. . . . Yes, she brought her back.'

He was talking on a telephone! It took me that long to work it out; it was such an unthinkable thing, to have a telephone in the Community, and here, right at its heart! He had one of those portable wireless telephones; *that* was what he had taken out of the drawer in the desk! He was talking to somebody on it! The deception of the man! And to think I had felt bad, felt like a *sinner*, dammit, for making a couple of calls from a telephone box in Gittering! For shame, brother! I had half a mind to burst in on him and denounce him to his face, but luckily that particular rush of blood to the head didn't last very long.

'. . . Well, not for long,' Allan said. 'I asked Uncle Mo to come up here; looks like we've persuaded her to take a holiday with him.'

So Mo *had* been calling Allan. My uncle must have dialled the wrong number in his cups, having the vague idea that he was ringing the Community but getting the Woodbeans' number, not Allan's. So, did wireless phones have answering machines too? I supposed they must have, or could link into one somewhere else. Perhaps that accounted for the few minutes of silence when Allan had first entered the storeroom; he had been taking his messages. Well, of course; he couldn't be seen with the phone, couldn't carry it around and have it ringing while he was amongst us.

'. . . Spayedthwaite; oop north,' Allan said, putting on a funny accent. ' . . . Tomorrow, with any luck. Why, what were you . . . ? . . . Really? . . . Flumes? . . . Well, it's not Spain, I suppose, but . . .'

Spain? Hadn't Morag been due to go there with Mr Leopold, her agent/manager? Good grief! Was he talking to *Morag*? Then why— ? I abandoned speculation to continue listening.

'. . . Oh, I see. Really. Well, everybody should have a hobby, they say. . . . So we might see you yet for the Festival? . . . It was a joke. I dare say she will, too. . . . Oh, getting crazier; latest thing was she had a private audience with the old man and offered herself to him; tried to get him to screw her. Can you believe that?'

What? I felt my mouth fall open as I stared at the door, black in front of my face, unable to believe what I was hearing. *What* was I being accused of now? Attempting to seduce my Grandfather when in fact he had practically tried to rape me? If I had felt there was ice in my veins a few minutes earlier, I could believe it was superheated steam now. The treachery of it! The calumny! The mendacity! This was . . . this was *evil*.

'. . . I know, I know,' Allan said. '. . . Well, of course nobody else was *there*, Morag, but I believe Grandfather, don't you? . . . Well, quite. . . . Yes. . . . I don't . . . . . . No. No idea. . . . Yes, me too. Sorry about the lateness of the hour. . . . What? . . . No, I don't suppose it is, really, not for you, but it is for us. Well, I'll say . . .'

I'd heard enough. I wasn't quite so sure of my route back to the curtains as I had been from them to the door but I got there without bumping into anything. I slipped back behind them again and adjusted the gap until it was the same as it had been before.

The storeroom door opened and Allan reappeared with the paraffin lamp and the little portable telephone; different centuries in each hand. He put the phone back in the drawer of the main desk, locked it and – apart from one sniff at the air, which seemed to satisfy him – left the office without further ado. I heard the key turn in the lock and listened to his footsteps fade as he climbed the stairs back to his room.

I stood for a while, trembling as though cold.

So, my brother was spreading lies about me to Morag. I had the distinct impression that they were not the first, either. And how long had he been able to call her? Why had I been sent to find her at all? Why had he made no mention of her apostasy? The world seem to tip around me again, out of kilter, out of joint, out of its head.

I stepped out from the curtains with a strange feeling of numbness. I made faces of disbelief into the darkness. Had I really heard what I had just heard? I shook my head. Here, now, was no place to stand wondering what was going on.

I pulled myself together as best I could and relit my candle – waving the match's cloud of smoke away with one hand – then returned to the typing desk by the door.

The piece of paper I was looking for was in a folder in the deepest drawer. I noted down the numbers for Morag in a kind of insensible daze, my mind still reeling with shock at what I'd heard. I almost put the sheet of paper back in its folder straight away, and on such a trifle, at that moment, did the whole fate and future course of our Faith potentially hang.

Instead of putting the paper away, then, I looked at the other names and addresses.

And saw that there was an entry for Great-aunt Zhobelia, whom we had always been told had gone off to find – and perhaps effect a reconciliation with – her original family and then effectively disappeared. Great-aunt Zhobelia whom Grandmother Yolanda was convinced had once hinted at . . . something. Something for sure, she'd said. By God, I would welcome anything sure in my world, just now. There was no actual address for Zhobelia, just a note that said she was 'Care of Unc. Mo'.

I looked at it, transfixed. *Now* what?

I half expected to find full addresses and telephone numbers for Aunt Rhea, or even Salvador's original family, but there were no more surprises. I looked through a few other folders and riffled through all the loose papers, in case there were any more revelations, but I think my courage was running out at that point; my hands were shaking. I put the desk back as I'd found it and lifted the candle carefully this time.

I stopped at Allan's desk and tried its drawers, but they were all locked, and I couldn't find a key anywhere; I strongly suspected that the only key was the one hanging round his neck. My teeth were starting to chatter, though I wasn't cold. The mantelpiece clock said the time was half past midnight. I decided it was time to retreat. I considered keeping the candle aflame when I went back through the storeroom, but I really did feel I had entirely used up my quota of good fortune for the night, and it would be just my luck for there to be a Luskentyrian or two wandering around out there in the formal garden or beyond, so I blew out the candle.

I forgot to walk backwards through the storeroom and banged a shin so hard I swear I actually saw lights – I think it was because I closed my eyes so hard; it was that or cry out. Doubled-up, limping and rubbing my shin, I got to the window, muttering quiet but vehement curses under my breath. It was only as I was climbing out of the opened window and saw starlight reflected in the pond on the ground below that it occurred to me that this was probably the window I had been thrown out of by my father on the night of the fire, sixteen years earlier.

Suddenly realising that, I experienced a second of dizziness as I straddled the opened sash-window, and for a moment I was terrified that I was about to totter and fall; certainly I was quite far enough above the ground to break my neck if I did. The moment

319

passed, but my tattered nerves, already stretched to their limit, could have done without the scare. I started to tremble again.

Perhaps because I was shaking so much, getting down to the ground proved more difficult than climbing up had been, and I hung on my fingertips for a good half-minute desperately trying to fit the welt of my boots into a crack, but I made my way down eventually and got back as far as the orchard wall before I came up with an idea.

I looked down the road towards the river.

*

'Is! What's wrong? Are you— ?' Sophi said, looking out from the hall with an expression of concern on her sweet face. She wore pyjamas and a dressing-gown.

'I'm fine,' I said, in a whisper. 'Sorry it's so late. Can I come in?'

'Of course.' She stood aside. 'Dad's in bed,' she said.

'Good.' I kissed her cheek. She closed the door and hugged me. 'Can I use your phone?'

'Of course. I might not wait up till you're finished, though,' she said, smiling.

I shook my head. 'This will be a proper call; voice.'

She looked pretend-shocked. 'Are you allowed to do that?' she asked, lifting the telephone off its table and pulling it through to the sitting room.

'Not really,' I said. 'But these are desperate times.'

'God, they must be.' She pulled the telephone's wire under the door and then closed it. 'Quieter in here,' she said, putting the phone on the sideboard. 'Need a chair?'

'No thanks,' I said, pulling from my pocket the sheet of paper I'd written Morag's numbers on.

I explained to Sophi what I'd done.

'Is!' she squealed in delight. 'You're a *cat* burglar!'

'There's worse,' I said, and watched her expression change to horror and then anger when I told her what Allan had said to Morag.

'That slimy bastard,' she said, her jaw set in a firm line. 'Is that who you're going to call? Morag?'

'Yes. She might hang up on me; if she does, will you call her back; be a sort of character witness?'

'Certainly. I'll go make us some tea, eh?'

'I'd rather you stayed here; she might want somebody to put a good word in for me anyway.'

'My pleasure, Is.' She sat on the arm of the sofa.

I dialled the first number, and got a voice telling me I'd got through to La Mancha; I thought the voice sounded particularly distorted, and so narrowly avoided the embarrassment of trying to hold a conversation with an answering machine. I left no message after the beeps. I dialled the next number.

'Hello?' It was her. It was Morag. I knew that voice – I had heard it going, 'Yes, yes, oh *yes!*' just a week ago – well enough to tell from just that one word.

I swallowed. 'Morag,' I said, gulping. 'Please don't put down the phone, but . . . it's Isis.'

There was a pause. Then, coldly, 'What?'

I glanced at Sophi for some moral support, which arrived in the shape of a wink. 'Did Allan just phone you?'

Another pause. 'What's it to you?'

'Morag, please; I think he's been lying to you. I just heard him lying to you.'

'How?'

'What?'

'How did you hear?'

'Well, overheard.'

'*How?*'

I took a deep breath, then shook my head. 'Oh, it's a long story, but the point is I did. I heard him say that I had tried to . . . seduce Grandfather.'

'Something like that,' said the cold, distant voice. 'It didn't surprise me, not considering what you've been doing to me.'

'What? What have I done?' I asked, hurt and confused. Sophi was biting her bottom lip, face creased into a frown.

'. . . Oh for God's sake, Isis!' Morag yelled, making me jump.

321

I jerked the handset away from my ear, startled. 'Following me; *stalking* me all round the country, for a start!'

'But I was told to!' I protested. 'I was on a mission!'

'Oh, *yeah*. I suppose you heard voices.'

'No! I was told to; I was *sent* on the mission to find you ... sent by Grandfather, by the Community; everybody.'

'Don't *lie*, Isis. God, this is so pathetic.'

'I'm not lying. Ask anybody in the Community; they all came to see me off. We had a meeting; two meetings, sub-committees—'

'I've just *been* talking somebody from the Community, Isis: Allan.'

'Well, apart from him—'

'I mean, he's even spoken up for you in the past; when all this crazy obsessive stalking stuff started.'

'What crazy obsessive stalking stuff?' I cried. 'What are you talking about?' I was feeling terribly emotional; there was a prickling behind my eyes. Sophi, sitting on the couch in her dressing-gown, looked concerned and slightly alarmed too.

'For God's sake, Isis; all the letters; asking me for—'

'What letters?'

'Isis, are you having black-outs or something? All the letters you've sent me, pledging undying love; sending me your knickers; asking me for *my* used knickers, for God's sake—'

'*What?*' I screeched. Sophi flinched and glanced upwards. She put her finger to her lips.

'Morag,' I said. 'You have to ... Look, I mean, I ... I like you; I always have ... I'm, that is ... we're friends, as ... as well as cousins ... but I don't have a *crush* on you or anything; I'm not obsessive about you. *Please* believe me; I haven't sent *any* sort of letter for about four years, soon after you started sending the open letters, to everybody, when you got busy, with; well, at the time we thought it was playing the baryton, but I suppose it was, um, actually the, ah, films really, but—'

'Don't lie, Isis,' she began, then broke off. '... Wait a minute,' she said. 'What do you mean, "films"?'

I grimaced. Sophi returned the look as though reflecting my

feeling of embarrassment. I cleared my throat. 'As, ah, Fusillada; you know.'

There was a long pause. 'Ah, Morag?' I said, thinking she had somehow rung off silently.

'You do know about that,' she said, sounding wary.

'Yes,' I said. 'I . . . Well, it's another long story, I suppose, but—'

'Allan just told me you hadn't found out,' she said flatly.

I caught a sniff of victory. 'That's what I'm *telling* you; Allan's a *liar*!' I said.

'How many people know about the films?'

'Well . . . everybody,' I confessed.

'Oh, shit.'

'Look, Morag, I don't think there's anything wrong in what you're doing. It's your body and you can do what you want with it, and the act of love is holy under any circumstances unless there is coercion involved; commercial exploitation is irrelevant in that respect and the reaction of Unsaved society is largely a result of its deep-seated fear of the power of sexuality and the repressed—'

'Is, Is . . . yeah, right; got all that. Jeez, you're sounding like some girl on the game who's just got an Open University degree.'

'Sorry.'

'It's all right. But none of this explains why you were chasing me round the fucking country in the first place.'

'I told you; I was on a mission!'

'For *what*?'

'To talk you back into the fold of the Saved and restore your faith in the Order.'

'Eh?'

I repeated what I'd just said.

'What are you talking about?'

'Morag; I saw the letter you sent.'

'What letter?'

'The one you wrote two weeks ago where you said you didn't want to be part of the Order or take part in the Festival; the one where you said you had found another faith.'

Morag laughed. 'Hold on, hold on. I wrote *ages* ago saying I wasn't coming to the Festival, after I started getting the weird letters from you. But I haven't written in a couple of months. As for finding some new faith, I know I'm not the best Luskentyrian in the world, but I'm not lapsed or anything.'

I stared at Sophi. She looked back, her expression half trepidatious, half hopeful.

'So,' I said into the telephone. 'Somebody's been sending both of us faked – forged – letters.'

'Yeah, if all this isn't you being a really *clever* stalker,' she said, but didn't sound serious. 'Oops; I'm getting battery low showing here. You got any other bombshells you want to drop?'

'I don't think so,' I said. 'But look, can I meet you? Can we talk some more about this? Wherever you want.'

'Well, I don't know. I heard from Allan you were going to stay with Uncle Mo . . .'

'What's that got to do with anything? Look, I'll come to Essex, or London; anywhere. But I'm not *stalking* you, for goodness' sake . . .'

'Well, the thing is, as you were going to be heading south – well, the north of England – but you know what I mean, and as we're stalled here with Frank's . . . ah, business dealings—'

'Ah yes. The VAT problems,' I nodded.

'How do you— ? Oh, never mind.' I heard her take a breath. 'Okay, look; yes, we'll meet, but I'm going to bring Ricky – the cute guy you saw at the house?'

'With Tyson.'

'That's right. And it'll be a public place, okay?'

'Fine by me.'

'Right. Well, the thing is, we're going to be in Edinburgh tomorrow.'

'Edinburgh!' I exclaimed.

'Believe it or not.'

'Why?'

'It's a long story. Let's meet at the Royal Commonwealth Pool, right?'

'Royal Commonwealth Pool,' I repeated. Across from me, Sophi looked surprised.

324

'Afternoon okay?' Morag asked.

'Perfect.'

'Three o'clock?'

'I'll be there. Shall I bring my costume?'

'Yes; we'll be at the flumes.'

'The whats?'

'The flumes.'

I frowned. 'Isn't that a thing they send logs down in the Canadian north-west?'

'Originally, Is, yes. God, you really are out of touch up there, aren't you?'

'And proud of it,' I said, feeling relatively cheerful for the first time in days.

'Nothing changes,' Morag sighed. 'Oh, and look, you won't be saying anything to Allan in the meantime, will you?'

'Absolutely not.'

'Right. Same here. See you tomorrow, then.'

'Indeed. Tomorrow. Goodbye, cuz.'

'Bye.' The phone clicked off.

I put down the handset and grinned at Sophi. I took her hands in mine and watched with joy as her face gradually lost all traces of worry and doubt and bloomed into a beautiful broad smile, expressing what I felt.

I laughed quietly. 'Light at the end of the tunnel,' I said.

C H A P T E R
T W E N T Y

'It is dreams, you see, Isis. Dreams.' Uncle Mo took another drink from his little plastic tumbler, nodding to himself as he watched the grass, cliffs and sea slide past our window. 'Dreams can be terrible things. Oh yes. Terrible, terrible things.'

'I thought they were called nightmares when they were like that,' I said.

Uncle Mo laughed in a watery way and leaned over the table to me, patting me on the forearm. 'Ah, Isis, bless you, child, you are so young. You see things so simply but that clarity is gone from me. This is what life does, what dreams do. You are not to know how terrible dreams can be. I,' he said, tapping himself softly on his waistcoated chest, 'I am not old; I am not an old man. I am in my middle ages, no more. But I have lived enough for an old man's memories. I could be old for all that matters. Ah, dreams.'

'I see,' I said, not seeing at all.

The train banked round a fast corner, tipping us towards the view of red-cliffed coastline and fractured rocks washed by a lazy, ruffled sea. On the pale blue horizon a grey speck was a ship. The sky was swathed in quiet layers of pastel cloud.

We were on the eleven o'clock train from Edinburgh to London King's Cross, due to change at York for Manchester. I was supposed to meet Morag at three in Edinburgh and right now I was heading south for England, getting further and further away from my cousin all the time. I had thought seriously about giving Uncle Mo the slip in Waverley station, and had worked out a plan to do just that, but I had changed my mind. I had another plan now. The timing was a little tight and there was no guarantee of its success anyway, but I judged it worth the effort and the risk.

'Dreams,' Uncle Mo said, unscrewing the top of another miniature bottle of vodka and tipping the bottle's contents into his plastic tumbler. He added a little soda from a larger bottle, shaking his head in time as he shook the miniature, forcing the last few drops

329

out of it. 'Dreams . . . dreams of ambition, dreams of success . . .
are terrible, my lovely niece, because they sometimes come true,
and that is the most awful of things for a man to suffer.'

'Oh,' I said. 'That sort of dream. I thought you meant dreams
when one is asleep.'

'Those as well, dear child,' Uncle Mo said, sitting wearily back
in his seat. We had a four-person table to ourselves, on the eastern
side of the train. I was on my Sitting Board, of course, still wearing
the leather trousers which I was growing to like, and the jacket
that Grandma Yolanda had bought me. Uncle Mo was dapper in
a three-piece suit and flamboyant tie, his camel-hair coat carefully
folded and placed lining-outwards on the luggage rack overhead.
He did not use a Sitting Board, claiming that he had a medical
condition and in any event was a Moslem now and had quite
enough to worry about what with remembering his prayer mat.
I had pointed out that Muslims were not supposed to drink.

'That is different,' he had said defensively. 'I was a Luskentyrian,
then an alcoholic, then a Moslem, you see?' I'd said I'd seen, but bit
my lip on a remark about which of his three faiths he seemed most
devout in serving. 'But I shall beat the demon drink,' he insisted,
'be in no doubt. I drink, and drink and drink and then—' he made
a sweeping, cutting motion with the flat of his hand. 'I stop. You
will see.'

I said I saw.

'All dreams can destroy a man,' he said, staring with heavy,
deeply lidded eyes at the calm vistas of sea and shore unreeling
beyond our window. I was glad I'd chosen this flank of the train; I
had not travelled on the line before, but I knew from maps and the
tales of other travellers that this was the best side for the view.

'Just men are destroyed by dreams?'

'Yes. And I say that as a man who is not a chauvinist, no; I am
aware of the equalness of women in most matters, and celebrate
and sanctify their ability to bring forth life. In this much I am in
advance of many of my co-religionists, I dare to admit, though
. . . well, the West is not the end all of being.' He leaned over
the table again, wagging the same finger and staring intently at
me. 'What good is equality if it is just the equality of being

330

disrespected just as much as men, and violence . . . done violence against?'

I nodded noncommittally. 'You may have a point there.'

'I have indeed.' He looked up, as though checking his camel-hair coat was still there. Then he looked back at me. 'What was I saying?'

'Dreams. Doing terrible things. To men, mostly.'

'Exactly!' he cried, waving his finger in the air. 'Because men are the obsessivists, Isis! Men are the driven half of our kind; they are the dreamers, the creatives who have brains in recompensation for not being the creationists with their wombs! We are even you might say the slightly mad half of the human races, because we are tormented with our visions, our ambitions, our ideas!' He slapped the table with his hand.

I was trying to think where I'd heard this sort of stuff before. Recently. Oh yes; Grandma Yolanda.

'It is men who are afflicted the worst by dreams,' he told me. 'That is our curse just as women have theirs.' He looked hurt, and touched his forehead with one set of fingers, closing his eyes, then held out one hand to me. 'I am sorry. I did not mean to be indelicate. Your pardon, Isis.'

'That is quite all right, Uncle.'

He held up the plastic tumbler with its almost-melted ice and its cargo of liquid. 'Perhaps I am drinking a little too much,' he said, smiling through the plastic at me.

'We're just enjoying ourselves,' I said. 'Nothing wrong with that. It passes the journey.' I raised my own tumbler, which was half full of beer. 'Cheers.'

'Cheers,' he said, swallowing. I sipped.

*

Uncle Mo had started drinking at the buffet bar in Stirling station after we'd been dropped there by the bus.

I had returned to my own room after my phone call to Morag from the Woodbeans'; I had already decided I would be departing for somewhere in the morning and, tempted though I was to stay

331

again with Sophi, I felt it appropriate and fitting to spend a night – at last – in my own old hammock in my own room in the Community, after so long away from it.

It had taken a good hour for my feverish thoughts to subside sufficiently to let me sleep, but I awoke at my usual time, dressed, packed and went down to the kitchen, where I informed a bleary-eyed Uncle Mo that I would be coming with him to Spayedthwaite. The atmosphere in the kitchen became glacial the moment I entered; much worse than the day before. When I made my announcement to Uncle Mo in the sudden silence, there was a muttered 'Good riddance' from somebody at the far end of the table, and no voice raised in my support.

I knew then that all my politicking yesterday had been in vain, and the scurrilous lie about the attempted seduction of Grandfather had already been disseminated.

I made to leave, but stopped at the door and looked back in at them.

'You have been deceived in this,' I told them. 'Wickedly deceived.' I was able to keep my voice low; the kitchen had probably never held such numbers and such silence at the same time. I was unable to keep the sadness and the hurt from my voice. 'With God's help I will prove this to you one day and reclaim your good regard.' I hesitated, unsure what more to say, and aware that the longer I stood there the greater became the possibility that somebody – perhaps the one who had wished me good riddance – would rob me of my chance to say my piece. '. . . I love all of you,' I blurted, and closed the door and walked quickly away across the courtyard, a strange high keening ringing in my ears, my fists clenched painfully, nails digging into my palms and my teeth clenched together so hard my nose hurt. It seemed to work; no tears came.

I ascended to the office to tell Allan I was leaving. I was given five pounds spending money; Uncle Mo would get my ticket for me. I found it surprisingly easy to look Allan in the face, though I suspect he found me cold and oddly unconcerned at leaving the Community again so soon. I should perhaps have made a show of regret or even distress, but could not bring myself to do so.

He assured me again that he would be doing all he could to help restore my reputation and my standing in the Community while I was away, and would both keep in touch and be ready to call me back on the instant that the situation improved and Grandfather's humour ameliorated. Please God that would not be long.

I just nodded and said I agreed.

Polite, restrained, dissembling, I stood there with an aspect outwardly quite banal, but in my heart, in my deepest soul, it was as though great cold stones slid grinding and grating across each other into some dreadful new configuration, like a vast lock fit to secure one continent to another, but now undoing, freeing its great ladings to the demands of their different influences, different courses, different velocities, and to the catastrophes incumbent upon their now opposed and antagonistic movements.

Within me there was now set in place a cruel desire; a will, a determination to seek the lode of truth amongst this flinty wilderness of lies and follow its path and its consequences wherever they might lead. I would seek to do no more than lay bare the truth, to mine the gold from this mountain of leaden falseness, but I would expose that vein of truth utterly and without fear, favour or qualification, and if the result of its revelation meant the destruction of my brother's reputation and his place within our Order, even if it meant the humbling of my Grandfather, then I would not shrink from it, nor hesitate to pursue this course to the very limit of my abilities, no matter what balances my actions shook or what structures my excavations threatened.

And, I decided – there and then, in the Community office in the mansion house, at the epicentre of my hours-old astonishment and wrath, with that key still hanging round my brother's neck, that locked drawer with its treacherous cargo not more than a few feet away – I would embark upon my mission sooner rather than later, before the trail or the dish grew cold, and before the results of these most recent infamies became too set in stone to suffer amendment.

My brother and I parted with an insincerity only I knew was quite mutual.

As I left the office I met Sister Amanda, coming downstairs with her and Allan's child, Mabon, in her arms. Amanda is a few years older than Allan, a slim, red-haired woman I've always been on good terms with. I said hello to her but she just hurried past me, averting her head and clutching the one-year-old to her chest as though I was a monster who might rip the infant from her arms and tear it asunder. The child looked back at me over her shoulder, his big dark eyes full of what looked like dismayed surprise. He and his mother disappeared into the office.

*

The bus took Uncle Mo and me into Stirling half an hour later. Brother Vitus was sent to see us off. He carried our bags and seemed monosyllabic with embarrassment or shame.

He waved back, once, perfunctorily, as the bus took us away, and I was left thinking that the contrast with the last time I had left High Easter Offerance – upon the slow rolling river in that misty dawn, with the well-wishes of all the Community sounding hushed but resonant in my ears – could not have been much greater.

I might have cried then, but there was something cold and stony and sharp in me now that seemed to have frozen all my tears.

*

When we got to the station at Stirling we had twenty minutes to spare before our connecting service with Edinburgh arrived, which time, Uncle Mo informed me – even allowing a couple of minutes for making our way to the appropriate platform – was exactly the decent minimum for drinking a large and comforting vodka and soda at a civilised pace, without unseemly gulping towards the end and an undignified gallop along the platform. It more or less behoved him so to do, therefore, and he wondered if I would join him in a fast-breaking drink, it being a very early hour in the morning for him, all things and current style of life considered. I accepted an orange juice and a sandwich.

Uncle Mo pronounced the vodka a particularly good one for

334

a public bar, and knocked the drink back as if it was water. He ordered another. 'One must make hay while the sun shines, Isis,' he said as he paid the bar lady. 'Grab one's opportunities. Seize the time!' He seized the glass and sampled that vodka, too. It turned out to be equally worthy of note.

I ate my sandwich quickly, but paced my sips of the orange juice so that I finished it a couple of minutes before our train was due. Uncle Mo managed to cram in another vodka and soda before we heard the train arrive and had to quit the bar quickly to run for the train. He purchased my ticket on board. It was a single, I noticed. I mentioned this.

He looked discomfited. 'Your brother gave the money,' he said. 'He will send additional funds for a ticket back later, along with some money for your keep.'

I nodded, saying nothing.

There proved to be a trolley service on the train from Stirling to Edinburgh. Uncle Mo found this out by asking another passenger. For a while he sat fretting and turning to look back up the aisle every few moments, then he announced he was going in search of the toilet. He reappeared a few minutes later with four miniatures of gin, a larger bottle of tonic and a small can of orange. 'I bumped into the buffet trolley,' he explained, setting his supplies down on the table and passing the orange juice to me. 'No vodka. Tsk.'

'Hmm,' I said.

I was already starting to reconsider my plans.

At Waverley, having dispatched the four gins with the swift contempt they apparently deserved for not being vodkas, Uncle Mo still did not seem particularly drunk, though he was slurring his words slightly on occasion, and his turn of phrase – tricky and ill-cambered at the best of times – seemed to be tightening.

There was a half-hour to spare; it seemed only natural to repair to the bar. Uncle Mo appeared to have hit a plateau by that time and managed to cruise through the thirty minutes on nothing more than a brace of vodkas (obviously not counting the twelve that went into his hip flask straight from the optic on the discovery that there was no off-licence in the station).

We left the bar, I picked up a timetable for the east-coast line from the information centre, and then we boarded the train which was due to take us to York. My original plan had involved getting on the train with Uncle Mo and then saying I was going to the toilet or the buffet car just before the train was due to depart. I deliberately stowed my kit-bag on the luggage shelf at the end of the carriage, near the door, and claimed the seat that faced in that direction from Uncle Mo after he sat in it originally, claiming that I got sick if I didn't have my back to the engine. All this meant that I could leave my seat, collect my bag and get off the train just before it left, and not even risk being seen as the departing train went past me.

However, I had been thinking.

Despite the obvious importance of everything else I had had to take on board over the last twelve hours – Cousin Morag's allegations and revelations, the promise that at long last I might catch up with her, Allan's sacrilegious use of a piece of high-technical electronic equipment within the Community, his lies to Morag, his lies to me, his lies to the whole Community and the sheer selfish greed for power that these symptoms hinted at, not to mention my Grandfather's profane, misguided weakness and his attempt to seduce me – I could not stop thinking about that note on the address list in the desk, the note alongside my Great-aunt Zhobelia's name. 'Care of Unc. Mo'.

I remembered Yolanda's words. *Something, for sure.*

It spoke of the corrupting atmosphere engendered by the deception that had been revealed to me that what had once seemed innocent, or at any rate of no great consequence, I now found deeply suspicious. Great-aunt Zhobelia's decision to seek out her original family and her effective disappearance as far as the Community was concerned had always seemed odd before, but certainly well within the normal parameters of human contrariness; people are constantly doing things we find incomprehensible for what they regard as good and obvious reasons, and I had never really wondered about Zhobelia's decision any more than I had about Brigit or Rhea becoming apostate, accepting that people just did do strange, even stupid things sometimes.

But now, in the infecting climate of mistrust and apprehension brought about by my discovery of Allan's mendacity and the realisation that behind the curtain of familial and religious trust and love was hidden the machinery of perfidious malevolence, much that I had previously taken blithely on trust now set me thinking what sinister purpose might be concealed therein.

Great-aunt Zhobelia. Care of Uncle Mo. I wondered . . .

I felt a moment of dizziness, just as I had the night before, perched on the storeroom window. The moment passed, as it had just the night before when I had teetered on the fulcrum of that window at the back of the mansion house, leaving me in a moment of giddy clarity.

I made my decision; my mouth felt dry and there was a metallic taste in it. Heart thumping; again. This was becoming habitual.

What the heck. I would stay on the damn train. The timetable said I could get off at Newcastle upon Tyne and catch a train back to Waverley in time to get to the swimming pool for my rendezvous with Cousin Morag. If everything ran to time, that was. I'd risk it.

The train started off. An announcement informed us the buffet car was open for the sale of light refreshments, soft drinks and alcoholic beverages.

'I think that means the bar's open, Uncle Mo,' I said brightly. 'Would you like me to go and get us something?'

'What a good idea, niece!' Uncle Mo said, and took out his wallet.

CHAPTER
TWENTY-ONE

'Dreams,' Uncle Mo repeated sadly, obviously getting into his stride with this theme. 'Dreams can destroy you, you see, Isis.'

'Really?'

'Oh, yes,' he said, and sounded bitter. 'I had my dreams, Isis. I dreamed of fame and success and being an admirable person, a person people would recognise without ever having met me. Do you see, Isis?' He reached across the table and grasped my arm. 'I wanted all this for myself you see. I was young and foolish and I had this idea that it would be wonderful to be loved without reason, just because people knew oneself from stage or film or the dreaded goggle-box; the television. But I was too young to see that it is not really *you* that they love; it is your part, your role, your persona, and in that much you are at the mercy of writers,' he grimaced, as though he had just bitten into something sour, 'producers, directors, editors and the like. Liars, egotists; all of them! *They* control the character you play, and they can destroy you with a few sentences typed on the typewriter, a few lines scribbled on a memo, a few words over a coffee break.'

He sat back, shaking his head. 'But I was young and foolish, then. I thought everyone would love me; I could not understand that there is so much cynicism and selfishness in the world, especially in certain professions of a so-called artistic bending. The world is a wicked place, Isis,' he said sombrely, fixing his watery gaze on me and lifting his plastic tumbler. 'A wicked, wicked place.' He drank deeply.

'I am starting to find that out, Uncle,' I said. 'I am finding wickedness and selfishness even in the heart of our—'

'It was ever thus, niece,' Uncle Mo said with a wave of his hand, that sour expression on his face again. 'You are the innocent now; you have your dreams and I hope they are not the source of bitterness that mine were for me, but now is your time and you

341

are finding what we all find, no matter where we go. There is much that is good in our Faith – well, your Faith – but it is still part of the world, the wicked, wicked world. I know more than you know; I have been around longer, I have kept in touch even though I was not there, you see?'

'Ah.'

'So I have heard much; perhaps more than if I had stayed in the Community.' He leaned forward, chin almost on the table again, and tapped his nose. I leaned forward too, but this time I led with my other arm; the one he'd been grabbing until now felt bruised and sore. 'I know things, Isis,' he told me.

'You *do*?' I said, in my most breathless-ingénue manner, and widened my eyes.

'Oh yes,' Uncle Mo said, and sat back again, nodding his head. He straightened his jacket, patting the bulge over where his wallet was. 'Oh yes. Mysteries. Rumours.' He appeared to think for a moment. '. . . Things.'

'Golly.'

'Not all sweetness and light, Isis,' he said, finger wagging. 'Not all sweetness and light. There have been . . . darknesses along the way.'

I nodded, looking thoughtful as the train swung briefly away from the coast to enter the town of Berwick-upon-Tweed. It slowed but did not stop as it passed through the station; we both watched the view unfold as the train curved out along a long arched stone viaduct across the river, revealing the jumbled old town on the steep north bank, the later, more uniform houses on the flatter south side, and the sloping road bridges between the two, outlined against the distant sea and clouds.

'Our Faith has had,' I said eventually, 'our share of sadness, I suppose.'

Uncle Mo watched the view, nodding. I refilled his glass with the last of the four miniatures.

'The loss of Luskentyre,' I said, 'my parents' death and Grandmother's death, and one might even say the loss of your mother, my Great-aunt Zhobelia, who is supposed still to be alive, but is lost to us all the same. All these thi—'

'Ah, you see!' Uncle Mo sat forward, taking my arm in his hand again. 'I know things there; things I am sworn to secrecy on.'

'You are?'

'Indeed. For the good of all . . .' He sneered. 'So I am told. Then I hear what is supposed to have happened . . .' He looked as though he had thought the better of saying any more, and took a long swallow from his tumbler instead. He finished his drink and looked around the bottle-strewn table.

'Shall I get us some more refreshments, Uncle?' I asked, quickly draining my beer.

'Well,' he said. 'I suppose . . . but I am drinking rather quickly today. I don't know. Perhaps I should have a sandwich or something. Maybe . . .'

'Well,' I said, holding up my empty plastic tumbler. 'I think I'll go and get another beer anyway, so if you . . .'

'Oh, very well. But I must slow down and have a sandwich or something. Here,' he said, digging inside his jacket for his wallet. He felt around inside, then had to open out his jacket with his other hand and look within to guide his seeking fingers, before finally taking out the wallet and carefully extracting a twenty-pound note from it. 'Here.'

'Thank you, Uncle. How many would you like— ?'

'Oh, well, I shall slow down, but best to stock up in case they run out. Say . . .' He waved his hand weakly and shook his head. 'Whatever that will buy. And whatever you wish, of course.'

'Right you are!' I said perkily. I tidied the table, shoving some of our debris into the little brown paper bag. I included my beer can, which was still half-full. I lifted out the can when I deposited the rest in a litter bin on my way to the buffet car.

I had kept a little of the change from the last order. I kept all the change from this one, wolfed down a sandwich at the bar, and came back swigging beer from the same can I'd taken away.

'Here we are!' I said, plonking down another rattling brown paper bag onto the table.

'Ah! There, now. I see. Well, there we are. Ah, you fine child,' Uncle Mo said, his hands waving like tendrils towards the bag's little folded paper handles.

'Allow me,' I said.

Outside, Lindisfarne, the Holy Isle, slid past beyond undulating meadows and long shallow dunes of golden sand and gently waving grass. Between the land and the island were empty acres of sandy tidal flats which in places were already inundated by the rising tide. A car was risking the crossing on the causeway across the sands, waves lapping at the roadway. A small castle rose dramatically in the distance on the island's only piece of high ground, a smooth, linear swell of rounded rock towards the isle's southern limit. Beyond, on the land facing the island, two huge obelisks rose before the miles of low dunes, and visible on the seaward horizon bulked a hazy prominence that – if I remembered my maps correctly – ought to be Bamburgh Castle.

'Did you get any sandwiches?' Uncle Mo asked plaintively, as I emptied the bag and poured him a drink.

'Oh, did you actually want a sandwich? I'm sorry, Uncle Mo; shall I—' I started to rise from my seat again.

'No, no,' he said, motioning me to sit down. 'Never mind. It's not necessary,' he slurred.

'Look; I got some ice in a separate glass,' I said, putting a couple of lumps into his drink.

'You are a good child,' he said, raising his tumbler and slurping at his drink. Dribbles ran down his chin. 'Oh, my goodness.' I passed him a napkin and he dabbed at his chin. He put down the glass, spilling a little, but did not seem to notice. He fixed me with his bleary, diluted, dilated gaze. 'You are a very good child, Isis. Very good.'

Not that good, I thought to myself, and had what I hope was the decency to feel guilty for my mendacity, and for my cynical use of Uncle Mo's weakness for the drink.

I sighed. 'I often think of Great-aunt Zhobelia,' I said, innocently. 'I hardly ever think of my mother and father, because I was so young when they died, I suppose, but I often think of Zhobelia, even though I can't remember her very clearly. Isn't that strange?'

Uncle Mo looked like he was going to cry. 'Zhobelia,' he said, sniffing, head bowed, looking into his drink. 'She is my mother and

I love her as a dutiful son should, but it must be said she has grown
... cantankerous with age, Isis. Difficult, too. Very difficult. And
hurtful. Most hurtful, also. You wouldn't ... No. But there you
are. Terribly hurtful. Terribly. I think now she likes especially to
hurt those who love her most. I have tried to do my best for her and
been the good steward for her charge ...' He sniffed sonorously
and dabbed at his nose with the napkin I'd given him. 'There is
some ... I don't know. I think they were always ... I think those
two knew more than they let on, Isis. I know they did.'

'What two, Uncle?'

'Zhobelia and Aasni; my mother and my aunt. Yes. There you
are. They knew things about ... things; I don't know. I would
catch things they said to each other when they weren't talking in
the old country's language, or the island language, which they also
knew something of, you know, oh yes. Indeed. I would catch a look
or a start of a sentence or phrase and then they would switch into
Khalmakistani or Gaelic or that mixture of those and English they
used which nobody else could understand and I would be lost, but
... Oh,' he waved a hand at me. 'I am ramp ... I am rambling now,
I know ... I ... I'm sure you think ... I'm just an old man but I'm
not, Isis. You know, at the last Festival, when I asked, well; didn't
really, but thought of asking ... well; did ask, I suppose, but not
such that ... that ... but ... you ...' He shook his head, his eyes
full of tears and his lips working in a strange, fluidly disconnected
way. 'Flippink dreams, eh, Isis?' he said, sniffing hard again and
looking at me. He shook his head, looked into his tumbler again
and drank.

I gave him a while to compose himself, then I got up and – taking
my Sitting Board – went round to sit next to him, putting an arm
round his shoulder and holding his other hand.

'Life can seem cruel sometimes, Uncle Mo,' I said. 'I know this
now, though you have known it longer. You are older and wiser
than I am and you have suffered more, but you must know in your
heart, in your soul, that God loves you and that They – or He, your
prophet's God, if you will – that God can be your comfort, just as
your family and friends can comfort you, too. You do know that,
don't you, Uncle Mo?'

He put down his drink and turned to me in the seat, putting out his arm; I leaned forward so that he could put his arm between me and the seat. We hugged each other. He still smelled of cologne. I hadn't realised how slight he was; shorter than me, and somehow packaged, bulked out with his fine clothes to look more substantial than he actually was. I was aware of his wallet pressing into my breast and, with my left hand, could feel what was probably the hardness of a portable telephone in another jacket pocket.

'You are such a good child, Isis!' he assured me again. 'Such a good, good child!'

I patted him on the back, quite as though it was he who was the child, not I.

'And you are a good uncle,' I said. 'And I am sure you are a good son as well. I'm sure Zhobelia must love you and must love to see you.'

'Ah,' he said, shaking his head against my shoulder. 'She has little time for me. I cannot get to see her as often as I would like anyway, Isis; they keep her up there, away from me; ha! I have to pay; my savings, you'll notice; mine. My money from my savings and the few parts I get and the restaurant money. It is a fine, good restaurant, Isis; I don't actually own it, you probably guessed that, if I ever gave that impression I didn't mean . . . didn't mean deceiving, but it is the best in the city, a most estimable place where one might lavish oneself and I am the *maître de* you see, Isis; I am the first public face of the establishment and so most highly important and influential with the minds and hearts of the diners, you see. We have a most extensive wine list and I was a fine wine waiter, a *fine* wine waiter I tell you as well and still can fill in . . . in the most exemplary manner.'

'Your mother should be proud of you.'

'She is not. She calls me a liqueur Moslem; innocent and sweet on the outside – even chocolate coloured – but open me up and I am full of alcohol. It is her family. Her other family.'

'Her other family?' I said, shifting my hand to stroke Uncle Mo's head.

'The Asis family. She says she wants to be in that home but she was happy in Spayedthwaite; they persuaded her, turned her against me, made her say she wanted to be nearer to them. And yet I still pay. I get some help from them and a little from your people but I pay most; I. Me. Mr Muggins McMuggins here. They talked about responsibility and blood ties and they wanted her near them and they made her say that she wanted the same thing too and so she away went, most unfairly. It isn't fair, Isis.' He squeezed my hand. 'You are a good child. You would have been good to your poor mother and father. I don't know I should be doing this for your brother, really. He holds the wallet strings, you know that, but I don't know that I should be taking you away like this. It is so hard to do the right things. I try, but I don't know. You must forgive me, Isis. I am not so strong a man. Not so strong as I should like to be. Then, who is? You are a woman, Isis, you would not understand. Such strength. Please understand . . .'

He put his head down upon my breast and sobbed then, and after a moment or two I could feel my shirt getting wet.

I looked out of the window. Trees whizzed past. The train rocked us. The trees parted dramatically, like a great green curtain upon a stage, revealing a small steep valley with a river curving through beneath. A flock of birds burst from somewhere underneath us and turned as one, a grey-black cloud of fluttering movement sweeping through the air between the banked walls of the trees. The trees rushed back up in a green blur. I looked upwards to the creamy layers of cloud.

'Where did they take Zhobelia, Uncle Mo?' I asked quietly.

Mo sobbed, then sniffed hard, so that I felt his whole body shake and vibrate. 'I'm not supposed . . . Oh, what does . . . ? You're not supposed . . .'

'I'd love to know, Uncle Mo. I might be able to help, you know.'

'Slanashire,' he said.

'Where's that?'

'It's Lanca . . . Lanarkshire; a horrid little town in . . . Lanark-shire,' he said.

That was a relief. I'd thought he was going to name somewhere in the Hebrides, or even back in the sub-continent.

'I'd so much like to write to her,' I said softly. 'What's her address?'

347

'Oh . . . The . . . what is that word again? Gloaming. Indeed. There. The Gloamings. The Gloamings Nursing Home, Wishaw Road, Mauchtie, Lancashire. Lanarkshire,' he said.

I got him to repeat the town's name, too.

'Near Glasgow,' he went on. 'Just outside. Well; near. Bloody horrid little place it is. Oh, excuse me. Don't go. . . . Miserable. . . . Write. She would love to hear you . . . hear from you. She would love to see you, perhaps. Well, maybe. She seems not to want to see us very much . . . Her own son . . . but . . . Well. Who knows? Who ever knows, Isis? Nobody ever knows. Nobody ever . . . knows nothing . . . at all. All dreams. Just . . . dreams. Terrible . . . . . .dreams.' He gave a single great, ragged sigh, and settled closer into me.

I held him for a while. He seemed very small.

After a while, I shifted one of my hands to Uncle Mo's head and gently placed my palm over his hair, cupping his head like some delicate goblet. I closed my eyes. I settled into the steady rhythm of the rushing, rocking train, letting its hurtling movement become stillness and its shimmering, steely racket become silence, so that I found – in that stillness and that silence – a place to prepare myself and gather my powers and await the awakening sensations that were the presentiment of my Gift.

It came eventually, tingling in my head and in my hand, and I became a conduit, a filter, a heart, an entire system. I felt my uncle's pain and sadness and broken dreams, felt their spare, bleak, numbing terror, felt the choking fullness of his emptiness, and felt it all flowing into me, circulating through me and being cleaned and neutralised and made good through me and then flowing back out through my hand and into him again as something made wholesome from poison, something made positive that had been negative, giving him peace, giving him hope, giving him faith.

I opened my eyes again and flexed my hand.

The trees outside the window gave way to farmland, then houses.

I watched the houses for a while. Uncle Mo breathed on, easily now, and nestled against me like a child.

The guard announced we would soon be arriving at Newcastle upon Tyne. Uncle Mo didn't stir. I thought for a moment, then looked at my hand, the hand that I had touched Uncle Mo's thoughts with.

'Oh, Uncle Mo,' I breathed, too quiet for him to hear, 'I'm sorry.'

I did some quick mental arithmetic and a bit of estimating, then I looked around to make sure nobody could see and shifted Uncle Mo a little in my arms. Then – asking God for Their forgiveness as I did it, and feeling quite wretched and triumphantly predatory in equal measure, yet excited as well – I took Uncle Mo's wallet from his inside jacket pocket.

He had eighty pounds. I took half, then gave him change for twenty-nine from the funds I already held, most of which, admittedly, Uncle Mo himself had unwittingly provided. I pocketed the notes, replaced his wallet and shifted him again, pushing him gently away from me so that he rested with his head partly against the side of the seat and partly against the window. I thought a little more, then reached into his other inside pocket and took his portable telephone. He muttered something, but seemed otherwise oblivious. I scribbled a quick note on a napkin and put it under his tumbler on the table in front of him.

The note said, *Dear Uncle Mohammed. I'm sorry. By the time you read this I will be on a train to London. Thank you for all your kindness; all will be explained. Forgive me. Love, Isis.*

P.S. Posting phone back.

I got up as the train was slowing, took my travelling hat down from the overhead luggage rack, lifted my Sitting Board and walked up the carriage to collect my kit-bag. I passed an elderly couple sitting in seats whose reservations labels read from Aberdeen to York, and pointed Uncle Mo out to them, asking them to wake him before York and make sure he got off. They agreed and I thanked them.

There was a train like ours pulling into Newcastle station from the south just as ours arrived from the opposite direction. I talked

349

to an official on the platform who told me the other train was a delayed Edinburgh-bound service. I sprinted over the footbridge and was back heading north even before the train carrying Uncle Mo set off again.

CHAPTER
TWENTY-TWO

I arrived back in Edinburgh with an hour to spare. It was a pleasantly mild day under high, patchy overcast; I went to the main Post Office, purchased a padded bag and posted Uncle Mo's telephone back to his address in Spayedthwaite, then I walked to the Royal Commonwealth Pool, stopping at a bookshop en route to search a motoring atlas for the town of Mauchtie, in Lanarkshire. It was there, indeed, not far from the town of Hamilton.

I continued on to the pool, in the shadow of Arthur's Seat. I took a walk round it and saw what had to be the flumes, at the back of the building; huge coloured plastic pipes which looked a little like the rubbish chutes one sees on buildings under renovation. There were four of these tubes: a broad meandering white one with an upper section which was either transparent or opaque, two steeper convoluted flumes in yellow and blue, and an abrupt black example which looked almost as steep as a rubbish chute.

I sat on the grass on the slopes of Arthur's Seat for a while, looking out across the buildings and soaking up a little soft, cloud-filtered sunlight, then presented myself at the ticket office of the pool, descended to the changing rooms, squeezed carefully into my tired and tight old costume (it was once yellow, but after years of swimming in the silty old Forth it had long since turned oatmeal) and – after some difficulty stuffing my kit-bag into the narrow locker I had been assigned – spent the next twenty minutes swimming lengths, admiring the sheer size of the place and taking an interest in the flumes, the four of which were entered via a tall circular staircase and three of which decanted into their own small pool. The fourth flume – which appeared to the one with black tubing I'd seen outside earlier – deposited its patrons into a long water-filled trough. Judging from the occasional shrieks and the speed with which people were ejected from the black mouth of this last flume, I gathered that this one was the most thrilling.

353

I'd been keeping an eye on the exits from the changing rooms, and after twenty minutes saw somebody I was reasonably certain was the young man Cousin Morag had called Ricky, whom I had met at La Mancha a week earlier. His trunks were brief and he presented a fine figure of a man: he was tanned, blond and muscled, and I was far from the only female looking at him. I imagined a fair few males were sizing him up too, most with jealousy. He walked halfway along the edge of the pool and stood at the side, his feet spread, his arms crossed bulkily beneath impressive pectorals. There was a frown on his face as he stared round the pool. I did the backstroke past him a couple of times but he didn't seem to notice.

Cousin Morag appeared five minutes later, and drew even more stares. She wore a one-piece, as I did, but there the resemblance ended. Her costume was glossy black. It rode high on the hip and featured sheer-looking black mesh side panels which rose from hip-hem to armpit, huggingly displaying her narrow waist. The swimsuit possessed what was technically a high neck, the concealing effect of which was, however, entirely undone by another deep and wide see-through panel which exhibited the swelling tops of her considerable breasts.

She joined the young man at the side of the pool, gods amongst mortals. They both looked out over the swimmers and those walking or sitting around the side; Morag glanced up at the flumes. She wore her long chestnut hair gathered up into a bun held with a black band. I raised my hand and waved as her gaze swept past me.

She waved back, an uncertain smile on her face. I turned onto my front and swam over to them, reckoning that – if she still believed herself to be in some way threatened by me – Morag would feel less so if I was in the water and beneath her and the young man.

I pulled in at the side; Morag squatted; the young man remained standing, looking down, frowning.

'Hello,' I said, nodding and smiling at both of them.

'Hi, Is. You've met Ricky, haven't you?'

'Yes. Hello again,' I said cheerily. 'How's Tyson?'

He scowled, and appeared to think. 'All right,' he said eventually.

'Good. I'm sorry if my friends and I alarmed you, back at La Mancha.'

'Wasn't alarmed,' Ricky said indignantly.

'I should have said annoyed,' I said, apologetically. 'Sorry if we annoyed you.'

'All right,' Ricky said, apparently appeased.

'So, how's things, cuz?' Morag asked with a small smile.

'Oh, pretty traumatic,' I said, smiling bravely. 'But I'm surviving.'

'Good,' she said, standing. She nodded across the pool to where the circular stairs led to the flume's entrance. 'Shall we flume?' she asked.

'Why not?' I said.

Morag dived gracefully overhead, entering the water behind me with a dainty splash. Ricky launched himself a moment later, creating a disturbance hardly any greater. I kicked away from the side and splashed inelegantly after their sleek shapes.

*

'Flumes are like life, see?' Cousin Morag said, as we neared the end of the queue on the spiral steps and approached the platform which supported the entrances to the four flumes. An attendant in white shorts and T-shirt was supervising the people – mostly children, already damp – who were queuing for the fun.

'Like life?' I said, shuffling forward and talking round Ricky's bulk. He had insisted on standing between Morag and me, seemingly not yet content that I wasn't in fact a stalker with murderous intent, though quite where he thought I could have secreted a weapon I couldn't really see. Perhaps he suspected I was going to up-end Morag over the side of the spiral railings and send her hurtling to the tiles below.

'Yes,' Morag said, round Ricky's impressive biceps as she

355

came to the front of the queue. 'You can take the short fast fun route, like the black chute here, or the long slow leisurely route like the white one, or something in between, know what I mean?'

'Sort of,' I said.

Morag got the nod and padded over to the mouth of the black tube, watched all the way by every pair of eyes within range. She lifted herself athletically into the gaping mouth of the black hole. Lights above the tunnel mouth changed from red to green. She pushed herself away and down, disappearing with a joyous whoop.

Ricky turned to me, grinning. 'She always does that,' he said. Then he strode across the moist tiles to follow her, hurtling silently down into the blackness a little later.

I thought it would seem churlish not to take the same route. I settled myself in the mouth of the drop, grabbing the chrome handles at the side of the flume entrance. When the red light went off I let myself go.

Terror. It only lasted about three seconds, but for those moments I felt scared witless. Air rushed around me, one shoulder burned with friction, water rushed up my nose, I was twisted this way and that and then hurtled from near vertical to perfect horizontality in a single body-jarring thud and blasted into the water-filled trough I'd observed earlier. I skidded to a stop near the end of the trough, coughing and spluttering and with a chlorine-burned nose. My swimming costume had tried to insert itself into my womanhood. I also suspected I now knew what receiving an enema felt like. I waved my arms around, red-faced and coughing.

Morag and Ricky pulled me out, laughing.

I thanked them, stood, stooped, spat out a little water and pulled my swimsuit into a more modest configuration.

'Wow!' I said, beaming at them.

'Again?' said Morag.

'Again!' I cried.

*

'In most flumes, just sit up to go slower,' Morag said, explaining how to apply the brakes. 'Though that wouldn't really work in something like the black run here.' She giggled. 'Also, you can put out your arms, or there's a way of lying down but arching your back so you get a vacuum between your back and the flume floor. But going slower isn't the point, is it?' She shook her head at me. 'If you want to go *faster*, you cross your ankles and put your hands round the back of your neck, forcing down your shoulder blades. That way you've got one heel and both shoulders in contact: minimum friction. There's more to it than that, naturally, for really fast runs; you have to throw yourself into the curves, know what I mean? Flex into the right shape, try to minimise collisions. You've got to *think* yourself down it. That's how to score really low times.'

'You carry a stop watch?' I asked as we moved spasmodically up the spiral steps.

'Not allowed any jewellery,' Morag said, displaying elegantly naked wrists in front of me. Ricky was ahead of us, content that I was not such a bad egg after all. 'A lot of fast flumes have a button you hit as you set off; you go through a beam or something at the bottom and your time's displayed on a clock at the exit pool. Really good fun, it is.'

'Oh.' I watched over the edge of the railings as somebody exited into the splash pool beneath us. 'Do you do a lot of this sort of thing?' I asked her.

'Oh God, yes; I've been to all the major flumes in England, the Costa del Sol and the Balearics. We were due to go off to the Canaries last week; I've heard there are some good ones there, but then this thing with Frank's VAT came up.'

'Hmm,' I said. 'I take it Allan knew you were supposed to be going on holiday?'

'Yeah. He knew.'

Of course; and if all had gone according to plan I'd have got to London, finally found out that Morag was away on holiday, and – if I hadn't decided to wait on my own initiative – would doubtless have received instructions to do so from High Easter

357

Offerance when I reported back by phone-code. 'How long were you going for?' I asked.

'A month,' Morag said. 'But then Frank had to talk to the Customs and Excise guys and I thought, well, I'll do the Scottish flumes then, except I was a bit worried about you. I was going to give Stirling a miss; reckoned they were a bit too close to home for comfort.'

'So there's lots of places with flumes, then?'

'God, yeah; hundreds. I mean, these ones here are all right, but you should see some of the big ones they got abroad, the big outdoor ones; fuckin' brilliant, they are . . .'

'Right, goin' for the Black Hole again, right?' Ricky said, getting to the front of the queue.

'Right, lover,' Morag said, holding him by one shoulder and then patting his behind when his turn came.

'So Ricky's your boyfriend?' I asked her.

'Yeah,' she smiled broadly. 'Hunk or what, eh?'

'Oh, a hunk,' I agreed. 'How does he feel about you . . . you know, in the films?'

She put her head back and laughed. 'Is he jealous? Na; I think he's proud, and he likes watching, anyway. Besides,' she lowered her head to mine and dropped her voice. 'Don't tell him, right? But sometimes, right, doing the porn? I just pretend I'm faking it.'

She giggled, winking at me.

I looked at her, frowning. 'You mean you fake faking an orgasm?' I said, confused.

'Yeah,' she said, nudging me. 'Don't want to hurt his feelings, do I?' She glanced round. 'See you at the bottom.'

*

Terror, again. But this time I kept my legs crossed and hence avoided any orificial invasions. I was starting to appreciate how, for Morag, fluming might present a refreshing contrast with her day job.

*

'How *did* you become a porn star?'

'I was giving a concert—'

'The baryton?'

'Yeah; of course. I was doing all right with that, too, though it wasn't like you could get many people to come along; very small scale and select it was . . . but I was on the tube train going there, kind of dolled up, I suppose, when this guy came up and gave me his card and asked would I like to have some photos taken for a magazine? And I said, What sort of magazine? And he said a men's magazine, but one of the class ones, like. Well, I wasn't bothered one way or the other, but then he mentioned the money and I said, well, I'd have to think about it. Thought about it, called him next day, said okay, went to this stately home a week later where they were doing the shoot, took off me togs, the photographer recommended Frank as a manager and he got me into the films. Simple as that, really. I know I should have said something, written or something, but the communal letters kept telling me how proud everybody was of me playing the baryton and I felt I'd be letting people down, and I mean after all I had *started off* doing what I'd said I'd do, and I still do the *occasional* concert, every few months, like, and so I reckoned it was sort of all right and maybe even kind of ordained, anyway, because if it hadn't been for the baryton and me going to that concert and meeting the guy on the tube train then I wouldn't have got into porn in the first place, would I?'

'Hmm,' I said. Obviously, formulating elaborate justifications for deceit was not an area in which I held a monopoly. 'Do you *enjoy* it?' I asked, frowning.

'What, the porn?'

'Yes.'

She looked thoughtful. 'You know what?' she said, nodding at me. 'I love it.' She shrugged. 'I like lots of sex, I like being admired and I like the money. Sure beats working for a living.' She laughed. 'I'll give it another few years, then I think I might open my own chain of exotic lingerie shops.' She looked thoughtful, her gaze directed far away. 'Or go into flume design or something.' She shrugged again and went on filing her fingernails. 'I mean, it's kind of technical and cluttered, right enough, but it's very pure, really.'

359

We sat wet-haired in the café, watching the pool and the swimmers. I am sure I looked bedraggled. Morag looked like some fresh, glowing, blue-jeaned mermaid. Ricky was at the counter, queuing to fetch us our drinks.

We had each tried the other three flumes, though Morag and Ricky both kept going back to the Black Hole. I didn't, preferring the two convoluted medium tubes because they gave you time to appreciate the ride rather than just be terrified by it. I even liked the broad, shallow white tunnel, the slowest of the lot, which Morag and Ricky tried because they felt they had to for completeness' sake but declared was really there for wimps and sportive old-age pensioners, but which had the additional attraction of having a view for the first, half-transparent section, and a damn fine view at that, of Salisbury Crags and Arthur's Seat rearing up all green and brown against the blues and whites of the sky.

After a couple of hours of intense fluming, producing raw heels, shoulders and other pointy bits, we did a few lengths of the pool for exercise, and then decided to call it a day. Once we'd changed we'd headed for the café.

Morag put away her nail file in her little shoulder bag and sat back in her seat, stretching with lithe magnificence, her hands at the back of her neck pulling her damp hair away from her blouse. Lifting her arms like that had a dramatic effect on her bosoms; the effect it had on those present, however, seemed to obey a sort of inverted inverse square law; she gave no sign whatsoever of noticing. I wasn't about to, either, but men sitting at nearby tables stole furtive glances, males further away looked on with appreciative directness, and those surrounded by toddlers and damp towels twenty yards off across the café floor suddenly sat up straight and adjusted the position of their little plastic seats for a better view.

I gave a small laugh, leaning over the table. 'So, cousin, do I take it you've absolved me of being a stalker or an obsessive or whatever it was you thought I was?'

'Yeah,' she said, looking a little bashful. 'Well, I'm sorry about that, but it wasn't my fault, right?'

'No, I know,' I said. 'I think I know who's to blame.'

Ricky returned from the counter with a tray. I had a little pot of tea, Morag a black coffee and a mineral water, and Ricky a cola and a cheeseburger.

'So, what do you think's going on, then?' Morag asked me in a business-like manner.

'At the Community?' I asked. She nodded. 'I'm not certain,' I admitted. 'But I think Allan wants to take over.'

She frowned. 'But he's not a Leapyearian; how can he?'

'He's the one helping Grandfather with the revisions at the moment; that might even be the whole reason for getting me out of the way in the first place. I can't see how he can remove Leapyearianism from the Faith entirely and leave anything worth believing in, but he might be able to persuade Salvador that a real Leapyearian is male and so I don't count, or that there should be a division between the Elect of God, who'd be just a . . . a sort of figure-head, and the . . . executive, I'd suppose you'd call it – whoever actually runs the Order and the Community. They'd hold the reins.'

I looked over at Ricky, who was staring at me over his cheeseburger, his jaws wrestling with the food.

Morag saw me looking and glanced at him too. 'It's all right, Rick,' she said. 'Just God talk.'

He nodded, mollified, and redirected his concentration back to the cheeseburger.

'Maybe it's just me,' I said, shrugging. 'Maybe he feels I've wronged him somehow and he wants to destroy me personally . . .' I shook my head. 'No. No; I think he's doing it for himself, and for Mabon, his son.'

'Maybe he's frightened of you.'

I opened my mouth to protest that this could not be the case, but then thought of Allan's face and the expression I had seen on it too many times to count, the first time on the day I brought life back into the fox lying dead in the field by the road. I closed my mouth again and just looked down, shrugging.

'Or what about Salvador?' Morag asked. 'Sure it isn't the old man behind it all?'

'Not sure, but . . . fairly so. I think he just took advantage of the situation.' I laughed bitterly. 'To try to take advantage of me.'

'Old bastard,' Morag said. Ricky looked up again.

'Please, Morag,' I said. 'He is still the Founder, still my Grandfather. It's just the man . . . and the drink, maybe, got the better of the prophet in him.'

'That's crap, cuz,' Morag said.

'He gave us everything, Morag,' I told her. 'Our whole way of life. I'll not deny the treasure he found just because the hand that opened the chest was human and soiled.'

'Very poetic,' Morag told me, 'but you're too bleedin' generous, that's your problem.' It was probably the least perspicacious statement she had made that afternoon.

'Well,' I said, 'I don't intend to be very generous with Allan, once I have my case ready to present before the Order.'

'Good,' she said, with relish.

'Will you help me?' I asked her.

'How?' She looked neutral, Ricky looked suspicious.

'Come to the Community? Back up my story? I mean; simply tell the truth about these letters and Allan's phone calls and what he's told you; how he's lied. Will you?'

'Think they'll listen to me?' She sounded doubtful.

'I think so. We mustn't let Allan suspect anything or he'll attempt to discredit you with everybody else beforehand, as he has me, but if we say nothing about us having met, we should be able to surprise him. If we had it all out in front of a meeting everyone attends, a full Service, there should be no opportunity for him to poison people's minds with rumours and lies. We ought to be able to denounce him without retort.'

'But what about the porn?' Morag asked warily.

'Well, it is hardly the most blessed of professions, certainly, but it was your apparent apostasy that alarmed us most, and I think there would be more rejoicing over your return to the fold than resentment due to the fact that your fame derives from an artistic area other than music, were you to return,' I said, with only a little more conviction than I felt. 'Salvador is upset apparently – at the deception more than the true nature of your

... career, I suspect – but I think he'll come round.' I smiled. 'You'll charm him.'

'I can try,' Morag said, with a smile that would have charmed blood from a stone.

'It might be best,' I said, thinking it through as I sat there, 'if you and I didn't turn up together. At around the same time, certainly, but not obviously together. Well, maybe.'

'All right. Whatever. It's a deal. But when?' she asked.

I nodded, still thinking. The next big Service would be on Sunday evening, for the Full Moon. That was only two days away and so probably too soon, but you never knew. 'Let's keep in touch, but it might be as early as . . . day after tomorrow?'

Morag sat back, looking thoughtful. 'We're here tonight,' she said, glancing at Ricky, who had finished his cheeseburger and was now picking little bits of melted cheese and blobs of pickle off the surface of the tray. He looked up guiltily. 'Leven and Dundee tomorrow,' Morag continued. 'We were going to go to Aberdeen next, but we could make it Perth instead, and do Stirling as well, now. I'll give you the hotel numbers where we'll be staying. How'd that be?'

I thought. 'Fine. It might take a few more days, though.'

'Whatever,' Morag said, nodding and looking determined. 'What have you got to do next?'

It crossed my mind to lie, shame upon me, but it also occurred to me that there comes a point in such a campaign when you just have to trust, and let it be known that you trust. 'I'm going to visit Great-aunt Zhobelia,' I said.

Morag's eyes widened. 'You are? I thought she'd disappeared.'

'Me too. Uncle Mo held the key.'

'Did he now? And how's he?'

I looked at the wall clock. 'Hung-over, probably.'

CHAPTER
TWENTY-THREE

I f you travel the same route as everybody else, all you will see is what they have already seen. This has expressed our Faith's attitude to travel and Interstitiality for many years, and so it was with some regret that I reviewed the course of my recent journeys as I sat on the train from Edinburgh to Glasgow the evening after I had met Morag and Ricky.

It had long seemed to me that the best way one of our Faith might travel from Edinburgh to Glasgow, or vice versa, would be to walk the route of the old Forth and Clyde canal, and I had travelled that route a few times in my mind and on maps while I sat in the Community library. Yet here I was, taking a train from east to west, just like any normal Bland. My only – and rather pitiable – concession to the Principle of Indirectness had been to take the slow rather than the express line from one city to another; the fast route takes a trajectory via Falkirk, the stopping service bellies south through Shotts. I would change at Bellshill for the Hamilton loop, so in a way this route was frustratingly more, not less, direct. However, it was slower than heading straight for Glasgow and changing there, which alleviated the mundanity somewhat.

Morag and Ricky had invited me to stay for dinner with them; they would be eating at an Indian restaurant that evening. I'd been sorely tempted, but I'd thought it best to head straight for Mauchtie in the hope of obtaining an audience with Great-aunt Zhobelia that evening. Morag and I had parted with a hug at Waverley station; Ricky had shaken my hand grudgingly but gently. Morag had asked me if I needed any money; I'd thought about it.

I had determined early on – in the Community office, that Monday almost a fortnight ago, in fact – that twenty-nine pounds was a blessed and significant amount to carry, but that had been before I'd realised I was up against a brother prepared to use something as underhand and outrageous to our principles as a portable telephone in the heart of the Community, and I had certainly never been under any illusions about the importance of adequate finance in this cruelly acquisitive society. I said I'd be grateful for a loan of twenty-nine pounds. Morag laughed, but coughed up.

The train ride through the sun-rubbed landscape of assorted fields, small towns, industrial ruins, faraway woods and still more distant hills was the first chance I'd had to concentrate on all that had happened over the last couple of days. Before, I had still felt shocked, or I had been with people, or – on the train journey back from Newcastle – I had been rehearsing what I would say to Morag, trying to plan out the conversation we might have, especially if she had returned to her former scepticism and distrust. I still had a similar interview with my great-aunt ahead, but its parameters were so vague that there was little to hang a serious obsessive fugue on, so I could stop and think at last.

I reviewed my actions so far. To date, I had stolen, lied, deceived, dissembled and burgled, I had used the weakness of a relative to winkle information out of him, I had scarcely talked to my God for two weeks and I had used the works of the Unsaved almost as they did themselves, telephoning, travelling by car and bus and train and plane, entering retail premises and spending an entire evening enjoying a large proportion of all the exorbitantly hedonistic delights one of the world's largest cities could provide, though admittedly this last sin had been while in the company of a forceful and determinedly sensualistic relative from an alien culture where the pursuit of fun, profit and self-fulfilment was regarded practically as a commandment. Beyond all that, I had made an adamantinely pitiless commitment to myself – again, standing in that office in the mansion house – that I would use whatever truth I could discover like a hammer, to lay waste all those about me who were vulnerable to its momentous weight, without knowing what fragility might exist even in those I loved.

What a pretty alteration had taken place in me, I thought. I shook my head as I looked out across that motley landscape. I wondered – for the first time, oddly enough – whether I really could go back to my old life. I had stood in my little room in the farmhouse just two days ago, thinking that my life was represented not by my possessions but rather entirely defined by my relationship with the people of the Community and the Order, and with the farm and the lands around us . . . but now I had been exiled from all that – not as successfully in terms of distance as my brother had intended, but determinedly, and with a continuance of ill-wished intent that I did not doubt – and I wondered that I did not feel more abandoned and ostracised, even excommunicated, than I did.

Certainly I had my Gift, but its uncanny – and now spurned – ability to cure others hardly constituted much of a comfort by itself; rather it provided another criterion by which I might be judged different, set apart.

Perhaps it was that I did not intend to stay cast out for very long, and that I nursed a fierce but perversely comforting determination to return gloriously, wielding the fiery sword of truth with which to smite those who had wronged me. Perhaps it was simply that my upbringing had forged in me a strength and independence that, while undeniably in part a result of all the support and affection I had received from my family, Faith and surroundings, now possessed an autonomy from all of them, just as the tender sapling, shielded from the wind's harsh blast by the encircling forest, grows gradually to adulthood and is later found – should those sheltering trees be felled – no longer to need their help, capable of standing alone, secure in its own vigour and fortitude, and itself capable in turn of providing protection for others, should that time come.

So I mused, at any rate, as the train puttered through little stations, rumbled between the green walls of cuttings and threw its shadow down the northern faces of embankments to the roads, fields, forests and hills beyond, taking me closer, I hoped, to my Great-aunt Zhobelia. My plans for the evening were to see Zhobelia and then either sleep rough near the village, or perhaps find a bed and breakfast. It had occurred to me that, if there was time to catch a train back, I might repair to Glasgow and look up Brother Topec, who was a university student there, but I was not sure about this.

369

Topec is a friend as well as a relation (his mother is Sister Erin, his father Salvador), and I could probably rely on his discretion regarding the fact that I had turned up on his doorstep rather than going with Mo to Spayedthwaite or heading to London, as I'd intimated in my note to my uncle; however I wasn't sure it would be right to implicate Topec in my deception unless I had to, especially as his mother seemed to be Allan's lieutenant.

The train was warm. I closed my eyes, trying to recall the exact lay-out of the map I had seen in the bookshop in Edinburgh, so that I'd know which way to walk out of Hamilton.

I fell asleep, but woke before Bellshill and was able to change trains after a half-hour's wait. I followed road signs from Hamilton to Mauchtie and arrived there before nine on a fine, clear blue evening.

The Gloamings Nursing Home was a substantial old building of red sandstone which had been inelegantly extended to either side with square, ugly wings covered with roughcast. The house stood a little way out of the drab main village in a garden of grass and sycamore. A lane between the Gloamings and a similar, unextended house led to farmland on the low ridge beyond; an electricity substation lay on the other side of the home, pylons humming over the flank of the hill. The Gloamings looked out over more fields on the other side of the road. I took the ramp that led to the front door rather than the steps.

'Yes?' said the harassed young woman who came to the door. She wore a blue overall, like a real nurse, and had wildly frizzy black hair, large round red glasses and a distracted appearance.

'Good day,' I said, tipping my hat. 'I'm here to see Ms Zhobelia Whit, née Asis.'

'Zhobelia?' the girl said, her face screwing into an exasperated expression.

'That's right. May I come in?'

'No, I'm sorry, dear,' she said, 'ye canny.' She had a high, nasal voice. Her glasses went up and down with each word. She glanced at her watch. 'It's past time, so it is.'

I gave her my most tolerantly condescending smile. 'I don't think you understand, young lady. It is very important,' I said. 'Allow me to introduce myself; I am The Blessed Gaia-Marie Isis Saraswati Minerva Mirza Whit of Luskentyre, Elect of God, III.'

She looked blank.

I continued. 'I believe I am expected. Our lawyers did send a letter to that effect. You haven't heard anything?'

'Naw, ah'm sorry . . . ah'm just here masel, no one's told me anything. But ah canny let ye in, see, 'cos ah'm just here masel, ye know?'

'Please,' I said. 'I really must see Ms Zhobelia this evening. I regret to say that if I have to, I am instructed to authorise an interdict to be issued which would require that you give me access to her, but obviously the proprietors of this establishment – and indeed I – would rather avoid such legal action if it can be avoided.'

'Aw, wait a minute,' the lass said, looking so tired and hurt that I felt a pang of guilt at subjecting her to this nonsense. 'Look, ah'm no allowed tae let ye in, hen; it's as simple as that. It's more than ma job, ye know what ah mean? They're dead strict wi' the staff here, so they are.'

'All the more reason to let me—'

There was pale movement in the dark hall behind the girl.

'Is that my Johnny?' said a weak and faltering old voice, and an ancient face, like translucent parchment stretched over bleached bone, peered round the girl's shoulder. I could smell antiseptic.

'Naw, it's naw, Miss Carlisle,' the girl shouted. 'Get back tae yer seat.'

'Is that my Johnny?' the old lady asked again, her thin white hands up near her face fluttering like two weak, chained birds.

'Naw, it's no your Johnny, Miss Carlisle,' the girl shouted again, in that flat, even raising of the voice that indicates one is talking not in anger or for emphasis but to somebody who is deaf. 'Now, you away back tae yer seat; ah'll be through to put you to your bed soon, all right?' The girl turned Miss Carlisle around gently with one hand and carefully blocked her from the doorway, half closing the door.

'Look,' the girl said to me. 'Ah'm awfy sorry, hen, but ah canny

371

let ye in; ah just canny. Ah've got ma hands full here as it is, ye know?'

'Are you sure it's not my Johnny, dear?' said the faint, shaky voice from the hallway.

'Well,' I said, 'I'm just going to stay here until you do let me in.'

'But ah just canny. Honest. Ah just canny. Ah'm sorry.' There was a crash from the background, and the lass glanced behind her. 'Ah've got tae go now. Ah've just got tae. Sorry . . .'

'Look; you're risking civil proceed—' I began, but the door closed and I heard a lock snick.

I could just make out the muffled words from behind the door. 'Naw, Miss Carlisle, it's no . . .'

I decided to wait. I would try again later and see if sheer persistence paid off. I wondered if this girl was the night shift or if she would be replaced. I put down my kit-bag on the step and sat on it. I fished out my copy of the *Orthography* and read a few passages by the slowly fading light from the still clear sky.

I couldn't settle, though, and after a while got up and walked round the house. There was a locked gate to one side but a clear passageway on the other. Tall wheeled rubbish bins in grey and yellow were lined against the roughcast wall beneath a black metal fire escape. The back garden was full of white sheets and grey blankets, hung out to dry and dangling limply in the still air. I walked round the back of the house. I tried the back door, gently, but it was locked.

Then I heard a tapping noise. I expected it was going to be the girl in the nurse's uniform, shooing me away, but it was the same old lady who'd appeared behind the nurse earlier: Miss Carlisle. She was wearing a dark dressing-gown, standing at a small window to the side of the wing that overlooked the farm lane. She tapped again and motioned to me. I went over and stood under the window. She fiddled with something at the bottom of the window-frame. After a while the window cracked open, pivoting horizontally about its centre line. She lowered her head.

'Ssh,' she said, putting one thin, milk-coloured finger to her lips. I nodded and mirrored the gesture. She motioned me in. I looked around. It was getting dark and hard to see well, but there didn't appear to be anybody watching. I pushed my kit-bag through first, then scrambled over the sill.

Her room was small and smelled . . . of old person; of bodily wastes that were somehow genteel because the failing system had done little processing on their raw materials, so that the offensive became unobjectionable. There was a faint scent of something pleasant, too; lilacs, I thought. I could make out a wardrobe, drawers, a dressing table and a small chair. There was a narrow single bed, its covers disturbed as if she'd just got up.

'I always knew you'd come back, dear,' she said, and gave me what was probably meant to be a fierce hug. She was tiny and so frail; really she just leaned against me and put her arms round my back. Her tiny head was against my breast. I looked down into translucent, wispily white hair; as my eyes adjusted to the gloom, I could see that the skin on her scalp was very pale pink, and covered in little faint brown patches. She gave a sigh.

I put my arms round her and gave her the gentlest of hugs, fearful of crushing her.

'Dear Johnny,' she sighed. 'At last.'

I closed my eyes, holding her lightly to me. We stayed like that, holding each other for a while, until it gradually dawned on me that she had fallen asleep.

I pulled carefully back, unclasped her hands from the small of my back, and laid her gently down on the bed, pulling out the covers to slide her feet and legs in, adjusting her trailing nightie and tucking her in properly. She gave a tiny snore and turned onto her side. From what I could see, there was a smile on her face.

I opened the door. There was a light on in the corridor; no noise. There was a faint smell of institutional cooking. Miss Carlisle's door had number 14 on it and a little plastic apparatus at about eye level which contained a slip of white cardboard with her name on it. I relaxed a little. That ought to make things easier. I looked back into the room. Through the window, I could see the girl in the nurse's uniform in the garden, bringing in the washing, grabbing the sheets and blankets off the line and throwing them into a wash basket. I hoisted my kit-bag and went silently out into the corridor, closing the door quietly behind me.

I checked all the names in that corridor; no sign of Zhobelia. There was a fire door with a glass and wire-mesh window to one side off the corridor, leading to the main house. I peeked through to a dimly lit hall.

The door creaked as I went through. I paused. I could hear music, and then a man's voice, distorted and professionally cheery, then more music. I went on, and found another couple of rooms with names on them, looking to the front of the house.

The first one I looked at said 'Mrs Asis'. I looked around, gave the gentlest of knocks for form's sake, then slowly opened the door and stepped into the darkened room.

It was bigger than Miss Carlisle's. I saw two single beds and worried that Zhobelia might be sharing; that would complicate matters. I need not have worried initially; there was nobody in the room. I was wondering what to do when I heard slow footsteps and two voices approaching.

There were two wardrobes. I opened one to find it almost full; trying to squeeze myself and my kit-bag in would probably take minutes and cause a commotion anyway. The other was locked. I tried the nearest bed; it was solid underneath, with drawers. The voices were at the door now. I pulled up the cover on the second bed. Bliss! It was an old iron-framed thing. Plenty of room. I pushed a plastic chamberpot out of the way and disappeared underneath five seconds or so before I heard the door open. The carpet under the bed smelled of old dust and – very faintly – of vomit.

'I don't *want* to go to bed, horrible child,' said a voice that I thought I recognised; a curious feeling – half familiar, half dizzyingly novel – ran through me.

'Now, Mrs Asis. Ye've got tae get yer beauty sleep, haven't ye?'

'I'm not beautiful, I'm old and ugly. Don't be stupid. You're very stupid. Why are you putting me to bed now? What's wrong with you? It's not even dark yet.'

'Aye it is; look.'

'That's just the curtains.'

The light clicked on. 'There ye are, that's better now, isn't it? Will we get ye tae yer bed now, eh?'

'I am not a child. You are the child. I should have stayed with the white man. He wouldn't treat me like this. How can they do this to me?'

'Now now, Mrs Asis. Come on. Let's get that cardie off.'

'Ach . . .' There followed a stream of what might have been Gaelic or Khalmakistani or a mixture of both. I have heard that there are no real swear-words in Gaelic, so from the sound and force of the utterances directed at the unfortunate lass either Zhobelia was making up her own or she was speaking the language of her ancestors.

I stopped listening after a while, not so much from boredom but because I was having to concentrate very hard not to sneeze. I pushed my tongue forcefully into the top of my mouth and forced one finger hard up underneath my nose until the pain alone brought tears to my eyes. This worked, as usual, but it was a close-run thing.

Eventually Zhobelia was installed in the other bed and the girl bade her goodnight, turned off the light and closed the door. Zhobelia muttered away to herself in the darkness.

I was now left with the ticklish problem of how to let my great-aunt know there was somebody there in the room with her without either giving her a heart attack or causing her to scream blue murder at the top of her lungs.

In the event, the dilemma was taken out of my hands by my own lungs, or my nose, anyway. The urge to sneeze returned, more powerfully this time. I tried to prevent it, but to no avail.

I kept my mouth shut and closed my throat with my tongue, so that the sneeze back-fired, repulsed into my lungs. Despite my attempts to silence my sneeze, however, it was still loud.

Zhobelia's mutterings stopped abruptly.

CHAPTER
TWENTY-FOUR

A charged, uneasy silence hung in the air.

Zhobelia mumbled something.

'Great-aunt Zhobelia?' I said quietly.

She muttered something else.

'Great-aunt?' I said.

'. . . I am, I'm hearing voices now,' she muttered. 'Oh no.'

'Great-aunt, it's me; Isis. Your grand-niece.'

'I'm going to die. That must be it. Hearing little Isis. It'll be her next, then him.'

'Great-aunt, you're not hearing voices.'

'Now they're lying to me, telling me I'm not hearing them. What have I done to deserve this?'

'Great-aunt—'

'Sounds like Calli, not Isis. Just a child. It'll be them next: Aasni and then the white man. I wonder what they'll say?'

'Please, Great-aunt Zhobelia; it really is me. It's Isis. I'm under the other bed. I'm going to come out now; please don't be alarmed.'

'No, it's still her. That's funny. I thought dying would be different . . .'

I got slowly out from under the bed on the far side, so that I wouldn't suddenly emerge right in front of her. I stood. The room was dark. I could just make out the dark masses of the furniture, and sense my great-aunt's bulk in the divan bed.

'Great-aunt; over here,' I whispered.

I sensed movement at the head of her bed, and heard skin or hair move on fabric. 'Oooh,' she breathed. 'Oooh! I can see it now. It's a ghost.'

Ye Gods, it was like being Miss Carlisle's Johnny again. 'I am not a ghost, Great-aunt. It's Isis. I'm really here. I am not a ghost.'

'Now the ghost is saying it's not a ghost. Whatever next?'

379

'Great-aunt!' I said, raising my voice in frustration. 'For good-ness' sake; will you listen? I am not a ghost!'

'Oh dear. I've upset it. Oh no.'

'Oh, Great-aunt, please; listen to me!' I said, stopping at the foot of the other bed. 'It's Isis. Your grand-niece; I've come here from the Community at High Easter Offerance. I have to talk to you. I am as human as you are and *not* a supernatural apparition.'

There was a silence. Then she muttered something in what I suspected was Khalmakistani. Then, in English: 'You're not little Isis. She's just . . . little.'

Oh, good grief. 'Grand-aunt, I am nineteen years old now. The last time you saw me I *was* little. But I'm not any more; I am a fully grown woman.'

'Are you sure?'

'What?'

'You're not a ghost?'

'No. I mean, yes, I'm sure I'm not a ghost. I am real. I would like to talk with you, if you don't mind. I'm sorry I had to hide in here in order to get to see you, but the young lady would not let me in. . . . May I talk with you?'

'Talk with me?'

'Please. May I?'

'Hmm,' she said. I sensed her moving. 'Touch my hand.'

I moved forward, then squatted near the bed and put out my hand, eventually finding her hand. It felt warm and small. The skin was loose and very soft and smooth.

'Oh,' she whispered. 'You're warm!'

'See? Not a ghost.'

'Yes. I see. You're not a ghost, are you?'

'No. I'm real. I'm Isis.'

'Little Isis.'

'Not little any more.' I stood up, slowly, still holding her hand, then squatted again.

'Are you really Isis?'

'Yes. Isis Whit. I was born on the twenty-ninth of February, nineteen seventy-six. My mother was Alice Cristofiori, my father was Christopher Whit. My brother's first name is Allan. You are my Great-aunt Zhobelia Asis; your sister was Aasni, who . . .' I had been going to say, 'who died in the fire that killed my parents', but I thought the better of saying that, and after a moment's hesitation said, '. . . who was my paternal grandmother.'

She was silent.

'Believe me now?' I asked, squeezing her hand gently.

'I think so. Why are you here? Have they sent you away too? I thought here was only for old people.'

'Well, yes, I suppose I have been sent away, but not to here. I came here to see you.'

'You did? That was very nice of you. Mohammed comes to see me sometimes, but not very often. He drinks, you know. The girls have been; Calli and Astar. And the Glasgow ones; they talk the old language. I can't understand them, usually. I keep telling them they must talk slower but they don't listen. People never listen, you know. Especially young people.'

'I'll listen, Great-aunt.'

'Will you? You're a good girl. You were very good as a baby; you hardly cried, did you know that?'

'Other people have—'

'Are you really Isis?'

'. . . Yes, Great-aunt.'

She was silent for a long moment. 'I missed you growing up,' she said, though without obvious emotion, unless it was mild surprise. I wished I could see her face.

'I was sorry you went away,' I told her. 'I think we all were.'

'I know. Perhaps I shouldn't have. This is very strange, talking to you like this. What do you look like? Shall we put on the light?'

'Won't the nurse see the light is on?'

'Yes. She can see it under the door.'

'I have an idea,' I said, patting her hand.

Zhobelia's clothes had been laid neatly on the bed I had been hiding under. I moved them to the top of the chest of drawers and pulled the cover off the bed. I rolled it up and placed it at the foot of the door.

'Here,' Zhobelia said, grunting. There was a click, and a little yellow electric lamp like a miniature strip-light came on above the bed. I stood up, smiling at my great-aunt. She sat up in the bed, blinking. Her nightie was pale blue, with little yellow flowers. She looked a little puffy and pale about the face, not as Asiatically dark as I remembered. Her hair was frizzy, quite long and still surprisingly black, though shot through with thick, crinkly white hairs. She felt on the bedside table and found her glasses. She put them on and squinted at me.

The room seemed to spin about me as the feeling of half-familiar dizziness I'd experienced earlier struck me again.

Zhobelia seemed oblivious. 'You look like your mother,' she said quietly, nodding. She patted the bed. 'Come and sit here.'

I went shakily forward and sat on the bed; we held hands.

'Why did you leave, Great-aunt?'

'Oh, because I couldn't stay.'

'But why?'

'It was the fire.'

'It was terrible, I know, but—'

'Do you remember it?'

'Not really. I remember the aftermath; the shell of the mansion house. It's been rebuilt now.'

'Yes, I know.' She nodded, blinking. 'Good. I'm glad.'

'But why did you leave, afterwards?'

'I was afraid people would blame me. I was afraid of Aasni's ghost. Besides, I'd done my bit.'

'Blame you? For what? The fire?'

'Yes.'

'But it wasn't your fault.'

'It was. I should have cleaned the pressure cooker. And burning the money was my idea; I saw it, after all. My fault.'

'But you weren't – pardon?'

'The pressure cooker. I should have cleaned it properly. The valve. That was my job. And I saw the money would cause a disaster. I knew it.'

'What money were you talking about?'

She looked as confused as I felt. Her eyes – their dark brown irises surrounded by yellowy whites magnified by her thick glasses – looked watery. 'Money?' she asked.

'You said burning the money was your idea.'

'It was,' she said, nodding.

'What money, Great-aunt?' I asked, squeezing her hand gently.

'The money. Salvador's money.'

'*Salvador's* money?' I asked, then glanced back at the door, afraid that I had spoken too loudly.

'The money he didn't have,' Zhobelia said, as though all this made perfect and obvious sense.

'What money he didn't have, Great-aunt?' I asked patiently.

'The money,' she said, as though it ought to be self-evident.

'I'm sorry, Great-aunt; I don't understand.'

'Nobody understood. We kept it secret,' she said, then turned down the edges of her mouth and shook her head, looking away. Suddenly a smile lit up her face, revealing long, thin teeth. She patted my hand. 'Now, tell me all that's happened.'

I took a deep breath. Perhaps we could come back to this mysterious money later. 'Well,' I said. 'When . . . when did you last talk to somebody from the Community? Was it recently?'

'Oh no,' she said. 'I mean, since I had to leave. I can't remember what *they've* said to me. No, no.' She frowned a little and gave the appearance of racking her brains, then apparently gave up and smiled broadly, expectantly at me.

It felt as though my heart slumped at the prospect, but I smiled gamely and squeezed her hand again. 'Let me see,' I said. 'Well, as I said, the mansion house was rebuilt . . . the old organ – remember the organ, in the farm parlour?'

She smiled happily and nodded. 'Yes, yes; go on.'

'That was installed in the mansion house to give us extra room in the farm; we always meant to have it properly looked after but we never did get round to it . . . Anyway, Salvador moved back into the mansion house . . . let's see; Astar had Pan, of course, Erin had Diana—'

'I'm cold,' Zhobelia said suddenly. 'I'd like my cardie.' She pointed at the pile of clothes on the chest of drawers. 'It's there.'

'Oh, right,' I said. I got her cardigan and settled it round her shoulders, plumping up her pillows and generally getting her comfortable.

'There we are,' she said. 'Now.' She clasped her hands and looked expectantly at me.

'Right,' I said. 'Well, as I was saying, Erin had her second child, Diana . . .'

I went through the litany of births, death and marriages and the various comings and goings of Communites and Orderites, trying to recall all the important incidents and events of the past sixteen years. Zhobelia sat nodding happily, smiling and cooing softly or widening her eyes and sucking air in through her pursed mouth or frowning and clucking her tongue as she felt appropriate for each related occurrence.

The story of our family and Faith led me naturally through to more recent events, and I gradually sharpened the focus of my tale to the point of my visit. I had little idea of how much my great-aunt was actually retaining of all this, but I felt I had to make the effort.

'The *zhlonjiz*?' she said when I got to that part of the story. She laughed. I glanced back at the door again.

'Ssh!' I said, putting a finger to my lips.

She shook her head. 'What a fuss. All a lot of nonsense, too. That was something else we never told the white man,' she chuckled.

'What?' I asked, puzzled.

'We could have made that,' she told me. 'It was easy to make. The main thing was . . . now, what was it? What do they call it? I should know this. Oh, old age is so . . . Ah; TCP!' she said triumphantly, then frowned and shook her head. 'No, that's not it.' She looked down at the bed cover, brows furled, mouth pursed, muttering in what I guessed was Khalmakistani. She switched to English. 'What *was* the blinking stuff again? I should know, I should know . . .' She cast her gaze to the ceiling, sighing mightily. 'Ah!' She pointed up with one finger. '. . .Sloan's Liniment!' she cried out.

I reached forward and gently placed my hand over her soft lips. 'Great-aunt!' I whispered urgently, with another glance at the door.

'And coriander, and other herbs, and spices,' she whispered, leaning closer. 'Our grandmother, old Hadra, sent us the recipe, you know, but it was all a lot of old nonsense anyway.' She nodded, clasping her hands and sitting back, looking smug.

'*Zhlonjiz*?' I asked. 'It was . . . ?'

'Sloan's Liniment,' Zhobelia confirmed, rheumy eyes twinkling. 'Embrocation. You rub it in. Chemists sell it. Not mail order.' She reached forward and tapped me sternly on the knee. 'Stuff and nonsense, you know.'

I nodded, slowly, not knowing what to think. I wondered what the other herbs and spices were. I wondered if it made any difference.

My great-aunt tapped my hand. 'Keep going,' she said. 'I like this. It's interesting.'

I continued my tale. As I had been telling it I had been turning over in my mind both how much detail to go into regarding Allan's duplicity, and whether to mention my Grandfather's sexual advances to me. I considered mentioning both only in passing, but in the end I told the full story much as I would have done to a close friend, though I did say that Cousin Morag made exotic rather than erotic films. I confess I also did not reveal the full extent of how I used poor Uncle Mo's weakness for the drink, and will not pretend that such diplomacy was principally for his benefit.

When I had finished, Zhobelia just sat there, hands clasped, looking unsurprised. 'Well,' she said. 'That's him. He was always like that. You're an attractive girl. He was always a one for the ladies. We knew that. Didn't begrudge him it; it was just his nature. As well have complained that he snored; he couldn't help it. Couldn't help himself.' She nodded. 'Helped himself. Yes; helped himself. Wouldn't want me now. I'm old and dried up. Prunes they give us for breakfast sometimes, yes. No, good for you, little Isis.' She looked up at the ceiling, frowning and seemingly trying to remember something. 'That Mohammed. You know what I call him?' she asked, sitting forward and fixing me with a stern look and tapped me on the knee. 'Do you? Do you know what I call him?'

'A liqueur Moslem?' I ventured.

'No!' she barked, so that I put my finger to my lips again. 'I call him a very silly boy!' she said in a hoarse whisper. '*That's* what I call him.'

'I think he's sorry,' I told her. 'Mohammed doesn't want to upset you. He wants to give up drinking, but he can't. Not yet, anyway. Perhaps he will, one day.'

'Huh. When I see it I will believe,' she said, dismissively. She looked away, shaking her head. 'This Allan, though.' She looked at me, squinting. 'Such a quiet child. Colic as a baby, you know. Yes. But after that, very quiet. Always watching. Always thought he was listening, knew more than he let on. Had a funny look sometimes. Sly.' She nodded. 'Sly. That's it. Sly.' She seemed very happy with this word, and looked at me with an I-told-you-so sort of look.

I despaired of ever getting my great-aunt to appreciate the seriousness of the situation. Well, my situation, anyway. I felt exhausted. It must have taken a good hour to tell the recent history of the Order and Community and the full tale of my adventures over the last fortnight. I had to stifle my yawns, clenching my jaw and pretending I was just stretching. Zhobelia gave no sign of noticing.

'The thing is, Great-aunt,' I said, 'he's lying about me. Allan; he's telling lies about me and I think he wants to take over the Order; I'm not just worried for myself, I'm concerned for everybody at the Community; for the whole Order. I think Allan wants to change it, make it . . . less than what it has been. More . . . commercial, perhaps. They have started to send out letters begging for money,' I said, trying to bring us back to that subject. 'We have never done that! Can you imagine, Great-aunt? Us; asking for money. Isn't that disgraceful?'

'Tsk,' she said, nodding in agreement. 'Root of everything, and such. Tut. Hmm. Yes.'

'We have always managed to do without money from others, that is what is so terrible.'

'Terrible. Yes. Hmm. Terrible,' she said, nodding.

'Money has played almost no part in our Faith's history,' I persisted, feeling desperate and slightly underhand.

Great-aunt Zhobelia sat there, gathered her cardigan around her and leaned forward, tapping my knee again. 'Do you want me to tell you about the money?'

'Yes, please. Do tell me.'

'You won't tell anybody else?' she whispered, glancing to either side.

What to say? She might not tell me if I refused to give such an assurance, yet – if this somehow affected my situation – I might need what she could tell me as ammunition. I wondered what the chances were of her finding out if I promised and then broke my promise, and started calculating the odds. Then some part of my brain further up the chain of command put a stop to such faithlessness.

'I'm sorry, I can't make that promise, Great-aunt,' I told her. 'I might need to tell somebody else.'

'Oh.' She looked surprised. 'Oh. Well, I shouldn't tell you then, should I?'

'Great-aunt,' I said, taking her hand. 'I will promise not to tell anybody else unless to tell them is make things better for all of us.' I didn't feel that really said what I meant, and Zhobelia looked confused, so I fell back and regrouped for another try at it. 'I will promise not to tell anybody else unless telling them is to do *good*. You have my word on that. I swear.'

'Hmm. Well. I see.' She looked up at the ceiling, brows gathered. She looked at me again, still puzzled. 'What was I talking about?'

'The money, Great-aunt,' I said, wringing my poor tired brain of its last drops of patience.

'Yes,' she said, waggling my hand holding hers up and down urgently. 'The money.' She looked blank. 'What about it?' she asked, her face like a little girl's.

I felt tears prick behind my eyes. I just wanted to lie down and go to sleep. I closed my eyes briefly, which was a mistake, because it seemed to encourage my tears, leaving me with blurred vision. 'Where did this money come from, Great-aunt?' I asked wearily, in a kind of befogged daze. 'The money you were talking about, from the time of the fire; where did it come from?'

387

'Royal Scotland.' She nodded.

'*Royal* Scotland?' I said, baffled.

'The Royal Scottish Linen Bank.'

I stared at her, trying to work out what on earth she was talking about.

'That's what it said on the bag,' she said, back in her isn't-it-obvious attitude.

'What bag, Great-aunt?' I said, sighing. I had the impression I actually was already asleep and this was just me sleep-talking or something.

'The bag.'

'*The* bag?' I asked.

'Yes; the bag.'

A feeling of déjà vu, intensified by tiredness, swept over me. 'Where did the bag come from?'

'Royal Scotland, I suppose.'

I felt like one of two people rowing a boat, only my partner wasn't actually rowing, just stirring their oar in the water, so that we kept going round and round in circles.

'Where did you find the bag, Great-aunt?' I asked, flatly.

'On the—' she began, then sat forward and beckoned to me. I leaned towards her so that her mouth was at my ear. 'I forgot,' she whispered.

'Forgot what, Great-aunt?'

'We don't have it any more. We burned it. Saw what would happen and thought we'd get rid of it. I'm sorry.'

'But where did you get the bag, Great-aunt? You said—'

'From the chest.'

'The chest?'

'Our special chest. The one he didn't have a key to. That's where we kept it. And the book.'

'The book?' Here, I thought, we go again. But no:

'I'll show you. I still have a box, you know. The chest we lost in the fire, but I saved the book and the other things!' She clutched excitedly at my shoulder.

'Well done!' I whispered.

'Thank you! Would you like to see it?'

'Yes, please.'

'It's in the wardrobe. You get it for me, there's a good girl.'

I was directed to the full wardrobe, which was stuffed with colourful saris and other, plainer clothes. At its foot, amongst a litter of old shoes and fragrant white mothballs, there was a battered shoe-box secured with a couple of dark brown elastic bands. The box felt quite light when I lifted it and brought it over to Zhobelia, who seemed quite animated at the thought of what was inside. She bounced up and down on the bed and motioned me to bring her the box, for all the world like a child waiting on a present.

She pulled the elastic bands off the old shoe-box; one band snapped, seemingly just of old age. She put the lid of the box down on the bed beside her and started sorting through the documents, newspaper cuttings, old photographs, notebooks and other papers inside.

She handed me the old photographs. 'Here,' she said. 'The names are on the back.'

She shuffled through the other stuff in the box, stopping to read occasionally while I looked at the old snaps. Here were the two sisters, looking young, wary and uncertain in front of their old ex-library van. Here they were with Mr McIlone, whom I recognised from the few other photographs that we had at High Easter Offerance. Here was the farm at Luskentyre, here the old seaweed factory, before and after renovation, and before and after the fire.

There was only one photograph of Grandfather, sitting in bright sunlight on a kitchen chair outside what I guessed was Luskentyre, turning his head away and putting his arm up to his face in an action the camera had captured as a blur. It was the only representation I had ever seen of him, apart from a couple of even more blurred newspaper photographs. He was barely recognisable, but looked very thin and young.

'Ah. Here now . . .' Zhobelia lifted a small brown book – about the size of a pocket diary, but much thinner – from the shoe-box. She looked inside the little book, taking off her glasses to read. A piece of white paper fell out. She picked it up and handed it to me.

389

I put the photograph of my Grandfather down on the knee of my leather trousers. 'Ah-ha,' she said matter-of-factly.

I unfolded the piece of paper. It felt crinkly and old, but also thick and fibrous. It was a bank-note. A ten-pound note, from the Royal Scottish Linen Bank. It was dated July 1948. I inspected it, turned it over, smelled it. Musty.

Zhobelia tapped my knee again. Having attracted my attention, she gave me a stagy wink as she handed me the small brown book.

I put the bank-note on my knee along with the photograph of Grandfather.

The little brown book looked faded and worn and very old. It was warped, too, as though it had once been saturated with water. There was a British Royal Crown on the front cover. It was really just two bits of card, one thinner piece placed inside the other thicker cover, and not secured. The inner card carried a list of dates and amounts of money, expressed in pounds, shillings and pence. The last date was in August 1948. That piece of card was marked AB 64 part two. I put it down on the bed cover. The other piece of card was marked AB 64 part one. It seemed to be some sort of pass book. It belonged, or had belonged, to somebody called Black, Moray, rank: private. Serial number 954024. He was five feet ten inches tall, weighed eleven stone five pounds and had dark brown hair. No distinguishing marks. Born 29.2.20.

The rest was a description of injections he had received and what sounded like army punishments: fines, detentions and losses of leave. Perhaps it was just tiredness that meant I didn't haul up short at the date of birth, for I found myself thinking that I had no idea what any of this had to do with anything, until I looked from the book to the photograph of my Grandfather as a young man, still on my knee.

The world tipped again, my head swam. I felt faint, dizzy and sick. A terrible shiver ran through me as my palms pricked with sweat and my mouth went dry. My God. Could it be? Height, weight; hair colour. Of course the scar wouldn't be there . . . And the birth-date, to settle it.

I looked up into the eyes of my great-aunt. I had to attempt to swallow several times before I had enough saliva in my mouth to make it possible to speak. My hands started shaking. I rested them on my thighs as I asked Zhobelia, 'Is this him?' I held up the small brown book. 'Is this my Grandfather?'

'I don't know, my dear. We found that in his jacket. The money was on the beach. Aasni found it.'

'The money?' I croaked.

'The money,' Zhobelia said. 'In the canvas bag. We counted it, you know.'

'You counted it.'

'Oh yes; there were twenty-nine hundred pounds.' She gave a sigh. 'But it's all gone now, of course.' She looked at the ten-pound note sitting on my knee. 'We burned all the rest, in the canvas bag.' She nodded at the white ten-pound note resting on my leg. 'That's the last one left.'

CHAPTER
TWENTY-FIVE

I sat with my great-aunt, gradually piecing together the story, going over it from what seemed like slightly different angles in her memory. The story of my Grandfather being found on the sandy ground outside the mobile shop at Luskentyre on the night of the storm was all true, but what we had never been told was that the sisters had found an army pay-book inside the jacket he had been wearing.

They had also kept quiet the fact that the next day, after the storm, Aasni had walked along the beach at Luskentyre and found a zippered canvas hold-all, washed up on the sands. It contained a pair of brown leather shoes, sodden with sea water, and a money sack containing two hundred and ninety ten-pound notes, all from the Royal Scottish Linen Bank.

They wondered if perhaps there had been a shipwreck during the storm, and Grandfather and the money had been washed ashore from the foundering ship, but when they asked Mr McIlone and some other locals, then and later, nobody had heard of a ship going down that night off Harris.

My Grandfather had been in no fit state to appreciate all this, lying with his *zhlonjiz* poultice over his head wound, hallucinating. When he eventually woke up days later and claimed to be called Salvador Whit, the sisters thought the better of disabusing him of this notion while he was in such an obviously fragile and fevered state. They had already agreed to hide the money in their special chest, worried that the small fortune they had found washed up represented the proceeds of some nefarious exploit; when Grandfather started pleading with them to look for just such a canvas bag, they became even more worried.

By the time my Grandfather was well enough to start looking for the canvas bag himself, both Aasni and Zhobelia had rather fallen for him, and jointly arrived at the conclusion that if he was given the money – whether it was rightfully his or not – he would probably disappear out of their lives. The two sisters agreed that they would share the white man, assuming that that was what he wanted, and they would keep the money safe, only revealing its existence if there should arise some emergency which could be dealt with in no other way except financially.

They also agreed that, one day, they would reveal the truth to their joint husband, if it seemed like a good idea, and they were certain that he wouldn't beat them or leave them or cast them out. Somehow, that day never did arrive.

Eventually, one afternoon at High Easter Offerance in 1979, they decided to dispose of the money altogether, after something that Zhobelia saw (she had so far been very vague as to exactly what it was that had had this effect). They originally intended to burn it in the tandoor oven in the farm kitchen, but even in the middle of the night people sometimes came down to the kitchen, so that might be risky. They decided they would incinerate the notes in the stove in the mansion-house kitchen, where the sisters usually carried out their experiments with Scottish-Asiatic cuisine.

Zhobelia didn't actually know what had happened in the kitchen on the night of the fire, but had managed to convince herself that the money – evil influence to the last – had somehow caused the pressure-cooker explosion and subsequent conflagration, and that it was therefore all her fault. She had seen Aasni's ghost in her dreams, and once, a week after the fire, she had woken up in her bed in the darkness, and been quite fully awake but unable to move or breathe properly, and knew that Aasni's ghost was there in the room with her, sitting on her chest, turning her lungs into a pressure cooker for her guilt. She knew that Aasni would never forgive her or leave her alone so she decided that night that she would leave the Community and seek out her old family to ask their forgiveness.

The Asis family had moved too, setting up home in the Thornliebank district of Glasgow, from where they ran a chain of food shops and Indian restaurants. There were still Asis family members in the Hebrides but they were a younger generation; the people Aasni and Zhobelia had known had all decanted to Glasgow, and apparently there had been great debate amongst them regarding whether they wanted Zhobelia back at all. Zhobelia had gone to stay with Uncle Mo instead – swearing her son to secrecy in the process – while the Asis family were making up their collective mind.

Then Zhobelia had had a stroke, and needed more constant care than Mo could provide alone; she was moved out to a nursing home in Spayedthwaite. Uncle Mo had eventually contacted both our family and the Asis clan, pleading for support, and received guarantees that the financial burden of looking after his mother would be shared by all three parties. Later, the Asis family insisted that Zhobelia be moved closer to them, and the Gloamings Nursing Home, Mauchtie was the result.

'They come to see me, but they talk too fast,' Zhobelia told me. 'Calli and Astar have been too, you know, but they are very quiet. I think they're embarrassed. The boy doesn't come very often at all. Not that I care. Stinks of drink, did I tell you that?'

'Yes, Great-aunt,' I said, squeezing her hand. 'Yes, you did. Listen—'

'They look after us here. That Mrs Joshua, though; she's a horror. Teeth!' Zhobelia shook her head, tutting. 'Miss Carlisle, now; soft in the head,' she told me, tapping her temple. 'No, they look after us here. Though you can lie in bed and nobody will talk to you. Sit in your chair; the same. Rushed off their feet. Apparently the owner is a *doctor*, which is good, isn't it? Not that I've ever seen him, of course. But still. Television. We watch a lot of television. In the lounge. Lots of young Australian people. Shocking.'

'Great-aunt?' I said, still troubled by something Zhobelia had said, and starting to link it with a couple of other things I'd been confused about earlier.

'Hmm? Yes dear?'

'What was it you saw that made you want to burn the money. Please; tell me.'

'I told you; I *saw* it.'

'What did you see?'

'I saw the money was going to bring a disaster. It just came to

397

me. Didn't do any good, of course, these things rarely do, but we had to do something.'

'Do you mean you had a vision?' I asked, confused.

'What?' Zhobelia said, frowning. 'Yes. Yes; a vision. Of course. I think the Gift passed on to you after me, except you got it as healing. Think yourself lucky; healing sounds easy compared to those visions; I was glad to see the back of them. It'll pass on from you, too, eventually; only one of us ever has it at a time. Just one of those things that has to be borne.' She patted my hand.

I stared at her, mouth agape.

'Grandmother Hadra's mother had the seeing, like me. Then when she died, Hadra found she could talk to the dead. When Hadra had her stroke back in the old country it passed to me and I started seeing things. I was about twenty. Then, after the fire, you started healing.' She smiled. 'That was it, you see? I could go then. I was tired of it all and anyway I wasn't going to be any more use to anybody, was I? I knew the seeing would stop after you started healing and I knew everybody else would look after you and, anyway, I knew Aasni would blame me for not seeing it properly in the first place and getting her killed; she was annoying that way and she'd always gone on at me for not treating the Gift with more respect; said it would have been better if she'd had the visions, but she didn't; it was me.'

I don't know how long the next moment lasted. Long enough for me to be aware that Great-aunt Zhobelia was patting my cheek and looking with some concern into my eyes.

'Are you all right, dear?'

I tried to talk, but couldn't. I coughed, finding my mouth and throat quite dry. Tears came to my eyes and I doubled up, coughing painfully but still trying to keep quiet. Zhobelia tutted and clapped me on the back as my face lowered to the bedclothes.

'Great-aunt,' I spluttered eventually, wiping the tears from my eyes and still swallowing dryly with every few words. 'Are you telling me that *you* had visions, not Grandfather; that you saw—'

'The fire; I saw a disaster coming, from the money. I didn't know it was going to be a fire, but I knew it was coming. That was the last thing I saw. Before that; oh, lots of things.' She laughed

quietly. 'Your poor Grandfather. He only ever had one real seeing;
I think I must have loaned him the Gift for the time he was lying
on the floor of the van, covered in all that tea and lard. Poor
dear; he thought it was this twenty-ninth of February thing that
made people different. There *was* something special about him,
though. There must have been. The only thing that ever really
surprised me in my whole life was him turning up like that; I
hadn't any inkling of that. None at all. That was how we knew
he was special. But visions? No, he had that one, and woke up
with it and started babbling, trying to make something of it. Just
like a man; give them a toy and they have to play with it. Never
content. All the rest though . . .' She set her mouth in a tight line,
shaking her head.

'All the rest . . . what?' I asked, gulping.

'The visions. The seaweed factory, the hammock, those Possil
people, Mrs Woodbean, your father being born, and then you,
and the fire; I saw all that, not him. And if I didn't actually
see it every time, at least I knew what I wanted – what
Aasni and I wanted, and got your Grandfather to do what
we thought was right, what we thought was needed, for all
of us. That's the trouble with men, you see? They think
they know what they want, but they don't, not usually. You
have to tell them. You have to give them a bit of a hand
now and again. So I told him. You know; pillow-talk. Well,
suggested. You can't be too careful. But if it's a warning of a
disaster, well, there you are; you see what happened with the
money.'

'You foresaw the fire at the mansion house?' I whispered, and
suddenly my eyes were filling with tears again, though this time
not because my throat was sore.

'A disaster, dear,' Zhobelia said matter-of-factly, seeming not to
notice the tears welling in my eyes. 'I saw a disaster, that was all.
If I'd seen it was going to be a fire then of course the last thing I'd
have suggested doing with the money would have been burning it.
All I saw was *a* disaster, not exactly what sort. Should have known
it would still happen, of course.' She put on a sour face and shook
her head. 'The Gift is like that, you see. But you have to try. Here,

my dear,' she said, pulling a handkerchief from her sleeve. 'Dry your eyes.'

'Thank you.' I dabbed at my tears.

'You're welcome.' She sighed, settling her cardigan about her. 'I was glad to see the back of it, no mistake. Hope it hasn't been the burden to you it was to me, but if it is, well, there's nothing much to be done, I'm afraid.' She looked concernedly at me. 'How has it been for you, dear? Are you bearing up? Take my advice: let the men-folk deal with the consequences. They'll take the credit for any good that comes from it, anyway. But it's so nice when it goes; that's the blessing, you see; that only one person has it at a time. It's such a relief to have surprises again. It was a lovely surprise to see you this evening. I had no idea you were going to appear. Just lovely.'

I handed the handkerchief back to Zhobelia; she stuffed its sodden ball up her sleeve; it was the shape of the inside of my fist. 'How long has this . . . Gift . . . ?'

'What, dear? How long will you have it? I don't know.'

'How long has it existed? Is it just in our family?'

'Just in the women; any of the women, but only ever one at a time. How long? I don't know. There are some silly ideas . . . I've heard certain daftnesses . . .' She shook her head quickly, dismissively. 'But you don't want to concern yourself with them. People are so credulous, you know.'

'Credulous,' I said, suppressing a laugh and a cough at the same time.

'Oh,' she said, tutting and shaking her head, 'you wouldn't believe.' She reached out and held my hand again, patting it absently and smiling at me.

I sat there, looking at her, feeling half hysterical with all the things she'd told me, wanting to howl with despair and rage at the madness of the world and burst out in screams of riotous laughter for exactly the same reason.

What was I to do? What mattered most out of all I had discovered? I tried to think, while Zhobelia sat blinking and smiling at me and patting my hand.

'Great-aunt,' I said eventually, putting my other hand on top of hers. 'Would you like to come back?'

'Back?'

'Back with me, to the Community, to the farm, to High Easter Offerance. To stay; to live with us.'

'But her ghost!' she said quickly, eyes childishly wide. Then she frowned and looked to one side. 'Though *you* weren't a ghost,' she muttered. 'Maybe it would be all right now. I don't know . . .'

'I'm sure it would be all right,' I said. 'I think you belong back with us.'

'But if it isn't all right? You weren't a ghost, but what if she is?'

'I'm sure she won't be. Just try it, Great-aunt,' I said. 'Come back for a week or two and see if you like it. If you don't, you could always come back here, or maybe stay somewhere nearer by us.'

'But I need looking after, dear.'

'We'll look after you,' I told her. 'I hope I'll be going back soon, too; *I'll* look after you.'

She seemed to think. 'No television?' she asked.

'Well, no,' I admitted.

'Huh. Never mind,' she said. 'All the same, anyway. Lose track, you know.' She stared at me vacantly for a moment. 'Are you sure they'd want to see me again?'

'Everybody would,' I said, and felt sure that it was true.

She stared at me. 'This isn't a dream, is it?'

I smiled. 'No, it isn't a dream, and I am not a ghost.'

'Good. I'd hate it to be a dream, because I'd have to wake up.' She yawned. I found myself yawning too, unable to stop myself.

'You're tired, dear,' she said, patting my hands. 'You sleep here. That's what to do.' She looked over at the other bed. 'There; have the other bed. You will stay, won't you?'

I looked round, trying to judge where I might sling my hammock. The room didn't look promising. In truth I was so tired I could have slept on the floor, and quite possibly might.

'Would it be all right if I stayed?' I asked.

401

'Of course,' she said. 'There. Sleep there.'

*

And so I slept in Great-aunt Zhobelia's room. I couldn't find anywhere to hang my hammock so I made a little nest for myself on the floor with bedclothes from the other bed and curled up there, in between Zhobelia and the empty bed.

My great-aunt wished me goodnight and switched off the light. It was quite easy to go to sleep. I think my brain had given up reeling by that point; it had gone back to being shocked. The last thing I recall was my great-aunt whispering to herself, 'Little Isis. Who'd have thought it?'

Then I fell asleep.

*

I was awakened by the noise of doors slamming and the rattle of tea cups. Daylight lined the curtains. My empty stomach was growling at me. My head felt light. I rolled over stiffly and looked up to see Great-aunt Zhobelia looking down at me from her bed, a soft smile on her face.

'Good morning,' she said. 'You're still real.'

'Good morning, Great-aunt,' I croaked. 'Yes; still real, still not a dream or a ghost.'

'I'm so glad.' Something rattled in the hall outside her door. 'You'd better be off soon, or they'll catch you.'

'All right.' I got up, quickly remade the other bed, took the cover from the bottom of the door and replaced Zhobelia's clothes on the bed. I ran a hand through my hair and rubbed my face. I squatted at the side of her bed, holding her hand again. 'Do you remember what I asked you last night?' I whispered. 'Will you come back to stay with us?'

'Oh, that? I don't know,' she said. 'I'd forgotten. Do you really mean that? I don't know. I'll think about it, dear, if I remember.'

'Please do, Great-aunt.'

402

She frowned. 'Did I tell you last night about the things I used to see? About the Gift? I think I did. I'd have told you before, but you weren't old enough to understand, and I had to get away from her ghost. Did I tell you?'

'Yes,' I told her, gently squeezing her soft, dry hand. 'Yes, you told me about the visions. You passed on the Gift of knowing about them.'

'Oh, good. I'm glad.'

I heard voices outside in the corridor. They went away, but I stood anyway and kissed her on the forehead. 'I must go now,' I told her. 'I'll come back to see you, though. And I'll take you away, if you want to come home.'

'Yes, yes, dear. You be a good girl, now. And remember: don't let the men know.'

'I'll remember. Great-aunt . . . ?'

'Yes, dear?'

I glanced at the shoe-box, which sat on her bedside cabinet. 'May I take the pay-book and the ten-pound note with me? I promise I'll return them.'

'Of course, dear. Would you like the photographs as well?'

'I'll take the one of Grandfather, if I may.'

'Oh, yes. Take the lot if you want. I don't care. I stopped caring a long time ago. Caring is for the young, that's what I say. Not that they care either. But you do. No; you take care.'

I put the photograph, pay-book and bank-note in my inside jacket pocket. 'Thank you,' I told her.

'You're welcome.'

'Goodbye, Great-aunt.'

'Oh yes. Mm-hmm. Thank you for coming to see me.'

I peeked through the curtains to check the coast was clear, slid up the sash window, dropped my kit-bag onto the path beneath and jumped out after it. I walked smartly away and was at Hamilton station within the hour.

A train took me to Glasgow.

*

403

I sat looking out at the countryside and the buildings and the railway lines, shaking my head and muttering to myself. I neither knew nor cared what sort of effect this behaviour had on my fellow passengers, though I noticed nobody sat beside me, despite the fact that the train seemed full.

Zhobelia. Visions. Money. Salvador. Whit. Black . . . All this on top of everything else I'd learned in the last few days. Where did this stop? What extremity of revelation could still lie in store for me? I could not imagine, and did want to envision. My life had changed and changed again in so many ways in such a short time recently. Everything I'd known had been exploded, thrown into chaos and confusion, mixed and tumbled and strewn, made nebulous and inchoate and senseless.

I scarcely knew what to think, where to begin *trying* to think so that I might piece everything back together again, if that were even remotely possible. At least I had had the presence of mind to ask Zhobelia for the ten-pound note and the pay-book. I supposed that I was clinging of necessity to the most practical course that presented itself, clutching at reality like a shellfish to a familiar rock while the waves of something unimaginably more vast and powerful washed over me, threatening to dislodge my sanity. I focused upon the immediate practicalities of the moment, and found some relief and some release in thinking through what had to be done now to bring the more mundane problems I was faced with to some sort of resolution. By the time the train pulled into Glasgow Central station, then, I had decided on the plan for the next part of my campaign.

CHAPTER
TWENTY-SIX

'Yeah?'
'Good morning. I would like to speak to Topec, please.'
'Speaking.'
'Brother Topec, it is I, Isis.'

'Is! Well, hello *there*!' My relation whooped, painfully loudly. I held the phone away from my ear for a moment. '*Really*?' he laughed. 'You're kidding! But, hey! You aren't *allowed* to use the phone, are you?'

'Not normally. But these are desperate times, Topec.'

'They are? Whangy-dangy! No one ever tells me anything. Where are you, anyway?'

'Glasgow Central station.'

'Yeah? Wow! Great! Hey; come on round and meet the guys; we're gonna have some brekkers and then head out for some jazz.'

'Breakfast would be appreciated.'

'Great! Brilliant! Hey,' he said, as his voice went echoey and small for a moment. 'It's my cousin Isis.' (Topec and I are not, of course, actually cousins; the real relationship is more complicated, but I understood the elision.) 'Aye. She's coming round here.' I heard a lean chorus of male cheers in the background, then Topec's voice again, still echoey. 'Yeah, the neat-lookin' one; the messiah-ess. Aye.'

'Topec,' I said, sighing. 'Don't embarrass me. I don't have the emotional resilience just at the moment.'

'Eh? What? Na, don't worry. So,' he said, 'how come you're using the phone, Is?'

'I think I might need some help.'

'What with?'

'Research.'

'Research?'

'In a library, or maybe a newspaper. I am unused to such things. I wondered if you might be able to assist me.'

407

'Dunno. Maybe. Give it a go, I suppose. Yeah; why not? You comin' over, then?'

'I shall be there directly.'

'Ha ha! I love the way you talk. Great. The guys are dyin' to meet you. You've got a fan club here.'

I groaned. 'See you soon.'

'You got the address?'

'Yes. I'll be about half an hour.'

'Okay-doke. Give us time to clean the place up.'

*

I could only conclude that Topec and the three male friends with whom he shared the flat in Dalmally Street had not bothered to do any cleaning whatsoever, or that they normally lived in a state resembling the interior of one of those municipal rubbish lorries which compresses each binload of refuse it picks up.

The flat smelled of beer and the carpet I first stepped onto in the hall stuck to my feet, like something designed to let astronauts walk in a space station. Topec gave me a hug which lifted both my kit-bag and me off my feet – the hall carpet only parted with the soles of my boots reluctantly, I believe – and proceeded to squeeze most of the breath out of me.

Topec is a lively lad, tall and skinny with outrageously good looks: he has long, black, naturally ringletted hair which – happily for him – suits, indeed thrives on, not being combed or cared for, and an electrifyingly dark, exquisitely sculpted face with eyes so piercingly blue the impression they give is of cobalt spikes. He put me down before I fainted.

'Isis!' he yelled, and took a step backwards, going down on his hands and knees, laughing and salaaming. 'I'm not worthy! I'm not worthy!' He was dressed in ripped jeans and a ripped T-shirt under a frayed check shirt.

'Hello, Topec,' I said, as tiredly as I felt.

'She's here!' Topec cried out, and jumped to his feet, dragging me through to the flat's living room, where three other young men sat grinning at a table, playing cards, drinking tea and eating greasy food out of cold aluminium containers with spoons.

I moved a pair of grubby-looking socks off the seat I was offered and sat down. I was duly introduced to Steve, Stephen and Mark and invited to share their breakfast, which consisted of the remains of a communal take-away curry and ditto Chinese from the previous night, bulked out by a plate piled high with huge soft floury rolls. Tea was provided, and such was my hunger I found the cold, oily debris from the previous night quite palatable. The rolls were more appearance than substance, seemingly composed mostly of air, but at least they were fresh.

I chatted to the other three young men, who all suffered from an interestingly diverse range of spots and related skin conditions. They seemed embarrassed by my presence, which I might have found flattering if I'd had the energy to spare. They kept on playing cards as they talked and ate, roundly abusing and cursing each other as though they were homicidally desperate outlaws gambling for the entire proceeds of a robbery rather than, I assumed, reasonably good friends and playing, apparently, for sweets called Smarties.

'Are those earrings, Topec?' I asked, as Topec – finding that some hairs were getting into his mouth as he munched on his lemon chicken and roll – flicked his hair back behind his ear and revealed a set of half a dozen or so small studs and rings set into the rearward edge of his left ear.

He flashed a smile at me. 'Yeah. Cool, eh?'

'Hmm.' I continued digging into my mostly-air roll.

Topec looked hurt. 'You don't like them?' he asked plaintively.

I forbore pointing out that body piercing was frowned upon by our Faith, just as I had questioning Topec's lack of a mud-mark on his forehead. 'I have always felt,' I said, instead, 'that the human body arrives with a more than sufficient number of orifices out of the box, as it were.'

They were all looking at me.

'Yeah,' sniggered the one called Mark. 'To name but one!'

The others snorted and laughed too, after a moment. I just sat and smiled, not entirely sure what the joke was.

Topec looked a little discomfited, but cleared his throat and asked politely what exactly it was I wanted help with.

While giving the details a wide berth, I explained to Topec that I wanted to investigate army records, events in 1948 as reported in newspapers, and possibly old currency. Even as I spoke the words I felt that just mentioning those three areas was already giving too much away, but Topec's eyelids remained unbatted, and I felt I had to involve him. I needed to do this quickly, I felt, and as a student Topec ought to know his way round a library, oughtn't he? Listening to the four lads chat and curse as they played cards, I wondered if this had been wise, but I had made my play now and would have to stick with it.

'Aw, shit, Is!' Topec exclaimed, when I made clear the need for haste. 'You wanna do this *now*? Aw, rats, man! This is Saturday, Is!' Topec said, laughing and waving his arms about. His pals nodded enthusiastically. 'We have to go out and get steamin' and listen to jazz and stuff and do a pub crawl or come back here and drink cans and bet on the football scores and go out and get paralytic and get black-pudding suppers and chips and go to the QMU and dance like maniacs and try and get off with nurses and end up back here having an impromptu soirée, like as not and throw up in the garden and throw things out of the window and call for a pizza and play bowls in the hall with empty cans!'

He laughed.

'You can't interfere with a . . . with a *months*-old tradition like that just because you need to do this *research* shit! Fuck, if we wanted to do *that* sort of stuff we'd be writing our *essays*! I mean, do we *look* like sad students? Come on; we're trying to resurrect a fine student tradition here. We have to *party*!'

'*Party*!' the others chorused.

I looked at Topec. 'You told me students were all very boring and exam-oriented these days.'

'They are, mostly!' Topec said, gesticulating. 'We party—'

'*Party*!' the other three chorused again.

'—animals are practically an endangered species!'

'I can't imagine why,' I sighed. 'Well, just—'

'Oh, come, Is; let your . . . I mean, get your party—'

'*Party!*'

'—hat on. We can do all that stuff on Monday.'

'Topec,' I said, smiling faintly. 'Just point me in the right direction. I'll do it myself.'

'You won't come out with us?' he asked, looking deflated.

'Thank you, but no. I'd like to get this done today. It's all right; I'll do it myself.'

'Not at all! If you won't come out with us, I'll come out with you; we'll do all this stuff. We'll all help! Except you have to come out for a drink with us tonight, right?' He looked round the others.

They looked at him and then at me.

'Na.'

'No, don't think so, Tope.'

'Nut; I wannae to go to the jazz.'

Topec looked crestfallen for a moment. 'Oh. Oh well,' he said, with an expansive shrug, waving with his arms. 'Just me, then.' He laughed. 'Fuck. Talked myself into that one, didn't I?'

The others murmured assent to this.

Topec slapped his forehead, staring at me. 'I suppose I have to wash your feet, too, don't I? I forgot!'

The others looked up, surprised.

I took a guess at the state of cleanliness of any basin, bowl or container suitable for feet-washing the flat might possess. 'That won't be necessary just now, thank you, Topec.'

*

'Currency,' Topec said, a little later in the kitchen as we tidied away the breakfast things.

'A bank-note,' I told him.

'Yeah. Cool. My Director of Studies collects stamps and stuff. I wonder if he knows anybody collects notes? I'll give him a call.' He grinned. 'Got his home number; I'm always calling in for extensions. Just chuck the stuff in there,' he said, pointing at one of three black polythene bags by the side of an overflowing bin. He strode out into the hall. I opened the black bag, averting

411

my nose from the smell that emanated from it, and dumped the crushed, empty take-away containers into it. I tied up the sack and did the same with the other two, breathing through my mouth to combat the stench.

I started cleaning dishes. Anything to be busy. I'd been right about the washing-up basin. Topec was back a few minutes later. He stared at the washing-up suds as though he had never seen such a phenomenon before, a thesis the state of the kitchen did nothing to contradict. 'Oh, yeah! Like, well done, Is!'

'What did your Director of Studies say?' I asked him.

'We need a notaphilist,' he said, grinning.

'A what?'

'A notaphilist,' he repeated. 'Apparently there's one in Wellington Street.' He glanced at his watch. 'Open till noon on Saturdays. Reckon we can make it.'

*

I found it quite easy to drag myself away from the washing-up. We caught a bus into the city centre and found the address in Wellington Street, a little basement shop under a grand, tall Victorian office building of recently cleaned fawn sandstone.

H. Womersledge, Numismatist and Notaphilist, said the peeling painted sign. The place was pokey and dark and smelled of old books and something metallic. A bell jangled as we entered. I tried to convince myself that these were not really retail premises. There were glass cases, counters and tall display cabinets everywhere, all full of coins, medals and bank-notes, the latter held in little transparent plastic stands or folders like photographic albums.

A middle-aged man appeared from the back of the shop. I'd expected some little old bent-over octogenarian sporting a patina of dandruff and dust, but this fellow was my side of fifty, smoothly plump, and dressed in a white polo-neck top and cream slacks.

'Morning,' he said.

'Yo,' said Topec, bouncing from one foot to the other. The man looked unimpressed.

I tipped my hat. 'Good morning, sir.' I brought out the bank-note

412

and placed it on the glass counter between us, over dully gleaming silver coins and colourfully ribboned medals. 'I wondered what you could tell me about this . . .' I said.

He picked up the note delicately, held it up to the dim light from the one small window, then switched on a tiny but powerful table lamp and studied the note briefly.

'Well, it's pretty self-explanatory, really,' he said. 'Ten-pound note, Royal Scot Linen, July 'forty-eight.' He shrugged. 'They were produced in this form from May 'thirty-five to January 'fifty-three, when the RSL was taken over by the Royal Bank.' He turned the note over a couple of times, handling it the way I imagined a card-sharp did a card. 'Quite an ornate note, for the time. It was actually designed by a man called Mallory who was later hanged for murdering his wife, in nineteen forty-two.' He gave us a suitably wintry smile. 'I suppose you want to know how much it's worth.'

'I imagined it was worth ten pounds,' I said. 'If it was still legal tender.'

'Not legal tender,' the man said, grinning and shaking his head. 'Worth about forty quid, mint, which this isn't. If you were selling I could give you fifteen, but even that's only because I like round numbers.'

'Hmm,' I said. 'Well, perhaps not, then.'

I stood, looking down at the note, just letting the time pass. The man turned the note over on the counter one more time.

'Well, then,' I said, after Topec had started to get agitated at my side. 'Thank you, sir.'

'You're welcome,' the man said, after a moment's hesitation.

I picked up the note and folded it back inside my pocket. 'Good day,' I said, tipping my hat.

'Yeah,' the man said, frowning, as I turned and walked to the door, followed by Topec. I opened the door, jangling the bell again. 'Ah, wait a minute,' the man said. I turned and looked back.

He waved one hand, as though rubbing out something on an invisible screen between us. 'No, no, I'm not going to offer you more or anything; that's all it's worth, really, but . . . could I have another look at it?'

413

'Of course.' I went back to the counter and handed him the note again. He frowned at it. 'Mind if I take a copy of this?' he asked.

'Will it be harmed?' I asked.

He smiled tolerantly. 'No, it won't.'

'All right.'

'Won't be a minute.' He disappeared into the back of the shop. There were a series of quiet, mechanical noises. He was back a moment later, with the note and a copy of both its sides on a large sheet of paper. He handed me the note again. 'You got a phone number I can reach you at?'

'Yes,' I said. 'Topec, do you mind . . . ? '

'Eh? What? Oh! Like, hey, no; no, on you go. Pas de probleme.'

I gave the man Topec's phone number.

'Now what?' Topec asked on the street outside.

'Army records, and old newspapers.'

*

There are occasions when I find pieces of technology I can't help liking. The fiche reader and built-in copying machine that I was directed to at the Mitchell Library proved to be one such device. It was like a large vertically oriented television set screen, but was really just a sort of projector, throwing onto the screen the highly magnified images of old newspapers, documents, journals, ledgers and other papers which had been photographed and placed – hundreds at a time – on pieces of thin, laminated plastic. In this manner, many years' worth of broadsheet newspapers that might have filled a room could be condensed into a small filing box that one could carry comfortably with one hand.

By working two small wheels, one could manipulate the glass bed the fiches rested upon and so rove at will across the hundreds of pages recorded on each plastic sheet. When one had found a sheet one wanted to record, all that had to be done was to press a button, and the contents of the screen would be transferred by a photocopying process to a sheet of ordinary paper.

I suspect it was something about the mechanical nature of

the whole business – despite the machine's obvious reliance on electrical power – that attracted me. If you held the fiches up to the light you could just make out the tiny shapes of the newspapers, easily identifying large headlines and photographs by the black and grey blocks they made on the white surface. It was obvious, in other words, that the information was physically there, albeit in microscopically reduced form, not macerated into digits or stripes of magnetism plastered on a bit of tape or a little brown disk and intrinsically unreadable without the intervention of a machine.

The fiches could probably be used without the machine, if one had a bright light and a very strong magnifying glass, and that seemed to me to define the limit of acceptable technology; Luskentyrians have traditionally had an almost instinctive suspicion of things which boast of having few or no moving parts. It makes us incompatible, as a rule, with electronics, but this device seemed just about tolerable. I was sure Brother Indra would like this machine. I thought again of Allan, using the portable phone in the office storeroom, and felt my teeth grind as I read the ancient headlines I had come here to inspect.

I was looking at old copies of Scottish and British newspapers from 1948. I glanced at one or two from the early months of the year, but was concentrating on the second half of the year. I was not entirely sure what it was I might find; I was just looking for something that caught my eye.

I sat alone at the machine, having given Brother Topec the task of finding out how one might investigate an individual who had been in the British Army; he had pointed me towards the Mitchell Library from an army recruitment centre in Sauchiehall Street. I had left him standing in a queue there; I was hoping he wouldn't join up by mistake, though with those earrings he was probably safe.

I had plenty of newspapers to choose from: *The Herald*, *Scotsman*, *Courier*, *Dispatch*, *Mirror*, *Evening Times*, *Times*, *Sketch* ... I started with the *Scotsman*, for no better reason than that was the paper Mr Warriston took, and I had once picked it up and surreptitiously read a few pages on the first occasion I'd visited his house in Dunblane.

I read of the assassination of Gandhi, the formation of Israel, the Berlin airlift, Harry S. Truman elected President in the United States, the founding of the two Korean republics, the austerity Olympics in London, continuing rationing in Britain and the abdication of Queen Wilhelmina in Holland.

What I was looking for were shipwrecks, bank robberies, mysterious disappearances, people being washed overboard from troopships or going missing from army bases. After a quick look through a selection of months, I decided to restrict my search to that of September 1948 initially, reckoning that the chances were that whatever I was looking for had taken place then. I had got to the last September issue of the *Scotsman* without success when Topec appeared in the little alcove off the upper gallery where the fiche reading machine was situated.

'Any luck?' I asked.

He sat down on another chair, breathing hard as though he'd been running. 'No; it's been fucking privatised, man.'

'What? The army?'

'No; the records. All the armed forces' records. Used to be some civil service department, but now it's something called "Force Facts plc" and you have to pay for each inquiry and they're not open over the weekend anyway. Hilarious, eh? Total.' He shook his head. 'How about you?'

'Nothing yet. Done the *Scotsman*; about to start on the *Glasgow Herald*. If you could take the right-hand side of the screen while I read the left, we'll get through this a lot quicker,' I told him, making room for his seat.

He scraped in beside me, glancing soulfully at his watch. 'The guys will be watching the jazz by now,' he said in a small voice.

'Topec,' I said. 'This is important. If you don't feel you can devote your full concentration to the task, just say so and run off to play with your pals.'

'No, no,' he said, pushing back his hair and sitting forward in his chair to peer intently at the screen.

I took the last *Scotsman* fiche off the glass plate and put the first *Glasgow Herald* fiche on. Topec continued to stare at the screen. 'Is?'

416

'What?'

'What am I looking for, anyway?'

'Shipwrecks.'

'Shipwrecks.'

'Well, maybe not actual shipwrecks,' I said, recalling that Zhobelia had said there hadn't been any shipwrecks at the time. 'But something like shipwrecks.'

Topec grimaced, looking up at the ceiling. 'Right. Cool. Anything else?'

'Yes. Anything that rings a bell.'

'Eh?'

'Anything that sounds familiar. Anything that sounds like it might be linked to the Order.'

He looked at me. 'You mean you don't know *what* we're looking for.'

'Not exactly,' I admitted, scanning my half of the display. 'If I knew exactly what it was there wouldn't be any need to look.'

'Right,' he said. '. . . So I've got to look for something, like, really carefully, but I don't know what it is I'm looking for except it might be something like a shipwreck, that isn't?'

'That's right.'

From the corner of my eye, I could see that Topec continued to study me. I half expected him to rise from his chair and walk out, but instead he just turned back to the screen and pulled his seat closer. 'Wow,' he chuckled. 'Like, Zen!'

An hour went by. Topec swore he was paying attention but he always claimed to be finished at the same time as me, and I know I read very quickly indeed. Still, I had calculated that we would be lucky to finish all the records of all the papers for September 1948 by the time the library closed, so I had no choice for now but to trust his word. After that first hour, Topec started humming and whistling and making little sibilant noises with his tongue, lips and teeth.

I suspected it was jazz.

The next hour grew to middle age.

I tried with all my might to concentrate, but occasionally I would drift away from my task and start reliving the previous night, hearing Zhobelia tell me in her matter-of-fact way that what I had thought a personal miracle – a blessed affliction, one wise wound upon another – was something I shared through time with generations of my female ancestors, including her. Did that make any more sense of what I felt when I envisioned something? I had no idea. It put my visions in a sort of context but it made the experience no less mysterious. Did it *mean* anything that God chose to order Their miracles in this manner? I could not shake off the feeling that if there was one thing Salvador had got right it was that we are not even capable yet of understanding the purpose God has in mind for us. We can only struggle through, doing the best we can and trying neither to hide behind ignorance nor over-estimate the reach of our knowledge. I kept having to drag myself back to the task in hand, trawling the past for the key to the present.

And found it.

It was in the *Glasgow Courier*, dated Thursday, 30th September, 1948. It was as well I was sitting down; the experience of dizziness induced by a familial revelation did not seem to be a condition I was becoming inured to, despite the frequency with which it had swept through me in the past few days. My sight seemed to go a bit swimmy for a while, but I just sat and waited for it to clear.

I read on, while Topec read, or pretended to read, beside me.

Civilian and military police are today seeking Private Moray Black (28) a private of the Dumbartonshire Fusiliers, who is wanted for questioning in connection with an incident at Ruchill Barracks, Glasgow, on Monday night when it is understood an attack took place on a junior officer in the Pay Corps and an amount of money was subsequently found to be missing. Private Black, who is described as five feet ten inches in height and weighing eleven stone five pounds with brown hair, is known to have connections in the Govan area . . .

The words seemed to dance in front of me. I let them settle down

418

. . . Mother believed to be an unmarried textile worker in Paisley
. . . brought up by his grandmother, a member of the Grimsby
Brethren, a charismatic sect . . . gang member . . . alleged racketeer
during War . . . national service . . .

'Finished!' Topec said.

I turned and smiled, wondering that Topec did not hear my
heart thudding in my chest.

'Right,' I said, and put the fiche back in its box. 'Topec, could
you ask a librarian whether it is permitted to have a glass of water
or a cup of tea here, at the desk? I'm thirsty, but I don't want to
leave . . .'

'Yup!' he said, and bounded out of his seat as though released
by a spring.

I put the fiche back in the machine and took a couple of copies
of it while he was away. I quickly searched the other papers.
They had the same story, though the *Courier* seemed to have
the most detail; their reporter had talked exclusively to Private
Black's grandmother. I went to another shelf and selected the box
with October's newspapers in it.

On Saturday the 2nd of October there was another report in the
Courier to the effect that Black was still being hunted. The junior
officer who had been attacked in the incident was recovering in
hospital, concussed.

On the same page, a familiar word attracted my eye; it turned out
to be the name of a ship. It appeared in a report which stated that
the SS *Salvador*, a general cargo vessel of 11,500 tons registered
in Buenos Aires, which had sailed from Govan docks on the
morning of the 28th September bound for Quebec, New York,
Colón and Guayaquil, had encountered heavy weather off the
Outer Hebrides on the night of the 30th, and suffered structural
damage. The ship was now limping back to Glasgow. Amongst its
cargo had been railway carriages and other rolling stock, bound
for South America. Several carriages lashed to its deck had been
washed overboard during the storm.

My God.

I read the article about the SS *Salvador* again, and looked up at
the ceiling.

419

My Grandfather was washed ashore after a *train wreck*?

*

We got back to Topec's flat. Stephen reported, drunkenly, that there had been a message from a Mister Wormsludge – har har – asking me to ring his home number.

I rang Mr Womersledge. He said the serial number on the ten-pound note I had shown him was one of a consecutive batch which had been stolen from the Army Pay Corps in September 1948. The note might be more valuable than he'd said originally, and he could now offer me fifty pounds for it. I said, Thank you, I'd think about it, and put down the phone.

As the final teetering keystone of my belief in my Grandfather finally tumbled down about me and the world I had known seemed to fall away like unseasonable sprink before the sudden thaw, Topec asked, Hey, were we, like, ready to go out for a drink, like, yet?

I – of course – said, Yes.

CHAPTER
TWENTY-SEVEN

I had thought that I might find release from my tormented thoughts in alcoholic oblivion, but it was not to be.

After making another couple of phone calls, I duly went out that evening with Topec and his pals, but as we sat quickly drinking beer in a bar in Byres Road – apparently the natural and normal preparation before a dance at something called the Queen Margaret Union – I found myself slipping behind in the beer-drinking, unable to stop myself thinking about the revelation of the inherited, bizarrely serial nature of my Gift and the treachery and mendacity of those close to me.

Barely had I started to come to terms with the betrayal of my own brother when I discovered that my Grandfather was a thief and a liar as well as a potential rapist; that particular scrofulously scabrous cat was scarcely out of the bag when it was revealed – in an almost off-hand manner! – that I was just the latest in a long line of visionaries, faith healers and mediums, dating back to who-knew-when!

Our whole Order had been constructed on a base more dangerous and shifting than the sands of Luskentyre themselves; everybody had been lying to everybody else! Far from being a single eruption of poison in our placid and serene environment, Allan's lies and machinations suddenly started to look like an unremarkable and even predictable continuance of a vein of evil and mendacity that had been intertwined with the roots of our Faith from the very start, and indeed which predated it. Was there no foundation of my life on which I could still rely?

I tried to comfort myself with the thought that the Community and the Order had some intrinsic merit independent of their genesis. In a sense, all I had discovered – about my Grandfather, at any rate – made no difference. The proof of our Faith's worth lay in the hearts and minds of all of us who believed, and in the commitment and dedication we displayed. Why should good not

423

come out of evil? Was it not a sign of the ineffable bounteousness of God that They wrought the gold that was our Faith from the base and toxic ore that had been my Grandfather's violence and thievery and my grandmother's and my great-aunt's deceptions and manipulations?

It might be argued that the subsequent deceits of my grandmother and great-aunt had been the balancing wrong that had redeemed my Grandfather's original sins, that sometimes two wrongs do make a right, and that of all the things Aasni and Zhobelia might have done – reporting the find of money and Grandfather's army pay-book to the appropriate authorities being the most obvious and strictly correct – their actual course of action, intrinsically dishonest though it was and including Zhobelia's exploitation of her own Gift and my Grandfather's need for guidance, had produced entirely the best and most fruitful outcome, and a harvest of enlightenment and happiness very few avowedly good and well-intentioned acts ever yielded.

But ancestry matters in the minds of men and women, and symbols are important. To discover that Salvador had been no more than a common thief on the run after an act of violence, and realise that had he been able to find his washed-up loot he would probably have disappeared from Aasni and Zhobelia's lives, could not fail to alter the whole way people thought of my Grandfather, and by implication the Faith he had engendered. We would all feel deceived, and our beliefs cheapened.

It could be argued that the worse Grandfather had been before his conversion, the more blessed he became in comparison afterwards; God may take little credit for turning a man already good into a slightly better one, but to perform the miracle of forging a virtuous man from a bad one signified serious divine accomplishment and deserved real appreciation. But would such considerations make up for the inevitable feeling of betrayal people were bound to experience?

How many followers would we lose if this truth came out, as I had vowed to myself it must? How many more converts could we hope to gain once my Grandfather's history became common knowledge? Ought I now to renounce my earlier oath and, like my grandmother and great-aunt, conceal the ugly truth to favour the general good? What, then, would my word be worth? What self-respect could I claim for myself if a commitment, so freshly made, so vehemently sworn, could be so quickly abandoned when its consequences proved even more wide-ranging and more grave than I had anticipated?

Well, my self-respect was far from being the most important point at issue, I supposed; what mattered was the good of the Order and the Community and the spiritual well-being of the great majority of blameless people therein. I was confident that should I go back on my vow and keep my Grandfather's dreadful secret to myself, I could rest easy with such contained knowledge, and its cosseting would not contaminate or poison me.

But would it be right to incorporate what would in effect be another lie into what was already a whole tangled web of them, when the truth might sweep them all away and let us start again, righteous, uncontaminated, and without the baleful, jeopardising threat of that deceit hanging over us? And was I right – and *had* I the right – to assume that our Faith was so fragile it required shielding from such unpleasant facts? In the long term, might it not be better to embrace the truth regardless, and suffer whatever falling away in belief and support such a course entailed, secure in the knowledge that what – and who – remained would be true and strong and fundamentally trustworthy, and proofed – tempered – against further harm?

And should I announce, *I* have the Gift, only me; I am the one and the line that comes from my great-aunt, not my Grandfather? Ought I to take it upon myself to alter the whole emphasis of our Faith and point out another false belief we had previously held so dear, another area of shifting sand we had before thought immovable bedrock?

And by God, even *my* Gift was not unquestioned, in my own mind; here I was suffused with self-righteous anger at my Grandfather for having lied to us when there was still a question hanging over the validity of my own renown, if people only knew. The problem of action at a distance, with which I had been struggling for over a decade, took on a new, shiftier significance in the present

climate of poisonous suspicion, and suddenly the hope I had clung
to that I might have a gift greater than people knew of, rather than
lesser, looked distinctly dubious.

'Cheer up, Isis; might never happen,' Topec's friend Mark said,
winking at me across the glass-crowded table.

I gave him a tolerant smile. 'I'm afraid it already has,' I told
him, and drank my beer.

I fell out of the system of buying rounds, unable and unwilling
to keep up.

I went to the dance with the lads, and continued slowly drinking
beer out of plastic pint containers, but my heart was not really
in the proceedings. I found the music boring and the men who
came up to our group to ask me to dance no more attractive than
the sounds. I could not bring myself to join in the dancing even
when Topec asked. Instead I found myself watching everybody
else dance, reflecting what a strange and comical activity it could
appear. How odd that we should get such pleasure just from
moving rhythmically.

I supposed you could link the urge to dance to the sexual
drive, and certainly there was both a correspondence between the
regularity of the movements the two activities tended to involve
and an obvious element of something between courtship and
foreplay in the coming together of two people on the dance floor,
but I had watched young children and very old people take part
in dances at the Community and had myself danced there when
I had been convinced there was no aspect of sexuality involved,
and had seen the obvious delight experienced by young and old
alike and felt a kind of transcendent joy in myself that I was even
more sure shared nothing with carnality except the feeling that
what one was experiencing was good and pleasant.

The elation I had felt while dancing, in fact, seemed to have
more in common with religious ecstasy, as I understood it, than
with sexual bliss; one could feel almost mystically taken out of
oneself, transported to another plane of existence where things
became clearer and simpler and more connected at once and one's
whole being seemed suffused with peace and understanding.

Certainly this effect was difficult – and took a long time – to

426

achieve while dancing (I thought of whirling dervishes, and African tribespeople, spinning through the night), and could only ever be a weak reflection of the intense rapture experienced by the believer . . . but one had to say that it would be better than nothing, if nothing was the only other choice. Perhaps there lay the explanation for the attraction so many young people obviously felt for dancing, in our increasingly Godless and materialist society.

A strange species, humanity, I found myself thinking, quite as though I was some visiting alien.

I do not belong here, I thought. My place is with my people, and their future rests in my hands now. I suddenly wanted to be away from the noise and the heat and the smoke of this place, and so borrowed a key from Topec, donated the remains of my pint to him and stood and made my apologies and left, stepping out into the clear black night and breathing in its cool air as though released from a fetid prison after many years' incarceration.

The stars were mostly hidden by the city's glare, but the moon, less than a day away from being full, shone down almost undiminished, and as coolly serene as ever.

I did not go straight back to the flat, but wandered the streets for a while, still troubled by my conflicting thoughts, my conscience and will buffeted this way and that by the opposing arguments that racked my soul.

Eventually, I stood on the bridge that carries Great Western Road over the river Kelvin, leaning on the stone balustrade and looking down into the dark waters far beneath while the traffic grumbled and roared at my back and groups of people went chattering past.

A feeling of calmness gradually stole over me as I stood there, thinking and thinking and trying not to think. It was as though the warring forces in my soul were both so evenly matched and so precisely targeted upon their opposite that they eventually cancelled each other out, fighting each other to a standstill, to exhaustion and a stop, if not a conclusion.

Let what would be, be, I thought. The shape of tomorrow was already half decided, and how exactly it would all end I would

427

simply have to wait and see, playing events as they fell rather than trying to decide precisely what I would do now. At the least, I could sleep on my decision.

Sleep seemed a very good idea, I thought.

I returned to the flat, extended my hammock between the wardrobe and the bed's headboard in Topec's room – both articles of furniture were massive enough to support the weight, and both were also of such an anciently elaborate design that there was an almost embarrassing choice of stoutly carved curlicues and knobbly extrusions on which to loop the hammock cords. I took off my jacket, shirt and trousers, climbed into my hammock and fell asleep almost instantly.

I was only dimly aware of a party going on much later. Topec crept in and whispered to me he'd got lucky and swapped rooms with Stephen so that he could be alone with his new conquest, but Stephen, true to Topec's guarantee, did not disturb me during the night and I awoke – to Stephen's unconscious snuffles and snorts – bright and early the next morning. I arose, washed and dressed before anybody else awoke.

The living room was carpeted with sleeping bodies. I stood at the hall table to write a note to Topec and a letter to Grandmother Yolanda, then left to find a post box.

Sophi – who had been the next person I'd telephoned after talking to Mr Womersledge last night – arrived in her little Morris half an hour later, to discover me sitting on the flat's doorstep, eating a filled roll from a wee shop down the road.

Sophi looked blithe and summery in jeans and a striped T-shirt; her hair was gathered up in a pony-tail. She kissed me when I got into the car.

'You look tired,' she told me.

'Thank you. That's how I feel,' I told her. I held out the white paper bag I'd got from the wee shop. 'Would you like a filled roll?'

'I had breakfast,' she told me. 'So.' She clapped her hands. 'Where first?'

'Mauchtie, Lanarkshire,' I told her.

'Righty-ho,' she said, and put the car into gear.

The day, and the last, decisive part of my campaign, had begun.

*

It had crossed my mind that if I did decide that discretion concerning Grandfather's misdemeanours was the prudent course, then bringing Zhobelia back into the bosom of our family and Community might prove unwise, even catastrophic. What were the chances that she would be able to hold her tongue regarding the pay-book and the money now that she had broken the dam of that secrecy? Having her staying with us might well mean that the truth would be bound to leak out eventually, and perhaps in the most damaging way: over time, through rumour and gossip.

But I could not leave her in that place; it had been clean enough at the Gloamings Nursing Home, Zhobelia had a generously sized room, she obviously shared and enjoyed some sort of social contact with the other residents, and she had not complained of much there, but it had all seemed so loveless, so cold after the warmth of the Community. I had to take her away. If doing so forced my hand concerning the telling of the truth, then so be it; I would not sacrifice my great-aunt's happiness to such expediency. Telling the truth was what I had sworn to myself I would do, after all, even if now my instinct was to conceal rather than to reveal.

Well, we would see.

We drove through the lightly trafficked city. I gave Sophi an edited version of my short but eventful travels with Uncle Mo, my meeting with Morag, my audience with Great-aunt Zhobelia and time spent with Brother Topec. I did not, for the time being, mention the things Zhobelia had told me, or the pay-book and the ten-pound note.

'So what were you looking for at the library?' Sophi asked.

I shook my head, and could not look at her. 'Oh, old stuff,' I said. 'Things I half wish I hadn't found out.' I glanced at her. 'Things I'm not sure about telling anybody else yet.'

Sophi looked briefly at me, and smiled. 'Well, that's okay.'

429

And seemed happy with that, bless her.

*

'She is my great-aunt and she's coming with us!'

'Look, hen, she's here in my charge, and I'm not supposed to just let any of these old dears start wandering off.'

'She is not "wandering off", she is coming of her own free will, back into the bosom of her family.'

'Aye, well, that's what you say. Ah don't even know you are her . . .'

'Great niece,' I supplied. 'Well, look, why don't we just ask her? I think you'll find she'll confirm everything I say.'

'Och, come on; she's not exactly the full shilling, is she?'

'I beg your pardon? My great-aunt may appear a little confused on occasion but I suspect that much of what seems to be encroaching senility is simply the effect of having to subsist within the insufficiently stimulating environment which is all that you are able to provide, despite what I am sure are your best efforts. After some time spent with the many, *many* people who love her and who are able to provide her with a more intense set of emotional and spiritual surroundings I should be most surprised indeed if she did not a show a marked improvement in that regard.'

'Yeah!' Sophi breathed at my side. 'Well said, Is.'

'Thank you,' I said to her, then turned back to the plump middle-aged lady who had let us into the hall of the Gloamings Nursing Home. The lady had introduced herself as Mrs Johnson. She wore a tight blue uniform like the one the young lass had worn the last time I'd been here, two nights ago, and unconvincing blonde hair. 'Now,' I said, 'I would like to see my great-aunt.'

'Well, you can see her, Ah canny stop ye seein; her, but Ah havny had any notification she's supposed to be movin' out,' Mrs Johnson said, turning to walk towards the rear of the house. She shook her head as we followed her. 'Ah don't know, ye get told nuthin' here. Nuthin'.'

Great-aunt Zhobelia was in a room full of old ladies, all perched on high-seated chairs watching the television. A large tray with tea things sat on a sideboard, and many of the old dears – Zhobelia actually looked the youngest – were sitting sipping cups of tea, their bony, fragile hands shakily clutching robust green china cups which rattled in their saucers. Zhobelia wore a voluminous bright red sari and a matching red hat in the style of a turban. She looked bright and alert.

'Ah, it's you!' she said, the instant she saw me. She turned to one of the other old ladies and shouted, 'See, you silly old woman? Told you she was real! A dream, indeed!' Then she looked back to me and put up one finger, as though raising some point of order. 'Thought about it. Made up my mind. Decided to come for a holiday. Bags are packed,' she said, and smiled widely. Mrs Johnson sighed deeply.

*

'A lion-tamer? Goodness gracious me!' said Great-aunt Zhobelia from the back of Sophi's car as we headed cross-country towards Stirling.

'I'm not really a lion-tamer, Mrs Whit,' Sophi said, slapping me on the thigh with her left hand, then laughing. 'Isis just tells people that because she thinks it sounds good. I'm an assistant animal handler; an estate worker and zoo-keeper, really.'

'What, no lions, then?' Great-aunt Zhobelia asked. She was sitting sideways across the car's back seat, her arm on the back of my seat. Her bags took up the rear footwells as well as the car's boot.

'Oh yes,' Sophi said. 'There are lions. But we don't tame them or anything.'

'You don't tame them!' Zhobelia said. 'My. That sounds worse! You must be very brave.'

'Nonsense,' Sophi snorted.

'Yes, she is, Great-aunt,' I told her. 'And dashing, too.'

'Oh, stop it,' Sophi said, grinning.

'Do you have tigers at this safari park?'

'Yes,' Sophi said. 'Indian tigers: a breeding pair and two cubs.'

'There used to be tigers in Khalmakistan,' Zhobelia told us. 'Not that I was there ever, but we were told. Yes.'

431

'Aren't there any there any more?' I asked.

'Oh no!' Zhobelia said. 'I think we caught and killed them all long ago and sold their bits to the Chinese. They believe tiger bones and such are magic. Silly people.'

'That's a shame,' I said.

'A shame? I don't think so. It's their own fault. They don't have to be silly. Good merchants, though. Canny. Yes. Give them that. Things are worth what people will pay for them, no more, no less; say what you like. Found that out all right.'

'I meant for the tigers.'

Zhobelia *hmph*ed. 'Generous with your sympathy. They used to eat us, you know. Yes. Eat people.' She reached over and tapped Sophi on the shoulder. 'Hoy. Miss Sophi; these tigers, in this safari park next door to the farm, they aren't going to escape, are they?'

'We've never had an escape,' Sophi said in her most reassuring voice. 'We're not next door to the farm, anyway; a couple of miles away. But no, they aren't going to escape.'

'Ah well,' Zhobelia said, settling back in her seat. 'I suppose I should not worry. I'm as tough as old boots, I am. A tiger is not going to eat a shrivelled-up old lady like me, is it? Not when there's young ones about, tender young things like you and Isis, eh?' she said, thumping me on the shoulder and laughing loudly in my ear. 'Nice and juicy young things like you, eh? Nice and tasty, eh? Eh?'

I turned and looked round at her. She winked and said, 'Eh?' again, and took out a handkerchief from somewhere in her sari, to dab at her eyes.

Sophi looked across at me, grinning and raising her eyebrows. I smiled, content.

*

We met Morag and Ricky in the foyer of the same Stirling hotel Grandmother Yolanda had stayed at. I had called Morag at her hotel in Perth the night before, after I'd rung Sophi. Morag and Ricky had checked in here for the night.

'Hey, Is,' Morag said, glancing at Ricky, who looked away,

embarrassed. 'We've decided if you can get this all sorted out, we would like to get married at the Festival; we'll come back after we've done all the Scottish flumes. Sound cool?'

I laughed and took her hands in mine. 'It sounds wonderful,' I said. 'Congratulations.' I kissed her cheek and Ricky's. He turned red and mumbled. Sophi and Zhobelia offered their congratulations as well; a bottle of champagne was ordered and a toast drunk.

There was still time to kill; the Full Moon Service would not take place until the evening. Ricky went off to check out the flumes at Stirling swimming pool. We four took tea. Great-aunt Zhobelia reminisced, rambling through her memories like a gracious lady through a flourishing but overgrown and unkempt garden. Morag sat poised in jeans and a silk top, twisting a gold chain on her wrist. Sophi chatted. I dissembled, nervous. Zhobelia said nothing to the others of the secrets she had revealed to me at the nursing home, though whether this was because she was being discreet or just absent-minded it was hard to say; either seemed plausible.

Ricky reappeared. We had a late lunch in the restaurant. Great-aunt Zhobelia yawned and Morag offered her the use of her and Ricky's room for a lie-down, which she accepted.

Morag and Ricky went off to the flumes. Sophi and I strolled through the town, doing a bit of window-shopping and just taking the air, walking round the base of the castle and through the strange old cemetery nearby under breezy blue skies and a damp wind. Looking west across the broad flood-plain of the Forth, we could make out the trees surrounding the bend in the river where the Woodbeans' house and the Community lay. I tried not to feel too sick with nervousness.

We thought we'd lost Great-aunt Zhobelia for a few minutes, arriving back at the hotel to find Morag and Ricky on the brink of telephoning the police because Zhobelia was not in their room, and nowhere else to be seen, either. Then she appeared from the hotel kitchens, accompanied by the chef, chatting.

We took more tea. I kept asking Sophi the time. The afternoon wore on. Zhobelia went back up to the room to watch a soap opera, but returned a few minutes later, saying it wasn't the same watching it without the old dears there. And then it was time to go, and we went; Great-aunt Zhobelia and I in Sophi's car, Morag and Ricky in the white convertible Ford Escort.

It took less than ten minutes to arrive at the entrance to the High Easter Offerance estate.

CHAPTER
TWENTY-EIGHT

W e left the cars at the gates and walked down the shady drive. My stomach felt huge and hollow, resounding to the beat of my thudding heart.

'Want me to come along?' Sophi asked, just before we got to her house.

'Please,' I said.

'Okay, then,' she said, winking at me.

We helped Great-aunt Zhobelia over the bridge across the Forth. She chuckled to see how dilapidated the bridge had become. 'Oh yes. I think we're safe from tigers here!' she laughed.

We walked slowly up the curving track to the buildings. Zhobelia nodded approvingly at the re-pointed orchard wall, but tutted over the state of the grass on the lawn in front of the greenhouses and verbally scolded the two goats concerned, which lay on the grass, chewing the cud and looking at us with insolent unconcern.

The gate had been drawn across the arched gateway that led into the courtyard. This was not uncommon when there was a big Service taking place. It occurred to me we might be better going round the long way anyway, so we opened the door to the greenhouse and walked through.

Zhobelia sniffed a few blooms on the way through and prodded the earth in the flower pots. I got the impression she was looking for faults. I rubbed my sweaty hands on my trousers.

A terrible thought occurred to me. I let the others walk on a little way while I stopped with Zhobelia, who was looking at a complicated arrangement of hydroponic pipe work.

'Great-aunt,' I said quietly.

'Yes, dear?'

'I just thought; did you ever mention that little book and the money and so on . . . to anybody else?'

She looked puzzled for a moment, then shook her head. 'Oh no;

437

never.' She brought her head closer to mine and lowered her voice. 'Glad I mentioned it to you though, oh yes. Been a burden off my back, I'll tell you. Best forgotten now, if you ask me.'

I sighed. Fine, but my confidence was shaken. If I hadn't thought of that until now, what else might have escaped me? Well, it was a little late to turn back now. Sophi, Ricky and Cousin Morag waited at the far end of the greenhouse. I smiled at them, then took Zhobelia's elbow gently in my hand. 'Come on, Great-aunt.'

'Yes. Lot of pipes, aren't there? All very complicated.'

'Yes,' I said. 'All very complicated.'

We exited the greenhouse's humid, mustily perfumed warmth beside the door I had crept out of on my way to burgle the office a few days earlier. We continued round, past the outhouses and some of the old buses and vans which had been converted into dormitories and extra greenhouses. Zhobelia tapped the bodywork of an old coach with her knuckles.

'Bit rusty,' she said, sniffing.

'Yes, Great-aunt,' I said, choosing not to point out that the bodywork was aluminium.

We entered the courtyard from the north. The sound of distant singing-in-tongues was sweet, and brought a lump to my throat. I took a deep breath and looked in through the windows of the schoolroom as we headed for the main doors of the mansion house. Somebody was standing at the far end of the room, drawing on the blackboard with coloured chalk. It looked like Sister Angela. The children were sat at their desks watching Sister Angela; some had their hands up. Little Flora, Sister Gay's eldest, turned round and looked at me. I waved. She smiled broadly and waved, then put up her hand and waved it urgently. I heard her shouting out. Other small heads turned to look at us.

I walked to the main doors and held them open for Great-aunt Zhobelia, Sophi, Ricky and Cousin Morag.

'Okay?' I asked Morag.

She patted my arm. 'Fine. You?'

'Nervous,' I admitted.

The singing was very loud in the front hall, swelling out of the meeting room's closed double doors to our left. Sister Angela opened the door on the other side of the hall. She looked surprised. She looked at Ricky and Morag, then Zhobelia. Her mouth opened.

'Sister Angela,' I said. 'Ricky. Sister Zhobelia. I believe you know Sister Morag. Shall we?' I nodded into the classroom.

'Little Angela, eh?' said Zhobelia as we trooped into the classroom. 'I don't suppose you remember me, do you?'

'Ah . . . not that . . . well, yes, but . . . ah; children? Children!' Angela shouted, clapping her hands. She introduced the others to them *en masse*, and the dozen or so little ones dutifully said Good Evening. Across the hallway, the sound of singing-in-tongues gradually subsided and then ceased.

'Would you tell my Grandfather that Sister Zhobelia would like to see him?' I asked Angela. She nodded, then left the room.

Zhobelia sat in the teacher's chair. 'Have you all been good?' she asked the children. A chorus of Yeses came in return. I took a piece of scrap paper from the pile on the teacher's desk and wrote a number on it.

Sister Angela came back. 'Ahm,' she said, seemingly uncertain whether to address me or Zhobelia. 'He'll—'

She was interrupted by Grandfather coming into the room.

'Are you sure— ?' he said as he entered the room. He was dressed in his best creamy-white robes. He saw me and stopped, looking more surprised than angry. I nodded to him and pressed the little sheet of paper into his hand. 'Good day, Grandfather.'

'What . . . ?' he said, looking round, glancing down at the bit of paper, and then staring at Zhobelia.

She waved. 'Hello, my dear.'

Grandfather started over to her. 'Zhobelia . . .' he said. He looked at Sophi and Ricky and then stared at Morag, who was half sitting on the teacher's desk, arms folded.

I kept near Grandfather's shoulder. 'I think you should look at that bit of paper, Grandfather,' I said quietly.

'What?' He looked back at me. His face reddened as his expression turned from shock to anger. 'I thought you'd been told—'

I put my hand on his arm. 'No, Grandfather,' I said quietly and evenly. 'Everything has changed. Just look at the paper.'

439

He scowled, then did as I asked.

I'd written a number on the scrap of paper.

954024.

For a while I was worried that it was too subtle a way of getting through to him, that too much time had passed and he'd simply forgotten. He stared down in silence at the number on the paper, looking mystified.

Damn, I thought. It's just a string of numbers. Meaningless to him now. What had I been thinking of? He probably hadn't thought of that number in forty-five years; he certainly wouldn't have seen it. Is, Is; you idiot.

The number my Grandfather was looking at was his old army serial number.

Eventually, after what seemed like a long time to me, and while I was still cursing myself for a damned fool and wondering how else I might get through to him, his face changed, and slowly lost that look of anger. For a moment he visibly sagged, as though deflated, but then seemed to drag himself back upright. Even so, his face seemed crumpled, and he looked suddenly five years older. I swallowed down a feeling of sickness and tried to ignore the tears pricking behind my eyes.

He stared at me with big, bright eyes. His face looked as white as his hair. The sheet of paper dropped from his fingers. I stooped and caught it, then – as he swayed – took him by one arm and guided him back towards the desk. Morag moved away as he sat down on the edge, staring at the floor, breathing quickly and shallowly.

Zhobelia patted Grandfather on his other arm.

'Are you all right, dear? You don't look that well, you know. My, we've got old, haven't we?'

Grandfather took her hand and squeezed it, then looked up at me. 'Will you . . . ?' he said quietly, then looked round at Morag, Sophi and Angela. 'Would you excuse me . . . ?'

He stood. He did not seem to notice my hand, still supporting him. He looked into my eyes for a moment, a small frown on his face, for all the world as though he had forgotten who I was, and for another moment I was terrified that he was going to have a heart attack or a stroke or something awful. Then he said, 'Would you come . . . ?' and pushed himself away from the desk.

I followed him. He stopped at the door and looked back at the others. 'Ah, excuse us, please.'

In the hall he stopped again, and again seemed to pull himself upright. 'Perhaps we could take a turn round the garden, Isis,' he said.

'The garden,' I said. 'Yes, that's a good idea . . .'

*

And so we walked in the garden, in the late-evening sun, my Grandfather and I, and I told him what I knew of his background and where I had found it, though not what and who had led me there. I showed him a copy I'd taken of the newspaper report and said that I had sent another one in a sealed envelope to Yolanda, to be kept by her lawyers. He nodded once or twice, a slightly distracted look on his face.

I told him, too, that Allan had been deceiving all of us, and that his lies would have to be dealt with. Grandfather did not seem very surprised or shocked by that.

At the far end of the formal garden there is a stone bench which looks down a steep grassy slope to the weeds, rushes and mud of the river bank. Beyond, the fields stretched to a distant line of trees, with the hills and escarpment beyond under a sky patched with cloud.

My Grandfather put his head in his hands for a moment, and I thought he might be about to weep, but he merely gave a single long sigh, then sat there, hands hanging over his knees, head bowed, staring at the path beneath us. I let him do this for a while, then – tentatively – put my arm over his shoulders. I more than half expected him to flinch at my touch and throw off my arm and shout at me, but he did not.

'I did a bad thing once,' he said quietly, flatly. 'I did one bad thing, Isis; one stupid thing . . . I was a different man then; a different man. I've spent the rest of the time trying to . . . trying to make up for it . . . and I have. I think I have.'

441

He went on like this for a while. I patted his back and made encouraging noises now and again. I still worried in a distant kind of way that he might suffer some attack or seizure, but mostly I was simply surprised at how unaffected I felt by all this, and how cynical my attitude seemed to have become. I did not comment on his claim that everything he had done since his crime had been to atone for it. Instead, I let him talk on while I turned over in my mind again my choice between the destructive truth and the protective lie.

I felt like Samson in the temple, able to tear it down. I thought of the children in the classroom with Sister Angela, and wondered what right I had to bring the stones of our Faith tumbling down on those innocent little heads. Well, I supposed, no more than I had the right to decide for them they should be brought up within a Faith founded on a great lie.

Perhaps I should just behave as everybody else seemed to behave, here as elsewhere, and settle the matter according to my own selfish interests . . . except I could not even decide in which direction that would take me either; part of me still wanted to take my revenge on the Faith by shaking it to its very foundations, to exercise the power – the real power – I knew I now possessed just by having discovered what I had, and bring as much as possible of it crashing down about those who had wronged me, leaving me to look on from outside, from above, at the resulting chaos, ready to pick up the resulting pieces and rearrange them however I saw fit.

Another part of me shrank from such apocalyptic dreams and just wanted everything to go back – as much as was possible – to the way it had been before all this had started, though with a feeling of personal security based this time on knowledge and hidden authority, not ignorance and blithe naïvety.

Another part of me just wanted to walk away from all of it.

But which to choose?

Eventually, my Grandfather sat upright. 'So,' he said, gazing at the mansion house, not me. 'What is it you want, Isis?'

I sat there on the cool stone, feeling calm and clear and detached; cold and still, as though my heart was made of stone.

'Guess,' I said, speaking from that coldness in my soul.

He glanced at me with hurt eyes, and for a moment I felt both cruel and petty.

'I'm not leaving,' he said quickly, looking down at the gravel path at our feet. 'It wouldn't be fair to everybody else. They rely on me. On my strength. On my word. We can't abandon them.' He glanced back, to see how I was taking all this.

I didn't react.

He looked up at the sky now. 'I can share. You and I; we can share the responsibility. I've had to live with this,' he told me. 'All these years; had to live with it. Now it's your turn to share that burden. If you can.'

'I think I could cope,' I told him.

He glanced at me again. 'Well, then; that's settled. We don't tell them.' He coughed. 'For their own good.'

'Of course.'

'And Allan?' he asked, still not looking at me. The breeze brought the noise of bird-song across the lawn, flower beds and gravel paths to us, then took it away again.

'I think it was he who put the vial of *zhlonjiz* in my bag,' I told him. 'Though he may have got somebody else to carry out the actual physical act. It was certainly he who forged the letter from Cousin Morag.'

He glanced at me. 'Forged?'

'She hasn't written for two months. It's true she wasn't going to come to the Festival, but the rest was all a fabrication.'

I explained about the holiday Morag and her manager had arranged, which had only been postponed at the last minute. I told him about Allan lying about me to Morag, so that she would avoid both me and the Community.

'He has a portable phone, does he?' Grandfather asked when I got to that part. He shook his head. 'I knew he crept down there most nights,' he said, sighing and wiping his nose with his handkerchief. 'I thought it was a woman, or maybe drugs or something . . .' He sat forward, hunching over, elbows on his knees. He wound the handkerchief round and round in his hands.

'I hear since I've been away he's been . . . helping you with the revisions to the *Orthography*,' I said.

443

He looked round at me, but then could not hold my gaze, and had to look away again.

'Tell me, what changes has he inspired, Grandfather?'

Grandfather seemed physically to grope for words, his hands waving in the air. 'He . . .' he began. 'We . . .'

'Let me guess,' I said, trying to keep the bitterness out of my voice. 'You have heard God tell you that primogeniture is back, that Allan and not I should inherit the control of the Order when you die.' I gave him time to answer, but he did not choose to do so. 'Is that right?' I asked.

'Yes,' he said quietly. 'Something like that.'

'And Leapyearians . . . what of us? Where do we figure in this new regime?'

'To be respected,' he said, still not looking back at me. I heard him swallow. 'But . . .'

'But without power.'

He didn't speak, but I saw him nod.

I sat there, looking at his back for a while. He was looking down at the handkerchief, still winding it round and round in his hands.

'I think that all has to be changed back, don't you?' I said softly.

'So that's your price, is it?' he asked bitterly.

'If you want to put it like that, yes,' I said. 'Restoration, Grandfather. My restoration. That's what I want.'

He looked back, angry again. 'I can't just . . .' he began, his voice raised. But again he could not maintain his gaze, and looked away from me, his words dying on his lips.

'I think, Grandfather,' I said, slowly and softly, 'if you listen hard enough for the Voice of God you may well hear it tell you something which could have the desired effect. Don't you?'

He sat for a while, then looked round, his eyes moist. 'I am not a charlatan,' he said, and indeed sounded genuinely hurt. 'I know what I felt, what I heard . . . back then, back at the start. It's just since then . . .'

I nodded slowly for a few moments, wondering what to say

about Zhobelia's visions. Eventually I said, 'I didn't accuse you of being a charlatan.'

He looked away again, went back to winding the handkerchief round his fingers for a moment, then stopped, made an angry noise and stuffed the hanky back in a pocket. 'What do you want of Allan?'

I told him what I wanted.

He nodded. 'Well,' he said, and sounded relieved. 'We'll have to put that to him, won't we?'

'I think we ought to,' I agreed.

'Your brother has . . . ideas, you know,' he said, sounding regretful.

'What, like asking our followers for money?'

'Not just that. He has a vision for the Order, for the Faith. According to him, we have to move ahead into the next century. We have the opportunity to build upon what we have here, to evangelise and expand and learn from other cults; send out more aggressive missions, build up bases overseas, almost like franchises, in Europe, America, the Third World. We could go into the specialist food market and capitalise . . . on . . .'

His voice trailed off as I slowly shook my head.

'No,' I said, 'I don't think so, Grandfather.'

He opened his mouth as though he was going to argue, then his head dropped. His shoulders rose and fell as he sighed. 'Well,' he said. And that was all. He shook his head.

'Have those . . . the begging letters gone out yet?' I asked, not trying to keep the contempt out of my voice.

He glanced at me. 'Not yet,' he said, sounding tired. 'We were going to wait and see who turned up for the Festival. Approach them personally, if possible.'

'Good. I don't think we should do any approaching of that nature, or send the letters. Do you?'

He hunched over his knees again. 'I suppose it isn't necessary any more.'

'Good,' I said. 'I'm afraid I won't be taking a fully active part in the Festival of Love, either, not that I need to; Morag and Ricky will be getting married at the Festival. I don't feel ready for that myself, yet. I don't know that I'll ever feel ready for that. We'll see.' I paused, then continued. 'I'm sorry.'

He seemed not to have heard me, then just shrugged and shook his head.

'Whatever you want,' he said quietly.

'Good,' I said, and felt a strange, hard elation course through me. 'So,' I said, putting my hands on my knees. 'Shall we head back?'

'Yes,' he said, standing when I stood. In the skies above us a lark trilled.

'We'll go to the library and call Allan to us there,' I said. 'See which way he's going to jump. All right?'

'All right,' he said, his voice flat.

'Good.' I started down the path, then became aware that he wasn't following me. I turned and found him looking at me with a strange half-smile on his lips. 'Yes, Grandfather?' I said.

He nodded as though to himself, and his eyes narrowed. I felt a twinge of fear, thinking that perhaps he was taking this all too calmly and that he was about to break down, to shout and scream or even to try to attack me physically.

I tensed, ready to run.

His smile widened and his gaze roved over my face, as though he was only now really seeing me for the first time. With what might have been admiration in his voice, he said, 'Aye.' He nodded again. 'Aye, you're my grandchild, all right, aren't you?'

We looked into each other's eyes for a moment, then I smiled and held out my arm. He hesitated, then took it and we walked slowly, arm-in-arm, back to the house.

CHAPTER
TWENTY-NINE

'What?' Allan shouted.

'Confession,' I said calmly. 'Or exile. I want you to stand in front of everyone, this evening, and confess you tricked them and manipulated them, lied about me, lied to me, lied to Morag, lied to our Founder, lied to everybody.'

'Well ... fuck *you*, little sister!' Allan roared, storming away from where I stood by the windows with Morag, Sophi and Ricky and striding from one end of the library to the other, his splayed hand tearing through his hair. He turned and whirled round by Grandfather's seat; Grandfather was sitting in a chair by the closed door to the hall. Zhobelia was still in the schoolroom, talking to the children. The meeting for the Full Moon Service was still in abeyance; Calli was reading from the *Orthography* while we had our conclave in the library, next door to the schoolroom. I felt good here, surrounded by the books and their lingering musty smell.

Allan dropped to his knees in front of our Grandfather and put his hands on the arms of his chair, shaking it. 'Salvador! Founder! *Grandfather*!' he shouted. 'Don't let her do this! Can't you see what she's up to?'

Grandfather shook his head and looked away. He muttered something but I didn't catch what it was.

Allan threw himself back up and came striding towards me, one fist clenched and raised by his shoulder. Ricky, who had apparently accepted that Allan was the bad 'un in all this, growled and stepped forward. Allan stopped a few paces away. He was dressed in grey robes of a similar cut to Grandfather's.

I looked my brother in the eye, keeping my expression neutral and my voice steady. 'I want you to admit you took the *zhlonjiz* and put it in my kit-bag, Allan,' I continued. 'And you'll admit you've been using a portable phone here in the heart of the Community to arrange all your lies and deceptions and manipulate people like Morag and Uncle Mo.'

449

'Ha!' Allan said, laughing. 'I will, will I? And that's all, is it?'

'No,' I said. 'I also want you to confess you lied about my attempting to seduce Grandfather and that you tried to influence him and the revisions of the *Orthography* for your own selfish, political purposes.'

'You're mad!' he exclaimed, his voice rising in pitch. He looked round all of us, his eyes wide, his face shining with sweat, his chest heaving in and out. He laughed again. 'She's mad!' he told Sophi, Morag and Ricky. He turned back and looked at Salvador, who was gazing at his grandson now. 'She's mad! She's fucking mad, I'm telling you! Do you hear what she's saying? I mean, are you *listening* to all this?'

'Do you deny any of it?' Salvador asked coldly.

'All of it!' Allan yelled, spinning round to glare at me.

I looked slowly at Morag, who was standing at my side. She was frowning at Allan, her arms folded. Allan looked from Morag's face to mine and then back. He blinked rapidly.

'Perhaps, Grandfather,' I said, 'you'd like to ask my brother for the key to his desk in the office. It was on the chain round his neck, last time I saw it.'

'Well, Allan?' Grandfather said.

Allan turned round to face our Grandfather again. 'Look,' he said, and took a deep breath. He gave a small, nervous laugh. 'Look, all right; I have got the phone. Yes, I mean, big deal. Big *fucking* deal. I've used it for everybody's good. Everybody's. Plus, it's there for emergencies . . . And yes, all right, there might have been some crossed lines with the letters from Morag, but Grandad—'

I found myself striding down the room to him.

He must have heard me coming; he turned round and my forearms thudded into his chest as I gathered two balls of material from his robes into my fists; my momentum carried him two tottering steps backwards until his shoulders thumped into the library door, just to the side of where Grandfather sat. I glared up into Allan's face; his eyes were wide, his breath rushed out of his open mouth and struck my face.

I pressed into him, my whole body quivering with rage.

'Listen, *Brother*,' I hissed, grasping his robes tighter and shaking him. 'I don't think you've really understood the situation. I *know* what you've been doing, I *know* what your plans were and now so does Grandfather. Everything I'm doing now and everything I'm saying now has Grandfather's authority. *Everything*. Is that right, Grandfather?' I said, without looking at him.

I watched Allan's eyes tear their gaze away from mine to look imploringly down and to the side.

Quietly, our Grandfather said, 'Yes, that's right, Isis.'

Allan's gaze swung back to me. I could see sweat on his top lip now. His eyes looked very big.

'Is it starting to register now, big brother?' I asked. 'It's every damn thing I say or nothing; there's no negotiations, no talks, no compromises, no deals. You just do exactly as I say, exactly as Grandfather says, or you're *out*!' I pushed him back against the door, banging his head off the wood. '*Understand*?' I shook him again. I think I was trying to lift him off his feet but he was too heavy for me. It was only my anger and his surprise that was letting me pin him here at all.

He stared into my eyes. He looked pale. His breath smelled of mint. He swallowed. I felt him bring his hands up to mine, trying to free his robes from my grip. 'Hey, Is,' he said, his voice small and shaky. 'Come on; you're taking this kind of hard, aren't you? I mean—'

'You piece of *shit*!' I said, the rage shining like a white star inside me. 'You tried to destroy my *life* here; you want to pervert everything this Community's stood for and you've lied to every single one of us, all for your own slimy ends and you think I'm going to take it as a *joke*?'

I let go with one hand, but just to pull down on his robes with the other fist so that my free hand could grip the chain with the key on it. I pulled the chain off; he yelped as it parted somewhere behind his head. I stepped back and he stood there, rubbing his neck and glaring at me. Muscles quivered at the hinges of his jaw beneath his ears.

'Well here's the joke, Allan,' I said, feeling a tingling in my eyes and hearing a high keening noise in my ears. I weighed the key and its chain in my fist. 'Either you confess, in public, now, to

451

everything, or you're out, brother. Forever, with nothing. Because if *you* don't tell everybody everything, we – Grandfather and I – will. We'll take your phone and we'll have the office searched, your rooms searched, we'll have the whole damn *place* searched, plus we'll be there at the bank in Stirling first thing tomorrow, just in case you were thinking of making off with any funds, you know? I think all that kind of makes your position . . . what's the word? Untenable. That's the sort of corporate-speak you understand, isn't it, *brother*?'

Allan put shaking hands to his chest and smoothed his robes back down. He looked again at Salvador, who was sitting with his hands on his knees, his head down.

'Grandfather?' Allan said, and sounded like he might be about to cry. 'What about the new revelations for the *Orthography*? The ones we were going to reveal—'

'Down the drain, brother,' I told him. 'Like the rest of your plans.'

He ignored me. 'Grandfather?' he said again. 'She's gone crazy,' he said with another nervous laugh. 'You aren't going to let—'

'Oh for God's *sake*, boy!' Grandfather bellowed, not looking up. Still his voice filled the room. Even I jumped. The effect on Allan was more dramatic; he staggered and shivered as if run through.

Grandfather looked slowly up and round at my brother. 'Just do,' he said, 'what she says.' He shook his head briefly. 'Don't protract this,' he muttered. He looked down again.

Allan stared down at our Grandfather, then looked back up to me. His eyes were staring, his face white. His mouth worked for a moment before any noise came out.

'And what,' he said hoarsely, then stopped to swallow a couple of times. 'And what would you leave me with, if I . . . if I did agree to . . . to this ridiculous confession?'

I breathed deeply, in and out. I looked at Grandfather for a moment. *So.*

'You can have most of what you have at the moment, Allan,' I told him. 'Well, most of what we all *thought* you had. I think a penitential pilgrimage to Luskentyre might be in order, but

452

when you come back you can have control of the day-to-day administration of the farm, as you've had before. Of course, from now on I'd want full access at any time I want it to all the books and accounts. To everything, in fact. Most importantly, I'll want to sign all the cheques and authorise any expenditure.'

'But that's more than Grandfather does!' Allan protested.

'I know, Allan,' I said. 'But it's what I want.' I paused. 'While you look after the farm, I shall be taking over the day-to-day running of the Community and the Order; Grandfather's position will not change in that he remains our Founder and our OverSeer. Equally, there will be no need for him to be troubled by all the details you've been looking after until now. I'll supervise that aspect of our affairs. And I think we'll have to make it clear to everybody in the Community that they're accountable to the Founder and to me.' I shrugged. 'And perhaps to a more formal structure, like an elected board or committee. We'll have to think about that. I'll be asking everyone for suggestions. You'll be welcome to contribute, after you return from your pilgrimage.'

Allan looked almost comical now. He opened and closed his mouth and blinked, trying to take all this in. He gave one last despairing glance down at our Grandfather. 'Grandad?' he said, voice faltering.

Grandfather continued to look at the floor. 'Whatever Beloved Isis wishes,' he said quietly.

Allan stared at the older man.

I turned towards the windows. Ricky looked bored. Morag still had her arms crossed. She was frowning, but gave me a small smile. Sophi looked half terrified but then, when I winked at her, broke into a relieved if nervous smile. I turned back.

Allan brought his arms up from his sides until they were straight out and level, his face still white, his eyes still huge. His voice seemed to come from somewhere a long way away. 'Whatever you say,' he breathed.

*

453

I sat on the small wooden chair on the podium, looking out over a meeting room full of astonished faces. My brother kneeled before me; he put the basin full of warm water to one side, accepted the towel from my Grandfather, and began to dry my feet.

Allan's face was still wet after weeping during his confession, which Grandfather had announced. His admission of guilt had been brief but comprehensive; I didn't think he'd left anything out. It had been greeted with utter silence and then, when it was over, with a rising tumult of noise that had taken all my Grandfather's authority, and volume, to quieten again.

Grandfather had asked for silence once more while the ceremony that had been unjustly neglected on my return a few days earlier was belatedly carried out now, then asked Morag to bring forward the bowl of water and the towel. There were a few gasps when she walked forward from the back of the meeting room, soon hushed by a scowl from Grandfather.

As my brother dried my feet in the stunned silence, fresh tears fell from his eyes, extending his task by a few seconds.

Soon it was over though, and after Allan had gone to sit in the body of the kirk again and I had risen to stand, bare-footed, at the lectern, my Grandfather called once again for quiet, then left the podium to me and sat in the front row of the pews.

There were more gasps of astonishment and mutterings at this unprecedented action. I waited for them to pass.

When they did, I looked out over my people, and smiled. I gripped the smooth, polished wood of the podium and felt the hard surface beneath the papery softness of my skin.

Suddenly I remembered the way the fox had felt in my hands, when I had lifted it from the field, all those years ago. That tiny, feathery hint of a beat, there as soon as I'd picked it up. I had always been unsure whether it had been my own pulse I'd been feeling, or the animal's, and then – beyond that, if it had indeed been the fox's heartbeat I'd sensed – uncertain whether the animal had simply lain there unconscious until we'd come along (and Allan had poked it with his stick) or whether it really had been dead, and my Gift – working at a distance, without touching, doubly miraculously – had brought it back to life.

Was my Gift real? Was it genuine? Could I be certain? All these questions – or that one question in those different guises – had come to depend, in my mind, on the precise physical state of that small wild animal, that summer's day with Allan in the stalk-stubbled field, when I had been a child.

I had never known the answer. For a time I had thought that I might come to know it, but now I could accept that I never would, and in that acceptance found a liberating realisation that it didn't really matter. Here was what mattered; here, looking out over these stunned, bewildered, awed, even fearful faces, *here* was action at a distance, here was palpable power, here was where belief – self-belief and shared belief – could truly signify.

Truth, I thought. *Truth*; there is no higher power. It is the ultimate name we give our Maker.

I took a deep breath and an abrupt, fleeting dizziness shook me, energising and intoxicating and leaving me feeling strong and calm and able and without fear.

I cleared my throat.

'I have a story to tell you,' I said.

455